The Seventh Cross

ANNA SEGHERS
THE SEVENTH CROSS

Translated from the German by James A. Galston

Foreword by Kurt Vonnegut

Afterword by Dorothy Rosenberg

A Verba Mundi Book
David R. Godine · *Publisher* · *Boston*

This is a Verba Mundi Book
published in 2004 by
DAVID R. GODINE, *Publisher*
Post Office Box 450
Jaffrey, New Hampshire 03452
www.godine.com

Library of Congress Cataloging-in-Publication Data

Seghers, Anna, 1900–
[Siebte Kreuz. English]
The seventh cross / Anna Seghers ;
translated from the German by James A. Galston ;
foreword by Kurt Vonnegut ;
afterword by Dorothy Rosenberg. — 1st ed.
p. cm.
ISBN 1-56792-253-8 (alk. paper)
I. Galston, James A. (James Austin), b. 1881. II. Title.
PT2635.A27S513 2004
833´.912—DC22
2004007383

Design and composition by Carl W. Scarbrough

FIRST PRINTING
Printed in Canada

Contents

Foreword

Kurt Vonnegut

A suitable flag for the ordinary working people of Europe in this century, it seems to me, might flaunt a kitchen table and a few wooden chairs. There is the center of the universe. Anybody who can make it back to the table and chairs is safe again.

This splendid novel about such people in Germany in the 1930s, before the outbreak of World War II, was written by a German woman when the infamous death factories with their gas chambers and crematoria had yet to be constructed. Things were already bad enough. A new prison has been built near the town where the story takes place, and the bodies and spirits of those believed to be critical of any aspect of the government are broken there. Smoke wafted from the new prison to the town is generated not by burning flesh, but by fossil fuel.

All the same, the political disease that has attacked the community is terminal.

It is the last stages of the disease which are most often shown in movies nowadays, with familiar actors playing SS officers in smart black uniforms or victims with their pathetic luggage, and with greasy smoke belching from the square brick chimneys of crematoria only a few paces away from the unlocked cattle cars. The disease has left politics far behind. It is nothing but madness now.

In February 1985 in London, I asked the great German writer Heinrich Böll, who would die that summer, how much ordinary tables-and-chairs Germans had known about the death camps. No more truthful man ever lived, and he said that they had known about local camps like the one in this book and were expected to fear them. Most, however, learned of the death factories which killed people by the millions only when the war was over. I cite this merely as a piece of historical trivia, and nothing more, since it was general acceptance of the local camps which made all subsequent ghastliness possible.

Thus was the immune system of the community against unlimited evil destroyed.

What does this book say about that immune system? That it is such a fragile thing.

Böll was a German soldier all through World War II, sometimes a corporal, sometimes a private. At the end of his life, he often seemed to be carrying German war guilt all by himself. He did not think the planet could ever recover from the crimes committed by his compatriots. I said to him, "When the war was over, what hope did you have for humanity?"

"Nothing," he said.

Was he too pessimistic? Well – he was surely old and sick, and had had a hard life, a Nobel Prize notwithstanding. But then I consider how many countries at this very moment are destroying their dissidents, their immune systems against evil, with police methods perfected in Germany in the 1930s. I have to believe that such limited horrors could again become unlimited at any time. What passes for civilized behavior in many places nowadays, in fact, consists of doing anything short of using nuclear weapons or starting up the gas chambers again. The arrest and torture and killing of political enemies or the dropping of high explosives on civilian populations are scarcely worth discussing.

Meanwhile, as in the 1930s, there are plenty of weapons for everybody, and all these ordinary people are sitting on their wooden chairs at their kitchen tables, modest in their expectations and bravery, maybe drinking coffee or tea or beer or wine, and waiting to hear what the latest news might be.

The Seventh Cross

LIST OF PRINCIPAL CHARACTERS

GEORGE HEISLER, *a prisoner escaped from Westhofen Concentration Camp*

WALLAU
BEUTLER
PELZER
BELLONI } *also escaped*
FUELLGRABE
ALDINGER

FAHRENBERG, *commander of Westhofen*

BUNSEN, *lieutenant at Westhofen*

ZILLICH, *sergeant at Westhofen*

OVERKAMP
FISCHER } *police commissars*

ERNST, *a shepherd*

FRANZ MARNET, *George's former friend, a worker at the Hoechst Die Works*

LENI, *George's former sweetheart*

ELLY, *George's wife*

HERR METTENHEIMER, *her father*

HERMANN, *a friend of Franz's working at the Griesheim Railway Shops*

ELSE, *his wife*

FRITZ HELLWIG, *a gardener's apprentice*

DR. LOWENSTEIN, *a Jewish physician*

MADAME MARELLI, *a former artiste*

PAUL ROEDER
LIESEL ROEDER } *friends of George's*

KATHERINA GRABBER, *Roeder's aunt, owner of a garage and trucking business*

FIEDLER, *a fellow worker of Roeder's*

GRETE, *his wife*

DR. KRESS
FRAU KRESS
REINHARDT, *a friend of Fiedler's*
A Waitress
An Upright Man Willing to Run Considerable Risk

Chapter I

Never perhaps in man's memory were stranger trees felled than the seven plane trees growing the length of Barrack III. Their tops had been clipped before, for a reason that will be explained later. Crossboards had been nailed to the trunks at the height of a man's shoulder, so that at a distance the trees resembled seven crosses.

The camp's new commander, Sommerfeld by name, immediately ordered everything to be cut up into kindling wood. There was quite a difference between him and his predecessor, the gallant Fahrenberg, conqueror of his own home town, Seeligenstadt, where to this day his father runs a humble plumbing shop on Market Square. The new commander had seen service in Africa as a colonial officer before the war, and afterward he had marched upon Hamburg with his old major, Lettow-Vorbeck. All this we learned much later. The old commander had been a fool given to unpredictable fits of cruelty; the new one was a methodical, matter-of-fact fellow whose every action was dictated by cold calculation. Whereas Fahrenberg might suddenly have had us all battered to bits, Sommerfeld would have the men lined up and every fourth one beaten to a pulp. That, too, we did not know as yet. What if we had

5

known it? What would it have amounted to, compared with what we felt when the six trees, and finally the seventh one, were cut down? A small triumph, assuredly, considering our helplessness and our convicts' clothing; but a triumph nevertheless – how long was it since we had felt the sensation? – which suddenly made us conscious of our own power, that power we had for a long time permitted ourselves to regard as being merely one of the earth's common forces, reckoned in measures and numbers, though it is the only force able suddenly to grow immeasurably and incalculably.

That evening was the first time our barracks were heated. It coincided with a change in the weather. Today I am no longer sure whether the billets we fed to our little cast-iron stove actually came from that kindling. At the time, we were convinced of it.

We crowded about the stove because our clothes were wet and because our hearts were deeply moved by the unaccustomed sight of an open fire. The SA guard turned his back upon us and looked indifferently toward the barred window. The slight gray drizzle, no more than a fog, had suddenly turned into a sharp rain, hurled against the barrack by gusts of wind. After all, even an SA man, be he ever so hard-boiled, can see autumn's entry but once a year.

The billets crackled. Two little blue flames appeared – the coal had caught fire. We were granted five shovelsful of coal, hardly enough for a few minutes' warmth in the drafty barrack, let alone for drying our things. But we were not thinking of that as yet. We only thought of the wood burning before our eyes. Softly, with an oblique look toward the guard and without moving his lips, Hans said: "Crackling!" Erwin said: "The seventh one!" On every face there was a faint strange smile, a mixture of heterogeneous elements, of hope and scorn, of helplessness and daring. We held our breaths. The rain beat fitfully against the boards and the tin roof. Erich, the youngest of us,

6

glanced out of the corners of his eyes, in which were merged his own inmost thoughts as well as ours, and said: "Where is he now, I wonder!"

i

Early in October, a few minutes before his usual time, Franz Marnet started on his bicycle from his uncle's farm in the township of Schmiedtheim in the Lower Taunus. Franz was a thick-set fellow of medium height, about thirty, with a quiet face which, when he was with other people, looked almost sleepy. Now, however, on the steep downgrade between the fields to the main road, his favorite stretch, it bore an expression of a strong and simple joy of life.

Perhaps it will be hard to understand later how, considering circumstances, Franz could have been in high spirits. No matter. He was; he even gave a happy little grunt as his bicycle bounded over two ridges in the road.

Tomorrow the flock of sheep, which had been manuring the neighboring field since yesterday, would be driven on to his uncle's large meadow with the apple trees. That's why they wanted the apples gathered today. Thirty-five gristly tangles of branches, curling vigorously into the bluish air, were hung thickly with golden globules. They were all so bright and ripe that now in the first light of the morning they sparkled like innumerable little round suns.

Franz had no regrets about missing the apple picking. He had dawdled away enough time in return for the paltry pocket money his uncle had given him. Still, he ought to have been thankful after all the years he'd been out of work, for surely his uncle's farm was far better than a work camp. Since the first of September he had been one of those who worked in the factory. He was glad of it for many reasons,

7

and so were his relatives, seeing that now he would be a paying guest for the winter.

Passing the neighboring farm of the Mangolds', Franz saw them adjusting the ladders and poles and baskets under their mighty pear tree. Sophie, the eldest daughter, a strong girl, stoutish but not ungainly, with very slender ankles and wrists, was the first to jump up on the ladder, calling out something to Franz as she did so. Though he could not make out her words, he turned toward her briefly and laughed. He had the overpowering feeling that he belonged here. People of feeble sentiments and feeble actions will not understand him easily. To them, "belonging" means a definite family, or a community, or a love affair. To Franz it meant simply belonging to that piece of soil, to those people, and to that early shift bound for Hoechst – above all, to the living.

When he had skirted the Mangold farm, he could look down upon the gently sloping land and the fog. Down a little farther, beyond the main road, the shepherd was opening the sheepfold. The flock came shoving out, immediately nestling close to the slope, still and thick like a little cloud, disintegrating at times into smaller cloudlets, contracting or puffing up at others. Ernst, the shepherd, a fellow from Schmiedtheim, also called out to Franz, who smiled. Ernst, with his fiery red neckcloth, was quite a bold and unshepherdlike rascal – in chilly autumn nights, compassionate farmers' daughters would come from the villages to his movable little hut.

In back of the shepherd, the land sloped down in placid, long-drawn waves. Though one cannot as yet see the Rhine from here, it still being an hour's train journey away, everything indicates the nearness of the great river: the wide, largely swelling slopes with their fields and fruit trees and, farther below, their vines; the factories' smoke, which could be smelled even up here; the southwesterly curve of the railroad tracks and the roads; the glistening and blinking spots in the fog; yes, even Ernst with his red neckcloth, one arm on his hip and one leg put forward as if he were watching an army, not merely a flock of sheep.

This is the land of which it is said that the last war's projectiles plow from the ground the projectiles of the war before the last. These hills are no chains of mountains. A child can have coffee and cake with relatives on the farther side and be back home when the evening bells toll. For a long time, though, this chain of hills meant the edge of the world; beyond them lay the wilderness, the unknown country. Along them the Romans drew their *limes*. So many races had perished here since they burned the Celts' sun altars, so many battles had been fought, that the hills themselves might have thought that what was conquerable had finally been fenced and made arable. It was not the eagle, however, nor the cross that the town down below retained in its escutcheon, but the Celtic sunwheel – the sun that ripens Marnet's apples. Here camped the legions, and with them all the gods of the world: city gods and peasant gods, the gods of Jew and Gentile, Astarte and Isis, Mithras and Orpheus.

Here, where now Ernst of Schmiedtheim stands by his sheep, one leg forward, one hand on his hip, one end of his shawl sticking straight out as if a little wind were blowing constantly – here the wilderness called. In the valley at his back, in the soft and vaporous sun, stood the peoples' cauldron. North and south, east and west, were brewed together, and while the country as a whole remained unaffected by it all, yet it retained a vestige of everything. Like colored bubbles, empires rose up from that country, rose up and as soon burst again. They left behind no *limes*, no triumphal arches, no military highways; only a few fragments of their women's golden anklets. But they were as hardy and imperishable as dreams. So proudly does the shepherd stand there and with such complete placidity that one might well think him aware of all that glorious past; or perhaps, though he may be unaware of it, it is because of it all that he stands thus. There, where the main road joins the motor highway, the armies of the Franks were assembled when a crossing of the Main was attempted. Here the monk came riding up, between the Mangold and Marnet farms, proceeding into the utter wilderness which from here no one had entered before – a slender man on a little donkey, his chest protected by the armor of Faith, his loins girded with the sword of Salvation. He was the bearer of the Gospels – and of the art of inoculating apples.

Ernst turned toward the cyclist. His cloth felt hot around his neck; he tore it off and threw it on the stubble field, where it lay like a battle pennant. One could have thought it a gesture watched by thousands of pairs of eyes. But there was only his little dog Nelly to see it. He resumed his inimitably scornful, haughty attitude, but now his back was toward the road, his face toward the plain where the Main flows into the Rhine. At the rivers' confluence lies the city of Mainz. Thence hailed the arch chancellors of the Holy Roman Empire. And all the flat land between Mainz and Worms was covered by the encampment of the imperial election. In this land something new happened every year, but every year the same thing: the apples ripened, and so did the wine under the gently befogged sun and the effort and care of man. The wine was needed by all and for all things: the bishops and landowners used it when they elected their emperor; the monks and knights when they founded their orders; the crusaders when they burned Jews – four hundred of them at one time in the square of Mainz which to this day is called the *Brand* – the ecclesiastical and secular electors when the Holy Roman Empire had crumbled but the feastings of the high ones were merry as never before;

the Jacobins when they danced around their liberty poles.

Twenty years later, an old soldier had stood guard on the floating bridge of Mainz. As the last ones of the Grand Army, ragged and dismal, dragged past him, he thought of how he had stood guard here when they marched in with their tricolors and their human rights, and he sobbed aloud. This guard, too, was withdrawn. Things quieted down, even in this part of the country. Then came the years of '33 and '48, thin and bitter, two little threads of congealed blood. They were followed by another Empire, which today is called the Second. Bismarck had his internal boundary posts put up not around the country but crossing it so that Prussia could take a piece in tow, for while the inhabitants were not downright rebellious they were altogether too indifferent, like people who had had all manner of experiences and would have more of them in future.

Was it really the Battle of Verdun the schoolboys heard as they lay on the ground beyond Zahlbach, or was it merely the continuous trembling of the earth caused by railroad trains or the marching of armies? Later, some of these boys had to stand trial – some because they fraternized with the soldiers of the army of occupation, some because they placed fuses under the rails. On the court building fluttered the flags of the Interallied Commission.

Hardly ten years ago these flags were hauled down and exchanged for the black-red-gold ones the Empire still had in those days. Even children were reminded of it the other day when the 140th Infantry Regiment once more marched across the bridge behind its merrily playing band. And the fireworks that night! Ernst could see them way up here. A burning and roaring city beyond the river! Thousands of little swastikas twistedly reflected in the water. Watch the little flames whisk across! In the morning, when the stream left the city behind beyond the railroad bridge, its quiet bluish-gray was in no way altered. How many field standards had it lapped against? How many flags? Ernst whistled to his little dog which brought him his neckcloth in its teeth.

We have now arrived. What happens now is happening to us.

ii

Where the country road joined the Wiesbaden Highway stood a roofed little soft-drink stand. Franz Marnet's relatives grew irritated every Sunday evening over their failure to lease it, for the brisk traffic had turned it into a veritable gold mine.

Franz had left home early because he much preferred riding by himself; he detested being wedged into the crowd of cyclists from the Taunus villages who made for the Hoechst Die Works every morning. He was therefore somewhat put out when he saw a chap he knew, Anton Greiner of Butzbach, waiting for him at the soft-drink stand.

The strong, simple joy of life disappeared from his face at once. He became narrow and dry, so to speak. This same Franz, who might have been ready unconditionally to offer his whole life, could not help feeling irritated because Anton Greiner never seemed to be able to pass the little stand without spending some money. He had a faithful little sweetheart in Hoechst to whom he would later slip his chocolate bars and little bags of candy. Greiner stood with his eyes toward the country road. "What's the matter with him today?" thought Franz, who, in the course of time, had become a fine judge of facial expressions. He knew that there must be some reason for Greiner's waiting for him. Greiner jumped on his bike and joined Franz. They hurried to get out of the crowd, which became denser and denser as the downgrade increased.

"Listen, Marnet, something's happened this morning," said Greiner.

"Where? What?" asked Franz, his face assuming the expression of sleepy indifference it always wore.

"Marnet, something *must* have happened this morning."

"What is it?"

"How should I know?" answered Greiner. "But something's happened sure."

"Ah, you're goofy. What could have happened so early in the morning?"

"I don't know, I tell you. But you take my word for it, something quite crazy must have happened. Something like on June 30th."

"Ah, you're crazy yourself. . ."

Franz stared straight ahead. How thick the fog still was down below. Quickly the level land came to meet them, with its factories and streets. Around them they heard cursing and the tinkling of bells. Suddenly the cyclists were split into two groups by two motorized SS men, Greiner's cousins, Heinrich and Friedrich Messer of Butzbach, who also were on this shift.

"Why didn't they take you along?" asked Franz, as though he were no longer curious to hear what Anton had to say.

"*Verboten!* They'll be on duty later. So you think I'm crazy. . . ?"

"Why, what makes you think so?"

"Aw, cut it. Listen. My mother, you know, has to go to see her lawyer in Frankfurt today because of the inheritance. So she took her milk across to Kobisch, seeing that she wouldn't be home for the milk collection. Young Kobisch was in Mainz yesterday, buying wine for the farm. So he got to drinking and didn't start for home until early this morning. They wouldn't let him pass at Gustavburg."

"Nuts, Anton!"

"Why nuts?"

"You know there's been a control station at Gustavburg for a long time."

"Listen, Franz, Kobisch isn't altogether a fool. He said the control was extra strict... and guards at the bridgeheads... and what a fog! 'Rather than run afoul of one of them,' said Kobisch, 'have them make a blood test, find I have alcohol in me – and I might as well kiss my driver's license good-bye – no sir – back to the inn in Weisenau and another bottle or two for me.'"

Marnet laughed.

"Go ahead, Franz, laugh! Do you think they'd let him go back to Weisenau? The bridge was closed. I'm telling you, Franz, there's something in the air."

The downgrade lay behind them. To the right and left, but for turnip fields, the level land lay bare. What could be in the air? Nothing but the motes in the golden sunbeams, turning gray and into ashes above the houses of Hoechst. "All the same," Franz thought, for suddenly he knew that Anton Greiner was right, "something *is* in the air."

They tinkled their way through the narrow, crowded streets. The girls screamed and scolded. At the street crossings and the entrances to the works a few acetylene lamps were burning. Perhaps it was because of the fog that they were being tried out for the first time. Their hard, white light deadened every face. Franz brushed against a girl who muttered angrily and turned her head his way. He felt as if her glance had pierced him deeply, even to the place he kept barred to himself.

The fire brigade's shrilling sirens over on the Main side, the crazily glaring acetylene lights, the cursing crowd, pressed against the wall by a lumbering truck – hadn't he yet become accustomed to all that, or was it somehow different today? He searched for a word or a glance for interpretation. He had dismounted from his bicycle and was pushing it. In the crowd he had long since lost both Greiner and the girl.

Once more Greiner joined him. "Over there at Oppenheim," said Greiner over his shoulder, bending over so far that his bicycle was almost torn from him. Their gates were at so great a distance from each other that after they had passed the first control station they might not see each other again for hours.

Marnet kept on the alert, but neither in the locker room nor in the yard nor on the stairs could he detect the slightest trace of an agitation other than the one that came every day between the second and third blasts of the whistle. Perhaps there was a little more confusion and squabbling, as there was every Monday morning. Franz himself, looking desperately for even the minutest sign of disquiet in the words he heard and the eyes he scanned, growled like the others, asked the same questions about the past Sunday, made the same jokes, and changed his clothes as gruffly. If someone had been watching him as persistently as Franz watched the others, he would have been equally disappointed. But Franz felt a pricking of hatred for all these people who were quite unaware of the fact that something was in the air, or refused to be aware of it. After all, had anything happened? Greiner's tales were pure gossip as a rule. Could his cousin, Messer, have set Anton to spy on him? "He surely wouldn't have noticed anything," thought Franz. "What was it he told me, anyway? Gossip, nothing but gossip. No more than that that fellow Kobisch got drunk while buying wine."

The last whistle put a sudden stop to his thoughts. As he

15

was still new at the works he had not yet got over a strong feeling of tension, even fear, at the beginning of the day. The first purring of the transmission belts made the roots of his hair tingle. Now the belts had assumed their clear steady humming. Franz's first, second, and fiftieth plate had long been punched; his shirt was sticky with perspiration. He drew a light breath. His thoughts became connected again, though but loosely, for he was meticulously exact in his work. Franz's work could never have been anything else, even if the devil himself had been his employer.

Up here there were twenty-five of them, and Franz watched with tortured attention for any sign of agitation around the stamping hammers. He would have been irritated if any of his stencils were inaccurate, not only because of a complaint that might do him harm but because the stencils themselves had to be accurate, even today. All the same, he thought: "Anton said Oppenheim. Why, that's the little town between Mainz and Worms. What's to happen there, of all places?"

Fritz Greiner, Anton Greiner's cousin, who was the foreman up here, stopped briefly at Franz's side, then went on to the next man. When Fritz parked his motorcycle and hung up his uniform in the locker he was just a stenciler among stencilers – except, perhaps, for the singular sound of his voice, noticeable only to Franz, when he called out to Weigand. Weigand was a middle-aged, hairy little man, nicknamed Noggin. It was a good thing that his little voice whirred high and thin, blending with the belts, for while removing the waste dust he said without moving his lips: "Have you heard? In the Westhofen CC [concentration camp]." Looking down, Franz saw in Noggin's clear eyes those tiny bright points for which he had so desperately waited: as if deep inside a person a fire were burning, and the last little sparks came flashing out of the eyes. "At last,"

Franz thought. Noggin was already at the next fellow's side.

Carefully Franz shifted his piece, placed it on the marked line, pressed down the lever again, again, and again. If only he could leave now and see his friend Hermann. Suddenly his thoughts snapped to attention again. There was something in this news that had a very personal meaning for him. It had shaken him powerfully, had hooked itself to his inside and kept gnawing, though he was still ignorant of the why and what. "A camp mutiny, eh," he said to himself, "perhaps even a big jail break." Here he realized suddenly what it was that affected him particularly: "George... What nonsense," he thought almost immediately, "to connect such news with George." Perhaps George was no longer even there. Or, what was equally likely, he was dead. But his own voice was joined by George's, far off and scoffing: *No, Franz, if anything happens in Westhofen I'm sure to be in it.*

During the past years he actually believed he was thinking of George as he did of all the other prisoners, as he did of any one of thousands of whom one thinks with rage and mourning. He actually believed that what tied him to George had long ceased to be anything but the firm bond of a common cause, one of their youthful stars of hope. No longer that other bond which at the time had so painfully bitten into their flesh and at which they had both tugged so violently. He had firmly persuaded himself that those old things were forgotten. George had become a different person, hadn't he, just as he himself had become different? For a second he caught a glimpse of the next man's face. Had Noggin said anything to him? Was it possible that he could continue to punch, carefully inserting one piece after the other? "If anything has happened there," thought Franz, "George is in it." And then: "Probably nothing at all has happened; it's just Noggin jabbering again."

When he stepped into the canteen during the noon hour

for his glass of light beer (he brought his lunch from home for he was saving up for a suit of clothes, though God only knew how long he would be permitted to wear it) he heard people at the bar say: "Noggin's been arrested... Because of last night. He got stewed good and proper and shot off his mouth... No, it wasn't that, it must be something else..." Something else? Franz paid for his beer and leaned against the bar. Since all had suddenly lowered their voices, a confused sound reached his ear. "Noggin, Noggin... He's put his foot in it," someone said to Franz. It was the man who worked next to him, Felix, a friend of Messer's. He looked at Franz fixedly. On his regular, almost beautiful face there was an expression of amusement. His strong blue eyes were too cold for a young face. "How's that?" asked Franz. Felix shrugged his shoulders and jerked up his brows, as if he were suppressing a laugh. "If only I could reach Hermann immediately," Franz thought again. But there was no chance of speaking to Hermann before the evening. Suddenly he discovered Anton Greiner trying to make his way to the bar. Under some pretext Anton must have procured a pass, because he never came to this building or to this canteen. "Why is he always looking for me of all people," thought Franz. "Why does he want to tell his tales to me?"

Anton took him by the arm, but released it at once as though the gesture might make them conspicuous. He stood next to Felix while he swallowed his light beer; then he went back to Franz. "He has decent eyes, hasn't he?" thought Franz. "He may be a little dense, but he's sincere and feels drawn to me as I do to Hermann..." Anton put his arm under Franz's and muttered, his voice cloaked by the noise of the general exodus at the end of the noon hour: "Over there on the Rhine, in Westhofen, some fellows have bolted, some kind of punishment squad. My cousin hears of these things. They say most of them have been caught. That's all."

18

iii

No matter how long he had pondered his escape, alone and with Wallau, no matter how many minute details he had weighed, or how much he had thought of the mighty course a new existence would take, during the first minutes of his flight he was only an animal escaping into the life-bringing wilderness, while blood and fur still clung to the trap. Since the discovery of the escape the wailing of the sirens had penetrated the country for miles, calling to life the little villages enveloped in the thick autumn fog. This fog smothered everything, even the powerful searchlights which at other times penetrated the darkest night. Now, toward six in the morning, they were drowned in a soupy fog to which they were hardly able to impart a tinge of yellow.

George crouched deeper, though the soil beneath him gave. He might be sucked under before he dared leave this place. The dry brambles bristled in fingers that had become bloodless, slippery, and ice-cold. It seemed to him that he was rapidly sinking deeper; he felt that he should already have been swallowed up. Though he had fled to escape sure death – no doubt that within the next few days they would have destroyed him and the other six – death in the swamp appeared to him utterly simple and without terror, as if it were another death than the one from which he had fled, a death in the wilderness, completely free, not death at the hand of man.

Six feet above him along the willowed embankment the guards and their dogs were running, crazed by the howling of the sirens and the thick, wet fog. George's hair stood on end; his skin crept. Near by, he heard someone cursing and recognized Mannsfeld's voice. So the blow with the spade with which Wallau had hit him in the head a while ago no longer hurt him! George let go of the brambles. He slid still deeper. But now his feet felt the projection which at this point could support a man. He had known of this when he had still had the strength to calculate everything in advance with Wallau.

Suddenly something new began. It was only moments later that he realized that nothing had begun, but something had ceased: the sirens. That was the new thing: the quietness, in which one could hear the sharply differentiated whistles and commands from the direction of the camp and from the outer barrack. The guards above him ran behind their dogs to the end of the willowed embankment. Other dogs ran from the outer barrack toward it. There was a slight report, another followed, a splashing sound, and the dogs' hard bark mingled with another thin bark that was quite powerless against the former. That could not have been a dog, or a human voice either. Quite likely that the man they were now dragging away no longer had the semblance of a human being. "Albert, I'm sure," thought George. There is a degree of reality that feels like a dream, though one has never been so far from dreaming. "Got him all right," thought George, as one thinks in a dream, "got him all right." It could not actually be that now there were only six of them.

The fog was still thick enough to cut with a knife. Two little lights flashed up, way beyond the highway – immediately behind the rush grass, one would have thought. These individual sharp points penetrated the fog with greater ease than the flat-beamed searchlights. By and by the lights went on in the peasants' houses, the villages woke up. Soon the circle of little lights was closed. "Such things can't be," thought George, "I'm dreaming it all." Now he had an over-powering desire to let his knees sag. Why involve himself any further in this hunt? A little knee-crooking, a gurgling sound, and all is over... First of all, calm down, Wallau used to say. Quite likely Wallau was squatting under some willow-bush nearby. Whenever Wallau said to a fellow: "First of all, calm down" he immediately became calm.

George grabbed at the brambles and crawled slowly to one side. He was now perhaps still twenty feet from the last bush. Suddenly he was shaken by an attack of abject fright which had nothing in common with any dream. He simply clung to the outer rim of the ditch, his belly flat against the ground. And as suddenly as it had come, it was gone.

He crawled as far as the bush. For the second time the siren started its howling. It must surely penetrate far beyond the right bank of the Rhine. George pressed his face into the soil. *Quiet, quiet,* said Wallau over his shoulder. George gasped once and turned his head. The lights had all gone out. The fog had become thin and transparent, a veritable tissue of gold. The lights of three motorcycles rushed along the highway like rockets. The howling of the siren seemed to swell. Again George pressed his face into the soil because above him he could hear them running back along the embankment. He barely squinted out of the corners of his eyes. There was nothing any longer for the searchlights to grasp, for the graying of the dawn made them feeble. If only the fog would not lift entirely!

All at once three of them came climbing down the outer decline not more than ten yards away. Again George recognized Mannsfeld's voice. He recognized Ibst by his cursing, not by his voice; it was quite thin with rage – a veritable old woman's screech. The third voice, appallingly close – "They are liable to step on my head," thought George – was that of Meissner, who used to come to the barrack at night summoning individual men. Two nights ago had been the last time that George himself had been called out. Even now there was a sharp impact upon the air after each one of Meissner's words. George thought he could feel the soft breeze they made. "You down there – straight ahead – come on – get going!"

A second attack of fright, a fist crushing his heart. Not to be human now, to be able to take root, a willow bush among willow bushes, to grow bark and branches instead of arms! Meissner stepped down onto the turf and began to roar like a bull. Suddenly he stopped. "Now he sees me," thought George. All at once he became entirely calm, no longer any trace of fear. "This is the end! Farewell all!"

Meissner climbed farther down to join the others. They were now waiting on the turf, between the embankment and the road. For a moment George was saved by the fact that he was much nearer than they could expect. If he had made a dash for it, they would surely have grabbed him now on the turf. Strange indeed that, wildly and unconsciously, he had stuck unwaveringly to his original plan. Plans evolved in sleepless nights – what power they retained in the hour when all planning comes to nought, when the thought occurs that another has planned for us. *And even that other one is myself.*

Again the siren subsided. George crawled sideways. One of his feet slipped. A marsh snipe gave such a violent start that fright made George loose his hold upon the shrubs. The snipe darted into the rush grass with a harsh rustling sound. George listened. They must all be listening now. *Why does one have to be a human being, and if so, why of all beings must it be I, George?* All the rushes had sprung back again; nobody came. After all, nothing had happened except that a bird had darted about in the swamp. All the same, George felt utterly unable to move. His knees were raw, his arms disjointed. Suddenly in the shrubbery he saw Wallau's pale little face with its pointed nose... All at once the shrubbery was alive with Wallau faces.

That passed. Again he became almost calm. Coolly he

thought: "Wallau and Fuellgrabe and myself, we'll get away. We three are the best of them. Beutler they've got. Belloni may get away, too. Aldinger is too old. Pelzer is too soft." He turned on his back and saw that it was already day. The fog had lifted. Golden-cool autumn light covered the land that might have been called peaceful. About twenty yards away George saw the two large flat stones with whitened edges. Before the war the embankment had been the driveway to a distant farm, long since deserted or burned down. It was then probably that the stones had been dragged up from the Rhine. Between them there was still some firm soil, long since overgrown with rushes. A kind of defile had been created through which one might crawl on one's belly.

The few yards to the first gray white-bordered stone were the worst, almost without cover. George clamped his teeth onto the shrubs, releasing first one hand, then the other. The twigs snapping back into place swished softly. A bird darted up, perhaps it was the same one. If only he were not so cold!

iv

For a long time after Fahrenberg, the commander, had received the report, he felt that this unbearable reality must be a dream from which he would presently awake; this whole ghastly business was not even a bad dream, but merely the memory of one. It is true that Fahrenberg seemed coolly to have taken all the measures called for by such a report. Actually, however, it had not been Fahrenberg, for even the most dreadful nightmare required no measures; someone else had thought them up for him to cover an event which must never be allowed to happen.

When, a second after the order had been given, the siren

began its howling, he stepped carefully over an electric extension cord – a dream obstacle – toward the window. Why did the siren howl? Out there before the window there was nothing: quite the proper view for a nonexisting time.

Fahrenberg gave no thought to the fact that this Nothing was something after all: a dense fog. What woke him to reality was Bunsen's becoming entangled in one of the cords that stretched between the office and Fahrenberg's sleeping quarters. Suddenly he began to roar, not at Bunsen, it goes without saying, but at Zillich who had just made his report. All the same, Fahrenberg was roaring not because he as yet understood the report – that seven prisoners in protective custody had escaped – but because he wished to rid himself of the nightmarish sensation.

Bunsen, a remarkably handsome six-footer, turned around, bent down with a "Beg pardon!" and plugged in the cord. Fahrenberg had a certain partiality for electric lines and telephone apparatus. In these two rooms there was a multitude of wires and interchangeable plugs which required a great deal of repair work and fitting. It happened that last week a prisoner had been discharged, Dietrich of Fulda, an electrician by trade. The discharge had come just after he had finished the new equipment, which turned out to be rather a mess. His eyes showing unmistakable amusement but his face blank, Bunsen waited until Fahrenberg had stopped roaring. Then he walked out. Fahrenberg and Zillich were alone. . . .

On the outer threshold Bunsen lighted a cigarette, pulled at it once, and hurled it away. Having had the night off, he would not go on duty for another half-hour. His future brother-in-law had driven him over from Wiesbaden in his car.

Between the commander's quarters, a solid brick building, and Barrack III, along which a number of plane trees grew, lay a kind of square which, among themselves, they called the Dancing Ground. Here, in the open, the siren pierced one's brain with a vengeance. "Bloody fog," thought Bunsen.

His men had lined up. "Braunewell! Nail this map to the tree there. Now come over here and listen!" Bunsen stuck the point of his compass into the red dot marked CAMP WESTHOFEN and drew three concentric circles. "It is now five past six. The break occurred at five-forty-five. By six-twenty the utmost speed would carry a man only to this point. So presumably they are stuck now between this circle and that one. Therefore – Braunewell! Close off the road between Botzenbach and Obereichenbach. Meiling! Same thing between Untereichenbach and Kahlheim. Nobody's to pass. Keep in touch with each other and with me. Can't comb the district yet. Reinforcements won't be here for another fifteen minutes. Willich! Our outer circle touches the right bank of the Rhine at this point, so block the stretch between the ferry and Liebacher Au!"

Fahrenberg in the meantime had forwarded the report to the Central Office. "Deucedly uncomfortable for the old guy," thought Bunsen. "The Conqueror of Seeligenstadt! Wouldn't like to be in his skin." As for his own skin, Bunsen was conscious of how well it fitted him. As though made to order by God, the master tailor! Again he was in luck. The damn break had happened while he was off duty and he'd got back a little ahead of time, just in time to be able to do his share. He turned toward the commander's quarters, trying to hear through the siren's clamor whether the old man had finished with his second burst of roaring.

Zillich, alone with his master, kept an eye on him while he tried to plug in for a direct phone connection with the Central Office. "This damn fellow Dietrich ought to be stuck in prison again for his lousy work." Zillich felt keenly how all this idiotic plugging was wasting time. Precious seconds during which seven little dots moved farther and farther out into an infinity where they could no longer be overtaken. At last he got the Central Office and made his report – the second time in ten minutes that Fahrenberg had to listen to it. While his face retained the expression of incorruptible severity long since indelibly stamped upon it in spite of a deplorable shortness of chin and nose, his lower jaw drooped. God, of whom he was only then reminded, could not possibly permit this report to be true. Seven prisoners escaped from his camp at one time! He stared at Zillich, who gave him in return a heavy, gloomy look full of remorse and sadness and contrition, for Fahrenberg had been the first one to have full confidence in him. That something untoward always seemed to happen when things were going well didn't surprise Zillich. Hadn't he got himself that nasty bullet wound in November 1918? Hadn't he lost his farm through a forced sale a month before the new law went into effect? Hadn't that slut recognized him fully half a year after the knifing and got him into stir? For two years now Fahrenberg had given him his confidence, entrusting to him what they called among themselves the "skimming" – forming the punishment squad, which consisted of prisoners to be treated with special harshness, and choosing the accompanying guards.

Suddenly the alarm clock which, following his old custom, Fahrenberg had put on a chair beside his field bed, started ringing. Six-fifteen – the usual day should have begun; Fahrenberg's usual day, the command of Westhofen.

The commander gave a start. The drooping jaw clicked shut. In a few short motions, he finished dressing, sliding a damp brush over his hair and cleaning his teeth. He approached Zillich, looked down upon the man's thick neck, and said: "We'll have them all back in quick order."

"Yes, *Herr Kommandant!*" The few suggestions Zillich made then were essentially those the Gestapo followed later, when no one gave any more thought to Zillich. The man's suggestions usually showed that his mind was clear and sharp.

Suddenly he interrupted himself. Both men listened. In the far distance they heard a thin and at first inexplicable sound, partly obliterated by the siren. There were words of command, and a new scraping of boots on the Dancing Ground. Fahrenberg and Zillich eyed each other. "Window!" said Fahrenberg. Zillich opened it, and the fog poured into the room, together with the sound. After listening briefly, Fahrenberg went out, Zillich with him. Bunsen was on the point of dismissing the SS squad when there was a commotion – Beutler, the first recaptured fugitive, was being dragged toward the Dancing Ground.

It was possibly thanks to a well-directed kick or two that Beutler was able to slide the last few feet in front of the squad all by himself – not on his knees, but sideways, face up. As he landed at Bunsen's feet, the latter realized what it was in that face that made it look so peculiar. It was laughing. Lying there in his bloody rags, blood oozing from his ears, the man actually seemed to be convulsed with silent laughter which exposed his large shiny teeth.

Bunsen forced his eyes from that face and looked up at Fahrenberg. Fahrenberg, gazing down on Beutler, drew his lips away from his teeth; for a moment it looked as if the two were laughing at each other. Knowing his commander, Bunsen knew what would happen now. His young face altered as it always did under those circumstances; his nostrils distended and the corners of his mouth twitched, a horrible change in features that were naturally endowed with the expression of a Siegfried or an archangel in shining armor.

Nothing happened just then.

Police Commissars Overkamp and Fischer had just come

through the camp gate and were being escorted toward the commander's quarters. Both men halted in front of the Bunsen-Fahrenberg-Zillich group. Realizing what was up, they said something quickly to each other. Then, without addressing anyone in particular, Overkamp said very softly, but in a voice hoarse with both rage and the effort to master it: "So that's what you call receiving prisoners. You'd better send out a hurry call for a specialist to patch up the man's kidneys, testicles, and ears before we can examine him. Clever! Clever! Congratulations!"

ν

By now the fog had lifted so far that it lay like a fluffy sky over the roofs and trees. Dimly and cozily, like a softly shaded lamp, the sun hung over the bumpy village street of Westhofen.

"If only the fog won't rise entirely now," some thought, fearful that the sun would harm the vines at the last moment before the grapes were gathered. "If only the fog would lift quickly," thought others, who wished for a last ripening touch of the sun on the vines.

There were not many in Westhofen with such worries, for the village raised cucumbers, not grapes. A little off the road from the Liebacher Au to the highway stood Frank's vinegar factory. Behind a broad, clean-dug ditch the fields extended to the edge of the path to the factory. WINE VINEGAR AND MUSTARDS – MATTHIAS FRANK'S SONS. Wallau had called George's particular attention to this signboard, for, emerging from the rushes, he would have to crawl about ten feet in the open; but then he would go down into the ditch; he must take care to choose the left turn that went along the fields.

When George stuck his head out of the rushes the fog hung so high that it revealed a clump of trees behind the vinegar factory; the sun at his back made the trees seem to blaze up as if they had suddenly caught fire. How long had he been crawling? His clothing had merged with the slimy soil, as if he were dragging the entire swamp along with him. A whistle from the direction of the Liebacher Au was answered by one so startlingly near that George dug his teeth into the soil. "Crawl!" had been Wallau's advice. Wallau had been in the War and in the Ruhr and in the fighting in Central Germany – why, the man had been wherever anything was happening. "See that you keep on crawling, George! Never think you've been discovered. Many are captured just because they think they've been found, and they do something foolish."

Between the faded shrubs George peered over the edge of the ditch. So near stood the guard – where the road across the cucumber field joined the highway – so disconcertingly near, that, far from feeling fright, he was enraged. Leaning against the brick wall, the man was so easily within his reach that it was torture to hide instead of jumping at his throat. The guard resumed his beat, pacing slowly past the factory and toward the Liebacher Au, two glowing eyes piercing his back. George thought the mill-like clacking of his heart would make the guard turn back any minute, though in reality his deathly fear made it beat softer than a bird's wing.

He slid farther along the ditch, almost as far as the spot where the guard had just been standing. Wallau had carefully explained that here was where the ditch went underneath the road; whether and how it went after that, Wallau himself hadn't known. At that spot even his foresight gave out. It was only now that George felt entirely forsaken. Calm! It was the one remaining word in his mind, a mere sound, a vocal amulet. "This ditch," he said to himself, "runs beneath the factory and serves as a drain." He would have to wait for the guard to turn. The man halted at the bank, whistling. From the Liebacher Au came the answering whistle. George could now calculate the distance between the whistles. He did a lot of calculating. Every part of his brain was occupied, every muscle tensed, every second filled – all life was singularly crowded, breathless, closely confined. But when he had forced himself into the nauseous, foul-smelling drain, he suddenly felt faint. This ditch was not meant to be crawled through but only to be suffocated in. Rage struck him at the same time – he was no sewer rat, this was no place for his final exit. Presently, however, it was no longer so pitch-dark in front of him. He thought he could see the swirling of a watery substance. Fortunately the factory grounds were not large, perhaps fifty yards wide. Where he emerged on the other side of the wall the field sloped gently upward to the highway, toward which a path led obliquely. In the angle between the wall and the path there was a heap of filth. George could go no farther. Squatting down, he was violently sick.

An old man with two pails slung across his shoulders by a rope was coming through the field. In Westhofen he was called Pigwidgeon. So doubled over with age was he that his shaggy cape-like felt cloak almost dragged along the ground. One did not need the stick with which Pigwidgeon tapped at every step to see that he was blind. Habit had made the tapping purely mechanical; he knew his daily route unfailingly. Six times on his short way to get rabbit fodder from the factory caretaker had the old man been stopped this morning. Six times had he had to identify himself: "Gottlieb Heidrich of Westhofen, called Pigwidgeon." "Something must have happened at the CC," thought Pigwidgeon as, hearing the wailing of the sirens, he proceeded slowly across the field, dangling the pails. "Something like last summer when one of those poor devils tried to make a bolt for it, and they shot him down. Even while the sirens were still howling he was full of lead." Such goings on would not have been tolerated in former days. Pity they had to build that CC here, right under the peasants' noses. But on the other hand, one could make a bit of money now instead of having to scrape along all the time, as used to be necessary when every morsel had to be driven to the market. "Is it true," Pigwidgeon wondered, "that the countryside the poor devils are now draining is to be leased out later? . . . No wonder they are trying for a getaway. . . And the rental, they say, is to be lower than over in Liebau." When his stick hit a flat boulder in his path, Pigwidgeon gave a little grunt of satisfaction, dropped his pails to the ground, and sat down on the stone for a brief rest. His cape slipped unnoticed from his shoulders, his head nodded forward, and he was asleep.

As for George, he stared blankly at the obviously blind man. *The cloak! Get it!* Wallau's counseling voice seemed to whisper to him. Noiselessly approaching the sleeping man, George stealthily took the cape and put it over his shoulders. His nausea over, he felt he must proceed. At first he had planned to go to Erlenbach, far from the Rhine, but now he did not dare cross the highway. He would have to change his plan. Shoulders hunched, head down, he trudged across the field, prepared for a hail or shots. He stabbed his toe into the loose earth and thought: "Any moment now, my dear fellow, there'll be a shout, a report, and your knees will buckle, bidding you irresistibly to throw yourself on the ground." Then came the thought: "They'll shoot me in the legs so they can drag me off alive." He closed his eyes. The cool morning wind against his face, he felt an excess of sadness, more than a man could bear. He stumbled on, faltered. At his feet lay a little green ribbon. He stared at it for a moment as if it had just fallen from the skies, then picked it up.

31

Suddenly, so suddenly that she must have sprung up from the ground, he saw a little girl standing in front of him. She wore a sleeved apron, and her hair was parted and braided. They stared at each other. The child shifted her gaze from his face to his hand. He gave her pigtail a little tug and handed her the ribbon.

The girl ran off to an old woman, her grandmother, who had also suddenly appeared on the road. "From now on you'll get a piece of string for your hair. There!" said the old woman, with a cackle. And to George: "She could do with a new hair ribbon every day." "Why don't you cut her braids off?" he asked. "What an idea!" tittered the old woman. Her glance, which had casually taken in George, wearing the cloak so familiar in her part of the country, fell upon Pigwidgeon, nodding on the stone near the vinegar factory close behind them. "Hey there, Pigwidgeon! Sleepyhead!" she shrilled. "If he misses his cape now," thought George, "there's going to be trouble." The blind man, called out of his drowsing by the old woman's familiar voice, but reluctant to cut short his usual forty winks, roused himself only sufficiently to wheeze out: "Ah you, Bagatelle." That's what everyone in Westhofen called her because all her life she carried rubbish around with her, useful things and useless ones, sticking plasters and bits of thread and cough drops. There was a time in her youth when she used to dance with Pigwidgeon, before his eyesight had given out, and once she had almost married him. Now she waved her skinny arms excitedly at the somnolent old man, her toothless mouth and her wrinkled little cheeks showing that grotesque vivacity which in old people takes the place of jolliness. One could almost hear a dancing skeleton's bones make little rattling sounds.

George, trudging off with the old woman and the child, felt as if, though for moments only, he had been claimed by the living. But the road across the field led not only to the village, as George thought; it forked into two roads, one to the village and the other to the highway. The old woman had stuffed the hair ribbon into one of her pockets with her other rubbish and was leading the little girl, who was swallowing her tears, by her pigtails. "Did you hear all the rumpus?" she cackled. "Oh my, oh my! What a tooting! Now it's quiet again. They've got him. No laughing matter for that fellow. Oh my, oh my!" At the fork in the road she stood still. "The fog's up. Look!"

George turned around. Sure enough, the fog had lifted. Pure and clear shone the pale-blue autumn sky. "Oh my, oh my!" said the old woman again as she saw two gleaming planes – no, now there were three – dart from the blue of the sky, fly close to the ground, then over the roofs of Westhofen, and cut wide circles over the swamp and the fields.

Keeping close to the woman and her grandchild, George walked toward the highway. They went a little distance along it without meeting anyone. The old woman fell silent. She seemed to have forgotten everything – George and the child and the sun and the planes – and to be brooding on things that had happened in the past, before George was even born. George, keeping close to her, felt like holding on to her skirts. This couldn't be real; it was only a dream that he was walking with the old woman and holding on to her skirts without her noticing it. He'd wake up presently and hear Lohgerber's voice in the barrack. . . .

To their right rose a long wall, its top encrusted with broken glass. They walked beside it for a few steps, in close single file, George bringing up the rear. Suddenly without sounding its horn, a motorcycle came rushing up from behind them; the woman and child hastily flattened themselves against the wall. Had Bagatelle before continuing on her way turned around, she must have thought the earth had swallowed George. The motorcycle flashed by. "Oh my, oh my!" wailed the old woman, trudging on. George had disappeared not only from her path but from her memory. He had scaled the wall almost with one leap and now lay panting on the other side of it. The cape had slipped off his shoulders, but anyone seeing it on the ground would have thought it belonged to the old woman pressed against the wall in panic. The broken glass had made George's hands bleed; there was a deep gash under his left thumb, and his clothing was cut through to the flesh.

Would they dismount now and come after him? No, the motorcycle had rushed on. Almost at once, or at least so it seemed to George, he heard another one tearing along from the other direction. It stopped abruptly. "Got me!" thought George, huddled against the wall. The SA patrol, spying the cloak, dismounted and looked at it with suspicion. Where was its owner? Bagatelle and the child had disappeared around the corner of the wall. The SA man, about to blow his whistle, heard Pigwidgeon's excited voice coming from the direction of the vinegar factory: "My cape! My cape! I can't find it!" As fast as he dared go, his stick prodding the ground all around him, the blind man came in the SA man's direction. "Hey you!" shouted the latter. "Here's your cape. Why can't you hold on to your things?"

"Where? Ah yes, it's mine. But how strange... I could have sworn..."

Grunting disgustedly, the SA man swung himself onto the seat of his motorcycle and was off with a roar.

From the agricultural school, a low, many-windowed red-brick building, came voices, high ones and low ones, and a whole chorus of the animated voices of boys. What word did they want to impress upon him, what sentence, in his hour of death? From the opposite direction another motorcycle came rushing. George felt no relief when it flew past, going in the direction of the Westhofen camp. Suddenly conscious

34

of the pain, he felt like biting off his hand above the wrist.

In front of the narrow left side of a school stood a greenhouse. The main entrance of the school and the stairway were on this side, opposite the greenhouse. Between the front of the school and the wall stood a shed which obstructed George's view. He eyed it musingly, then crawled toward it. Inside, it was quiet and dark; there was an odor of bast. His eyes were soon able to distinguish the thick bundles of bast fiber hanging on the wall. There was also any number of tools, baskets, and articles of clothing. Now that everything depended no longer on his quick judgment but on what is usually called luck, he became cool and calm. From the lining of a jacket he tore himself some rags and, using his teeth and his right hand, bandaged the injured member. Taking his time to inspect the clothes, he finally picked out a thick brown jacket of Manchester velvet with a zipper and an old pair of dusty work pants. He put them on right over his own bloody, sweaty tatters. The shoes were of excellent quality. He was inspecting the sizes when he suddenly realized that he could not get out of the shed. Peering through a crack between the boards, he saw people behind the school windows; there were others in the greenhouse. One chap came down the steps and went toward it, but at the door he stopped and turned toward the shed. A voice called him from one of the windows, and he went back into the school building. It was quiet again. The sun glistened on the windowpanes and on the metal parts of a partly packed piece of machinery that was lying near the stairway.

George suddenly dashed to the door and took out the key. Laughing to himself, he sat down, his back against the door, and regarded his shoes for two or three minutes. It was the last retreat within himself, when all is lost outside and no one cares a straw. If they came now, should he pitch into them with the hatchet or the rake? He didn't know what it was that snapped him back to reality. Perhaps the pain in his hand, perhaps the ghost of Wallau's voice in his ear. He put the key back in the keyhole and opened the door a crack. Impossible to get over the wall and back on the highway.

Between the glass-studded top of the wall and the sky he could see the spur of a vine-covered hill. The air was so clear that one could almost count the little points on the topmost row of vines as they protruded above the pale-brown edge of the hill. He was looking up dully when a sudden thought struck him. Where it came from George had no idea – perhaps from Wallau in the Ruhr, or a coolie in Shanghai, or some soldier in Vienna who had escaped from danger by carrying something on his shoulder that distracted attention from himself; for such a load bespeaks a purpose and lends the bearer a certain identity. Thus George in his shed was reminded by his invisible adviser that once before someone in a similar situation had escaped in that manner from a house in Vienna, a farm in the Ruhr district, or a guarded street in Tshapei. Not knowing whether this invisible adviser's face was Wallau's familiar one, or a yellow or a brown one, George still understood its counsel: *Pick up the machine part near the stairs. You'll have to get out of here some way. You may not succeed, but there's nothing else you can do. Your situation is desperate, but so was mine. . .*

Whether he had not been noticed at all or had been taken for an employee of a machine works, or for the man whose jacket he was wearing – at any rate, carrying the piece of machinery on his shoulder, he succeeded in making his way between the greenhouse and the school that faced the fields. The pain in his left hand was so violent that at times it deadened his fear. George went along the road that ran parallel to the highway past a few houses, all of which faced the fields; from their top windows one could see the Rhine. The planes were still droning, the deep blue of the sky had

36

overcome the haze, it would soon be noon. George's tongue was parched, and he was conscious of a painful and uncontrollable thirst; his stiff, dirt-encrusted clothes under the jacket tortured his skin. A tag with a firm's name on it dangled from the machine part he was carrying. He was just ready to put down his load and catch his breath when he was halted.

Probably one of the motorcycle patrols on the highway had noticed, through a gap between two houses, a harmless-looking man trudging through the fields under the quiet noonday sky, a load on his shoulder. He was stopped because everybody was being stopped; there was no other reason. As soon as George offered the tag as identification, the patrol waved him on. Possibly George might have gone on unmolested as far as Oppenheim or even farther – his invisible adviser counseled him to take that direction.

He could hear the gentle but insistent voice: *Keep on! Keep on!* But the patrol's challenge had been a blow to his nerve. Suddenly he sheered off. . . get as far as possible away from the highway. . . go across the fields toward the Rhine and the village of Buchenau. The more violently fear made his heart pound, the more imperceptible became the voice counseling him against the field road, until finally it was entirely drowned by his heartbeats and the noonday bells. Their sound was clear and bitter, like a knell tolled for an execution. A glassy sky arched over the village of Buchenau. As he entered it, he had the feeling that it would be a trap.

Suddenly the village was in an uproar. Whistles sounded from one end to the other. "Everybody into their houses!" Heavy gates creaked. George put down the piece of machinery, slipped through the nearest gate, and hid behind a pile of wood. It was slightly past noon. The trap was sprung.

*   *   *

37

Franz had just entered the canteen in Griesheim. No sooner had he learned of Noggin's arrest than Anton grabbed him by the wrist and told him all he knew.

At that very moment, Ernst, the shepherd, rapped against the kitchen window at Mangold's. Sophie opened the door, laughing. She was well-rounded and strong, but her joints were finely molded. Would she warm his potato soup? His thermos bottle was kaputt. – Why didn't he join the others inside? Nelly could keep watch in the meantime.

Ah, his Nelly, said Ernst, was no dog, she was a little angel. But after all he had a conscience and he was being paid to attend to his job. "Sophie," he said, "I'd rather you'd heat the soup and bring it to the field. . . Don't look at me that way, Sophie. When you do, your darling little eyes go through and through me."

He walked across the fields to his hut. He spread a layer of newspapers on a sunny spot on the ground and put his cloak over them. Squatting on his heels, he waited. He looked forward to Sophie's coming with delight. "Like little apples," he thought, "so round, so ripe, and such fine little stems."

Sophie brought him his soup and some of her potato dumplings and pear cake. "Funny," she said, sitting down beside him.

"What?"

"That you of all people should be the shepherd."

"That's what they said to me the other day down there," said Ernst, pointing toward Hoechst. "'You are a strong man, and nature has meant you to be something else.'" It was incredible how quickly Ernst could change the expression of his face or the sound of his voice. Sometimes he was Meyer of the employment department, sometimes Gerstl of the Work Front, then again Mayor Kraus of Schmiedtheim, and sometimes, but not often, himself.

" 'Why don't you let a man older than yourself have your job?' "

"Well, I told them," Ernst continued, after swallowing a few spoonsful of soup, "I said, in my family shepherding is hereditary from the days of Wiligis."

"Willy – what?"

"That's what they asked me down there too," said Ernst, mashing a dumpling against a piece of pear cake. "I suppose none of you were paying attention at school when that was taught. Then they asked me why I wasn't married, while others who were and had children had a much harder time earning their living."

"What did you say to that?" asked Sophie, a little hoarsely.

"Oh," said Ernst innocently, "I told them I'd already taken the first steps."

"How's that?" Sophie was tense now.

"Because I'm already engaged," answered Ernst, eyes downcast, though it didn't escape him that Sophie had become a bit pale and limp. "I'm engaged to Mariechen Wielenz of Botzenbach."

"Oh," said Sophie, her head bent, smoothing her skirt over her legs. "Why, she is still a schoolchild, your Marie-chen Wielenz of Botzenbach."

"That doesn't matter. I like to watch my intended grow up. But that's a long story. I'll tell you all about it someday."

Sophie was fussing with a blade of grass, smoothing it out and drawing it through her teeth. Scornfully but sadly she murmured: "In love, engaged, married. . ."

Ernst, who was having his fun with her and wasn't missing a thing – not her emotion, or the erratic movements of her hands – licked the two plates clean and put them on top of each other. "Thanks, Sophie. If you're as expert in every-thing as you are in making dumplings, you're a bargain for

39

any man. Look at me, will you? Come on, look at me... When you look at me, you make me forget Mariechen for all eternity, if not longer."

He looked after Sophie bustling away with her plates. "Nelly!" At his call, the little dog hurled itself against his chest, then put its paws on his knee and looked up at him, a little black bundle of unquestioning devotion. Ernst dipped his own face against its nose, fondled its head between his hands in a sudden burst of tenderness. "Nelly, do you know whom I love best of all? Do you know her name, Nelly? The one I like best of all the females in the whole world? Her name is Nelly."

In the meantime, the headmaster of the Darré School had rung the noonday bell fifteen minutes late. Young Hellwig, a gardener's apprentice, dashed out to the shed. He wanted to get twenty pfennigs from his purse in his velvet jacket. He owed the money to one of his fellow pupils for two tickets in the winter-aid lottery. Throughout the year the school gave courses, principally for the sons and daughters of the peasants from nearby villages. There was also an experimental farm on which the pupils worked; in addition, a few gardeners and apprentices were regularly employed.

Hellwig, a lanky, blond young fellow with clever eyes, searched the whole shed for his coat. At first he was surprised, then alarmed, then enraged. He had bought it only last week, after he'd had his first girl. He probably couldn't have bought it so soon, except for that prize he'd won in a competition. He shouted to his schoolmates, already seated at the lunch table. The light dining room with its clean-scrubbed wooden tables was festively decorated, as usual. Garlands of seasonal flowers and foliage were draped around pictures of Hitler, of Darré, and of some landscapes on the walls.

At first Hellwig thought that his comrades were playing a joke on him – they were forever teasing him because the jacket was sizes too large for him, and because they envied him his girl. The young lads, with their healthy honest faces in which, as in Hellwig's, there were traces of both boyishness and manliness, reassured him, offering to help him look for it. Cries soon went up: "What kind of spots are these?" "My lining's been ripped out!" "Somebody's been in here." "Your coat's been stolen." At this, Hellwig fought back his tears. The teacher on duty in the mess hall came to find out what mischief the boys were up to now. Pale with rage, Hellwig said that his jacket had been stolen. The other teachers were sent for, and the principal came out. When the door of the shed was opened wide, the spots on the clothing and the torn lining of an old blood-spattered jacket could be seen plainly. The old pants, forgotten by a former apprentice who'd gone into the Army, were not missed.

Ah, if they had only contented themselves with tearing the lining out of his coat! Now there were no traces of manliness in Hellwig's face; rage and sorrow made him childlike. "If I catch that fellow I'll kill him!" he shouted. He didn't feel a bit comforted, either, when Mueller missed his shoes. Mueller, the only son of a wealthy farmer, could easily afford a new pair. But for him, it meant saving again, saving, saving.

"Calm yourself, will you, Hellwig?" said the inspector, who had been lunching at home when the principal summoned him. "Calm yourself, and describe your coat as minutely as you can. This gentleman here belongs to the Criminal Police, and he can get it back for you if you'll just describe it carefully."

"What was there in the pockets?" asked the pleasant strange little man when Hellwig had finished his description. (He had had to swallow hard when he came to the words "inside zipper too.") Hellwig reflected. "A purse," he said, "with one mark and twenty pfennigs. . . a handkerchief. . . a knife. . ." All that he'd said was read over to him, and then he had to sign his name. "Where can I get my jacket?" "You'll be notified about that, my boy," said the inspector.

There was scant consolation in that for Hellwig, although in a way his misfortune was glorified because the thief was no ordinary thief. No sooner had the principal inspected the shed than he put two and two together. Merely as a matter of form he asked the inspector whether he should telephone.

By the time Hellwig came out of the building, the whole space between the school and the wall was surrounded. The place where George had damaged the fruit in jumping over the wall had already been marked. Guards were stationed at the wall and at the shed. There was a crowd of teachers and gardeners and pupils behind the guards. The noonday recess had to be extended; a hard layer had formed on the pails of pea soup with pork.

Kohler, a middle-aged gardener, who came from the same village as Hellwig, was repairing the road a few yards from where the cordon was drawn, obviously unaffected by all the excitement. Hellwig's pale face had by now become red, and he was answering all questions eagerly and with an air of importance. He stopped again in front of old Kohler, probably because the fellow hadn't asked him a single question.

"I am to get my jacket back," said Hellwig.

"That so?"

"I had to describe it very minutely."

"And *did* you describe it very minutely?" asked the gardener coolly, without looking up from his work.

"I sure did; I had to," said the lad.

The principal was ringing the bell the second time; lunch was resumed. There was a rumor that the Hitler Youth of Liebau and Buchenau would be allowed to join the search.

Hellwig was questioned, but now he had become taciturn, apparently struggling against a new and more secret attack of grief. He suddenly remembered that his membership card for the Buchenau Gymnasts had been in his jacket. Ought he to make an additional report about it?

What use could the thief make of the card? He might simply put a match to it. But how could a fugitive get hold of a match? Or he might tear it up and throw it into a toilet. But could a fugitive walk in wherever he pleased? "Why, he'll simply stamp the scraps somewhere into the ground," thought the lad, strangely reassured.

He went out of his way to pass old Kohler once more. Hellwig had taken just as much notice of this man, who to him was definitely old, as young people do of old ones whose presence is taken for granted and who draw attention to themselves only because occasionally they die. There was really no reason why he should have stopped again behind Kohler. Hellwig, a strong, frank, and handy boy, was generally well liked in the Hitler Youth and among the gardeners, and he always got along very nicely. He was fully convinced that the men interned in the Westhofen Camp belonged there just as insane people belong in an asylum.

"I say, Kohler," he ventured.

"What?"

"I had my membership card in my coat."

"Well. . ."

"Wonder if I ought to make an additional report about it."

"Why, you've already reported everything; you had to, hadn't you?" For the first time he looked up at the boy. "Don't worry, you'll get your jacket back."

"Do you think so?"

"Certainly. They'll catch him without a doubt, today probably. How much did it cost?"

"Eighteen marks."

"Why, that must have been quite a coat," said Kohler, as though he wished to reawaken the boy's grief. "There's still a good deal of wear in it. While you're still sporting it when you go out with your girl, that fellow" – vaguely pointing across the land – "will be dead a long, long time."

The boy frowned. "Well, so what?" he asked suddenly, gruffly and snappily.

"Oh, nothing," answered the gardener, "nothing at all."

"I wonder why he looked at me so strangely just now," thought young Hellwig.

vi

In the yard in which George lay hidden behind a pile of wood, laundry lines were stretched in all directions. Two women, one young, the other middle-aged, came out of the house carrying a laundry basket. The older woman was robust but stern in appearance; the younger one's face was tired, and she walked with her body bent forward.

The two women felt the wash. The older one said: "It's still too damp. Wait with the ironing."

"It's ready to be ironed," the younger woman answered, as she started to take the wash off the lines.

"It's much too damp," maintained the older.

"Good enough for ironing."

"Too damp."

"Everyone to his own way. You like to iron dry, I like to iron wet."

Swiftly, with an almost desperate haste, they emptied the lines.

The village was in an uproar. "Just listen to that!" the young woman exclaimed.

"Ah, well. . ." sighed the other.

"Listen! Listen, will you?" called out the younger one, her voice almost at the bursting point.

"I'm not deaf yet," the other replied. "Push over the basket, will you?"

At that moment an SA man came from the house into the yard. The younger woman said: "For goodness' sake! Where are you coming from so suddenly, all booted and spurred? Not from the vineyard, I'm sure."

"Are both you women crazy?" he shouted. "Doing your washing now, of all times. Why, it's enough to make me ashamed of you. One of the Westhofen prisoners is hiding in the village. We're searching everywhere."

"Go on!" she replied. "If it isn't one thing it's another. Yesterday it was the harvest thanksgiving, the day before that the welcome to the 140th Regiment, today an escaped prisoner, tomorrow the *Gauleiter* will be passing through. What about our turnips? And our wine?. . . And the wash?"

"Aw, shut up," said the man, stamping his foot on the ground. "Why isn't the gate closed, I'd like to know?" He stormed through the yard. Only one side of the gate was open. To close them both, the other one had to be moved back until the two fitted into each other. The old woman helped him close it.

"Wallau, O Wallau," thought George.

"Anna," said the woman, "shoot the bolt." Then she added: "Last year I could still do it myself."

The younger one mumbled as she braced herself, "Why, *I'm* here, am I not?"

No sooner was the bolt in its place than a new and distinct noise rose above the other noises in the village – the rough and hollow impact of boots, and a drumming against the gate that had just been closed. When Anna had unbolted the gate, a few young lads came rushing in, shouting, "Let us in, will you? We're on duty, and we're searching. Fellow hiding in the village. Come on, let us in!"

"Easy! . . . Easy does it," said the young woman. "Don't act as if you were in your own home. And you, Fritz, into the kitchen with you. The soup is ready."

"Aw, Mother, let them in, will you? You must. I'll take them around."

"You'll take them where?" asked his mother.

With remarkable strength the older woman took her by the arm. The boys, Fritz in the lead, hurdled the wash basket one after the other, and presently their little whistles could be heard from the kitchen, the stable, the rooms. Crash: They'd broken something.

"Anna," said the old woman, "don't take all this to heart so. Look at *me!* There are some things in this world that we can change. But there are others that we can't. These things we have to bear. Do you hear, Anna? I know, Anna, that you got Albrecht, the worst of my sons, for a husband. His first wife was a bad one like him – the place always looked like a pigsty. But you've made a real farmhouse of it. Look at Albrecht, who used to work by the day in the vineyard whenever it suited him and idled away the rest of the time! All of a sudden he's learned a thing or two. And see what a change you made in the children of that slut who was his first wife. As if you'd made them all over again. Trouble with you is, you're so sensitive. These things now, one has to put up with them. They'll pass away in time."

The young woman had calmed down a little. There remained in her voice only a note of mourning for a life to which, in spite of her truly great efforts, a blessing had been denied.

"I know," she said, "but then *this* comes!" She pointed toward the house filled with the sound of the impertinent little whistles, and toward the hubbub outside the gate.

"That has undone everything I was trying to do, Mother. I sweat blood over the children trying to straighten them out, but now they're the same rowdies they were when Albrecht and I were married. And nowadays he himself is the same beast of a man he used to be. Oh dear!"

She pushed a log back into the woodpile with one foot. She listened attentively, then clapped her hands to her ears and wailed: "Why did the fellow have to hide in Buchenau of all places? The wretch! To come piling into a decent village on a Monday morning like a mad dog. If he had to escape, why the devil didn't he hide in the swamp?"

"Take the other handle of the basket," said the old woman. "The wash is wet through. Couldn't it have waited until after dinner?"

"We all do as our mothers taught us. I do my ironing wet."

At that moment a fearful howling came from the street beyond the gate, a howling that a human voice could never produce. But at the same time it was no animal sound either. It was as if some hitherto entirely unknown creature had suddenly come forth. When George heard it, his eyes began to glow and he bared his teeth. His throat tensed as if he himself were harboring something that he must now bellow forth with those of his own kind. At the same time, though, an invulnerable, unquenchable inner voice arose, soft, pure, and clear; and he knew that he was now ready to die as, to be sure, he had not always lived, but had always desired to live: bravely and quietly.

The two women had put down their basket. A black network of wrinkles, rough and wide-meshed in the young one, fine and closely knit in the old one, showed on their pale faces. Out of the house, through the yard, and into the street streamed the boys.

Again there was a drumming against the gate. The old woman shook off her stupor, grasped the heavy bolt, and, perhaps for the last time in her life, pushed it open by herself. A crowd of boys, old women, peasants, and SA men crowded into the yard, shouting: "Mother! Mother! Frau Alwin! Mother! Anna! Frau Alwin! We've got him. Look, look! Next door at Wurm's house! He'd been crouching in the dog house. And Max and Karl had been in the field. Oh, and spectacles, yes, the fellow wore a pair of glasses. Ha, ha, he won't need them any more. They're taking him away in Alger's car. Right next door at Wurm's. Too bad. Look, Mother! Look!"

The young woman came out of her daze and walked toward the gate. Hers was the face of a person who is irresistibly attracted by the one sight she is forbidden to view. She rose on her toes, cast a single glance over the heads of the people crowding round Alger's car, then turned away, crossed herself, and ran into the house. Her mother-in-law followed her, head wagging as if she had suddenly become an old, old woman. The basket was left behind. The yard was quiet and empty.

"Spectacles," mused George. "That must have been Pelzer. What did he want to come here for?"

An hour later, Fritz found the piece of machinery outside the yard wall. His mother and his grandmother and a few neighbors crowded around it, filled with wonder. The tag said that it had been shipped from Oppenheim and was intended for the Darré School. As one of the Algers went to get the car again – it wasn't more than a few minutes' drive to the school – they plied him with questions as to what his brother, who was in the field again, had said about the fugitive's delivery at the camp.

"Did they give him a beating?" asked Fritz with sparkling eyes, shifting his weight from one foot to the other.

"A beating?" repeated Alger. "You're the one who ought

to get a good beating someday... But I really was surprised how decently they treated the fellow..."

They had even helped him down from Alger's car. His body, tensed in the expectation of blows and kicks, had gone limp when they took him by the arms and led him inside very considerately. Deprived of his spectacles, he was unable to tell what manner of consideration it was the faces expressed; there was a blur over everything. The man was overcome with an abysmal exhaustion, for now everything was lost. He was taken not to the commander's quarters, but to the room Overkamp had equipped for himself. "Sit down, Pelzer," said Commissar Fischer amiably. His voice and eyes were those of a man whose profession it is to get something out of someone else: diseased organs, secrets, confessions.

Overkamp was sitting at one side, curled up in a chair, smoking. Apparently he was willing to leave Pelzer to his colleague.

"A brief excursion, eh?" said Fischer. His eyes contemplated Pelzer, the upper part of whose body began to sway slightly. Then he started to thumb the dossier in front of him. "Pelzer, Eugene, born 1898, in Hanau. Correct?"

"Yes, sir," said Pelzer softly, uttering his first words since his flight.

"That you should lend yourself to such a stupid thing, Pelzer, you of all people... To let yourself be talked into it by a fellow like Heisler. You see, Pelzer, it is now exactly six hours and fifty-five minutes since Fuellgrabe made his attack with the spade. Tell me, for heaven's sake, how long ago did you start hatching this plot?" Pelzer remained silent. "Didn't it occur to you at once that it was a harebrained idea? Didn't you try to dissuade the others?"

In a low voice, for every syllable bit into him, Pelzer replied: "I didn't know anything."

"Come, come," said Fischer, still restrained, his voice soft. "Fuellgrabe gives the signal, and you run. Why did you start to run?"

"Everyone did."

"Exactly. And you mean to tell me you weren't in on the secret? Why, Pelzer!"

"No, sir."

"Pelzer, Pelzer!" said Fischer. Pelzer felt like one who, still deathly tired, hears the shrilling of an alarm clock and wants to ignore it. Fischer went on: "Fuellgrabe hit the first guard when the second one was standing near you, and at that moment you threw yourself upon him, as had been agreed."

"No, sir."

"I beg your pardon?"

"I did not throw myself."

"I see. Excuse me, Pelzer. Let's put it another way: the second guard was standing near you when Heisler and... let's see... oh, yes... Wallau jumped this guard who happened to be standing near you, as had been agreed upon."

"No, sir."

"What do you mean: 'No, sir'?"

"It was not agreed upon."

"What wasn't?"

"That he happened to be standing near me. He came because, because..." He tried to remember, but he might as well have been trying to lift a leaden weight.

"Why don't you lean back? Do," said Fischer. "So it wasn't agreed upon, and you weren't in on the secret. You simply started to run. When Fuellgrabe attacked, Wallau and Heisler threw themselves on the second guard who just happened to be standing near you. Is that right?"

"Yes, sir," said Pelzer slowly.

"Overkamp!" Fischer's voice was loud.

Overkamp stood up as if their ranks were reversed.

50

Pelzer gave a start; he hadn't even noticed that there was a third man in the room. He listened attentively as Fischer said: "Let's get Albert Beutler in here." Overkamp picked up the telephone receiver... "I see," he said, after a short phone conversation. Then to Fischer: "Not yet quite in shape for examination."

Fischer remarked: "It's one thing or the other; either 'not in shape' or 'not yet in shape.' What do you mean by 'not yet quite'?"

Overkamp walked over to Pelzer and, in a sharper tone than Fischer had used but still not harshly, said: "Pelzer, you must pull yourself together now, for Beutler has just told an entirely different story. Come now, Pelzer, pull yourself together; summon your memory and the last remnants of your intelligence."

vii

George was lying out there under the gray-blue sky in a furrow in the field, about a hundred yards from the highway to Oppenheim. Not to get caught now! To be in the city by nightfall. The city! It was like a cave with hiding places and winding passages. From the beginning he had planned to be in Frankfurt and to go on at once to the suburbs and Leni. Once with Leni, everything else seemed simple to him. In a case of life and death, an hour and a half on the train shouldn't be an insuperable obstacle. The only trouble was that he was about three hours behind his schedule. True, the sky was still blue, but a haze rising from the river was already invading the fields. Soon the cars on the highway would have to switch on their lamps in spite of the afternoon sun.

Stronger than all fear, stronger than hunger and thirst and the damned throbbing in his hand (blood had long since soaked through the rag), stronger than all this was an overpowering desire to remain lying there and trust in the approaching night. *Even now the fog is covering you; the sun has already paled behind this haze above your face. During the night they won't be looking for you here. You'll have peace.*

He tried to imagine what Wallau would advise. There was no doubting what he would say: "If you want to die, stay where you are. Tear a rag from your jacket for a new bandage. Go on to the city. Anything else is nonsense."

George turned over on his belly. Tears came to his eyes as he pulled the blood-encrusted rag from his hand. He felt nauseated once more when he looked at the stiff, blackish-blue little lump that was his thumb. He rolled over on his back after he had tightened the knot of the new bandage with his teeth. Tomorrow he'd have to find someone to fix up his hand. Suddenly he realized that he was expecting all kinds of things of the morrow, as if time in its flux carried one along automatically.

The denser the haze over the fields became, the stronger grew the blue of the saffron in the meadow. Only now did George notice the flowers. If he didn't succeed in reaching Frankfurt before night, he might send Leni a message. Should he spend on it the mark he'd found in the coat? Since his escape he had not thought of her, except as he thought of some guiding mark in the road, or of that first gray stone. How much energy he'd wasted on dreams, how much precious sleep! Dreams of this girl whom luck had put in his path three weeks to the day before his arrest. "I can't picture her to myself any more," he thought. Wallau, yes, and all the others too. He visualized Wallau clearest of all, but it was the billowing fog that made the others seem blurred.

The first lights were whisking along the highway. George climbed over the ditch. A sudden flash through his mind: "You'll never get me!" The same flash propelled him on to a brewery truck. At first he was dizzy with pain, for he'd had to use his injured hand in jumping. Almost immediately, so it seemed to him, but actually in about fifteen minutes, they drove into a yard on a street in Oppenheim. Only now did the driver notice that he had a passenger. "Beat it!" he growled. Perhaps it was something in George's leap down and his first staggering steps that made the driver turn his head again. "Going to Mainz by any chance?"

"Yes."

"Wait here!"

George had put his injured hand into his coat pocket. So far he had seen the driver only from behind. Even now he couldn't see his face because he was writing something on a pad against the wall. Then the driver walked across the yard and out of the gate.

George waited. The street in front of the gate sloped up gently. There was no fog here as yet; it was as though a summer day were fading out, so soft was the light on the pavement. Across the street was a grocery store, next to it a laundry, and then a butcher's. The bells tinkled as the shopdoors opened and closed. There were two women with packages; a boy was biting into a piece of sausage. How in times past he had despised the strength and glamour of everyday life! Now to be able to walk in instead of waiting here, to be the butcher's helper, the grocer's errand boy, a guest in one of these homes! How differently, when he was in Westhofen, had he pictured a street to himself. Then he'd felt that every face and every paving stone reflected shame, that sadness muffled every step and every voice, even the children's games. But this street was quite peaceful, and the people seemed to be in good spirits.

"Hannes! Friedrich!" An old woman in the window above the laundry hailed two SA men who were walking by with their girls. "Come up, I'll make you some coffee."

"All right!" shouted the two couples, after whispering briefly to one another. As they bustled into the house, the woman closed the window with a pleased and contented smile because now she would have good-looking young people around her. George was seized with as strong an attack of sadness as he had ever known in his life. He would have wept had not that voice soothed him, the voice that even in our saddest dreams tells us that presently all will be as nothing. "And yet there *is* something," thought George. The driver returned. He was a robust man, with little black birdlike eyes in a fleshy face.

"Get up here," he said curtly. "We're not allowed to pick up riders." He nodded at a sticker which stated tersely MIT-FAHRER VERBOTEN! "But I'm short a helper on this trip. Here, put on his cap there just in case."

George fumbled in the dashboard compartment and found the uniform cap, marked above the visor GELTZ'S BREWERY. He thought of the street scene. "Not a butcher's or grocer's helper, but a brewer's."

Outside the town, evening had already come. The driver cursed the fog. "What're you going to Mainz for?" he asked suddenly.

"Hospital."

"Which one?"

"The one I was in before."

"You seem to like the stink of chloroform," said the driver. "Me, they couldn't drag me into a hospital with a team of horses. Last February when the roads were icy. . ." They came near bumping into two cars that had been stopped suddenly by the SS patrol. The truck driver slammed on his brake and cursed again. After the SS man had waved the two cars on, he approached the brewery truck. The driver handed down his truck papers.

"And how about you up there?"

"Well, it hasn't been such a bad show," thought George. "I made two mistakes. Too bad one can't practice these things beforehand." He had exactly the same sensation he'd had when he was first arrested, when the house was suddenly surrounded – a quick sorting of all sentiments and thoughts, a lightning jettisoning of all rubbish, a cleancut farewell, and finally. . .

He wore a brown coat of Manchester velvet, there could be no doubt about that. The SS patrol compared descriptions. "It's surprising how many Manchester jackets are to be dug up between Mainz and Worms within three hours," Commissar Fischer had said, when Berger had brought in a velvet-coated fellow a while ago. "This particular type of apparel seems to enjoy a certain popularity among the people of this district." Except for the clothing, the details given in the warrant of arrest were taken from the fugitive's papers when he was admitted in December, 1934. "But for the jacket," mused the patrol, "this man in no way fits the description. This fellow here could be the fugitive's father; the man in the warrant was about his own age, a healthy fellow with a smooth, fresh face. Compare this description with this man's flat, pushed-in mug, with its thick nose and pouting lips!" Then he noticed for the first time the brewer's uniform cap and his preoccupation with Manchester jackets and descriptions that didn't tally faded from his mind. He waved them on. "*Heil Hitler!*"

Without a word, they rolled along for a few minutes at a fifty-mile clip. Suddenly, for the second time, the driver braked on the empty, open road. "Get down," he ordered. George wanted to say something. "Get down," the driver repeated threateningly. His fleshy face grew distorted as George still hesitated. He prepared to throw George out forcibly. George jumped down, bruising his hand again and barely suppressing a howl of pain. He staggered on as the truck speeded up, its lights soon swallowed by the fog that had thickened during the past few minutes. Cars whistled past him at brief intervals, but he dared not hail one. He didn't know whether there were hours of walking ahead of him, or whether he had already been walking for hours. While he was still trying to figure out exactly where he was – he knew he was between Oppenheim and Mainz – he came to a little village with bright lights in the windows. He could not chance asking its name. He heard a tinkling not far ahead and saw tracks that ended in a little square, presumably the village square. Now he was among the people waiting at a streetcar terminus. He spent thirty pfennigs of his mark. At first the car was almost empty, but at the third stop, a factory, a crowd got on, and George kept his eyes down. He looked at nobody, content to give himself up to the warmth and presence of all these people; he felt safe and almost sheltered. But when anyone pushed against him or glanced at him casually, he grew cold.

George got off at Augustinerstrasse, and walked along the rails toward the center of the town. He was suddenly wide awake. But for his hand, he might have felt light-hearted. That was because of the street, the crowd, and the town generally, which leaves nobody to himself, or at least gives that impression. One of these thousands of doors would surely open hospitably, if only he could find it! He bought two rolls in a bakeshop. All this babbling of the women, old and young, around him, about the price of the bread and its quality, about the children and men who would eat it – had it actually gone on uninterruptedly all this time? "What a fancy, George," he said to himself. "It has never ceased, it will never cease." He ate his rolls while he walked, brushed some flour dust from Hellwig's jacket. Looking through a gate into a yard, he saw some boys drinking water from a fountain there; there was a cup attached to a chain. After he had had a drink, he walked on. Finally he came to a very large square which looked foggy and empty, in spite of lamp posts and the people in it. He would have liked to sit down now, but he didn't dare.

In the meantime, bells had begun to peal, so near and strong that the very wall against which exhaustion had forced him to lean seemed to reverberate. The crowd in the square began to thin. He was certain that the Rhine could not be far distant. The child he questioned answered him briskly: "What's the matter? Do you want to drown yourself tonight?" Only then did he realize that this person, although thin and weakly, was not a child, but a bold and greedy grown woman. She hung around, thinking he might ask her to accompany him down to the river. But nothing was further from his mind; on the contrary, she had made him focus his whirling thoughts and come to a decision: On no account must he cross the river over one of the large bridges; he must spend the night here in the town. Now of all times the bridgeheads were sure to be doubly guarded. To keep on the left bank, though more hazardous, was the more reasonable thing to do. He'd have to find another chance to cross farther downstream. "Don't try to reach your destination by a direct route; make a wide detour!" He looked after the girl blankly.

In the meantime the bells had ceased. The sudden silence in the square and the absence of the reverberation in the wall against which he was once again leaning made him realize how strong and powerful their sound had been. He took a step forward and looked up at the spires, but grew dizzy before he found the highest one. Above the two squat steeples near by a single spire towered into the autumn sky with so effortless a daring and ease that it hurt him. Suddenly it occurred to him that in so vast an edifice there ought to be no dearth of chairs. He looked for the entrance; it was a door, not a gate. Still marveling at actually being able to get in, he collapsed on the nearest end of the nearest bench. "Here," he thought, "I can rest." Only then did he look about him. Not even under the vast expanse of the sky had he felt so tiny. When he saw the three or four women scattered here and there, as tiny as he himself, realized the distance between himself and the nearest pillar, the distance between one pillar and another, and realized too that from where he sat he could see no ending either above or in front of him, but only space and again space, amazement rose within him. And perhaps the most amazing thing of all was that for a moment he forgot his own self.

The sexton, however, quickly put an end to his amazement. Treading firmly – you see, he was used to the place, and besides he was doing what he was supposed to do – he came stalking along between the pillars, announcing in a loud and crusty voice that it was closing time. To the women who seemed unable to tear themselves from their prayers he said – rather as an adviser than a comforter – that the dear Lord at any rate would be there again tomorrow. George jumped up in alarm. The women got up slowly and went past the sexton and through a near-by door. George went back to the door through which he had entered, but it was already closed. He was hurrying across the nave to catch up with the women when a thought flashed through his mind. He slowed his pace and ducked behind a large baptismal font. The sexton locked the door.

Out of the fog came the shrilling of the sirens of Hoechst and the roar of the railroad trains. The factory was changing shifts. Everywhere, women were preparing the evening meal. The first of the homebound bicycles could be heard on the highway. Ernst walked to the edge of the ditch beside the road. Standing with one leg forward, his arms crossed on his chest, he gazed down to where the road ascended after it passed the Grape Inn. Over his features flitted a smile of superior scorn, meant apparently for God and the world. Every evening he derived amusement from the fact that men and women had to dismount there and push their wheels up the hill. Ten minutes later the first ones were passing him, sweaty, gray, tired. *Hello, Hannes! Hello, Ernst! HEIL HITLER! HEIL! Hello, Paul!*

"I say, Franz!" said Ernst.

"Sorry, Ernst, I'm in a rush." Franz was pushing his bicycle over the ridges in the road over which he had bumped so merrily in the morning. Ernst turned around and looked after him. "What's the matter with the fellow?" thought Ernst. "I bet it's some girl." All at once he was certain that he was not particularly fond of Franz. "What does he need a girl for? If there's anybody that needs one, it's me." He set his face toward Mangold's kitchen window.

When he got home, Franz went right into the kitchen. "Evening!" "Evening, Franz," growled his aunt. The soup was already in the plates – potato soup with little sausages. Two sausages to each man – old Marnet, his eldest son, his son-in-law, and Franz – one sausage to each woman – Frau Marnet and Augusta – half a sausage to each child – Hans and Gustav. There was milk for the children and beer for the grown-ups. There hadn't been too much soup, so there was bread and another kind of sausage. During the war Frau Marnet had learned how to provide – by milking and slaughtering and maneuvering skillfully with all kinds of ordinances and restrictions – almost everything a family could need.

Plates and glasses, clothes and features, the pictures on the walls and the words the family spoke – everything proclaimed that the Marnets were neither rich nor poor, citified nor rustic, pious nor unbelieving.

"It's quite a good thing for the young fellow that he didn't get his leave right away. He found out that he can't push his stubborn head through a stone wall," said Frau Marnet, speaking of her youngest son who was serving with the 140th Regiment down in Mainz. Everybody except Franz assented. "It'll do the young man a great deal of good to be properly sweated. Anyway it's a blessing that the beggars are being taught to obey orders for a change."

"Why, today's Monday, isn't it?" said Frau Marnet to Franz, who had no sooner finished eating than he got up from the table. They had all hoped that he would help bring in the last apples. They kept on grumbling after he had gone. But after all, there wasn't much to be said against him – he'd always been decent and ready to help. The only thing against him was that he was forever going to Breilsheim to play chess with Hermann. "If he had the right kind of a girl," said Augusta, "he wouldn't be frittering his time away."

Franz mounted his wheel and rode along the field road down to Breilsheim. The town, formerly an independent village, had been united with Griesheim after the new settlement had come into existence. Since his second marriage, Hermann had lived in the settlement. His job at the railroad works had given him the right of priority. As a matter of fact he had suddenly enjoyed any number of rights and privileges, and the devil only knows how many loan possibilities, since his marriage in the spring to Else Marnet, a young cousin of the Marnets. There were times when Hermann asked himself whether he had done right to take an eighteen-year-old girl for a second wife. But he had been lonely for years – unbearably so during the last three years – and she was sweet and clinging.

Else was singing to herself in the kitchen. Her voice was not particularly strong or particularly pure, but because she sang entirely without restraint it came bubbling forth like a little brook, sad at times, at other times merry – whatever her mood was at the moment.

Hermann frowned because of a slight twinge of conscience. He and Franz put the chessboard between them and without thinking made the three moves with which they usually started the game. Franz began his tale. He'd been waiting for this minute so feverishly all day long that now that it had arrived and he had the chance to tell everything, his speech grew a bit confused. At times Hermann broke in with brief questions. Yes, indeed, he himself had heard some vague stories. At any rate, everything would have to be held in readiness. There was a chance after all that it was more than a rumor and that somebody in need of help would show up. Hermann concealed even from Franz what he himself had heard: the former District Leader Wallau, an exceptionally fine man whom he had known personally, had escaped from the Westhofen Camp. He had even heard that Wallau's wife had a hand in the matter, a fact that worried him greatly. For if this was really true, no one should have known a thing about it. As for that fellow George about whom Franz asked again and again, no, he hadn't heard a word about him. "We must think carefully," he said, "for a successful escape is of some importance after all."

viii

Franz was not the only one to lie awake that autumn night, thinking: "What if my friend is one of them?" He was not the only one to torture himself with the thought that the man he was thinking of could be one of the fugitives from the camp. He tossed back and forth on his bed in the attic chamber he had demanded for himself when he began paying something for his keep.

Why of all people should he, George, his old friend, be one of them, he asked himself for the hundredth time. But wait a minute – was George really his friend? "He certainly is," thought Franz suddenly. "He's my best and only friend!" This realization was quite disconcerting.

When had he first met George? It was in '27, in the Fichte Vacation Camp. Why, no, it wasn't, either. It was much earlier. He'd already known him when they played soccer at Eschenbach, soon after they left school. Because Franz had always been such a poor player that nobody ever gave a hoot about him, he was forever ridiculing fellows like George, who thought of nothing but soccer. "George," he'd say, "you've got a football on your shoulders instead of a head." The pupils of George's eyes would grow small and pointed. Franz was sure that it was no accident when George's ball caught him in the belly the following afternoon. After that, realizing that he was at a disadvantage, Franz stayed away from the soccer field, although he felt drawn there again and again.

Four years later he had met George again at a course he himself was giving at the Fichte Vacation Camp. George told him that what had attracted him to the camp was the inexpensive instruction in jujitsu. As for this course of Franz's only boredom had induced him to take it. He'd had no idea that Franz the teacher was his old Franz, his rotten old Franz of the soccer days – now suddenly become a teacher. Again George's eyes became mere slits, the pupils minute pinpoints of hate, as if there were something to be avenged, some outrage or disgrace. He seemed to have made up his mind to wreck the course Franz was giving. When the disturbances he created met with no response from the rest of the class but were on the contrary opposed, he simply stayed away. But Franz never stopped watching him. George's handsome tanned face often held an expression of contempt. He carried himself almost too erect, as if he felt sorry for everyone less strong and handsome than he. Only

62

when he was rowing or wrestling was he different; his expression grew pleasant and happy, as if he had escaped from himself. Actuated by a strange curiosity, Franz got hold of George's questionnaire; he found out that he was an automobile mechanic by trade, but had been out of work ever since he had served his apprenticeship.

The following winter Franz met George again at the January Demonstration. Again he was wearing his fixed, almost contemptuous, smile. Only when he was singing did his face soften. Later, after the parade was over, he met him at party headquarters. George was having trouble with one of his gym shoes; the sole had loosened in the slushy city snow. The thought had flashed through Franz's mind that George was a man who, if need be, would walk barefoot in the demonstration from beginning to end. He asked George what size shoes he wore, and in reply was given a terse: "My mother's son can attend to his own repairing." Franz asked him if he'd like to see some snapshots of the vacation camp sometime. George, he said, was in some of them. Of course George would like to see them, especially since he appeared as one of the participants in the swimming meet and in the jujitsu matches.

"Why, yes, I might have a look at them someday."

"Have you anything on for tonight?" asked Franz.

"What should I have on?" replied George. Without any apparent reason, both grew embarrassed. All the way down to the Altstadt they didn't speak a word to each other. Now Franz wished he had some pretext for leaving George. Why had he gone to the trouble of having this fellow come to see him? He had meant to do some reading. Franz went into a store and bought some sausage, cheese, and oranges. George waited outside, minus his usual smile, his expression almost black. Franz, utterly unable to understand the reason, kept looking at George through the store window.

In those days Franz lived in the Hirschgasse under one of the beautiful humpbacked slate roofs. His room was small and had a sloping ceiling; a door led to the staircase.

"You live here quite alone?" asked George.

Franz laughed. "I haven't acquired a family yet."

"So you live here all by yourself," George said again. "Ah, well!" His face was as black as thunder.

Franz guessed that George must be living in crowded quarters with a large family. His "Ah, well!" meant: *Ah, well, that's how* YOU *live. No wonder you're getting along.*

"Would you care to move in here?" asked Franz.

George stared at him. In his face there was no trace of a smile, no haughtiness. It was as if he had been taken unawares too suddenly to arm himself with his usual expression. "I? Here?"

"Why, yes."

"Are you serious?" asked George softly.

"I am always serious."

As a matter of fact, he hadn't really meant it seriously; it had just slipped out. Later it became serious, bitterly serious even. George turned pale. Only then did Franz realize that his casual offer was infinitely important to George, that it represented a turning point in his life. Franz grasped him by the arm. "It's all settled." George withdrew his arm.

"He turned away from me at once," thought Franz in his attic. "He turned to my little window, completely filled it. It was evening, winter. I turned on the light. George sat down, straddling a chair. His brown hair stood out thick and stiff. He was peeling oranges for himself and me. I took the pitcher to get some water from the tap on the landing. I was standing in the door, and he looked at me from his chair. His gray eyes were quite calm; those funny pointed dots which I'd been so afraid of when I was a boy were gone. He said: 'You know, I'll give all this a fresh coat of paint. I'll make you a stand for your books out of that box there, and a little wardrobe out of that fine chest over there with the lock. All like new! Just watch me!'"

It was not long after that that Franz lost his own job. They pooled their dole money and their occasional earnings. "What a winter," mused Franz. Not to be compared with anything he had experienced before or since. A small slanting room, now painted yellow; snowy blankets on the roofs. No doubt they'd been hungry a lot of the time.

Like everyone who has actually thought of hunger and actually fought against it, they were least of all impressed with their own hunger. Together they worked, studied, and went to political demonstrations and meetings. Together they were called upon whenever their district needed two fellows of their type. And when they were alone, the mere fact that George asked questions and Franz answered them created for them "our common world," which grew younger the longer one dwelled in it, and expanded the more one took from it.

That, at least, was how it all looked to Franz. As for George, he grew more silent as time went on, and asked fewer questions. "I must have offended him somehow," thought Franz. "Why the devil did I want to force him to read? It undoubtedly tormented him, and he felt it." George said frankly, what was the use, he couldn't retain all that stuff; he wasn't built that way. And then he began staying overnight with his old soccer chum, Paul, who ridiculed him because all of a sudden he was so highfalutin' and was always wanting to make speeches. George, apparently bored whenever Franz was away, took to staying overnight with his family again. Now and then he'd bring back his youngest brother, a tiny, lean little devil with merry eyes. "That's when it began," Franz decided. "Unconsciously he must have felt disappointed. He probably thought that by sharing my room and having my companionship... The room soon bored him, and I was so different from him. I probably made him feel the disparity between us, although in reality there was none; it was just that I was using the wrong yardstick."

Toward the end of the winter George became restless. He went out a good deal. He changed his girls rather frequently, and for the strangest of reasons. He suddenly left the most beautiful girl in the Fichte group and took up with a silly, slightly crippled little thing, a milliner at Tietz's. He devoted himself to the baker's young wife until there was a row. Then he suddenly spent a weekend with a lean, bespectacled little girl. "She knows even more than you do, Franz," he said later.

"You're no friend of mine, Franz," he said once. "You never say anything about yourself. I bring you every one of my girls for inspection, and I tell you everything. I'm sure you've got something up your sleeve, something exceptionally fine and steady."

"That's because you can't imagine anyone being able to live alone for a while," Franz had answered...

"I met Elly Mettenheimer," mused Franz, "on March 20, 1928, about seven in the evening, just before the mail closed. We were standing at the same window in the post office. She wore coral earrings. The second time I saw her, in the park, she took them off at my request and put them in her purse. I told her that only Negro women wore such trash in their ears and noses. She laughed. As a matter of fact, the coral was beautiful against her brown hair."

He said nothing to George about Elly. One evening he and Elly met George accidentally in the street. Later, George said: "Well, well!" Every Saturday evening when Franz came home George would say with a sly smile: "Well, how was it?"

66

"She's not that kind," Franz would reply frowning.

One day Elly canceled their date. Franz blamed it on her father, who he knew was very strict. The following Monday he waited for Elly at her office, but she called out that she was in a hurry and ran for a streetcar. All that week he noticed that George never stopped watching him. Franz would have gladly kicked him out. When the weekend came, George got himself up with particular care. When he left, Franz was laying out his books on the window sill for a lecture he had to prepare on Sunday. "Have a good time, Franz!" he called.

Sunday evening George came back, tanned and gay. Franz was sitting at the window sill as if he had never left it. "That, too, has to be learned," said George. A few days later Franz unexpectedly met Elly in the street. His heart leaped. Her face was hot and red.

"Franz, dear," she said, "I think I'd better tell you myself. George and I... Don't be angry with me. One can't help these things, you know. There's no cure for it."

"That's all right!" he replied, and hurried on.

For hours he wandered around, surrounded by complete darkness except for the two glowing-red little points of the coral earrings.

George was sitting on his bed when Franz came home. Franz started at once to pack his things. George watched him sharply. His glance had the power to make Franz look at him, although he had but one wish, never to see George again in his life. George was smiling slightly. Franz had a burning desire to hit him square in the face, preferably in the eye. The moment that followed was probably the first one in their life together in which they understood each other completely. Franz felt that all the desires which up to that second had determined his actions were wiped out, all but one. George, perhaps for the first time in his life, earnestly desired to be free of all entanglements and to start working toward a single goal beyond his hitherto chaotic and troubled life.

"You needn't move on my account, Franz," he said quietly. "If it goes against the grain to live with me any longer – you must admit it now, it always did a little – I'll get out. Elly and I will get married at once."

Franz had not intended to say anything, but now it escaped him. "You? Elly?"

"Yes, why not?" asked George. "This is different from all the others. This is forever. Her father will get me some work."

On his narrow bed in the attic, his arms crossed under his head, Franz recalled every word that had been spoken at the time, every change in George's expression. For years he had carefully kept it out of his mind. Whenever, in spite of himself, some memory of that period had drifted into his thoughts, it had given him a sudden start. But now he permitted everything to pass slowly in review. He was conscious of nothing but surprise.

"It doesn't hurt any more," he thought. "It's all the same to me now. Fearful things must have happened in the meantime, that all this no longer hurts me."

Three months later, Franz saw George from a distance. George was sitting on a bench in the Bockenheimer Park with his arm round a woman so incredibly fat that it couldn't reach all the way. Before the birth of her child, Elly had gone to live with her parents again. But her father, so some neighbors told Franz, suddenly urged her to go back to her husband, for he was of the opinion that since she had married him and was to have a child by him, she must try to get along with him. In the meantime George had lost his job because, as his father-in-law put it, he'd been chasing around. Elly went back to her old job. Shortly before Franz left town he learned that Elly had gone back to her people for good.

Of so outstanding importance to Franz was this affair which, had others been concerned, would simply have ended in a fistfight, that he grew sick of the town. But for people like Franz, everything is of far-reaching importance. He decided he wanted a change of scenery, so he went to live with a married sister in Northern Germany, where his mother, whom he hadn't seen in years, was living also. Franz took root there. The change broadened his whole outlook on life. At times he even forgot the reason for his coming to the new place; he became absorbed in his new home and his new comrades. As far as his outward life was concerned, he was merely one of the host of unemployed drifting from one place to another. Altogether he was not unlike a student who transfers to another college. He might have been happy if he had been able to persuade himself that he was actually in love with the quiet decent girl with whom he lived for a time.

After his mother's death, toward the end of '33, he went back to a place near the town where he had formerly lived. In this he was swayed by three things: up around his sister's place he'd become too well known and things had got too hot for him, whereas down here he had been forgotten and, because of his familiarity with people and conditions, could make himself useful to the movement. Moreover, he was sure of a livelihood with his Uncle Marnet. Old acquaintances whom he happened to run across thought to themselves: "This fellow used to talk differently:" Or: "Another one who has changed his colors."

One day Franz came across the one man in his immediate vicinity who knew all about him: Hermann, an employee in a railroad yard. Hermann told him quietly, even a shade more quietly than usual, that the night before a deplorable arrest had been made. Deplorable, because the man who had been arrested had held all threads in his hand. He had been assigned to his job but a very short time ago, and that due only to his predecessor's arrest. Quietly and calmly, but none the less plainly, Hermann discussed the possibility of the man squealing, through either weakness or inexperience. Even though his distrust might possibly be unjustified, it was nevertheless his duty to do what his doubts dictated: to change all connections and to warn those concerning whom this man had information. He interrupted himself suddenly to ask Franz curtly if by any chance he'd known the fellow when he'd lived here before; his name was George Heisler.

Franz mastered his emotion, but not sufficiently to hide from Hermann his utter bewilderment on hearing the name again after so many years. In a few sentences Franz tried to paint a just picture of George, a thing he probably could not have done even when he was calmest. Hermann put his own interpretation on Franz's confusion.

Franz thought to himself: "All those precautions we took were superfluous. We need not have changed a single connection or warned any comrades. Nor was there any reason for my fear and trembling."

A few weeks later Hermann had arranged for him to meet a man who had been discharged from Westhofen. The man had had this to report about George: "They tried to make him an example to show how a lion of a man like him could be made to eat humble pie in no time at all. The very opposite happened. They only succeeded in showing that there is nothing that can humble a man of his stamp. But they continue to torment him, for now they want to see him dead. What an expression he always shows them! They get beside themselves with rage when he smiles. And then his eyes, with so many pointed dots in them! But now his handsome face is beaten into a pulp, and the man's entire body has shrunk."

Franz got up out of bed and stuck his head out of his little window as far as he could. It was utterly quiet. But for the first time this quiet failed to give him a sense of peace – the world wasn't quiet, it was speechless. Involuntarily he pulled his hands out of the moonlight which, like no other light, has the faculty of clinging to every surface and penetrating every crevice. "How could I have foreseen," he asked himself, "what kind of man he really is? How could anyone have known that beforehand? All of a sudden our honor, our glory, and our safety are in his hands. All that happened before, all his affairs, all his pranks, they were but irrelevant nonsense. But no one could possibly have known that in advance. If I'd been in his place I might not have held out, although I was the one who. . ."

Suddenly Franz felt very tired. He went back to bed. "Perhaps he isn't one of the fugitives," he mused. "He should be entirely too weak physically now for such an undertaking. But regardless of who has escaped, Hermann is quite right; an escaped prisoner, that is what counts. It always creates an upheaval. It raises a doubt as to their own omnipotence. It is a breach."

Chapter II

i

When the doors had been locked and the sexton had gone and the last sound had disintegrated in a distant vault, George realized that he had been granted a reprieve, a respite so tremendous that he almost confused it with actual deliverance. He was filled with a burning sensation of safety for the first time since his flight, even since his imprisonment. This sensation was as violent as it was short-lived. "It's damned cold in this hole," he said to himself.

The twilight was so acute that the colors in the windows grew blurred. It had reached the point when walls recede, vaults lift up, and pillars in endless rows merge into nebulous distances that may be nothing at all, but then again may be infinity. George suddenly felt that someone was watching him. The idea paralyzed him body and soul, and he fought against it. He stuck his head out from under the font, and started to crawl out. When he was sixteen feet away from the next pillar he met the gaze of a man who, with staff and miter, leaned against his sepulchral slab. The twilight dissolved the glory of his billowing vestments, but not of his features. They were clear and innocent, but at the same time threatening; his eyes followed George as he crawled past him.

The twilight did not penetrate from outside, as it usually does. Instead, the cathedral itself seemed to dissolve, to melt. Those vines on the pillars, the distorted faces, and the pierced naked foot over there were just imagination, an illusion. Everything that was stone began to turn into vapor; George alone was stone – petrified with fear. He closed his eyes and drew his breath a few times. And then it was all over, or perhaps the twilight had become a little more acute, and thereby more reassuring. He looked for a hiding place. He darted from one pillar to another, crouching low as if he were still being watched. Against the pillar in front of which he squatted leaned a well-rounded healthy man, who from his marble slab stoically looked beyond George, on his ample face the brazen smile of power. In each hand he held a crown which through eternity he would bestow on two dwarfs, the anti-kings of the Interregnum. With one leap George made the next pillar, as if the intervening spaces were full of eyes. He looked up at a man whose clothes were so ample that he could have wrapped himself in them. He gave a violent start at the face he saw bending over him, full of sadness and compassion. *Why do you struggle on, my son? Resign yourself, for even at the beginning you are at the end. Your heart is throbbing, and your injured hand, too, is throbbing.* George discovered a suitable hiding place, a niche in the wall. Holding his left arm out like a dog with a sore paw, he slid across the aisle, under the eyes of six arch-chancellors of the Holy Roman Empire. He tried to make himself comfortable. He rubbed the joint of his injured hand where it had grown stiff. He rubbed his knees, his ankles, his toes.

He was already feverish. His injured hand must not

make any trouble for him before he reached Leni's. Once there, she would bandage it, and he could wash, eat, drink, sleep, and be cured. He started up. In that case he ought to wish that the night which a moment ago he had desired so ardently, be over as quickly as possible. Again he tried to picture Leni to himself, a conjurer's trick that succeeded at times and failed at others, depending upon place and time. This time he succeeded: a slender nineteen-year-old girl with long slim legs, her blue eyes almost black under their heavy lashes, her face a golden tan. This was the substance of his dream. In the light of remembrance and in the course of their separation this girl, who in reality had impressed him at first as a bit odd because of her long arms and legs that gave her walk a certain awkwardness, had become a fairy creature that occurs only on rare occasions, even in myths. As their separation lengthened, she had become more delicate and more evanescent with every subsequent dream. Even now, as he leaned against the icy wall, he poured out upon her a wealth of endearing terms, partly to keep himself from falling asleep.

Countless similar protestations and any number of unsubstantial adventures had followed the one time they had actually had together. On the very next day he had to leave town. In his ears rang the assurances, monotonous and desperate: "I'll wait here till you come. If you have to flee I'll go with you."

From his place George could still make out the man at the corner pillar. In spite of the darkness, distance seemed to make the face even clearer. The curved lips seemed to pronounce the last and utmost offer: Peace instead of deathly fear, mercy instead of justice.

The little flat in Niederrad, shared by Leni with an older sister who was away at work most of the time, was favorably located either for a hiding place or for flight. Considerations of this kind had followed him even when he was crossing the threshold of the tiny room, although the room made him forget almost everything else, his past love affairs and long periods of his earlier life. Not even when the walls of the room had merged into one another like impenetrable hedges had the thought ceased to glimmer in his head that this would be a good hideout in an emergency. Once while he was in Westhofen he'd been told there was a visitor to see him, and for a moment he'd been afraid that the authorities had chanced upon Leni. At first he hadn't recognized the woman who confronted him. It might just as well have been any peasant girl, so far from his thoughts was this Elly whom they had brought in.

He must have been on the point of falling asleep when fright woke him up. The cathedral was filled with crashing sounds. A bright light traversed the entire edifice and shone on his extended foot. Should he flee? Was there still time? Where to? All the gates but the one through which the light was coming were locked. Perhaps he could still get to one of the side chapels. He supported himself on his injured hand, stifled a cry of pain, and collapsed.

He no longer dared to crawl across the ribbon of light, for the sexton's voice ran out: "Slovenly womenfolk! If it isn't one thing it's another!" His words resounded like pronouncements of dooms day judgments. An old woman, his mother, called out: "Why, there's your work bag." Another voice, that of the sexton's wife, joined in, reflected by the walls and pillars into a veritable howl of triumph: "I told you, didn't I, that I put it between the benches when I was cleaning?" The two women withdrew. The noise of their footsteps sounded like giantesses dragging their feet. Again the door was locked. Sound was all that remained; it was shattered, reverberated once more as if it would never subside, died away in the most distant corners, and was still trembling when George had ceased to tremble.

Again he leaned against the wall. His eyelids were heavy. Now it was entirely dark. The flicker of the solitary lamp somewhere in the blackness was so feeble that it no longer lighted up the vault, but only accentuated the all but impenetrable darkness. A moment ago George could have wished for nothing better; but now he breathed heavily and uneasily. "You must take your things off now," Wallau counseled him, "for you will be too weak later." He yielded, as he had always yielded to Wallau and, doing so, was amazed to feel his exhaustion subside.

Wallau had been imprisoned two months later than himself. "So you are George." In these four words, the older man's greeting, George for the first time had sensed his own full worth. Some discharged prisoner must have spoken about him outside. While he was being tortured to death at Westhofen, his home village and the towns he'd lived in were forming their judgment of him – an imperishable tombstone. Even now, leaning against the ice-cold wall, George thought: "If in all my life I could meet Wallau only in Westhofen, I would go through everything again. . ." For the first time, perhaps for the last, a friendship had come into his young life at a moment when it was a matter not of bragging or belittling, of withholding desperately or giving oneself entirely, but merely of showing one's true worth and being loved for it.

The darkness was no longer so dense to his eyes. The plaster on the wall gleamed faintly like newly fallen snow. His whole body seemed to warn him that it stood out darkly. Should he change his place once more? When would they unlock the gates for early mass? There would be countless minutes of safety before morning came. He had as many minutes before him as, let us say, the sexton had weeks. For, after all, even a sexton is not immune to danger all his life.

Far away, toward the main altar, a single pillar was plainly visible as the light played along its grooves. This one illumined pillar seemed to support the entire vault. But how cold it was. An icy world, as though no human hand had ever touched it, like a human thought. As if he had been cast away on a glacier. With his uninjured hand he rubbed his feet and all his joints. In this refuge one might freeze to death.

"A triple somersault! That's the most the human body is capable of." Belloni, the acrobat, his fellow prisoner, had explained it to him minutely. Belloni, whose everyday name was Anton Meier, had been arrested straight from his trapeze because in his luggage a few letters had been found that had come from the artists' lodge in France. How often had Belloni been waked up out of his sleep to do some of his stunts. A dark silent man, a good comrade, but very aloof. "I tell you, there are perhaps only three performers living now who can do that. Oh, well, yes, this one or that may manage it once in a while, but never steadily, one day right after another." Belloni of his own accord had approached Wallau and said that he himself would attempt an escape under any circumstances. They were doomed here anyway. In his flight he relied on his own agility and his friends' readiness to help. He had given George an address where, whatever happened, he would leave some money and clothing for him. A decent fellow most likely, but one could never quite make him out. George didn't care to use the address.

On Thursday morning he would send Leni to some old friends in Frankfurt. If, in addition to his brains, Pelzer had had Belloni's sinews and muscles, he probably would have got away too. Old Aldinger surely had been recaptured by now. He could have been the father of all those blackguards, who even now perhaps were tearing his hair out and spitting into his old peasant face which failed to lose its dignity even when its owner no longer seemed to be in his right mind. The mayor of the neighboring village had denounced him because of an old family feud.

Of the seven, Fuellgrabe had been the only one he had known before. Often, from his till behind the counter, Fuellgrabe had contributed a mark, for his name was on George's collection list. Even in his greatest despair he had never been able to rid himself entirely of a certain resentment. He had just drifted into it, he would grumble; they had persuaded him; he had never been a man to say no.

Albert probably was no longer alive. For weeks he had put up with everything, protesting the trifling nature of his offense – some foreign-currency affair or other – until he had fallen into a frenzy of rage and been transferred to Zillich's punishment squad. How many relentless blows this Albert must have suffered before the last spark had been hammered out of his dulled heart.

"I shall freeze to death here," thought George, "and they will find me. The children will be shown a piece of wall: Here, on an autumn night in those wild days, a fugitive was once found frozen to death." What time was it? Almost midnight. With a new and perfect darkness surrounding him, he thought: "I wonder if anyone still remembers me. My mother? She was forever scolding. On painful feet she used to waddle up and down the street, short and fat, her breasts large and softly swaying. I suppose I'll never see her again, even if I stay alive." As far as her outward appearance was concerned, he had always been conscious only of her eyes, young and brown, but dark with reproach and helplessness. Even now he was ashamed of having been abashed before Elly, who for three months had been his wife, because his mother had such breasts and so funny a Sunday dress.

He thought of his old school chum, Paul Roeder. For ten

78

years they had played marbles in the same street, and soccer for another ten years. Then he had lost sight of him
because he himself had become another person, whereas little Roeder had remained the same. He thought now of Paul's
round freckled face as of a landscape, beloved and forever
barred. . . . Franz came to his mind. "Franz was good to me,"
thought George, "he took a great deal of pains with me.
Thanks, Franz. We had a falling out later. What was it all
about? What has become of him? A quiet fellow, decent,
loyal."

George held his breath. Across the aisle fell the reflection
of a stained-glass window, possibly lighted up by a lamp in
one of the houses facing the cathedral square or by a passing car. An immense carpet, glowing with all the colors of
the rainbow, suddenly unrolled in the darkness. Vainly and
for nobody's benefit it was thrown night after night across
the tiles of the empty cathedral, for even here visitors like
George did not appear more than once in a thousand years.

While it burned, that light outside, perhaps serving to
quiet a sick child or speed a departing man on his way, also
served to illumine all the saintly pictures. "Ah," thought
George, "these must be the two who were driven from Par-
adise; these the cattle gazing into the manger that sheltered
the Child for whom there was no place anywhere else; there
the Supper, when He already knew that He was being
betrayed; there the soldier thrusting the spear as He hung
on the cross. . ." George had long since forgotten most of
the pictures. Many of them he had never known, for in his
home such things were given scant attention. Anything that
mitigates solitude has the power to comfort. Not only other
people's suffering paralleling ours, but also the suffering
others have gone through in bygone days.

George listened. A motorcar was going by outside. He
heard the squealing and laughter of the men and women

who obviously had been squeezed into a car much too small to hold them all. They drove away. Quickly the colors of the window were reflected between the pillars, withdrawn again, farther and farther away from him. His head fell forward upon his chest.

He slept.

When he slumped over on his wounded hand, the pain made him wake up. The deepest part of the night had passed. The plaster on a piece of wall in front of him began to gleam. In an order opposite to that when the evening had come, the darkness at first began to dissolve, then pillars and walls were seized with a ceaseless rippling, as if the cathedral were built of sand. Struck by the feeblest rays of the morning light, the pictures in the windows slowly came to life; they did not flash out, but appeared in dull and somber colors. At the same time the rippling stopped, and everything began to solidify. The vault of the nave became petrified in the immutable laws that had guided the Imperial House of the Hohenstaufens when they had built it, product of individual architects' intelligence and the inexhaustible power of the people. Petrified became the vault into which George had crawled, that vault which in the days of the Hohenstaufens had already been venerable. Petrified likewise the pillars, and all the hideous faces and animal heads in their capitals. Petrified anew on the marble slabs before the pillars the bishops in their stately wakefulness of death, and the kings of whose coronation they had been so inordinately proud.

"No time to lose," thought George. He crawled out. Of his shirt and other things he had discarded he made a little bundle, drawing it together with his teeth and his uninjured hand. He slid it between a slab and a pillar. His whole body tense and his eyes shining, he waited for the moment when the sexton would unlock the doors.

ii

Ernst greeted his little Nelly with a deep chesty tone so familiar to the dog that she trembled with joy. "Nelly," said the shepherd, "Sophie, the silly goose, didn't come after all. She doesn't know what's good for her, Nelly. But we didn't lose any sleep over it, did we? And it didn't cause us any torment either."

At the Mangolds' everything was still quiet, but in Marnet's stable somebody was already busy. Ernst took his towel and the oilcloth bag in which he kept his shaving things and went to Marnet's pump. Shuddering with cold and enjoyment, he soaped himself, washed his neck and chest, and brushed his teeth. Then he hung his pocket mirror on the garden fence and commenced shaving.

Far away, in the thick fog down by the Main, the lamps were going out to the accompaniment of grumbling and yawning. Out of the yard gate of Liebau's most outlying house stepped a girl of about fifteen or sixteen, a kerchief round her head. The cloth was so white that it accentuated her fine brows below it all the more. With an expression of quiet expectation, admitting of no doubt that the man would turn up any moment on the path behind the wall of the yard as he had done every morning, she disdained even to look in the direction from which he would come but kept her eyes straight in front of her. Presently young Hellwig, the same Fritz Hellwig of the Darré School, came from behind the wall and stepped into the gateway. Without an exclamation, almost without a smile, the girl raised her arms, and they embraced and kissed. From a kitchen window two women, the girl's grandmother and an elderly cousin, watched them without envy or approval, just as one watches things that are a daily occurrence.

In spite of their youth, the two youngsters were considered engaged to each other. Today, the kissing over, Hellwig took the girl's face between his hands. They were playing the game Who'll Laugh First? but neither of them felt much like laughing. They gazed into each other's eyes until they were quite lost in them. Suddenly the girl's lids blinked a little.

"Fritz," she said, "now you'll be getting back your jacket."

"Hope so," said the boy.

"If only they haven't soiled it too much," added the girl. "You know that fellow Alger, who got hold of him last, is an awful ruffian."

The night before, the sole topic of conversation in the nearby villages had been the fugitive that had been captured in Alger's yard.... When the Westhofen Camp had been opened more than three years before, when barracks and walls had been built, barbed wire put up and guards posted, when the first column of prisoners had passed by to the accompaniment of jeers and kicks – in which even then the Algers and fellows like them had taken part – when screams could be heard at night, and howling, and on two or three occasions shots, a general feeling of depression had prevailed. People crossed themselves: What a neighborhood! Some, whose way to work took them far afield, had become used to seeing guarded prisoners at work on outside jobs, and many had thought to themselves: "Poor devils!"

It happened in those days that a young riverman openly cursed the camp. He was arrested almost at once and locked up in the camp for several weeks so that he could see for himself what was going on there. When he came out he had a strange look in his face and refused to answer questions. He found a job on a tugboat and later, so his people said, he settled permanently in Holland, a story which at the time had greatly surprised the village.

On one occasion two dozen prisoners had been taken

through Liebau; even before they reached the camp they had been in so deplorable a condition that people were horrified, and one woman in the village had wept openly. In the evening, the young new mayor of the village had summoned the woman to his house. Even though she was his aunt, he made it clear to her that her blubbering could bring incalculable harm not only to herself but to her sons, his cousins; one of the cousins was also his brother-in-law. It had been the younger people in the village, boys as well as girls, who could explain to their parents exactly why and for whom the camp was there – young people professed to know everything better than the old ones. In the old days the youngsters had claimed to have a superior knowledge of what was good, but now their knowledge ran to what was evil. Since nothing could be done about the camp, the villagers had come to accept the many orders for vegetables and cucumbers and to welcome the profitable intercourse that always follows in the wake of maintaining a large number of people.

But yesterday morning, when the sirens began their racket, when guards seemed to shoot out of the earth in every street, when rumors of the escape began to spread, and when an honest-to-goodness fugitive was captured in their very midst at noon, the camp, to which they had long ago become accustomed, was erected all over again, as it were. It was as if new walls were being built, new barbed wire spliced. The woman who had received a warning from her nephew, the mayor, almost three years ago, wept openly last night for the second time. Why had it been necessary, as long as the fugitive had been caught anyway, to crush one's heels down on his fingers when he tried to cling to the edge of the car?

Young Hellwig had been witness to all this. Ever since he had begun to think independently the camp had been there, and so had the explanations for its being. He had no other

83

knowledge. He had still been a boy when the camp had been built. Now he was almost a youth, and it was being built once more, so to speak.

Surely all of them in there couldn't be scoundrels and madmen, said the people. That riverman, for instance, he hadn't been a scoundrel, had he? When Hellwig's quiet mother said: "No!" young Hellwig looked at her. He felt strangely uneasy. Why had everything been called off for tonight? He was fond of his usual companions, liked noise, war games, marching. He had grown up in the midst of a din of trumpets, fanfares, *Heils*, and marching steps. Suddenly, this evening, everything had come to a stop for two minutes. Music and drumming had ceased, and one could hear the faint little sounds that at other times were inaudible. Why had the old gardener looked at him so strangely this noon? There were others who commended Hellwig. Because of his detailed description, they said, the fugitive had been caught.

Up the field path and over a rise walked Hellwig. He saw the older Alger among his beets and called out to him. Alger, red and perspiring from his work, came to the edge of the path. "Just think of all he's been through today," said Hellwig to himself, as if he felt he must defend the man. Alger described everything to him; he might have been describing a hunt. A moment ago he had been only a peasant going to his field earlier than the others. His description made him Storm Trooper Alger, a man who might advance to be a Zillich if he were given the chance. Once Zillich himself had been just an Alger, a peasant from Wertheim am Main. He, too, had got up early in the morning and sweated mightily, though in vain, for he had lost his tiny farm at a forced sale. Hellwig knew Zillich personally, for occasionally he came in from Westhofen when he was off duty, and dropped in at the inn and discussed village affairs. As Alger was telling him about the hunt, Hellwig lowered his eyes. At the end Alger said: "Your jacket? How do I know? No, that must have been another one of them. You'll have to catch him yourself, Fritz. Mine wasn't wearing a coat." Hellwig shrugged his shoulders. Relieved rather than disappointed, he trudged on toward the school, whose yellowish facade beckoned across the fields.

iii

On this Thursday morning, Alfons Mettenheimer, the sixty-two-year-old paperhanger, who for thirty years had been employed by Heilbach, Interior Decorators, in Frankfurt, received a summons from the Gestapo.

When something unusual and incomprehensible befalls a man, he searches within the incomprehensible for the one point that touches the periphery of his everyday life. Hence Mettenheimer's first thought was to tell his firm he could not come to work. When Siemsen, the manager, came to the telephone, he told him that he would have to have the day off. Since Mettenheimer was his best workman, this was rather inconvenient for Siemsen, for the Gerhardts' house on Miquelstrasse was to be ready for occupancy by the end of the week. Brand, the new tenant, had had everything fumigated that might have been contaminated by Jews, a request with which the firm of Heilbach had been glad to comply.

"What's the matter?" asked Siemsen.

"I can't tell you now," answered Mettenheimer.

"Can't you at least come in after lunch?"

"I can't tell yet."

Every man who is faced with the possibility of a calamity inevitably plants himself upon the bedrock of his individual character. For one man this may be an idea; for another, his faith; for a third it may be love of family. Some there are

85

who have no such bedrock, who find themselves standing on quicksand. The whole outer life, with all its terrors, may avalanche upon them, burying them inexorably.

After he had quickly reassured himself that "God" was still there – he usually gave scant thought to Him, being content to leave churchgoing to his wife – Mettenheimer sat down on a bench near the streetcar stop at which he usually boarded the car that took him to his work in the western part of the city.

His left hand began to tremble. This, however, was but an aftereffect, a merely outward manifestation. His first consternation had passed. Now he thought not of his wife and children, but exclusively of himself. Of himself who seemed to be in a fragile body which, for God knows what reason, might be tortured.

He waited until his hand had ceased to tremble. Then he got up, intending to continue on foot. He had plenty of time. His summons said nine-thirty. He'd rather get to his destination, though, and wait there. By this, too, he showed that in his way he was courageous.

He walked along down the street until he came to Police Headquarters. His thoughts were now quite calm. After all, the cause of his summons could only be something connected with George, the onetime husband of his second daughter, Elly. But this fellow was behind lock and key, had been for years. There couldn't be any new developments along that line because he himself, George's former father-in-law, had been questioned about that affair at the end of '33. And that occasion had shown clearly that he himself had strongly opposed the marriage and that, as far as George Heisler was concerned, he was entirely of one mind with his questioners. They had advised him at the time to persuade Elly to get a divorce. True, he hadn't done it. But that really had nothing to do with the matter, thought Mettenheimer, that was something entirely different.

He sat down on the nearest bench. "In that house over there, number 8, I once did a papering job. How they used to quarrel, husband and wife, whether it was to be flowers or stripes, blue or green, for the front room. I advised them to take yellow. I papered your walls, you two, and I shall continue to do so. I am a paperhanger."

They surely could only want to see him about something connected with that fellow. He had never been one of those fathers to get into arguments with clergymen on matters of religion. His youngest child would keep on at school, but only until Easter. He could not for the life of him see pugnosed little Liesbeth in the role of champion of the Church. Nor had he hesitated to explain this to the priest, when the latter put out a feeler. Let the child do what the school demanded of her; let her take her part in all the other girls' activities. He wouldn't have her do the things that were frowned upon, but would insist that she do what all the others were doing – except, perhaps, on high feast days. He felt confident that in spite of all the tomfoolery girls were being taught these days, he and his wife would be able to make a decent person out of Liesbeth. He had confidence in his ability to make a decent person even out of Elly's little boy, that child without a father.

"Alfons, the son of your second daughter, Elisabeth, familiarly known as Elly, was living at your flat all the time from December '33 to March '34, and during the daytime from March '34 to today. Is that correct?"

"Yes, *Herr Kommissar*," said Mettenheimer. He thought to himself: "What the dickens does he want with the child? He couldn't possibly have summoned me on his account. How does he know all this, anyway?"

The young man in the armchair under Hitler's picture could hardly be more than thirty. As if the room were divided into two zones by a line drawn across the desk, Mettenheimer was breathing with difficulty and perspiring all over, while the young man facing him looked brisk and the air he breathed was no doubt cool.

"You have five grandchildren. Why are you taking care of this child?"

"My daughter works in an office during the day."

"What does he want of me, anyway?" asked Mettenheimer of himself. "I'm not going to let myself be intimidated by such a young squirt. This room is like any other and this young man is just like other young men. . . ." He wiped his face. The young commissar watched him attentively out of his alert gray eyes. The paperhanger kept his crumpled handkerchief in his hand.

"There are children's homes. Your daughter is earning money. She has been earning 125 marks since April of this year. That ought to enable her to take care of the child."

Mettenheimer switched his handkerchief to his other hand.

"Why are you helping out this daughter of yours when she is quite able to take care of herself?"

"She is alone," answered Mettenheimer. "Her husband..."

The young man looked at him briefly. Then he said: "Sit down, Herr Mettenheimer."

Mettenheimer sat down. He suddenly felt that in another minute he would have collapsed. He put his handkerchief into his coat pocket.

"Your daughter Elly's husband was sent to Westhofen in January '34!"

"*Herr Kommissar!*" exclaimed Mettenheimer, half rising from his chair. Then he dropped back again and said calmly: "I never wanted to have anything to do with that man. I

88

told him never to darken my door again. Toward the end my daughter wasn't living with him."

"In the spring of '32 your daughter was living in your home. In June and July of that year she lived with her husband again. After that she went back to you. Your daughter is not divorced?"

"No, sir."

"Why not?"

"*Herr Kommissar*," said Mettenheimer, looking in vain for his handkerchief in his trouser pockets, "while she married that man against our wishes. . ."

"Nevertheless, you, her father, were opposed to her getting a divorce."

The room was not an ordinary room after all. What made it so terrible was the fact that it was quiet and light, delicately speckled by the foliage of a tree, quite an ordinary room looking out on a garden. What made it even more terrible, this young man was such a very ordinary young man with gray eyes and light hair, and yet he was all-knowing and all-powerful.

"You are a Catholic?"

"Yes, sir."

"And for that reason you were opposed to the divorce?"

"No, but matrimony. . ."

"Is sacred to you? Right? To you being married to a scoundrel is something sacred?"

"One can never tell in advance whether somebody is going to turn out a scoundrel," said Mettenheimer softly.

The young man contemplated him for a little while and then said: "You put your handkerchief in your left coat pocket."

Suddenly he banged on the table. "What kind of an upbringing did you give your daughter to have her take such a blackguard?" he shouted.

"I've brought up five children, *Herr Kommissar*. They've all done me honor. My eldest daughter's husband is a storm-troop leader. My eldest son. . ."

"I did not ask you about your other children. I'm only asking about your daughter Elisabeth. You let your daughter marry this fellow Heisler. Late last year you even went with her to Westhofen."

At that moment Mettenheimer realized that he still had his last resort in an extremity, his bedrock. With utter calmness he replied: "That is a sad errand for a young woman." To himself he thought: "This young man is the same age as my youngest son. How dare he speak to me in that tone? The presumption! He must have had the wrong kind of parents, and the wrong kind of teachers too. . ." The hand on his left knee started to tremble again. "It was my duty as her father," he added calmly.

There was silence for a moment. Mettenheimer frowned and looked down at his hand which continued to tremble.

"You won't have another opportunity to perform this duty, Herr Mettenheimer."

Mettenheimer, starting up, said: "Is he dead?"

If the questioning had been arranged with this end in view, the commissar must have been disappointed. The paperhanger's voice carried an unmistakable tone of genuine relief. The fellow's death would have settled everything with one stroke. Strange duties these, which Mettenheimer had imposed upon himself in the few decisive moments of his life; strange also his partly sly and partly harassed attempts at a possible evasion of these duties.

"What makes you think he is dead, Herr Mettenheimer?"

Mettenheimer stuttered: "You said. . . Why, I didn't mean anything."

The commissar jumped to his feet. Leaning far over the

table, he asked, his voice very mild: "Why do you assume, Herr Mettenheimer, that your son-in-law is dead?"

The paperhanger imprisoned his jerky left hand in his right. "I am not assuming anything." His calmness was gone. Thoughts of a different kind killed his every hope of being definitely rid of that fellow George. He reminded himself that, if the stories one heard were to be believed, these stubborn young fellows were tortured beyond imagination, so that his death must have been unimaginably painful.

"You must have had some reason for assuming that George Heisler is dead." Suddenly he roared: "None of your tricks here, Herr Mettenheimer!"

The paperhanger gave a violent start. Then he set his teeth and looked silently at the commissar.

"Your son-in-law was a robust young man, wasn't he? No special ailment? Therefore you must have a definite reason for your assertion."

"Why, I made no assertion." The paperhanger had grown calm again, even let go of his left hand. If he hit this young man square in the face now with his right hand, what then? Undoubtedly he would be shot down on the spot. The young man's face would be suffused with red; a whitish outline would show where Mettenheimer's hand had struck. It was the first time since his youth that so foolhardy and utterly impossible an idea had entered his old, harassed mind. The thought came: "Ah, if I had no family!" He suppressed a smile by feeling for his mustache with his tongue. The commissar stared at him.

"Now you listen to me carefully, Herr Mettenheimer. In view of your depositions, which not only confirm our own observations but, in some important points, even supplement them, we should like to warn you. We should like to warn you, Herr Mettenheimer, in your own interest, in the interest of your whole family, whose head you are. Abstain from taking any step, or making any remark, which is in any way connected with the former husband of your daughter Elisabeth Heisler. And if you have any scruples, or need any advice, do not turn to your wife or to any member of your family, do not seek assistance from your priest, but come to our central office and go to Room 18. Do you understand, Herr Mettenheimer?"

"*Jawohl, Herr Kommissar,*" said Mettenheimer. He had not understood a word. What had he been warned about? What had been confirmed? What scruples might he have? The young face he had just wanted to strike had suddenly turned to stone, the impenetrable image of power.

"You may go now, Herr Mettenheimer. You live at Hansa-strasse 11 and are employed by the firm of Heilbach?... *Heil Hitler!*"

A moment later, Mettenheimer was standing in the street. The city lay flooded by the light of the warm, caressing autumn sun which imparted to the crowds that general air of festive cheerfulness which is usually the prerogative of spring. The crowd carried him along.

"What did they want of me?" he thought. "What was the real reason for that summons? Perhaps it was because of Elly's child, after all. They could deprive one of – what is it called? – the right of provision." Suddenly he felt quite cheerful. He considered it a settled fact that someone in authority had interrogated him about some official matter. How could a thing like that have disturbed him so? He had not the slightest inclination to keep on puzzling his brain about it. He wanted the smell of paste in his nose, to crawl into a suit of overalls, to merge so deep with his usual life as to be undiscoverable. At that moment the streetcar came rolling along. He pushed aside some people and jumped on. He himself in turn was pushed into the car by a man who jumped on behind him. He was a plumpish man, not much younger than himself; his new felt hat seemed to be perched on the top of his head rather than put on. They outdid each other in puffing and blowing. "At our age," said Mettenheimer, "I call this enterprising."

The other replied angrily: "I should say so!"

When Mettenheimer arrived at his place of work, Siemsen greeted him: "If I had only known, Mettenheimer, that you'd be here so soon. Why, I thought you'd had a fire, or your wife had fallen into the river."

"Just some official business," said Mettenheimer. "What time is it?"

"Half-past ten."

Mettenheimer slipped into his overalls. At once he began to scold: "Again you've pasted the border first. What does that look like? No contrast at all. All you're afraid of is that the paper will smear. You'll have to be careful, that's all. It'll have to come down, that's all there is to it." He mumbled: "A good thing I got here in time." He hopped up and down the ladders like a squirrel.

iv

George had been successful. No sooner had the cathedral been opened than he assumed the role of early churchgoer. He was one of only a few men among a good many women. Recognizing him from the night before, the sexton thought to himself with a feeling of satisfaction: "Aha, another one who got it just in the nick of time. . ." It took George some little time to stand up straight. Painfully he dragged himself outside. "He won't last more than a few days," thought Dornberger, the sexton. "He'll collapse in the street." George's face was gray, as if he had some fatal disease.

If only his hand were not causing him so much trouble. Why must there always be some tiny bit of nonsense to ruin everything? "When and where did this happen to my hand? On the glass-encrusted wall, about twenty-four hours ago. . ." He felt pushed along by the people through the side door of the cathedral and into a short little street, framed by low houses in which the shops were already lighted.

When the cool damp air hit his face, George was done for. His legs slid from under him, and he found himself in a heap on the pavement. Two elderly ladies, spinster sisters, were coming out of the church. One of them forced a five-pfennig piece into his hand. The other scolded. "You know that's forbidden!" The donor bit her lips. She had been scolded these fifty years.

In spite of everything, George had to smile. How fond he had been of life! He had loved all of it: the sweet little lumps on the seeded cakes and even the chaff they put into the wartime bread; the cities and the rivers and the country and its people; Elly, his wife; and Lotte and Leni and little Katy and his mother and his little brother; the party slogans to make people come alive; the little songs to the accompaniment of a lute; the sentences Franz used to read to him, which contained great thoughts that upset his whole life; and even the babbling of old women. How good the whole had been; only the single parts were evil.

He pulled himself together and, propped against the wall, looked hungrily and miserably toward the market whose stalls were being put up under the fogbound lanterns. He felt his blood surge to his heart as if, in spite of everything, he were being loved in return, though perhaps for the last time, by all people and by all things, with a painful and helpless love. He stumbled the few steps to a pastry shop. Fifty pfennig he would have to keep as capital. He put a few coins on the counter. The woman poured a plateful of crumbs, broken ends of toast, and burnt edges of cakes on a piece of paper. She glanced briefly at his jacket; it seemed to her much too good for such a purchase.

Her glance brought George fully to his senses. Outside, he stuffed all the crumbs into his mouth. Chewing very slowly, he dragged himself to the edge of the square. The street lights were still lit, but they were useless. The opposite row of houses was already visible through the haze of the autumn morning. George walked on and on through a maze of streets that wound like yarn around the market; he finally emerged again upon it. He noticed a sign: DR. HERBERT LOEWENSTEIN.

"Here's the man who's got to help me," thought George. He walked up the stairs.

For a moment there was silence as he entered the waiting room. Everyone there looked at him briefly. There were two groups of patients. On the sofa near the window sat a woman and a child and a youngish man in a raincoat. At the table, an old peasant and a middle-aged citified man with a boy, and now George.

The peasant was talking. "Now I am here the fifth time. He has not helped me any, but there is a certain relief, yes, a certain relief. I hope it'll last at least until our Martin is home from his military service and gets married." His monotonous voice showed that even talking caused him pain. But he was partly repaid for it by the satisfaction he had in telling his story. "And you?" he added.

"I haven't come here on my own account," said the other drily, "but because of the lad here. He's my only sister's only child. The child's father has forbidden her to send him to Loewenstein. So I just took the boy and brought him myself."

The old man sat clasping his hands round his abdomen, probably the seat of his pain. He said: "As if there were no other doctor to go to."

The other man said quietly: "Well, you yourself come here, too."

"I? I've been to all the others, too: Dr. Schmidt, Dr. Wagenseil, Dr. Reisinger, and Dr. Hartlaub." Suddenly he turned to George: "What's the matter with you, eh?"

"My hand."

"Why, this is no doctor for hands, he's internal."

"I have some internal trouble too."

"Automobile accident?"

The waiting-room door opened. Quite overcome by pain, the old peasant leaned on the table and against George's shoulder. It was not only fear that filled George, but a child's irrepressible anxiety in a doctor's waiting room. He remembered having had the same sensation when he was a little boy no older than the jaundiced lad at his side. As in those days, he caught himself continually plucking at the fringes of his chair.

The doorbell rang. George gave a start. But it was only another patient, a half-grown dark girl, who went past the table.

At last he was facing the doctor. Name, address, occupation please. He said whatever came into his mind. The walls were beginning to sway; he felt himself gliding down an abyss of white and glass and nickel, a meticulously clean abyss. While he was gliding he heard the doctor's voice make obligatory reference to his being a Jew.* A smell reminded him of the aftermath of all cross-examinations when iodine and bandages were being applied. "Sit down," said the physician.

On first seeing George, he had thought that this patient made a thoroughly unfavorable impression. He was quite familiar with the symptoms: no gaping wounds, no ab-

*In Nazi Germany at this time a Jewish physician was required by law to inform his Aryan patients that he was a Jew.

96

scesses, a very delicate, thin shading above and below the eyes – in this case it had already grown into a blackish compact shadow. What could ail the man?

He began to undo the ragged bandage. An accident? Yes. A physician through and through, he was immediately under the spell that every wound and every disease exerted upon him. Yet through it all he was aware of his uneasiness at the mere sight of this man, a feeling that grew stronger when he saw the bandage. From the lining of a jacket? He undid it very slowly. What kind of man was this, anyway? Old? Young? His preoccupation grew.

He looked at the hand which now lay exposed before him. Undoubtedly it was badly messed up, but not so badly as to justify the symptoms displayed on this man's forehead and in his eyes. Why the terrible exhaustion? He had come because of his hand. Without question, perhaps unknown to himself, he was also suffering from some other ailment. The glass splinters had to be removed now. He would have to give the man a hypodermic injection; otherwise he might faint. He had said he was an automobile mechanic.

"In a couple of weeks," said the doctor, "you'll be able to go back to work." The man did not reply. Will he be able to stand the injection? The man's heart, though not entirely sound, was not in a particularly bad condition. What was the matter with him? Why did he not follow his impulse to find out what ailed the man?

And why had the man not gone to the nearest hospital immediately after the accident? The dirt in the wound had certainly been in there at least over night. He wanted to ask these questions, if for no other reason than to distract the man's attention from his hand.

Now he set to work with the pincers, but the man's eyes restrained him. He stopped short. Again he looked closely at the hand briefly at the man's face, at his jacket, at his

97

whole person. The man twisted his mouth slightly, gazing at the doctor obliquely but firmly.

Turning away slowly, the physician felt himself go white to his very lips. As he looked at himself in the mirror above the wash basin the dark shadows had spread to his own face. He closed his eyes. He soaped his hands and washed with infinite slowness, letting the water run.

"I have a wife and children. Why does this man have to come and see *me?*... To have to tremble every time the bell rings... And what I have to go through anyway, day in and day out!"

George looked at the doctor's white back. He thought: "Not you only!"

The physician was holding his hands under the water, making it squirt. "It's unbearable, really, what I have to go through. And now this into the bargain! Why, it's unbearable that anyone should have to suffer so."

George thought again, his brows knit, while the water gushed forth like a spring: "But not you only!"

The doctor turned off the water and dried his hands on a clean towel. For the first time he smelled the chloroform as only his patients usually smelled it. "Why did the man come to me of all people? To me? Why?"

Again he turned on the tap. He washed a second time. "See here, this doesn't concern you at all. It was just a hand that came into your consulting room, a sick hand. Whether it dangles from the sleeve of a scoundrel or from under the wing of an archangel must be a matter of indifference to you." He turned off the water and dried his hands again. Then he adjusted his syringe. Turning George's sleeve back, he noticed that the man was not wearing a shirt. "That does not concern me," he said to himself. "I'm concerned only with the hand."

Later George slid his bandaged hand into his jacket and

said: "Thanks very much!" The doctor had meant to ask for some money, but the man had thanked him in a tone that suggested he believed himself treated without charge. Though he reeled a bit when he left, the doctor thought now that after all the chief trouble had been his hand.

As George was going down the stairs, the janitor, a little man in shirt sleeves, planted himself in front of him on the bottom landing. "You coming from the second floor?"

With no time to reflect whether truth or untruth would be wiser, George quickly lied: "From the third."

"Oh, I see," said the little man. "I thought you might have come from Loewenstein's."

When George got out on the street he saw on a stoop two houses away the old peasant of the waiting room. He was staring toward the market. The fog had lifted. The autumn light lay on the large umbrellas which, mushroom-like, were stretched above the stalls. Only when George bent his head far back could he see the top of the spire, a golden pinnacle by which the whole city could be borne upward. After he walked a few steps, past the peasant who stared after him, he saw high above the roofs the effigy of Saint Martin on his horse, cutting up his cloak. George went where the crowds were densest. Apples, grapes, and cauliflowers danced before his eyes. His hunger was at first so greedy that he had to restrain himself from plunging his face into the various stands and eating his fill. After a while he felt nothing but loathing. Now his condition was the most dangerous of all. Dizzy with exhaustion, too feeble to think clearly, he reeled about among the stalls and finally stopped in front of the fish stands. Leaning against a lamp post, he watched a man scaling and disemboweling a huge carp. He wrapped it in a piece of newspaper and handed it to a young woman. Then the man scooped up some little frying fish from his tub, gave each one a quick slit, and threw a handful on his scales. George felt nauseated, but at the same time compelled to watch closely.

The old peasant on the stoop looked dully after George until he lost sight of him. For a little while longer he watched the people hurrying about in the autumn sun. The whole market seemed obscured by his pain. The upper part of his body swayed to and fro.

"And for this," he thought to himself, "the scoundrel made me pay him ten marks, not one pfennig less than Reisinger." There was no use arguing with Reisinger. As for the Jew Loewenstein, he'd get his son to attend to him. He pulled himself upright with his stick and dragged himself across the square to an automat. Looking out through the window, he saw George again, his hand freshly bandaged, leaning against the lamp post. So steadily did the old man stare at him that George turned his head toward the window. He was uneasy. Though from where he stood he could distinguish nothing behind the window, he forced himself to leave and went past the fish stands toward the Rhine.

By this time Franz had already punched a hundred little plates. In Noggin's place, after his arrest, there was quite a young lad who swept off the dust. At first all of them had paused for a moment because they had been so accustomed to seeing Noggin. But this lad was such a brazenly merry youngster that almost immediately they nicknamed him Snapper. Now, instead of "Noggin! Noggin!" they called: "Snapper! Snapper!"

The night before, in the locker room, all the men had not been so much excited over Noggin's arrest as over the sudden and unaccountable increase in the number of punched aluminum plates. Only during the day had the meaning of this become clear. One of the men said that one part of the machine had been changed so that the lever could be pressed down four times a minute instead of three; the plates, once inserted, now rotated automatically after each punch instead of having to be pushed by hand into their new position. Another workman considered the wage increase that they expected on the first was the main point after all. Still another, an older man, said he'd never been so dead tired as he was the night before. Several of the men answered that on Monday night one was always dead tired.

Such talk and its cause and the tone of it would ordinarily have furnished Franz with considerable material for thought. He would study the basic process that gave birth to a number of other processes, each more important in its way than the fundamental process, the disclosure of human nature, and the manifestation of man's true state of mind. But now Franz was disappointed, even disturbed, at the failure of the news that filled his mind day and night to be absorbed into the arid soil of everyday life.

"If I could only just go to Elly and ask her," thought Franz. "Is she living with her parents again? No, I couldn't risk that, unless I happened to run into her by chance."

He decided to make careful inquiries in her street to find out whether she had gone back to her family. Possibly Elly was no longer even in town. Oh, he still felt drawn in that direction, eh? The wound which either stupidity or a childish whim had inflicted upon him in those days was still rankling. It was important – vitally important.

"Why that's utter nonsense," thought Franz. "I bet Elly has grown fat and ugly. If I saw her again, I'd probably feel grateful to George for having cut me out when he did. And besides, she doesn't concern me at all any more."

He decided he would ride over to Frankfurt after work. He wanted to buy something at a store in the Hansastrasse, and then he might ask about the Mettenheimer family... Snapper was beside him, reaching under his elbow. Franz lifted his arms slightly and spoiled his plate. Rattled, he spoiled the next one too; even the third one was still not perfect.

Suddenly Franz saw and heard the whole shop where he worked as he had seen and heard it five weeks ago, in the first minute of his work there. He heard the humming of the belts that cut into one's brain and through all one's thoughts but could not drown the fine rasp the metal ribbon made as it rubbed against the bearings. He saw the faces which were quite bleak in the steady light but which twitched every time the lever had to be pressed down.

At no great distance from where Franz worked, a half hour's ride on a bicycle, a crowd had collected in a busy street near the Central Railroad Station in Frankfurt. People were craning their necks. There was a big hotel, the Savoy, in one of the blocks of houses, and a sneak thief was being hunted. Nobody seemed surprised to see not only an unusually large squad of policemen but also a number of SS men. This sneak thief, they said, had got away several times, but now he had been caught red-handed in a hotel room after stealing a few rings and some pearls.

"Just like a film," they said. "All we need is Greta Garbo." Their faces wore a smile of surprise and mild amusement. A girl screamed; she had seen something – or at least thought she had – up there on the edge of the hotel roof. The size of the crowd and its tension continued to increase. Every second they expected to witness a rare spectacle, something of a cross between a ghost and a bird. Even the fire department had now appeared, with its ladders and nets.

The object of pursuit, Belloni, known in everyday life as Anton Meier, was crouching behind a chimney on the Savoy roof. But where was his everyday life now? Where Belloni, the acrobat? To the last he had still been a stranger to George

102

and the others, though he was probably a decent enough chap. Belloni himself had been well aware that he and George were still strangers. To become friends, they would have had to be together longer.

Belloni's view from behind his chimney was limited. He could not see the streets full of people who were avidly following the search, eager to take part in it. Above the low iron grating of the sloping roof he could see only the outmost edge of the plain. High up in the west, he saw the shimmering sky in its calm pale blue, birdless and cloudless. While the crowd waited down below, he, on his roof, also waited with the bold calmness that he had learned as a child, the same calmness with which, as an acrobat, he had charmed the audience. People never quite realized what it was in his simple stunts that so fascinated them.

Three hours ago they had tried to arrest him in a flat owned by the mother of one of his former fellow performers. This chap had been a member of his troupe until an accident disabled him. The police, however, had, among other things, made up a list of all the troupes to which he had ever belonged. To keep a watch on all these performers involved hardly more difficulty than surrounding a few blocks of houses. Belloni had jumped through a window and run through several streets in the direction of the Central Station. After two hair's-breadth escapes, he dashed into the hotel through the revolving doors. He was wearing the new clothes he had gotten the day before, and his bearing was so calm and correct that he crossed the lobby without being stopped. The little money he had in his pocket made him once more entertain a slight hope of taking a train away from the city.

Now it was less than half an hour later, and he no longer had any hope. But on this last stretch of the road, this stretch without hope, he meant to fight for his freedom. To do this he had to get down to the next roof. Carefully and calmly he slid down the sloping roof a few yards until he reached a small walled-in chimney near the railing. He still thought he had not yet been discovered. He peeked under the railing and saw the black crowd hemming in the block of houses. Then he realized that he was lost. Worse than lost. He knew that these people crowded the streets to make a fugitive's escape impossible. The infinite shimmering space seemed to invite an artistic performance that he felt was beyond him. Should he try to climb down, or should he simply wait? Either one was senseless; the manifestation of fear as senseless as the evidence of courage. But he would not have been Belloni, had he not chosen the latter. He stretched his legs downward until his feet reached the railing.

Belloni had been seen when he was squatting behind the second chimney. "Into the feet," said one of the two men who were hiding behind a signboard on the edge of the next house. The other one took aim as the first man had ordered him to; when he shot he had to master a slight feeling of nausea, or perhaps only excitement. Then the two clambered skilfully and bravely onto the hotel roof after Belloni.

In spite of the pain, the fugitive had not loosened his grip; he held on all the more firmly. Creeping between the chimney and one corner of the roof, he left a trail behind him. Then he rolled against the railing. Once more he summoned all his strength and swung himself over the low railing, before they could get to him.

He plunged into the hotel yard, so that in the end the crowd had to disperse, cheated out of the expected experience. Afterward, in the conjectures of the idlers, in the excited reports of the women, Belloni kept floating above the roofs for hours, part ghost, part bird. When he died in the hospital toward noon (he had not been killed immediately) two men were still arguing about him.

"All you have to do is issue a death certificate," said the younger of the two physicians to the older one. "What do you care about his feet? They were not the cause of his death." Overcoming a slight feeling of nausea, the older man did as the young one suggested.

$\mathcal{V}$

It was now half-past ten. The sexton's wife was in charge of a number of cleaning women who worked according to a fixed plan clearly set forth in the regulations of Mainz Cathedral. If this plan were followed, every inch of the cathedral would get its turn at being cleaned at least once a year.

Hence it was the sexton's wife who found the little bundle behind the archbishop's marble slab. George would have done better to shove it under a bench. "Why, just look at this, will you?" she said to her husband who was just coming from the sacristy.

Dornberger looked at the shabby object but kept his thoughts to himself. "Get on with your work!" he said harshly. He took the little bundle across the yard and into the diocesan museum. "Father Seitz," he said, "look at this, will you?"

Father Seitz, like his sexton a man in his sixties, opened the bundle on a glass showcase, in which on a background of velvet lay a collection of baptismal crosses, neatly numbered and dated. A filthy rag made of drill. Father Seitz raised his head. The two men looked into each other's eyes.

"Tell me, why did you bring this filthy rag to me, my dear Dornberger?"

"My wife," said the sexton somewhat slowly, so as to give Father Seitz time for reflection, "just found this behind Bishop Siegfried of Epstein."

The priest looked at him with surprise. "See here, Dornberger," he said, "are we a lost-and-found office or a diocesan museum?"

The sexton stepped quite close to him and said softly: "I wonder if I oughtn't to take it to the police."

"To the police?" Father Seitz was greatly surprised. "Why, are you in the habit of taking every woolen glove you find under a bench to the police?"

"There were some stories going around here this morning. . ." Dornberger mumbled.

"Tales! Tales! I suppose you don't hear enough of them as it is. Will there be another one tomorrow, I wonder, about people coming to the cathedral to change their clothes? Phew, what a stink! You know, Dornberger, you could easily catch something from this. I'd burn it if I were you. But I wouldn't put it in my kitchen stove, it's too filthy. I tell you what, I'll put it right in here."

The little iron stove had been lit the first of October. Dornberger stuffed everything in and left the room. There was a stench of burning rags. Father Seitz opened the window a crack. His expression of geniality had disappeared; his face became serious, even somber. Once more something that had happened might as well evaporate through the crack of the open window as consolidate into a fearful stench that would be apt to suffocate one in the end.

While his bloodstained rags were turning into a thin wisp of smoke and escaping through the crack of the window much too slowly and with entirely too much smell to suit Father Seitz, George had found his way down to the Rhine and was now trudging downstream along the raised sandy promenade beside the highroad. Earlier, when he was still a boy, he had sometimes been taken along on excursions into this district. He knew the villages and little towns west of Mainz offered innumerable possibilities of getting to the other bank on a boat or ferry. When he had thought about this, especially at night, it had all struck him as nonsensical, empty hopes that depended on a thousand-and-one contingencies. But as he walked along, pondering these contingencies and possibilities, surrounded by danger, things did not seem so entirely hopeless. He went back over the last few hours in his mind. "Who saw me? Who can furnish a description of me?" Once caught in this circle he was already half-lost. Fear is the condition in which a certain idea begins to overrun everything else. Out of a clear sky, on this quiet path where no eyes were turned in his direction, he was seized with it. It was a new attack of fear, a sort of intermittent fever that occurred at ever-increasing intervals. He leaned on the railing. For the space of seconds, sky and water were obscured. Then the fear was gone – automatically, so George thought. As his reward because it had gone he now saw the world neither obscured nor exaggeratedly real, but in its usual everyday splendor: calm water and gulls, whose cries did not disturb the quietness but, on the contrary, made it perfect. "It is autumn," thought George. "The gulls are here."

At his elbow someone was leaning over the railing. Looking at him, George saw that he was a riverman in a dark-blue pullover. Whenever anybody leans over the railing here, he never stays alone very long. Soon there is a chain of rivermen off duty, anglers who just don't feel like angling, and old people. The flowing water, the gulls, the ships loading or discharging cargo – all this seems to be kept in motion for the benefit of those who watch it steadfastly. Beyond the riverman five or six others were already lined up.

"What do they charge here for a jacket like that?" asked the riverman.

"Twenty marks," answered George. He meant to walk

away, but the question had loosened a thought in his mind.

Down the highroad below the railing came a bald, fat riverman. "Hello, down there!" Cries from above were hurled down on the man's bald head. He looked up, laughing, and grabbed the legs of the man above him, who braced himself. In the twinkling of an eye and in spite of his bulk, he hoisted himself up, his large bald dome appearing between the other man's legs. More questions came. "Hey, there! How goes it?" "All right," answered the newcomer; it was immediately evident that he was a Dutchman.

At that moment there came from the direction of the city a little man with a fishing pole and a tiny pail, such as children play with in the sand. "Ah, there comes Pickerel," said the fat fellow, chuckling. As far as anyone knew, Pickerel with his rod and pail was as integral a part of the place where the city went fishing as the wheel was on the city's escutcheon.

"*Heil Hitler!*" shouted Pickerel.

"*Heil Pickerel!*" returned the Dutchman.

"Now we've caught you," said one chap; he'd been hit in the nose in a fight, putting that member, temporarily at least, slightly on the bias. It seemed that at any moment it might right itself again. "You are buying your whitebait in the market."

To the Dutchman he said: "What's the news in the wide world?"

"Well, there's always something doing," said the Dutchman, "but I hear that a couple of things have been happening around here, too."

"Oh, yes!" said Crooked Nose. "With us everything goes like clockwork and is in apple-pie order. Honestly, we no longer need a *Führer!*" And when they all stared at him aghast, he added: "Because we have one already whom the whole world begrudges us." Everybody laughed except the speaker; he pressed his thumb against his nose.

"Eighteen marks?" the riverman asked George.

"I said twenty," replied George. He had lowered his eyelids because he was afraid the brightness of his eyes might betray him.

The riverman felt the material. "Does it wear well?" he asked.

"It sure does," answered George. "Only trouble is it isn't very warm. Woolens keep a fellow warmer."

"My girl knits me a pullover every season."

"Ah," said George, "when the heart's in it. . ."

"Want to swap?"

George closed his eyes as if he were figuring. "Try it on, why don't you?"

"Let's go into the toilet." George didn't mind the general laughter; he did not care to have them see that he was wearing no shirt.

When the exchange had been made, George went on downstream at a run rather than at a walk. Carrying himself extra straight in his new jacket, one hand on his hip, the other raised in salute, the riverman joined the other men, his broad face displaying his conviction that once again he'd got the best of a fellow.

"To keep it would have been dangerous," thought George, "but to swap it was dangerous too. Well, now it's done, for better or worse."

Suddenly someone at his side called out: "Hey, there!" With his pail and rod Pickerel came prancing after him, as light-footed as a little boy. "Where are you bound for?" he asked.

George pointed straight ahead. "Following the Rhine."

"Aren't you from this part of the country?"

"No," replied George. "I was in a hospital here. I am going to visit some relatives of mine."

Pickerel said: "I hope you don't mind my company. I'm naturally very sociable."

George kept silent. He gave the little man another brief sideways look. From his early childhood George had had to fight against a strong feeling of discomfort whenever there was something wrong with a person, be it a twist of the brain or of the soul, or some physical defect. Only Wallau at the camp had succeeded in curing him entirely of such aversions. "Here you have an example, George," he'd said, "of how a fellow can come by such a thing." In this round-about way, George began to think of Wallau again. He was seized with an unconquerable sadness. "Whatever of life there is in me now," he thought, "I owe to him, even if I have to die today."

Pickerel, in the meantime, was babbling on endlessly. "Were you here the other day when we had the great celebration? How funny it all seems! Were you here at the time of the occupation? How those Moroccans rode through the city on their gray horses! How red their cloaks were! I say, why are you running so? Do you intend to be in Holland by nightfall?"

"Is this the way to Holland?"

"Well, to begin with, you'll get to Mombach, where the asparagus grows. Is that where your relatives live?"

"Farther below."

"In Budenheim? In Heidesheim? Are they farmers?"

"In a way."

"In a way," repeated Pickerel.

"Shall I get rid of him?" said George to himself. "How on earth can I manage it? No, it's always much better to be with someone. It shows that you have some ties." They passed the little swing bridge across the Flosshafen.

"Good Lord, how company makes the time pass!" Pickerel spoke as if George had been assigned there by somebody for the express purpose of making the time pass.

George looked across the Rhine. Over there, on an island – how near it was! – stood three low white houses close to each other, their reflections mirrored in the water. The middle house looked like a mill. Something in these houses seemed familiar and attractive to George, as if someone of whom he was fond were living there. Arching over the island to the distant bank was the span of the railway bridge. They passed the bridgehead on which was stationed a guard. "He looks fine," said Pickerel approvingly. George followed the little man from the path and across the meadow. Once Pickerel stood still, sniffing the air. "Nut trees!" He stooped and picked up two or three nuts which he put in his pail. George searched frantically, cracking the nuts frenziedly with his heel against a stone. Pickerel began to laugh. "Why, you seem crazy about these nuts." George pulled himself together. He was perspiring and exhausted. After all, this damn Pickerel wouldn't be tagging along after him forever. Somewhere he'd have to begin fishing. "Just keep cool and you'll see," he answered when George put out a gentle feeler in this direction. Willow bushes began to make their appearance, reminding George of Westhofen. His displeasure mounted. "Here we are," said Pickerel.

George was staring straight ahead. They were standing on a point of land. Before them and to the right and left lay the Rhine; there was no going ahead.

Pickerel, observing George's startled face, began to laugh. "Ah, there's where I fooled you. I caught you, all right! Just because you were in such a hurry. You didn't expect this, did you now?" He had put down his rod and pail and was rubbing his hands against his thighs. "As for myself, I at least had some company," added Pickerel. The little man had no idea how near death he had been only a second ago. George turned away and covered his face with his uninjured hand. With a tremendous effort he said: "Well, so long!" "*Heil Hitler!*" answered Pickerel.

At that moment the willows parted and a policeman with a tiny mustache and a lock of hair falling over his forehead said cheerfully: "*Heil Hitler*, Pickerel! Come on now, let's see your fishing license."

"Why, what do you mean? I'm not fishing, am I?"

"What about your rod?"

"Oh, I always carry it with me, just like a soldier carrying his rifle."

"And the pail?"

"Just look. Three little nuts."

"Pickerel, Pickerel!" said the policeman. "Well, what about you over there? Got your papers?"

"That's a friend of mine," interjected Pickerel.

"All the more reason," said the policeman. At least he meant to say it, for George, who had at first taken a few slow, casual steps toward the willow bushes, was now walking faster. He parted the branches and finally began to run. "Halt!" shouted the policeman, all his cheerfulness and affability gone. "Halt! Halt!" he shouted again in a thoroughly policemanlike voice.

Suddenly the two of them were running after George, the policeman and Pickerel. George let them pass him. How like the Westhofen stench it all was: silvery puddles and willows, the sound of whistles, and the violent beating of his heart that must betray him. Over there at the nearby bank there was a bathing beach – logs washed by the water, and between the logs a raft.

"There he is," shouted Pickerel. Now the whistles sounded on the bank. All that was lacking was the siren. Worst of all, though, was this dragged-down feeling – his knees like putty

– but there was also the feeling of being dragged down into unreality, for this could not actually happen to one, it must be some wild dream – but still one kept running and running. George fell flat on the ground; he noticed that there were rails under him. He had turned away from the river into a factory district. From behind the walls came a continuous whirr, but no whistles and no human voices.

"Finished," he said, not knowing himself what he meant by it, whether it was his strength or his weakness that was finished. Without a thought he waited a little while for outside help, for an awakening, for a miracle. But there was no miracle, and no outside help either. He got up and walked on. He came to a wide highway with a double row of tracks. The road was lonely because it was lined not by rows of houses but by some manufacturing plants. Telling himself that the riverbank might be guarded now, he walked again toward the city.

So many hours lost! "She must be waiting for me now," he thought, until he became aware of his stupidity in not realizing that Leni could not be waiting because she knew nothing. Nobody to help him, nobody to wait for him. Was there really no one to wait or to help? His hand hurt, for he had fallen on it again. A pity: the nice clean gauze was quite dirty.

Booths were being dismantled in a little market place, an offshoot of the large market. Before an inn a fleet of trucks was drawn up. He went in and sat down to a glass of beer. His heart leaped wildly, as if there were a tremendous amount of space inside him; but with every leap his heart bounded hard against his ribs. "I shan't be able to stand this very much longer," he thought. "Hours perhaps, but never days."

A man at a neighboring table eyed him sharply. *Haven't I met this fellow somewhere today? Well, there is no help for it now, none whatsoever. I've got to make a break. Up, George!*

There were as many people outside the inn as there were inside, guests and people from the market. He took in everything carefully. A young fellow was helping an elderly woman who was loading a truck. George walked up to him as he stepped down from the truck and went to a pile of baskets. "See here! What's the name of the woman up there?"

"That one? That's Frau Binder."

"That's the one," said George. "I have a message for her."

He waited beside the baskets until the motor was running. Then he went up to the truck. Looking up at her, he said: "You are Frau Binder, aren't you?"

"What is it?" asked the woman with distrustful surprise.

George looked at her firmly. "Just let me get up there a minute," he said, "and I'll tell you. I'm going that way myself." The truck started, and George swung himself up. Very slowly and with great detail he began to spin some yarn about the hospital and a distant relative.

In the meantime the man who had sat at the neighboring table had come out and accosted the young chap with whom George had just spoken. "What did that fellow ask you just now?"

"Why, whether that woman was Frau Binder," the young man said with surprise.

vi

Mettenheimer was in the habit of going home for lunch, if where he happened to be working was not too far away. But today he went to an inn and ordered pork chops and beer. He treated the tiny apprentice to a bowl of pea soup and later a glass of beer; and he asked him some questions in the assured manner of men who have themselves brought up a number of sons. Somebody came through the door and ordered a glass of light beer. Mettenheimer recognized the newcomer by his new felt hat as the man he'd ridden with on the streetcar that morning. For a moment, and hardly consciously, he had a slight feeling of uneasiness. He stopped talking to the apprentice and swallowed his last few bites quickly. He was in a hurry to get back to his work to fix up whatever in his opinion had been ruined because he had to be late that morning. He had said nothing to his wife about the summons, and now he decided he wouldn't tell her at all. He was anxious to forget all about his questioning, about this crazy summons. He'd never make any sense of it, anyway. Most likely there was none.

Mettenheimer fussed and scolded because the border had been pasted wrongly. He wanted to come down from his ladder to see that everything on the ground floor was being done properly, but a sudden dizzy spell made him hold fast. He swayed on his ladder. A voice from the staircase shouted: "Knock off!" In a rage, Mettenheimer shouted back: "It's still up to me to say when to knock off!"

At the streetcar depot he once more came across the felt-hatted man who had ridden with him in the morning and had had a drink at the same inn. "I suppose he also works somewhere around here," thought Mettenheimer, watching him board the car. Mettenheimer nodded to him.

Suddenly he remembered that again he had forgotten to pick up the package of wool for his wife at the porter's desk. The night before, she'd given him an awful scolding when he'd come home without it. He got off the car again and went back, hurrying so as not to miss the next car. He was very tired now. He looked forward to his supper and to being at home. Suddenly he felt his heart contract under the impact of a strange chilly uneasiness. The man with the new hat whom he had left on the first streetcar had suddenly materialized again on the front platform of this car. Not trusting his own eyes, the paperhanger changed his seat. There could be no mistake about it. By now he was quite familiar with the man's hat, his shaved neck and his short arms. Mettenheimer had intended to ride to the Zeil and walk the rest of the way, instead of changing cars. Now, however, he got off at the Central Police Station and took another car.

He breathed more easily when he saw that he was alone. But no sooner was he on the platform of this car than he heard hurrying steps behind him and the sound of a little grunt as a man jumped on. The felt-hatted man's gaze brushed lightly past him, entirely unconcerned, yet very precisely. Then he turned his back, for Mettenheimer would have to pass him anyway when he got off. The paperhanger now realized that the man would get off after him and it would be impossible to escape him. His heart pounded with panicky fear. His shirt, which had long since dried on his body, was wet through again. "What does the fellow want of me anyway?" thought Mettenheimer. "What have I done? What shall I be doing next?" He could not resist the temptation to turn around once more. Among the hats the evening crowd was wearing – overdue summer hats and early fall hats – he saw the one he was looking for approach at a moderate speed, as if its wearer knew in advance that the paperhanger would be in no mood tonight for unexpected ventures. Mettenheimer crossed the street. Before entering his house he turned around quickly again in an excess of courage typical of people who, in a corner of their hearts, are ready to put up a defense in an emergency. The pursuer's face was close behind him – a flabby, lazy face with poor teeth. His clothing was rather shabby, with the exception of the new hat. Perhaps the hat was not new, just less shabby. All in all, there was nothing fearsome in the man himself. For Mettenheimer, the fearsomeness was the inexplicable contradiction between obstinate pursuit and utter unconcern.

When Mettenheimer reached the vestibule of his house, he put the package of wool on the stairs and started to close the front door. During the day it was fastened back against the wall by a hook.

"Why are you doing that, Father?" suddenly asked his daughter Elly who was just coming down the stairs.

"There's a draft," replied Mettenheimer.

"How can you feel that up in your flat?" asked Elly. "They'll be closing the door at eight anyway." The paperhanger stared at her. His whole body told him that the man had planted himself over there on the opposite side of the narrow street and was watching him and his daughter.

She was his favorite daughter after all. Perhaps the man standing guard over there knew this. In what secret emotion did he expect to surprise him? In what open misdeed? Wasn't there some fairy tale about a father promising to give as a gift whatever he saw first coming out of his house? So far he had kept it a secret from his whole family, even from himself, that this child was dearest to his heart. Why? Even now he didn't know. Perhaps because of two contrary emotions. Because she was good-looking, and because she always brought him sorrow.

Elly touched his arm. In its frame of thick curly hair, her face looked small like that of a child. Her expression was one of sadness and affection. She recalled the day when, on the bench of a Westhofen inn, her father had pressed her head to his shoulder and roughly told her to cry to her heart's content. Neither of them had ever again referred to that day. No doubt, though, they both thought of it whenever they met.

"I'd better take the package of wool with me," said Elly, "since I am going to start it anyway."

117

The paperhanger could almost see the piercing glance of the man on the opposite side of the street fasten upon the little package. He felt as if his daughter were cramming some baleful object into her shopping bag, although he knew that there was nothing in the package except a few pieces of colored wool. Elly's face had become serene again. Her eyes, golden brown like her hair, spread a warm glow over her whole face. "Where did that fellow George have his eyes," he thought, "that he could leave her?" Her serenity cut into his heart. He tried to put himself in front of her so that no glance from across the street would fall upon her.

"If a trap has been set," he thought to himself, "this child in any event is innocent." But Elly was tall and robust, while he was short and shriveled. He could not shield her. Tensely he looked out into the street and watched her walk away, light and erect, swinging her shopping bag. He breathed more easily, for he had seen the pursuer turn his back and look into the window of the perfumery store. Elly passed him unnoticed.

Mettenheimer, however, failed to observe the agile young man with the little mustache who darted out next to the perfumer's and nudged the man with the felt hat lightly with his elbow as he went past him. Their eyes met in the mirror surface of the show window. Like anglers staring at the same water and going after the same fish, they both saw in the mirror the opposite side of the street, the paper-hanger's front door, and Mettenheimer himself.

"You want me to plunge my family into some calamity," Mettenheimer thought, "but you shall not succeed." Suddenly at peace with himself, he mounted the stairs. The man with the felt hat went into the public house from which the young one had hurried, and sat down at the window. The mustached young man, walking with long springy steps, soon caught up with Elly. He had to admit to himself that her legs and hips made his tedious job quite bearable.

In his living room Mettenheimer stumbled over Elly's boy, who was building something on the floor. Elly had left the child here overnight. Why? His wife shrugged her shoulders. Her face betrayed that she had many things on her mind, but her husband paid no attention to that. On any other evening he would have had his fun with the child, but now he asked: "What does she have her own room for?" The little boy grabbed his grandfather's forefinger and laughed. The old man did not feel like laughing. He gently pushed the child away. Now he could remember every word that had been said during this morning's questioning. He no longer felt as if he had been dreaming. His heart was as heavy as lead. He went to the window. The perfumer across the street had lowered the roller shutters of the shop. Mettenheimer was not deceived. He knew that one of the blurred shadows in the window of the public house had its gaze trained upon his house. His wife called him to supper. "I'd like to know when you're ever going to do some papering in your own home," she said, as she always did.

Franz, on his way home from work, dismounted from his bicycle shortly before reaching Hansastrasse. He was pushing his wheel and trying to decide whether to go into a store and ask about the Mettenheimer family. At that moment, what he had hoped for, and perhaps also feared, actually happened – he caught a glimpse of Elly. He clung to his bicycle. Lost in thought, Elly failed to see him. She had not changed at all. She was as straight and slender as ever. Her quiet movements were somewhat subdued and melancholy, but this had been true even when there was no cause for melancholy. She was still wearing her earrings. Franz was glad, for he rather liked them against her thick brown hair. Had Franz been a man to put what he felt into words, he might have said that the Elly of tonight was much more like her real self than the Elly he had carried in his memory. It hurt him that she went past him, though he realized she did not see him, could not see him. He would like nothing better than to do what he had done when he first met her at the post-office window: take her in his arms and kiss her lips. "Why should I not possess what is meant for me?" he thought to himself. He forgot himself, forgot that he was an insignificant-looking man with plain features that had no outward animation, that he was poor and awkward. He let Elly pass him. The young man with the mustache also passed him, although Franz could have no idea that he had any connection with Elly.

Franz turned his bicycle and pedaled after Elly for about ten minutes, until he saw her enter the house in which she lived as a subtenant with her child. From top to bottom he scrutinized the house that swallowed her. Then he inspected the surroundings. Diagonally across from the front door there was a baker's and confectioner's shop. He went in and sat down.

The only other customer there was the slender, rather neat young man with the mustache. He was sitting at the window, looking out. Even now Franz paid no attention to him. He felt like complimenting himself on his common sense in not rushing into Elly's house at once. But the day was not over yet. She might go out again. At any rate, he determined to wait there in the store as long as possible.

Elly in the meantime had changed her clothes, combed and brushed her hair, and, in short, done everything else she ought in her opinion to do to induce the guest she expected this evening actually to come, stay for a meal and – this thought, too, Elly did not entirely reject – perhaps even stay the night. With an apron over her clean dress, she went to her landlady's kitchen, beat and salted two cutlets, put lard and onions in a pan, and had it ready to put on the fire as soon as the bell would ring.

The landlady, a woman of about fifty, watched her with a smile. She was not a bad sort; she was fond of children and quite in agreement with all the robust manifestations of life. "You are quite right, Frau Heisler," she said, "one is young only once."

"Right? What do you mean?" asked Elly. Her face had suddenly changed.

"Oh, just that you're having supper with someone outside of your family for a change."

Elly, on the point of replying "I'd much rather eat by myself," decided to say nothing. She knew very well that she was anxiously waiting to hear the front door slam and firm steps resound on the stairs. She was waiting, certainly; but on the other hand she was also possibly entertaining a secret hope that something might intervene. "I'll make a pudding too," she thought. She poured out some milk, put in some cornstarch, and began stirring. "If he comes – all right," she suddenly decided, "if he doesn't come – all right, too."

She was waiting, to be sure. But how miserable this waiting was, compared with what she had once waited for. . .

There had been a time when she had waited for George's steps week in and week out, night after night. At that time she still dared to stake her young life against the empty night. Today she felt instinctively that her waiting had been neither senseless nor ridiculous, but something infinitely better and more to be proud of than her present humdrum life, when she had lost the very strength to wait. "Now I'm like all others," she thought sadly. "Nothing is very important any longer." She would certainly not stay awake the following night waiting, if her friend failed to come tonight. She would yawn and go to sleep.

When George had told her the first time that she need

wait no longer, she had not believed a word he had said. True, she had gone back to her parents, but that had only meant changing where she waited. If waiting had the power to draw people into each other's presence, George would have returned to her at that time. But there is no magic in waiting; it has no power over anyone else; it belongs only to the one who is waiting, and for that very reason it requires courage. It had brought no reward to Elly, unless it was the calm and never eloquent sadness which at times lent an unexpected beauty to her pretty, young face. These thoughts were also in the landlady's mind as she watched Elly cooking. "By the time you've eaten your cutlets," she said reassuringly, "your pudding will have cooled."

When George had made it clear to her that there was no longer any sense to her waiting – not roughly but with firm decision, because her waiting was irksome to him – when with calm and clever words he had explained to her that marriage was no sacrament and even the expected child no extraordinary event, Elly had at last given up their room for which she had secretly been paying the rent all the time.

But still she continued to wait – even during the night when her child was born. What better night could one have chosen to return suddenly? After a few days' searching, Mettenheimer had at last succeeded in dragging that rascally son-in-law of his to Elly's sickbed, but he repented it later, when he saw his daughter after George had gone. From the beginning he had counseled Elly against this marriage, and subsequently against a divorce; but now he realized that, come what may, his daughter must not wait any longer for it. Therefore, at the end of the second year – that was the year of '32 – he called at the official registration department, in an effort to locate his son-in-law. Not even George's own parents knew where he was keeping himself. . . .

The year '32 drew to a close. Elly soothed her baby, who

had been torn from sleep by the explosions of toy torpedoes and shouts for a happy '33. George remained undiscoverable. Whether one shrank from searching too assiduously, or whether Elly's mind was diverted by the care of her child, the whole affair began to sink into oblivion. Elly could still remember the morning when she had ceased to wait. Toward the end of the night she had been awakened by an automobile horn, and she'd heard steps in the street that might be George's, but they had passed by. Along with the diminishing ring of those footsteps Elly's waiting had also diminished. A last fading sound, and her waiting was at an end. No illuminating thought had come to her, no decision. It was simply that her mother had been right, as older people usually were. Time heals all wounds, and even the hottest irons grow cold. She had fallen asleep again quickly. The following day, Sunday, she had slept till noon. Rosy and refreshed, a new, sound Elly, she had appeared at mealtime in the living room.

Early in '34 Elly had received a summons. Her husband had been arrested and sent to Westhofen, they told her. Now at last, she had said to her father, the man had been found; now he could be sued for divorce. Her father had looked at her with surprise, as one looks at a beautiful and costly object on which a blemish is suddenly revealed.

"Now?" he had repeated.

"Why not now?"

"This must have been quite a blow to the fellow."

"I too have had to stand many a blow," Elly had replied.

"But after all, he is still your husband."

"That's all over and done with," Elly had said.

"You don't need to stay in the kitchen," said the landlady. "When the bell rings I'll put on the cutlets."

Elly went to her room. At the foot of her bed stood her

child's empty crib. Though her guest was already overdue, she would indulge in no idle waiting. She opened the package, felt the wool, and began to knit.

The man for whom she was now waiting – not very intensely, though – had been a chance acquaintance, a certain Heinrich Kuebler. A girl friend from her office had persuaded Elly to go to a dance. At first she had been sorry for having yielded. At the dance, a waiter behind her had dropped a glass. She had turned around, and at the same time this fellow Kuebler who happened to be walking through the hall had also turned. He was a tall, dark-haired man with strong teeth. A faint resemblance to George in his carriage and smile had lent added beauty to Elly's face, so that Kuebler had become aware of her, stopped short, and approached her. They had danced till morning. Seeing him at close range, she realized that there was really no resemblance to George at all. Kuebler was a decent enough chap. He took her to a few dances and to the Taunus on Sundays, and he'd kissed her a few times.

Elly had casually told Kuebler about her husband. "It was a bad break," was the way she put it. Heinrich had urged her to get rid of George definitely. She had decided to take care of this by herself.

One day, Elly had received a visitor's permit for the Westhofen Camp. She ran to her father; she hadn't asked his advice in a long time. "You must go," he said, "and I'll go with you." Not only had Elly not requested the permit, but she wished it had not come. Whoever arranged for it had had his own reasons for doing so.

Since neither blows nor kicks, hunger nor solitary confinement had any effect on this prisoner, they conceived the idea of having his wife come to see him. Seeing one's wife and child is bound to make a certain impression upon most men.

Both Elly and her father asked for a day off from work, but said to the family nothing about their painful journey. On the way to the camp, Elly was longing to be at her type-writer or lying in a Taunus meadow with Heinrich, and Mettenheimer was thinking about a papering job. When they had left the train and were walking along the highroad through several grape-growing villages, Elly reached for her father's hand as though she were suddenly a little girl again. She felt dry and brittle. Their minds were heavily oppressed.

When they came to the first houses on the outskirts of Westhofen, people's glances followed them with a sort of casual pity, as if they had been going to a hospital or a ceme-tery. How painfully they were aware of the general activity and the cheerful excitement that prevailed in the wine vil-lages... Why couldn't one simply be one of these people? Why not the one who was trundling this vat across the street to the tinsmith's? Or that woman cleaning her sieve on the window sill? Why couldn't one help to flush the yard before the wine press was set up? But instead, one had to walk a strange road, oppressed by an unbearable uneasiness. A young fellow who looked more like a riverman than a peas-ant stepped up to them and said quietly and earnestly: "You'll have to go round that way, across the field."

Mettenheimer decided that he would wait for Elly in the garden of an inn. Now that she would have to go on alone, she was seized with fear. But she repeated to herself that George was no concern of hers. She would permit herself to be moved neither by his unenviable position nor by his familiar face, his eyes, or his smile.

At that time, George had already been in Westhofen a long time. He had behind him countless grillings, and suf-fering, and agonies, enough for a whole generation swept by war or some other catastrophe. These agonies would con-tinue to be inflicted, perhaps tomorrow or perhaps even the next minute. Even then George was well aware that only death could help him. He knew the fearful power that had crushed his young life, and he also knew his own power. He knew now who he was.

Elly thought at first that they had brought the wrong man into the room. She lifted her hands to her ears, a rather attractive motion she had of assuring herself that her earrings were fastened securely. Then her arms fell to her side. She kept staring at the strange man flanked by two S A guards. Why, George was a tall man; this one was almost as short as her father, his knees were bent under him. She finally recognized him by his smile. It was the old unmistakable smile, partly cheerful and partly contemptuous, with which he had taken her in at their first meeting. But now, to be sure, it was decidedly not a question of enticing a young woman away from a friend whom one loved only too well.

He tried to form a thought in his tortured brain. Why had they brought this woman to see him? What was their object? He was afraid that his exhaustion and his physical suffering might make him overlook something of importance, some trap.

George stared at Elly. To him she was as strange as he was to her: her rakish little felt hat, her curly hair, and her earrings. He kept watching her. He began to remind himself of what she'd meant to him before – little enough. All the while five or six pairs of eyes were watching closely for the slightest emotion in the features still disfigured by the latest outrage. "I'll have to say something to this man," thought Elly. So she said: "The child is well."

He pricked up his ears. His gaze sharpened. What could her remark have meant? It surely must have a particular meaning; perhaps she was bringing him a message. He feared he was too weak to make out its meaning. With a questioning look he said: "Is that so?" She would certainly have recognized him by that look now. As strongly and warmly as it had that first time, it clung to her partly opened lips. What message would there be, to fill his life anew with strength and energy?

After a long and agonizing pause, while she was probably searching for the right word to say, she continued: "He'll soon be going to the kindergarten."

"I see," said George. How excruciating it was for his brittle head to have to think so quickly and acutely! What did she mean by his going to the kindergarten? It probably had some connection with the change in plans Hagenauer had told him about when he came to Westhofen about four months ago, after some of the party functionaries had been arrested. His smile grew more intense.

"Would you care to see his picture?" asked Elly. She searched in her handbag upon which not only George's eyes but also those of the guards were fastened. She lifted up to him a small photograph pasted on a piece of cardboard. George bent over the picture of a child playing with a rattle, his brows painfully knitted in his effort to recognize something important. He looked up, gazed at Elly, and down again at the picture. He shrugged his shoulders. Again he looked at Elly, this time darkly, as though she were making fun of him.

A guard called out: "Time's up!" They both gave a start.

George asked quickly: "How is my mother?"

"All right," Elly replied. She had not seen the woman who had always been a stranger to her, almost repugnant to her, in more than a year and a half.

Again George asked: "And my little brother?" He seemed suddenly to have come alive; his whole body twitched. It seemed to Elly no less terrible that George's appearance was becoming more human second by second. "How is. . ." He was grabbed on either side, turned around, and led out.

Back home once more, Elly had sat down and written a letter to Heinrich. He was not to call for her at the office and he must stop seeing her.

Undeterred, Heinrich waited for her at the office. He plied her with questions as to whether that fellow George had made an impression on her again, whether she'd suddenly grown fond of him again, whether she was sorry for him, and whether she would take him back again after his discharge. Elly listened with surprise to what seemed to her only nebulous and nonsensical conceptions of something about which she alone really knew. Calmly she answered him. No, she was no longer fond of George, would never return to him even if he were free; that was over for all time. But since she had seen George, Heinrich's company no longer gave her any pleasure. She simply didn't care for it any more, that was all.

Heinrich's position was similar to Franz's a few years earlier, when George had suddenly taken Elly away from him. But Heinrich, not being a particularly serious man himself, refused to believe in the finality of Elly's decision. What would be the sense of it? Oh, sure, if she still cared for George! But as it was. . . What good would it do her to stay all by herself? George would never know about her constancy, he'd not even believe it if she had an opportunity to tell him later. Why create difficulties artificially?

That, too, had been more than a year ago. Today she had invited Heinrich, the cutlets were prepared, the pudding had been stirred. She had made herself pretty for him. "Why has all this suddenly come over me again?" Elly asked herself. "Why should I want him again?" It had not been a particularly hard job to make up her mind. Nothing of any importance had happened. But a year is a rather long time. It was tedious to be all alone every evening. Elly, a very average type of girl, was not cut out for it. Perhaps Heinrich was right: "Why do all this for the sake of a man who has become such a stranger to one?" In the course of a year even the horrible face, disfigured by many blows, had faded somewhat from her memory. Mother was right, and so were all the old people – time does heal all wounds, and even the hottest irons do grow cold.

At the bottom of her heart Elly still entertained a faint hope that Heinrich would stay away. She would have been unable to explain what difference it made, since, after all, she had invited him.

Below in the confectioner's shop, Franz was looking out into the street. The street lights went on. Warm as the day had been, there could now be no doubt that summer had long since gone. The little store was poorly lighted. The woman at the counter was noisily rattling some plates. She would undoubtedly have welcomed it had her two tenacious customers left. Suddenly Franz grabbed the little table in both his hands. He could not believe his eyes. Between the lampposts and toward Elly's house George was coming along, a few flowers in his hand. Franz's mind spun round and round in a mad whirl. There was nothing missing in that whirl: fright and joy, rage and fear, happiness and jealousy. Then, as the man came nearer, it was all over. Franz, calm again, was thoroughly angry with himself. This man bore a faint resemblance to George only at a distance, and then only if one happened to be thinking of George.

In the meantime, the confectioner had got rid of at least one of her two customers. The young man had flung a coin on the table and rushed out. Franz ordered another cup of coffee and a second portion of seedcake.

At the sound of the doorbell Elly's eyes shone in spite of everything. A moment later Heinrich was standing in the room, holding a bunch of carnations in his hand. Quite disconcerted, he looked at the young woman sitting on the edge of her bed. She did not seem to have been waiting for him very anxiously; a ball of colored wool in her lap prevented her from getting up. Elly raised her face and laughed. Then she reached for her bag and stuffed her knitting in it, her embarrassment prompting her to do this with exaggerated slowness. She got up and relieved Heinrich of his carnations.

From the kitchen came the odor of frying meat – Elly had to smile at the promptness of kindhearted Frau Merker. Heinrich's face was so serious that she stopped smiling. Under his firm look she turned her face away. He took her by the shoulders, increasing the pressure until she lifted her head and looked at him. Oblivious of everything else, Elly was now quite sure that this man's coming was a happy event.

At that moment there were voices and steps on stairs and landing. Had somebody actually called it, or was it merely a thought: "Gestapo!" Heinrich's hands slid down; his face became rigid as if he had never smiled in his life and would never smile again.

Although Franz was by no means a fast thinker, he had no difficulty in finding an explanation for what he saw from his table at the confectioner's during the next few minutes. For a while there was some heavy traffic in the quiet little street, although not so heavy as to attract undue attention. A large dark-blue motorcar had stopped at the nearest corner. At the same time, a taxicab drew up at Elly's house; the driver kept his motor running. Not a second later came another taxicab which did not overtake the first one but stopped immediately behind it with a shriek of its brakes.

Hardly had the first taxi stopped, when three young men in ordinary street clothes jumped out. After a very brief stay in the house, they got in again, escorting a fourth person. Franz could not have sworn that this fourth person was the man he had mistaken for a second for George, for the other three, either by design or by accident, blocked the view between the taxi and the street door. What he did notice was that this fourth person did not go along quietly and decently; in contrast with the quick, erect movement of his companions, he rather gave the impression of one drunk or ill. After they drove away in the cab, the second taxi also stopped in front of Elly's street door. Its two passengers ran into the house and in a short time returned with a woman.

A few passers-by had stopped for a moment. One or two people might have been looking from near-by windows. But the little strip of pavement in front of the street door was intact and clean in the glare of the street lights; it was not the scene of an accident, it was not spattered with blood. If perchance these people had any suspicions, they took them with them to the bosom of their families.

Franz fully expected that he, too, would be arrested at any moment, but he managed to get away on his bicycle unmolested.

"So, after all, George is one of the fugitives," said Franz to himself. "They are keeping a watch on his relatives, his erstwhile wife, and certainly also his mother. They suspect that he is here in the city. Perhaps he actually is hiding somewhere. But how does he expect to get out of here?"

In spite of what George's fellow prisoners had told him, Franz had never been able to picture George in his present condition, the condition Elly had seen him in. But the memory of the old George rose within him suddenly and distinctly. He saw him so plainly that he felt like shouting out loud. Centuries ago, in times as dark as the present, people had shouted in like manner when in a crowded street or in the bustle of a gay celebration they thought they

131

had seen the one person whom a forbidden memory – or call it their conscience – had conjured up. Franz now visualized George's boyish face, his expression – both bold and sad – and his dark hair that grew down thick and attractive from the crown of his head. He saw George's head supported by his cupped hands, a head resting on two shoulders – a head representing an object – a head representing a prize. Franz scorched along the road as if his own safety were threatened.

In a frenzy of emotion, which fortunately was not fully apparent in his somewhat coarse and heavy features, he arrived at Hermann's house, but was even then prevented from unburdening his heart because Hermann had not come home from his work yet. "A meeting," explained Else, looking at Franz's upset face with her round eyes which were as curious as they were pure.

Feeling instinctively that Franz needed comforting, Else offered him some licorice drops from a box. Hermann occasionally brought her sweets because the first time he'd given her a present, he had been moved when he saw that so trifling a thing could bring such a glow of happiness to her face. Franz, who regarded her as a child, stroked her hair, but he regretted it at once when he saw her start and blush. "So he isn't home," said Franz, so lost in his despairing thoughts that a groan escaped from his lips. She gazed after him as he pushed his bicycle up the road and, childlike, felt deeply affected by a sorrow of which she had no comprehension.

vii

George ran on into the evening, so misty and still that it gave him a sense of elusiveness. At every step he told himself that the next step would surely be the last one. Every step, however, was but the next to the last. Shortly after passing through Mombach he had been ordered to get off the market truck. There were no longer any bridges here, but there was a landing place at every village. George had left one after another of them behind him. The moment to cross to the other bank had not yet come. If a man's energies are focused upon one point, everything – instinct as well as reason – will transmit a warning to him.

As on the evening before, he lost his sense of time. Foghorns were sounding from the Rhine. On the highroad which ran beside the river on an embankment, lights were flitting past at ever-increasing intervals. A tree-covered island in the near foreground obstructed his view of the water. Beyond the reeds gleamed the lights of a farm, but they filled him neither with fear nor with confidence. So deserted was this part of the country that they looked like will-o'-the-wisps. The view-obstructing island extended a long distance – perhaps it, too, had already come to an end. The lights might be those of a ship or they might come from the opposite bank which was no longer hidden by a tree-covered island but by the fog. A fellow might perish here in a very ordinary way, a victim of common exhaustion. To have two minutes now of Wallau's company, no matter in what hell...

If Wallau succeeded in getting to a certain Rhenish town, there was hope that he could get out of the country from there. People who had carefully prepared the next stage of his flight were waiting there.

When Wallau was imprisoned the second time, his wife was convinced that she would never see him again. Her requests for a visitor's permit having been denied roughly, even threateningly – she had personally gone to Westhofen from Mannerheim, where she was now living – she had decided to save her husband at no matter what cost. She followed up this decision with the uncanny perseverance of a woman whose first step in approaching an impracticable plan is the elimination of her sense of judgment, or at least of that part of it whose function is to pass on the practicability of things. Wallau's wife was guided neither by previous experiences nor by information vouchsafed by those around her, but by two or three legends of successful escapes. For instance, Beimler's from Dachau, Seeger's from Oranienburg. Legends, too, contain certain information and certain experiences. She also knew that her husband, a man of iron determination, had centered all his energies on the burning desire to live, and that he would thus grasp the slightest chance. Her refusal to distinguish in her quest between what was possible and what impossible did not prevent her handling many details skillfully. In the establishment of connections and in the transmission of news she used her two boys, especially the older one. In earlier days he had been well taught by his father and, burning with zeal, he was now in on the secret regarding his mother's plans. A dark-eyed, persevering lad in the Hitler Youth uniform, he was burned rather than enlightened by the flame that was almost too much for his heart.

Now, on the evening of the second day, Frau Wallau knew that the jail break itself had been successful. She could not know when her husband would arrive at the bungalow on the allotment garden plot near Worms, where money and clothing were stored for him. Perhaps he had already passed through there last night. The bungalow was the property of a family named Bachmann. The man was a streetcar conductor. The two women had gone to school together thirty years before, and their fathers had been friends, as their husbands also had been. Both women had shared all

134

the burdens of a common life and, during the past three years, the burdens of an uncommon one as well. Bachmann, to be sure, had been in prison only a short time early in '33. He had been working ever since and had not been molested.

It was this man, the conductor, for whom Frau Bachmann was waiting now, while Wallau's wife was waiting for her husband. Although Frau Bachmann knew that it would take her husband ten minutes to get from the car barn to his home, she was greatly disturbed, a fact which manifested itself in minute twitching motions of her hands. Perhaps he had had to take another man's place – he would not be home before eleven. Attending to her children, Frau Bachmann grew somewhat calmer.

"Nothing can happen," she said to herself for the thousandth time. "Nothing can be found out. And even if it should be discovered, nobody could prove anything against us. He may simply have stolen the money and clothing. We've been living here in the city, and none of us has gone to the bungalow for weeks... If one could only go and see whether the things are still there. Ah, this is almost unbearable. I don't see how Frau Wallau can stand the strain."

Frau Bachmann had said to Wallau's wife at the time: "Do you know, Hilde, this thing has changed all the men, ours included?"

Hilde had replied: "Nothing has changed Wallau."

"Ah, if once Death has been so close that one could look him straight in the eye..."

Frau Wallau had interrupted her: "Nonsense! How about us? And me? It was nearly all over with me when I had my oldest one. And a year later another."

Frau Bachmann had said: "They know everything about a person."

"'Everything' is saying too much. They know just what one is willing to tell them," Frau Wallau had replied.

Frau Bachmann, sitting quietly and alone, noticed that her hands had begun to twitch again. She got some sewing. That soothed her. "Nobody can prove anything against us," she said to herself again. "We'd say it was some burglar."

She heaved a sigh of relief when at last she heard her husband's steps on the stairs. She got up to prepare his supper. He entered the kitchen without saying a word. Even before Frau Bachmann had a chance to turn around she felt, not only in her heart but all over her body, as if the temperature of the room had gone down several degrees when her husband came in.

"Anything the matter?" she asked when she saw his face. He did not reply. She put the full plate of soup between his elbows. The steam from it went up into his face. "Otto," she asked, "are you ill?" Still he did not answer.

The woman became mortally afraid. "But," she thought, "it can't have anything to do with the bungalow, for after all he is here. The thing must be weighing on his mind. I wish it were all over."

"Don't you want to eat?" The man did not reply. "You mustn't always think of it," said his wife. "If we always have it on our mind we'll go mad." From the man's partly closed eyes veritable rays of agony were darting. Frau Bachmann had again taken up her sewing. When she looked up she saw that her husband had closed his eyes. "What is the matter with you? Do tell me!"

"Nothing!" But how he said it! As if his wife had asked him whether there was nothing in the world left for him, and he had truthfully answered: "Nothing!"

"Otto," she said, sewing, "perhaps there is something, is there?"

But the man replied vacantly and quietly: "Nothing, nothing at all!" When she looked into his face, quickly raising her eyes to his from her sewing, she knew that there truly was nothing at all. All that he had ever had was lost.

The woman felt cold as ice. She hunched her shoulders and turned her body away, as if it were not her husband sitting at the head of the table but... She sewed on and on. She did not think; she asked no question, for fear that the answer might destroy her whole life.

And what a life! An ordinary life, surely, with the usual struggle for one's daily bread and stockings for the children. But at the same time a bold, strong life, with a burning interest in everything that was worthy to be experienced. Add to it what they – she and the Wallau woman – had heard their fathers say when they were still two little pigtailed girls who lived on the same street, and there was nothing that had not resounded within their four walls: struggles for the ten-hour day, for the nine-hour day, the eight-hour day; speeches that were read even to the women as they bent over the truly fiendish holes in the stockings; speeches from Bebel to Liebknecht, and from Liebknecht to Dimitroff. Even their grandfathers, the children were told proudly, had been imprisoned because they had taken part in strikes and demonstrations. Ah, to be sure, in those days no one had been murdered and tortured for such misdeeds. What a straightforward life! And now that a single question, a thought even, had the power to undo it all! But here it was already, the thought. What ailed her husband? Frau Bachmann, a simple woman, was fond of her husband. Lovers once, they had been together now for many years. She was not like the Wallau woman who had managed to add a good deal to her knowledge. Ah, but the man at the end of the table was not her husband at all. He was an unbidden guest, strange and sinister.

Where had the man come from? Why had he been so late? While he had been a different man for a long time, now he seemed utterly destroyed. Ever since he had suddenly been discharged from prison that day, he had been a changed man. Though his wife had been glad and shouted with joy, his face had remained vacant and tired. A voice within her whispered: "Would you actually want him to share Wallau's fate?" The woman wanted to answer: "No! No!" But a voice, far older than she and at the same time much younger, had already replied: "Yes, it would be better." "I can't stand the sight of his face," Frau Bachmann thought. As if she'd spoken aloud, the man got up and walked to the window, his back to the room, although the shade was drawn.

George must surely have stumbled past a number of sheds like the one he finally found. Inside there was nothing except piles of willow baskets, evil-smelling and unused.

"Only to sleep now," thought George, "nothing else. To sleep and not wake again." Slinking off into a corner, he knocked against a stack of baskets, tumbling them. Terror recalled him to wakefulness. The fog had gone. The moonlight shone through the empty doorframe onto the well-trodden floor that lay still as snow. Quite plainly one could see the old tracks and George's fresh ones.

He actually fell asleep. Perhaps he slept for only a couple of minutes. He dreamed he had arrived at Leni's. He put his fingers in her hair; it was strong and crackly. He dug his whole face into it and breathed deep, knowing that now at last everything was no longer a dream, but sheer reality. He twisted the hair round his wrist so that she could not escape him again. His foot knocked against something, and he heard the splintering of glass. Again terror roused him from sleep.

He felt a pain in his head, so acute and sharply confined that he instinctively put up his hand to feel if his head were bleeding. Further sleep was unthinkable. "I really believed," he thought to himself, "that by this time I would be with

138

her." Wherever his thoughts turned, he felt perplexed. The emptiness in his mind was almost akin to despair.

In the distance, something, man or beast, was slinking across the field. Gradually, without growing perceptibly stronger, the sound came nearer over the soft soil – light, short steps. George dragged something in front of him, bags and baskets. Too late now to do anything more. The doorframe was filled; it grew dark inside. It was a woman's shadow, for he had been able to see the hem of a skirt.

Softly she whispered: "George?" George wanted to scream, but the sound stuck in his throat.

"George," the girl said once more, somewhat disappointed. She sat down on the floor of the shed near the door. George could see her low shoes and thick stockings, and between her knees the skirt of coarse material on which her hands lay. His heart beat so violently that he thought she must hear it. But she was listening for something else. Firm steps approached over the field, and joyfully she called: "George!" She drew her knees together and smoothed her skirt. George could now see her face. It looked exceedingly beautiful to him. But what face would not have been beautiful in that light and in the expectation of love?

The other George stooped through the door and sat down at once beside the girl. "Ah, there you are," he said, adding contentedly, "and here am I." She embraced him peacefully. She put her face against his without kissing him, perhaps even without a desire to kiss him. They spoke to each other so softly that not even our George could understand what they said. Finally the other George laughed. . . . Again it was so still that our George could hear his namesake stroke the girl's hair or brush his hand against her dress. He said: "My darling!" and again: "My all and all!" "I don't believe you," said the girl. He kissed her heartily. The baskets were tumbled about, except those George had in

139

front of him. "If you only knew how much I love you," said the girl, her voice changed and much clearer.

"Really?" asked the other George.

"Yes, more than anything... Oh, don't!" she exclaimed suddenly. The other George burst out laughing. The girl said crossly: "No, George, come on, behave now."

"Oh, I'll behave all right. Soon you'll be entirely rid of me."

Dismayed, the girl said: "How's that?"

"Well, next month I'll have to join up."

"Oh, Lord!"

"Why, that's not so bad. It'll put an end to this eternal drilling every night that leaves no spare time, not even a minute."

"Won't they pester you more than ever in the Army?"

"That's different when one is a regular soldier," explained the other George, "the other is just playing at it. Alger says the same thing... Say... Look here, didn't you go to a dance in Heidesheim with Alger last winter?"

"Why shouldn't I have?" replied the girl. "I didn't even know you then. And it wasn't like it is with us."

The other George laughed shortly. "Not this way?" He held her fast, and the girl no longer objected.

It was much later when she said sadly, as if her lover had been lost in a storm or in the darkness: "George!"

"Yes?" he answered merrily.

They sat again as they had been sitting at first, the girl with her knees drawn up, one of the man's hands in both of hers. They looked outside, in perfect harmony with each other, with the field, and with the tranquil night. "Over there, remember, we used to walk there?" said the other George. "I've got to go home now."

The girl said: "I shall be afraid if you go away."

"I'm not going to war," replied the man, "only into the Army."

"I don't mean that," said the girl. "I mean if you go away from me right now."

The other George laughed. "You're a crazy little loon. I can come back again tomorrow. For goodness' sake, don't start to weep now." He kissed her eyes and her face. "There you are, now you're smiling again," he said.

"My laughter and my tears come out of the same little pot," she answered.

As the other George was walking away across the field and the young woman gazed after him in the pale light, no longer silvery but somewhat mealy, our George noticed that far from being beautiful her face was really round and flat. For the girl's sake he was greatly afraid that the other George would not return tomorrow. Her face too held a suspicion of fear. She puckered her face as if she wanted to find a small fixed point in the far distance. She sighed and got up. George moved a little. At the place near the door where a moment ago there had been everything, there was now only the thinnest of moonlight, and even that was almost gone because the dawn was breaking.

Chapter III

i

The very night of his arrest Heinrich Kuebler was taken to Westhofen for arraignment. At first he had been almost petrified, letting himself be taken from Elly's room without a word. But on the way a sudden fit of rage had welled up in him and he struggled like any normal man who had been set upon by robbers.

Only partly conscious as a result of the terrific blows they had used to subdue him, his wrists manacled, himself apathetic and unable to find any reason for his present predicament, he had lurched across his captors' arms and knees like a bag of oats during the ride to the camp. When they arrived and the SA guards saw that he had already been beaten up, they knew at once that the commissars' order not to touch prisoners before their examination could not possibly refer to this man; the order was obviously meant only when prisoners arrived in sound condition. For a moment there was absolute quiet, then there came the brief deep growl that is an unfailing preliminary sound, then the piercing scream of one man, then minutes of roaring upheaval, and then an apparent quiet again.

Unrecognizable from being beaten, Heinrich Kuebler was at last taken away unconscious. Fahrenberg received the report: Fourth fugitive captured – George Heisler.

Ever since the calamity that had befallen him two days ago, Commander Fahrenberg had had as little sleep as any of the fugitives. His hair began to turn gray; his face commenced to shrink. At the mere thought of what was at stake for him or if he tried to realize clearly all that he had already lost, he writhed and groaned, finding himself inextricably enmeshed in a tangle of electric-light wires and telephone cords, hopelessly knotted and now totally useless.

Between the two windows hung the picture of his *Führer* who, so he flattered himself, had made him powerful. Almost – if not quite – all-powerful! To be the master of men, to rule them body and soul, to have power over life and death – how enviable a position! To have full-grown vigorous men lined up before oneself and be permitted to break them, quickly or slowly; to see their bodies, erect only a moment ago, become four-legged; to be able to relish the sight of bold, insolent fellows turning gray and stammering with deathly fear! Some had been finished off, some driven to turning traitor; some discharged, their necks bent, their wills broken.

In most cases the taste of power had been well-nigh perfect. But in a very few, at some of the questionings – especially of that fellow George Heisler – things had not gone entirely according to schedule. Ah, if only there weren't that delicate slippery thing which in the last analysis spoiled one's whole taste because, supple like a little lizard, it slipped between one's fingers, elusive and unseizable, unkillable, invulnerable. Always, at Heisler's grillings, in the end there had remained that certain look, that smile, that indefinable light in the man's face, no matter how many blows had been rained upon it. With the precision that at times is the property of insane imaginations, the report made Fahrenberg visualize how that smile on George's features would at last be erased and covered forever by a few shovelsful of soil.

Zillich came into the room. "*Herr Kommandant*. . ." He could hardly breathe, so great was his consternation.

"What is it?"

"They've brought in the wrong man. . ." He froze when he saw Fahrenberg start toward him. Probably Zillich would not have moved even if Fahrenberg had struck him. Until now Fahrenberg had never reproached him for anything. But even in the absence of an uttered reproach Zillich's thickset, powerful body was filled to overflowing with a general dull feeling of guilt and despair. He gasped for breath. "The fellow they grabbed in Frankfurt last night in Heisler's wife's room is not our Heisler. It was a mistake."

"Mistake?" Fahrenberg repeated.

"Yes, sir. Mistake. . . mistake. . ." Zillich, too, repeated the word, as if it were a delectable morsel on the tongue. "Some unimportant fellow with whom the woman consoled herself. I had a look at him. Although his face will never be the same again, I know the other fellow too well."

"Mistake," said Fahrenberg again. He seemed suddenly to reflect upon something. From under his heavy lids, Zillich watched him, motionless. All at once, Fahrenberg in a frenzy of rage roared: "What kind of a light is this in here, anyway? Must I knock my head against everything? I suppose there isn't a man here who can change a bulb. That isn't being done here, is it? And out there! What time is it? What kind of a fog do you call this? Good Lord, it's the same thing every day."

"It's the fall that does it, *Herr Kommandant*."

"Fall? And what about those goddam trees out there? They need trimming. Have them clipped, and be damn quick about it."

Five minutes later there was great activity in and outside the commander's quarters. Under the supervision of S A men several prisoners were trimming the plane trees that grew the length of Barrack III. In the meantime, another prisoner, an electrician by trade, was changing some of the bulbs. Fahrenberg could hear the cracking of the severed branches and the whining of the saws outside.

The electrician lay on his belly, fumbling with the switches. Happening to look up, he met Fahrenberg's gaze. He described it two years later: "Never in all my life have I ever seen such a look. I thought that any moment the man would trample on me and make jelly of my spine. But he only gave me a little kick in the behind and said: 'Hurry, damn you, hurry!' Finally they tried the lights and they worked all right. Then they switched them off. It was light now anyhow, because the plane trees had been trimmed and, besides, it was already daytime."

Meanwhile, Heinrich Kuebler, still unconscious, had been placed in the care of the camp doctor. Commissars Fischer and Overkamp were convinced that Zillich was correct and that this man was not George Heisler. There were others, too, who, after a look at the fellow, who'd been beaten to a pulp, had their doubts and shrugged their shoulders. Commissar Overkamp persisted in making the little whistling sounds – they were hardly more than a wheeze – that were his way of relieving himself when cursing became inadequate. Fischer, telephone receiver braced between head and shoulder, waited until Overkamp had finished wheezing. Overkamp had no hankering for light. In their room it was still night; the shutters were closed and only an ordinary desk lamp was burning. The 100-watt lamp was used for questioning only in certain cases. Fischer suppressed a desire to explode this lamp right in his superior's face to make him stop his infernal wheezing.

"They've got Wallau!" Fischer exclaimed.

Overkamp reached for the receiver and began to scratch on a pad. "Yes, the four of them," he said. A little later: "Seal the flat. Bring them here." Then he read Fischer what he'd written.

"When the various lists were examined in the respective cities day before yesterday, it appeared that in addition to the members of Wallau's family a number of persons in all these cities were involved. All these people were questioned again yesterday. Of the five selected from the final lists, a certain Bachmann fell under suspicion. The man is thirty-three, a streetcar conductor, served two months in the camp, and was discharged to enable us to keep watch on his associates.

"By the way, you remember, don't you, that this kind of watching led us to the address at which Arlsberg was receiving his letters? Well, as I was saying, this fellow Bachmann has not been active politically since his discharge.

"At his first and second questioning he denied everything. But yesterday he was put under pressure and he softened up. He admitted that Wallau's wife had cached things in his bungalow near Worms, though he pretends not to have known the why and wherefore. He was released under surveillance so we could continue to watch his associates. Wallau was arrested on this bungalow plot at eleven-twenty at night. So far he has refused to say anything. Bachmann did not leave his house again and did not report for duty at six; there's a suspicion of suicide. No news here of his family.

"That's all."

He had Fischer release the news to the press and radio: they'd just be in time for the early-morning news. Overkamp had fought those who opposed this procedure. He held that the immediate publication of all the facts was efficacious because it enlisted the aid of the public, especially when the escape of two, or at the most three, prisoners was involved. This exact and plausible number was adaptable to certain circumstances surrounding an escape; if the facts were properly released, they were likely to enlist public sentiment. If, on the other hand, the escape was a matter of seven, six, or even only five prisoners, making known a jail break of this magnitude would hardly help in the recapture of the fugitives. It would leave room for conjecture that an even larger number might be involved, and give rise to surmises, feelings, doubts, and rumors. All these arguments had now become untenable because with Wallau's capture the plausible number had been reached.

"Did you hear the news just now, Fritz?" were the girl's first words when the young man entered the yard gate.

"Hear what?"

"A little while ago, on the radio," said the girl.

"Huh, radio!" the boy replied. "With all the to-do I've got to put up with in the morning. Paul going to the vineyard with Father, Mother hustling to deliver the milk, me going to the stable for Mother – and all before half-past seven. I say, to hell with the old noise box!"

"Yes, but this morning," said the girl, "there was something about Westhofen and the three fugitives and that they killed Dieterling, the S A man, with a spade and committed a burglary in Worms and then fled in three different directions."

The boy said quietly: "That so? That's funny. Last night at the inn, Lohmeier from the camp and Mathes said that

147

the man they'd attacked with the spade was a lucky stiff: just a cut across the eye and nothing but a bit of sticking plaster over it. Three, you said – "

"Too bad," interrupted the girl, "that they've not caught your man yet."

"Ah, that fellow's got rid of my jacket long ago," replied Fritz Hellwig. "Don't think he's as foolish as all that, to run around this long in the same clothes. You can bet that he'll tell himself that they've broadcast a description of his clothes. Perhaps he's sold it, and it's hanging now in someone's closet or a store. Or perhaps he's thrown it into the Rhine, with stones in the pockets. . ." The girl looked at him with surprise. "At first I felt badly about it," said Fritz. "But now I've got over it," he added.

Only now did he step close to the girl. He made up for what he had not yet done this morning: he took her by the shoulders, shook her gently, and kissed her a few times. He held her fast for a moment. He thought to himself: "The fellow knows that he'll never get out alive if they catch him." He was thinking of course of the one fugitive of them all with whom he was personally concerned. Last night, in a dream, he had passed Alger's garden. There, behind the fence among the fruit trees, he had seen a scarecrow with an old black hat, the few sticks from which it was made covered by his velvet jacket. This dream seemed quite amusing in plain daylight, but it had frightened him to death in the night. He could feel himself shudder even now. From the girl's freshly laundered kerchief that lay against his chest came the crisp cool odor of newly bleached linen. He felt as if he had never before been so conscious of its odor, as if something new had come into his world that divided its constituent parts into the rough ones and those that were tender.

When, ten minutes later, he arrived at school, he happened upon the gardener. The fellow was at him again: "No news yet, eh?"

"What about?"

"About your jacket. Now it's on the radio."

"The jacket?" asked Fritz Hellwig with a start, for the girl had not mentioned it.

"He was last seen dressed as follows..." recounted the gardener. "I suppose by now it's ruined under the arms with perspiration."

"Aw, leave me alone," growled the boy.

When Franz entered Marnet's kitchen for a quick cup of coffee before starting off on his bicycle, Ernst, the shepherd, was sitting near the kitchen stove, spreading jam freely on a piece of bread. "Have you heard, Franz?" he asked.

"What?"

"The fellow from around here, who is in it – "

"Who? In what?"

"Well, if you don't listen to the radio," said Ernst, "you can't expect to be up-to-date." He now addressed himself to everyone that was sitting around the large kitchen table. The whole family were at their second breakfast; they'd already put a few hours' work behind them. The apples had to be sorted, for an appointment with two wholesale buyers had been made for tomorrow morning at the Frankfurt market. "What would you do," Ernst asked them, "if you found the fellow hiding back there in your shed?"

"Lock the shed," said the son-in-law, "bicycle down to the telephone, and call the police."

"You wouldn't need the police," broke in the brother-in-law. "There's enough of us here to tie him up and take him to Hoechst. Am I right, Ernst?"

The shepherd was spreading the jam so thick that he was

eating jam and bread rather than bread and jam. "Why, I won't be here tomorrow," he said, "I'll be over at Messer's."

"Well, he could be in Messer's shed, too," said the son-in-law. Franz was listening with breathless attention.

"Oh, of course, he could be hiding anywhere," admitted Ernst, "in a hollow tree, in any old shed. But wherever I'd be looking, he'd be sure not to be."

"Why not?"

"Because I wouldn't look there in the first place. That's not a sight I'd enjoy." Silence. Everybody was looking at Ernst, who was holding a piece of bread and jam in front of his mouth; its huge indentation made it look like a horse's head harness.

"You can afford to talk that way, Ernst," said Frau Marnet, "seeing that you have no farm and no property at all. If the poor devil was caught in the morning and told where he'd been the night before, you'd find yourself in prison."

"In prison?" cackled old Marnet, a wizened little peasant, thin as a rail, although the same fare and the same life had made his wife broaden out like a pudding. "You'll talk yourself into the C C yet, and never get out again. What's to become then of all your things? The whole family'll get into trouble."

"Well, I can't say about that," replied Ernst. He licked his mouth clean with his incredibly long, pliant tongue, the children watching him wide-eyed. "All I have is a little furniture in Oberursel that was my mother's, and my savings-bank book. I haven't any family yet, only my sheep. In this respect I'm like the *Führer*, I have neither wife nor child. I have only my Nelly. As for the *Führer*, he used to have a housekeeper; I read in the paper how he himself went to her funeral."

Suddenly Augusta said: "One thing I can tell you though, Ernst, I've put Marnet's Sophie wise to you. How could you lie to her, saying you were engaged to Mariechen of Botzen-bach? And you proposing to Ella Sunday before last!"

"That kind of a proposal has nothing whatsoever to do with my sentiments for Mariechen," Ernst answered.

"Why, that's downright bigamy," said Augusta.

"Not at all," replied Ernst, "that's talent."

"He got that from his father," explained Frau Marnet. "When he fell in the war all his girls joined Ernst's mother in weeping for him."

"And were you one of the weepers, Frau Marnet?" asked Ernst with a twinkle in his eye.

With a glance toward the insignificant little peasant, she replied: "Oh, I might have shed a tear or two."

Franz, listening with bated breath, expected that the thoughts and words of the people in Marnet's kitchen would automatically have to turn toward the place his heart was indicating to them. Far from it! The family's thoughts and words ran merrily in every conceivable direction. Franz pulled out his bicycle from the shed. He hardly knew how he got down to Hoechst. The hubbub around him and the continual shrieking in the narrow streets were mere empty sounds.

"Didn't you know him?" asked one of the men in the locker room. "You used to be in the neighborhood before."

"Why him, of all people?" asked Franz. "The name is entirely unfamiliar to me."

"Have a look at him," said another, shoving a newspaper under his nose.

Franz looked down at the pictures of three men. Even though it was a blow to see George's familiar face look up at him, the two police pictures flanking George's hit him hard. He felt ashamed that his thoughts were always only with George.

"No," he said aloud, "this picture means nothing to me. . .

Ah, the things one hears these days!" The paper circulated among some dozen hands. "Don't know him. – Good Lord, three at one time! – Perhaps there are even more. – Why did they run? – Silly question. – Killed with a spade. – Not a chance in a million. – Why not? They got away, didn't they? – Yeah, but for how long? – I wouldn't like to be in their place. – Look at this one! He's quite old already. – This one looks familiar to me. – They were certainly done for as it was; they had nothing at all to lose."

One man, his voice somewhat muffled, perhaps because he was bending over his locker or tying his shoelaces, asked quietly: "If there should be a war, what's to become of the camps?" A chill passed through the men who were shoving and hurrying to get themselves ready for work. In the same tone, the man added: "What then would be best for safety at home?"

Who was it who had just said that? The face had not been visible because the man was bending down. But the voice? We ought to know that voice! What was it he said? Nothing objectionable. A brief silence; and there wasn't one of them who, when the second blast of the whistle sounded, did not give a violent start. As they were running through the yard, Franz heard somebody behind him ask: "Is Albert still in there, I wonder?" And another replied: "I believe he is."

Binder, the old peasant who had been in Dr. Loewenstein's waiting room, was on the point of shouting to his wife to turn off the radio. Ever since his return from Mainz, he had tossed on his oilcloth-covered sofa, sicker than he'd been before, he thought. All at once he got up, his mouth hanging open. Life and death, which were having a tussle inside him, were forgotten. He roared to his wife to help him into his coat and shoes, and to be quick about it! He had his son's car brought around. Did he wish to be revenged upon the doctor who was unable to help him, or upon the patient with the bandaged hand who had gone calmly on his way yesterday, although, as he had just learned, he, too, ought to be at death's door? Or did he think this action of his would make him more thoroughly part of the living?

ii

George crawled out of his shed, fearing that his possible discovery might endanger others. He felt so miserable that it seemed senseless to him to put one foot before the other. But the buoyancy of a new day, more powerful than the terrors of the night could ever be, will sweep along everyone who has endured to await its coming. The damp asparagus ferns beat against his legs. A wind rose, so gentle that it could waft the fog only lightly. Although the fog blurred George's sight, he nevertheless felt the new day touching him and everything around him. Soon the little berries on the bushes began to glow in the rays of the low-hanging sun. At first George thought it was the sun shining beyond the foggy bank; but, as he approached it, he became aware of a fire that was burning on the headland. Slowly but perceptibly the fog drew off; now he could see a few flat buildings on the headland, its treeless point surrounded by moored boats, and the open water. Before him in the field, on the path leading from the highway to the river, lay the house from which the lovers might have come last night. Suddenly, from the peninsula, came the sound of rolling drums, a sound that made George's teeth chatter. As there was no time to hide, he walked on stiffly, prepared for the worst. But everything remained quiet; no sign came from the farmhouse. From the headland drifted the voices of boys which, by the very fact of not being men's voices, seemed to George beautiful and of an angelic clearness. Presently there came the splashing of oars approaching the bank, and the fire on the headland was quenched.

"If you can no longer get out of people's way," Wallau had taught him, "you must walk straight toward them, into their very midst."

These people, from whom there was now no escaping, were a crowd of about two dozen lads who, shouting like wild Indians invading the hunting grounds of a hostile tribe, were jumping out of their boats, unloading knapsacks, cooking utensils, baskets, tents, and flags. The turmoil subsided, and presently the boys formed into two groups. George saw that this was brought about by the commands curtly issued by a lean straw-thatched boy whose voice was raucous but still quite childlike. Two of the boys passed a pole through the rings and handles of the cooking utensils and pails and marched off toward the farmhouse, escorted by four heavily burdened comrades and two drummers, and led by a seventh who carried the little flag. George had sat down on the sand and was looking after them, not as if he had outgrown his childhood but as if he had been robbed of it. "At ease!" ordered the lean lad, after the others had formed in line and counted off, as he had ordered. Only now did the youthful commander become aware of George. Some of the boys were looking for flat pebbles, and already one could hear them counting the number of impacts as they skipped over the water. The others sat upon a bit of grass only a couple of feet away from George, around a shaggy, brown-haired little lad who was whittling something in his lap. George, listening to the boys' advice and expert opinions, almost forgot his own plight. Some of the youngsters assumed poses and spoke as children do who know that they are being observed by a grownup who unconsciously attracts them.

The whittler jumped up, ran past George, swept back his arm, and, his face tense and serious, threw what he had been whittling high into the air. It came down at his feet in obedience to the law of gravity, but apparently greatly to the boy's disappointment. He picked it up, looked at it with a frown, sat down again, and continued his whittling. His comrades' curiosity was fast giving way to ridicule.

George, who had taken in everything, said with a smile: "You want to make a boomerang, don't you?" The boy gazed straight at him with a strong, calm look that pleased George. "I can't help you because I hurt my hand," he said, "but I may be able to explain..." His face became gloomy. Wasn't it boys just like these who had tracked down Pelzer in Buchenau yesterday? This one with the quiet, steady look – was he one of those who had drummed against the yard gate? The boy lowered his eyes. The others gathered round George rather than round the whittler. Before he knew it, George was entirely hemmed in by a circle of boys. Unlike the Pied Piper, he hadn't even needed a pipe. An unfailing instinct seemed to tell these lads that there was something unusual about this man, some adventure, or strange misfortune, or some fatality. True, they had only a hazy conception of all this. They moved closer around him, prattling and looking sideways at his bandaged hand.

About this time, Overkamp had before him the report that, while George Heisler himself was, alas, still at large, the garment that was known to have covered his worthless carcass, the brown Manchester-velvet jacket with the zipper, had fallen into the hands of the law. Shortly after the barter, the riverman had taken the jacket to a second-hand dealer, intending to spend the proceeds in drink. His girl was forever knitting him sweaters, so the trade had been a windfall for him. The dealer, however, who had once or twice before been guilty of receiving suspicious goods, had been warned and had immediately called a policeman. The riverman, at first loath to turn over this valuable object to the police, calmed down when told he would be reimbursed. He had no difficulty in proving his own innocence, for at least half a dozen men had witnessed the exchange. These men said they were under the impression that the other party to the exchange had gone off, with someone else, in the direction of Petersau. In the course of the questioning the companion's name presently came up: Pickerel.

Pickerel was easily located. The result of it all was that Overkamp issued several instructions. He was now under the impression that this muddled-up affair had been given a new and encouraging impetus.

Among the reports that had come in was a highly significant one from a certain Binder, of Weisenau. This man claimed to have noticed a suspicious man in the waiting room of a Dr. Loewenstein; his appearance checked with the police description. During that same morning he had seen the man, his hand newly bandaged, walking in the direction of the Rhine. Every one of these people was questioned at once. Their depositions made it possible definitely to trace Heisler's trail until noon yesterday, and to draw conclusions as to his further progress.

The boys had inched from their bit of grass to the sand around George; the whittler was relegated to a place on the outskirts of the tight-packed circle. Suddenly, at the sound of a boat approaching from the headland, they all turned their heads. A man with a knapsack got out, and with him a tall youth whose somewhat long but regular features revealed a certain boldness that could no longer be called boyish. "Give it to me," this lad said to the whittler. He took one step forward and threw the thing into the air with a deliberate, peculiar motion that made the piece of wood whirl and his own body turn around on its own axis.

In the meantime, the other group of boys had returned from the farmhouse. The teacher said a few words of praise to the lean boy for having arranged everything so quickly and so well. Once more the boys had to line up and count off before proceeding on their way. George also got up. "You have a nice group of boys there, *Herr Lehrer,*" he said.

"*Heil Hitler!*" said the teacher, making amends for an obvious omission. He had a tanned and very youthful face which, because of its almost forcibly retained youthfulness, gave one a somewhat rigid impression.

"Yes, it's a good class." Although George said nothing more, he added of his own accord: "They come from good stock. I've made what I could of them. I was fortunate in keeping the class when they were promoted at Easter."

George thought to himself: "The fact of having kept the class seems to have been a matter of some consequence in this man's life." It cost George no effort at all to converse quietly with this man. The night lay suddenly far behind him. So serenely flows the everyday life that it carries along him who sets his foot in it. "Is it far to the next landing place?"

"Hardly twenty minutes' walk," replied the teacher, "that's where we are going."

"Here's the man to take me across the river," thought George. "He *must* take me across."

"March! March!" the teacher called out to the boys. He had failed to become aware of the spell that emanated from this stranger because he was already under its influence. The tall youth who had come in the boat with the teacher was walking beside him. The teacher put his hand on the lad's shoulder. George, had he been allowed to choose from among all the boys a companion for his wanderings, would

157

have chosen not the handsome boy at the teacher's side, or the clever-faced lean one, but little Boomerang. More than once he felt the boy's clear gaze directed toward him, as if he could see more than the other children.

"Did you spend the night in the open?" asked George.

"Yes," answered the teacher. "We have a shelter near the river, but for the sake of the practice we spent the night in the lee of the house. Last night and this morning we did our cooking over an open fire. Yesterday we tried to figure by means of maps how the heights over there could be strategically occupied today. Then we went back through history, if you know what I mean, and saw how an army of knights would have done it, how the Romans did it..."

"You make a fellow wish he could go to school again," said George. "You're a fine teacher."

"What we are fond of doing we do well," was the reply.

By now they had walked the length of the peninsula along the riverbank. At their side flowed the open stream. Now one could see that the headland that had obstructed the view with its few bushes and clumps of trees was just a narrow triangle among countless projections and other headlands. George said to himself: "If I get across, I can be with Leni before the day is over."

"Were you in the war?" asked the schoolmaster. George realized that this man, who was really about his own age, thought him much older.

"Yes," he answered.

"What a pity we didn't know. You might have told my boys about it. I never miss such an opportunity."

"I should have disappointed you," said George, "for I'm no good at telling stories."

"Same as my father. He never would tell me about the war."

"Let's hope that these boys will keep their sound bodies."

"It's to be hoped that they will," the teacher replied, adding: "What I mean is, I hope they'll keep them sound, but not by shirking the issue."

George felt his heart beat faster when he saw the piles and steps of the landing place not far ahead. Still, so powerful within him was the compelling habit of producing an effect upon others, that even now he answered: "Having one's heart and soul in one's profession is an issue, too."

"I am not talking now of that kind of an issue," said the schoolmaster. His words were meant for the ears of the boy who, holding himself very erect, was walking beside him. "I was referring to occasions when the issue is one of life and death. One's got to go through... I say, what made us talk about such things?" He looked his strange companion over once more. If the walk had only been longer, he would have liked to reveal his thoughts to this man. How many confessions are offered on the way to those of a reserved nature! "Here we are! I say, would you mind taking some of the boys across?"

"Why, not at all," said George, whose heart was in his throat.

"I'll stay here with the others, and we'll hunt for things in the sand while we wait for the next boat." "Perhaps little Boomerang will come with me," thought George. But when for the third time the boys were lined up and counted off, Boomerang unfortunately was in the teacher's group.

Pickerel was being questioned in Westhofen. He proved himself an apt describer, accurate and witty. Idlers of his type are usually excellent observers. Since it is never up to them to act, observations stick in their minds like unexploited treasures. For this reason they are often invaluable informers for the police. Facing the commissars, Pickerel reported in detail how his companion of yesterday had seemed frightened to death at finding himself at the point of Petersau.

"His bandage was new," he said, "though somewhat soiled. At least five of his teeth were missing, let's say three on top and two below, because the gap above was larger than the one below. And on one side of his mouth – " here Pickerel crooked his forefinger and put it into his own mouth – "there was a rip or – what shall I call it? – as if someone had tried to make the corner of his mouth reach his left ear."

Pickerel was dismissed with a *Heil!* and thanks. There remained the identification of the coat. All they would have to do then was to send out the new description over the network that covered the entire country, to all the railroad stations and bridgeheads, all the police stations and guards, and all the landing places and inns.

"Fritz, Fritz," they were shouting to him at school, "your jacket's been found!" When Fritz heard these words he felt everything whirl around inside of him. He ran outside. The road repairs back of the shed had been completed. He glanced into the greenhouse. The gardener was picking the seeds from the begonias, preparatory to sorting them. "My jacket's been found."

Without turning round, the man said: "Uh-huh? That means that they're close on his heels. Well, you ought to be glad."

"Glad? A sweaty, filthy, bespattered jacket, worn by such a fellow?"

"Well, have a look at it anyway. Who knows, perhaps after all it isn't yours."

"It's coming," shouted the boys. The motor exhaust could already be heard in the still air. The rays of the morning sun seemed to aim straight at the pilot's neckcloth, at a bird in flight, at the white river wall, and at the point of a church spire far away in the hills, as if these things above all others were worthy of leaving a deep and lasting impression. There was a scurrying down the few stone steps to the landing place, premature, for the boat had not come alongside yet.

George could see the guard at the opposite landing. Did he always stand there? Was he stationed there on his account? The boys surrounded him, pushing him down the gangway, crowding him into the boat. George, however, had eyes only for the guard.

"Heads apart, boys! Let me through, I'm jumping overboard! Not the worst kind of an end, if there's going to be trouble!" These thoughts flashed through George's mind. He raised his face. Far behind him he saw the Taunus Range, where he had often gone to gather apples with someone – who could it have been? – ah, Franz. It's apple time there again, for, true enough, it is autumn. Is there anything more beautiful in all the world? And the sky is no longer hazy, but a cloudless grayish blue.

The boys interrupted their babbling and looked in the direction of the man's strange gaze. But there wasn't anything to be seen – perhaps the bird had flown away. The pilot's wife was collecting the fares. George changed his fifty-pfennig piece. Forty-five left. The boat was already beyond the middle of the stream. The guard looked motionlessly toward the incoming boat. George dipped his hand into the water without taking his eyes from the guard. All the boys also dipped their hands in the water. "Ah, this is all a hallucination! But if they should get you now, send you back, and torture you, you'll be sorry that you didn't take this easy way out of it all."

* * *

It wasn't more than five minutes by car from the Darré School to Westhofen. Fritz had always imagined Westhofen to be something infernal. All he could see now was clean-looking barracks, a large well-swept square, a few trimmed plane trees, and the tranquil sun of an autumn morning.

"You are Fritz Hellwig? *Heil Hitler!* Your coat has been found. There it is." Fritz cast an oblique glance toward the table. There lay his jacket, brown and clean, not at all filthy and blood-spattered as he had seen it in his imagination. Only at the seam of one of the sleeves there was a dark spot. He glanced questioningly at the commissar, who nodded at him with a smile. Fritz stepped to the table and touched the sleeve. He drew his hand back.

"Well, that's your coat all right," said Fischer. "What?... Put it on," he said smiling, when Fritz still hesitated. "Come on," he said somewhat louder. "Isn't it yours?"

Fritz lowered his eyes and said almost inaudibly: "No, sir."

"No?" repeated Fischer. Fritz shook his head firmly in spite of the general consternation his words had caused. "Look at it very closely," said Fischer. "Why isn't it your jacket? Do you see any difference?"

With downcast eyes, stammering at first and then speaking quite circumstantially, Fritz began to explain why this was not his jacket. His had a zipper on the inside pocket, while this one had a button. Here there had been a small hole made by a lead pencil, here where the lining was of a lighter color. This jacket had a ribbon loop with a firm's name; his mother had sewn on two loops at the armholes of his coat for him to hang it up by; the ribbon loops always ripped loose. The better he got going, the more differences he could think of, for the more accurately he described the jacket the better he felt. In the end he was interrupted roughly and dismissed.

When he got back to school he explained: "It wasn't mine at all." Everybody laughed in surprise.

In the meantime George had got out of the boat and, hemmed in on every side by the boys, passed the guard. After saying good-by to them all, he continued on his way along the motor road that goes from Eltville to Wiesbaden.

Overkamp was in great form; he wheezed to himself without letup until Fischer, sitting opposite him at the table, felt his hands tremble. This lad would have been overjoyed to get back the jacket whose loss he had so violently lamented. Lucky he was honest enough to reject it. Since this coat was not the one that had been stolen, the man who'd swapped it could not be the one they were looking for. Also there was that Dr. Loewenstein who had been arrested – for no reason, it now appeared, even if the man whose hand he had bandaged yesterday was the same man as the jacket-swapper.

Overkamp would have continued his wheezing endlessly had not the whole camp been brought up with a jerk. Somebody came rushing in: "They are bringing Wallau!"

Much later, someone telling about that morning said: "The bringing in of Wallau made upon us prisoners about the same impression as the fall of Barcelona or Franco's entry into Madrid or some other event that showed clearly that the enemy had all the power in the world on his side. The flight of the seven men had the most catastrophic consequences for all of us. Nevertheless, with equanimity and at times even with scorn, everyone bore being deprived of food and blankets, the increased hardness of the work, and the hours of being grilled to the accompaniment of blows and threats. Our attitude, which we seemed unable to hide, incensed our tormentors all the more. So strongly did most of us consider these fugitives to be part of ourselves that we felt as though they were our emissaries. Although we had known nothing of the plan, we had the sensation of having succeeded in some rare undertaking. To many of us the enemy had seemed all-powerful. The strong can afford to be wrong at times without loss of prestige, because even the most powerful are after all only human – yes, their mistakes make them all the more human – but he who claims omnipotence must never be wrong because there can be no alternative to omnipotence except insignificance. If one stroke, no matter how tiny, proved successful against the enemy's alleged omnipotence, everything was won. This feeling soon gave way to terror and even despair when one after another was brought back comparatively quickly and, so it seemed to us, with scornfully little effort. During the first two days and nights we asked ourselves whether they'd ever get Wallau. We hardly knew him. After his admission he had been with us for a few hours, but he had soon been taken off again for a grilling. Two or three times after being questioned we had seen him led away reeling, one hand pressed to his abdomen; but with the other he made a tiny motion toward us as if he wanted to tell us that all this was of no conclusive importance and that we must be of good cheer. Now that Wallau himself had been caught and brought back, we bawled as if we had been little children. We were all of us lost now, we thought. Wallau would be murdered, as all the others before him had been murdered. In the very first month of the Hitler regime hundreds of our leaders had been murdered in every part of the country, and every month more were murdered. Some were executed publicly, others were tortured to death in the concentration camps. A whole generation had to be annihilated. These were our thoughts on that terrible morning; then for the first time we voiced our conviction that if we were to be destroyed on that scale, all would perish because there would be none to come after us. Almost unprecedented in history, the most terrible thing that could happen to a people, was now to be our fate: a no-man's-land was to be established between the generations, which old experiences would not be able to traverse. If we fight and fall, and another takes up the flag and fights and falls too, and the next one grasps it and he too falls – that is natural, for nothing can be gained without sacrifice. But what if there is no longer anyone to take up the flag, simply because he does not know its meaning? It was then that we felt sorry for the fellows who were lined up for Wallau's reception, to stare at him and spit on him. The best that grew in the land was being torn out by the roots because the children had been taught to regard it as weeds. All those lads and girls out there, once they had gone through the Hitler Youth, the Work Service, and the Army would be like the fabled children nurtured by animals who finally tore their own mothers to pieces."

iii

That morning, Mettenheimer had started for his place of work even earlier than usual. In his heart he had determined that, come what might, he would henceforth give no thought to anything but the work he was doing. Neither the questioning of yesterday, nor his daughter Elly, nor the felt-hatted shadow that had attached himself to his heels – today no less than yesterday – should in the least prevent him from doing his work properly. Though he suddenly felt himself threatened, spied upon from all sides, and in constant danger of being torn away from his wallpapers, his trade appeared to him now in a new light, almost exalted, vouchsafed to him in a desultory world by him who gives man his vocation.

Because of his effort to be exceptionally early after yesterday's lost time, he neither heard nor read anything that morning. Hence he failed to notice the glances the whitewashers exchanged upon his arrival. Today in his silent haste, interrupted only by short, growled-out orders, everyone helped him willingly as they never had before, although this fact entirely escaped him. Far from interpreting their boss's dogged zeal as the fruit of exalted thoughts on the importance of their trade, the men ascribed it merely to the natural dignity of an old man whose family has been stricken by terrible misfortune. His best workman, Schulz, who was working beside him, suddenly said with a sidelong glance at the old fellow's stern little face: "These things can happen anywhere, Mettenheimer."

"What things?" asked Mettenheimer.

In a somewhat stilted but sincere voice, such as is used on an occasion of mourning when we have not yet found our own words to express what we feel but have only the conventional ones available, Schulz added: "Such things can happen in any German family these days."

"What is it that can happen in any German family?" asked Mettenheimer.

This was too much for Schulz; it made him angry. At the moment more than a dozen men were busy decorating the interior of the building. About half of them had been regularly employed by the firm for many years, and Schulz was one of them. In such a community events in one's life cannot remain a secret for any length of time. They all knew that Mettenheimer had several pretty daughters and that the prettiest of them all had married against her father's will and had got herself into a mess. There had been no getting along with old Mettenheimer at the time. They also knew that the son-in-law had finally landed in a concentration camp. Listening to the radio and reading the paper this morning had recalled many things to mind which the stern features of the old man seemed to confirm. Schulz felt that as far as he was concerned there was really no need for Mettenheimer to try to play a part. It never occurred to him that the old man did not know about everything that had happened.

At the noon hour, several of the men went down to the janitress's flat to warm up their food. With exaggerated urgency they invited Mettenheimer to join them. Paying no attention to their manner, the old man accepted, for in his hurry he had forgotten to bring his sandwiches and he did not care to go to a restaurant. Here, in the corner of the staircase which a familiar group of whitewashers, young and old, had selected for their noonday meal, he felt safe. They kept teasing the diminutive apprentice, chasing him all over the place, bidding him get some salt from the janitress or some beer from the inn. "Give the lad a chance to eat his own lunch, will you?" said Mettenheimer.

Among the dozen or so men there were a few to whom the State was a sort of firm, like Heilbach. They were indifferent to everything, as long as they were made to feel that their honest labor was duly appreciated and they received what in their opinion was a just wage. The arguments of these men did not confine themselves to the simple fact that now as before they were papering luxurious flats for a very modest return; they were more concerned with individual, and at times odd, questions, such as religion, for instance. Schulz, on the other hand, the man who had tried to comfort Mettenheimer, had from the very beginning and at all times been against the State. He could distinguish between what, in the various professional competitions and other similar things, was hocus-pocus and what was expedience. He also knew that whatever was expedient was at the same time of benefit to the trade and to anyone who made a living from it. Furthermore, he knew that people were always being baited with what they were most likely to nibble at. Schulz was looked up to by those who felt instinctively that, as the saying goes, at heart he had remained unchanged. To be sure, one ought not to use the term "remain unchanged" for what actually signifies the greatest conceivable difference, whether the most important thing in man manifests itself in action or withdraws to his most secret point. Stimbert, one of the men, was a rabid Nazi. Everybody thought he was a spy and an informer, but this did not worry the rest of the men nearly so much as might have been expected. They were on their guard with him, but so were those who according to their own views were really more or less his associates. They all regarded him as, from the very days in kindergarten, in every community one is apt to regard the freakish individual – pathological tattletale or just an inordinately fat fellow – who unfailingly appears.

But all these men who were eating their lunch in the corner of the stairs would undoubtedly have rushed at Stimbert and given him a sound lacing if they had seen the mean and sneering look with which he was watching Mettenheimer at the moment. Everybody's eyes, though, were turned in the old man's direction, many of the men even forgetting to eat and drink.

Mettenheimer, who had picked up a newspaper that happened to be lying near by, was staring at a certain place; he grew pale. The men, realizing that only now had he learned the facts, held their breath. Mettenheimer slowly raised a face which had been utterly destroyed behind the sheet of printed paper. There was an expression in his eyes as if he had been cast into Hell. As he looked up, he saw himself surrounded by whitewashers and paperhangers. The diminutive apprentice was there too; he'd at last been able to eat, but had stopped again. Stimbert, the rabid one, smiled impertinently over the boy's head. Upon all the other faces there was an expression of sorrow and reverence. Mettenheimer drew his breath. He had not been cast into Hell – he was still a man among men.

During the same noon hour Franz was standing in the canteen, listening. "I think I'll take in the movies at the Olympia in Frankfurt tonight," said one.

"What are they showing there?"

" *Queen Christina.*"

"I prefer my little cutie to your Greta any time," said a third one.

The first one replied: "Cuddling and ogling are two entirely different things."

"How can such tripe still give you any pleasure?" remarked still another. "Me? – I prefer the pleasures of home life."

"Well, everyone to his taste; I'll take a movie ticket myself."

Franz was listening, outwardly sleepy but bursting inside. Again, so it seemed to him, everything was utterly hopeless. This morning, at least, there had been a minute, a breach. . . He gave a sudden start. These Olympia movies gave him the idea he'd been wrestling for all morning. Only through her parents' flat could he reach Elly without danger. Should he go up himself? Wouldn't the street door be watched? And letters too? "I'll just cycle over after work," he said to himself. "I'll buy two tickets. Perhaps I'll be lucky in what I plan to do. And if I should be out of luck, nobody will be any the worse for it."

George pursued his way on the Wiesbaden highroad. He decided to go on until he reached the next viaduct. There was nothing in particular he could expect from this goal, but some goal there had to be, every ten minutes. He let the rather numerous automobiles pass him – freight trucks loaded with goods, autos full of soldiers, the fuselage of an airplane, private cars from Bonn, Cologne, and Wiesbaden; the latest model of an Opel, still new to him. Which one should he thumb? That one? None at all? He walked on, chewing dust. A foreign car, a rather young man alone at the wheel. George raised his hand. The car stopped at once. Seconds before, the driver had noticed George trudging along the road. In an excess of boredom and solitude which is apt to deceive one into believing that one has been attracted to another person from the first, he may even have imagined he had actually expected George's hail. He cleared the seat beside him of rugs, raincoats, and other things. "Where to?" he asked.

They looked at each other briefly, but sharply. The driver was a tall, thin, rather pale man; his hair, too, was colorless. His calm blue eyes, shaded by colorless lashes, were not particularly expressive either of seriousness or of gaiety. George said: "Toward Hoechst." When he had said it, he was frightened.

"Oh," replied the stranger, "I'm for Wiesbaden. But never mind, never mind. Are you cold?" Again he stopped the car. He put one of his plaid rugs across George's shoulders and George wrapped himself up tight. They smiled at each other. The man started his car. George shifted his gaze from the driver's face to his hands on the wheel. These flipperlike, colorless hands were more eloquent than the face. There were two rings on the left hand. George thought that one of them was a wedding ring until a casual motion showed him that it was only turned round and that on the inside gleamed a flat yellowish stone. It tormented George to look at all these details so minutely, but he felt compelled to do so. "Farther around that way," said the driver. "But more beautiful."

"What's that?"

"Up there woods, down here shorter, but dust."

"Up, up!" said George.

They turned off, climbing at first almost imperceptibly

between the fields. With a sort of terror George presently saw the heights approach. The air already smelled of woods.

"Will be nice day," said the driver. "How the Germans name the trees? No, over there, whole forest. All red."

George said: "Beech."

"Beech, all right. Beech. You know monastery Eberbach, Rüdesheim, Bingen, Loreley? Very beautiful."

"We like this section better," answered George.

"Yes? I see. Will you have a drink?" He stopped the car once more, fumbled among his luggage, and unscrewed the top of a bottle. George took a pull and made a wry face. The man laughed. His teeth were so large and white that one might have taken them to be artificial, had not the gums receded so far.

For ten minutes they climbed at a considerable angle. The overpowering smell of the woods made George close his eyes. At the edge of the woods the car turned into a forest lane. The driver turned around, expelled an "Ah!" and an "Oh!" and motioned to George to admire the view. George turned his head, but kept his eyes closed. To look at all the expanse of water, fields, and woods was more than he could stand at present. After following the lane a short distance they turned off. The morning light dropped golden flakes into the beech forest. At times this flaky light made rustling sounds, but of course it was really only the falling leaves. George braced himself. He was close to tears. After all, he was quite weak. They were now skirting the forest. The man said: "Your country very beautiful."

"Oh, the country," repeated George.

"What? – Much forest, roads good. People also. Very clean, very orderly." George remained silent. Now and then the man looked at him, because after the manner of foreigners he identified the individual with his people. George no longer looked at the man, only at his hands. These robust, but colorless, hands aroused a slight feeling of antagonism in him.

They left the wood behind them and went through a mowed field and then through vineyards. The unbroken quiet and the seemingly unpeopled countryside gave them the sense of being in a wilderness, in spite of the abundant cultivation of the land. The driver cast a sidelong glance at George; he noticed that George was staring at his hands. George gave a start. The driver, however – queer fellow – stopped the car for no other purpose than to turn his ring right side up. He showed it to George. "You like very much?"

"Yes," George admitted hesitatingly.

"Take it, if you like," said the stranger calmly, with a smile that was a mere drawing back of the lips.

With great resoluteness George said, "No!" and when the man did not withdraw his hand at once, he repeated harshly as if somebody tried to force something on him, "No! No!" Then the thought came to him that he might have pawned the ring because not a soul could possibly know it. But now it was too late.

George's heart beat more and more violently. For the past few minutes, ever since they had left the edge of the wood above the valley and were driving through the mountain quiet, a thought had been in his mind, the merest seed of a thought that he was still unable to grasp fully. But his heart, as if it were quicker to understand than his mind, kept pounding and pounding. "Nice sun," said the stranger. He was driving at a mere thirty miles. "If I did do it," thought George, "what with? Whatever this fellow is, he's no cinch. Those hands aren't made of putty. He'll put up a fight." Slowly, very slowly, he let his shoulders sag. His fingers were already touching the crank near his right shoe. "Let him have it on the head, and then out with him. It'd be a long time before they found him. Hard luck for him that he met me, but such are the times. One life is worth another. By the time they find him I'll be out of the country in this nice, lovely bus." He withdrew his arm, pushing the crank aside with his right foot.

"What name is the wine here?" asked the stranger.

"Hochheimer," George answered hoarsely. "Don't get into such an awful stew," he exhorted his heart, just as Ernst, the shepherd, talked to his dog. "You know I wouldn't do such a thing. Come on, take it easy. All right, if that's what you want, I'll get out here."

Where the vineyard-flanked road joined the highway stood a milestone: HOECHST, TWO KILOMETERS.

Even though Heinrich Kuebler was still unfit to be questioned, he could at least be looked at, after he was bandaged and propped up. All the witnesses who had been detained for this purpose filed past, staring at him. He stared back at them, although he would not have known any of them even if he'd been fully conscious: Farmer Binder, Dr. Loewenstein, the riverman, Pickerel – people, all of them, whose road he would never have crossed if things had been permitted to take their natural course. Pickerel said gaily: " 'T may be him, and then again 't mayn't," though he knew full well that it wasn't George. Those who are not directly concerned in something are never satisfied unless it is carried to extremes. Binder declared almost morosely: "Not the man; just looks like him." Dr. Loewenstein furnished conclusive evidence: "There's nothing on his hand." As a matter of fact, the hand was the only part of the suspect that had not been hurt.

Thereupon, all the witnesses, with the exception of Dr. Loewenstein, were taken at the State's expense back to where they had come from. Binder rode through a pain-beclouded world back to his home in Weisenau and his sofa. It had all been in vain; his death was now as inevitable as it had been before his departure. Pickerel and the riverman wanted to be put down at the landing place near Mainz, where the swap had taken place the day before.

Shortly thereafter Elly was ordered to be released, but her person and house were to be kept under surveillance. Perhaps the real Heisler would still make an attempt to communicate with her. Kuebler, in his present condition, could not be discharged.

Elly, in her cell, had at first been petrified. When evening came and she was permitted to stretch out on her wooden bed, her numbness subsided and she tried to make some sense of what had happened. Heinrich, she knew, was a good man, the son of decent parents; he had not deceived her. Could it be that he had been guilty of something like George? She remembered he had at times grumbled about the taxes, the endless street collections, the flag waving, and the one-dish meals, but he'd grumbled no more than any of the others.

Didn't her father grumble whenever something displeased him and should be abolished, and didn't her brother-in-law in the SS grumble about the identical thing because he liked it but found it still imperfect? Perhaps Heinrich had listened to some forbidden foreign broadcast, or had borrowed a forbidden book from someone.

In contrast to most people who are spending their first night in prison, Elly fell asleep quickly. She was exhausted as a child whose day is crowded with more than its share of events. On the following day, too, she had been distressed only when her thoughts turned to her father. Everything being so unintelligible, she had not fully recovered her senses, but rather was in an unreal state between expectation and recollection. She felt no fear. She was also aware that the family would take good care of the child. Though she was not conscious of it, these considerations were motivated by her being prepared for everything.

When, early in the afternoon, she was taken from her cell, she was filled with a kind of courage that perhaps was nothing but disguised melancholy.

The depositions made by her father and her landlady had left little doubt as to her circumstances. Her release had been ordered promptly for, if the fugitive should attempt to get in touch with her, she would be much more valuable if she were free. Elly was told she could go home, but was warned that she'd risk never seeing her child or her parents again if she were arrested another time for withholding valuable information or being so foolish as to undertake anything in connection with Heisler without the knowledge of the authorities. At this, she opened her mouth and raised her hands to her ears. When a moment later she found herself in the open, she felt as if she had been away from home for years.

Her landlady, Frau Merkler, received her in silence. Her room was in fearful disorder. Strewn about on the floor lay balls of wool, children's garments, and pillows. The room was filled with the strong odor of Heinrich's carnations, standing fresh in the glass of water. Elly sat down on her bed. Her landlady came in, her face a sullen mask and, without preamble, gave Elly notice to vacate the room by November first. Elly, without answering, looked full in the face of the woman who had always been kind to her. Her course of action was the result of much brooding, dire threats, bitter self-accusations, tormenting considerations for her only son whom she supported, and an ultimate yielding.

The afternoon had progressed. After his arrival in Hoechst, George in despair had waited for the change of shifts that would fill the streets and taverns. Now he was standing jammed in tightly in one of the first crowded streetcars that rolled out of Hoechst.

Irresolute, Frau Merkler was standing in Elly's room. She seemed to be waiting to find comforting and soothing words for the young woman she had always liked well enough. Let the words be not too warm-hearted though, lest they lead to a reminder of the dictates of pure kindness.

"My dear Frau Elly," she said finally, "you must not take it amiss. Life is what it is. If you but knew what is in my heart." Still Elly said nothing. The doorbell rang. Both women were so frightened that they stared at each other wildly. At any moment they expected to hear shouts, noise, the door broken in. But there was only a second ring, decent and orderly. Frau Merkler pulled herself together. Presently her relieved voice called from the hallway: "It's only your father, Frau Elly."

Mettenheimer had never come to see Elly at this flat which, even though his own was by no means luxurious or particularly roomy, still impressed him as being unsuitable for his daughter's home. The vague rumors he'd heard about Elly's arrest made his face grow pale with joy at seeing her unharmed before him. He took her hand in both of his, pressing and caressing it, something he'd never done before. "What are we going to do now?" he asked. "What are we going to do?"

"Nothing at all," answered his daughter, "There's nothing we can do."

"But if he comes here!"

"Who?"

"That fellow, your husband."

"He'll certainly not come to us," said Elly sadly and calmly. "He'd never give us a thought." Her joy at her father's coming and the thought that she was not entirely alone in the world began to evaporate when she saw that he was even more perplexed than she herself.

"Never mind," said Mettenheimer, "a man up against it will think of everything." Elly shook her head. "But what if he should come after all, Elly? What if he should come to my flat, because that's where you lived last? That flat is being watched, and so is yours. If I were standing at the living-room window and saw him coming, Elly, what then? Should I simply let him come in and be caught in the trap? Or should I warn him?"

Elly looked at her father, who seemed to have taken leave of his senses entirely. "No, I'm sure of it," she said sadly. "He'll never come again."

The paperhanger was silent. Openly and undisguisedly his face reflected the dire distress of his conscience. Elly watched him with surprised tenderness. "God in Heaven – " Mettenheimer gave the three words the accents of a sincere prayer – "if only he won't come. If he does come, we are lost one way or another."

"Why lost one way or another, Father?"

"Oh, why can't you understand? Imagine that he comes and I signal him a warning. What will happen to me, to us? – And then imagine he comes, and I see him coming but make no sign. He isn't my son, is he? He's a stranger; and he's worse than a stranger. Well, so I make no sign. He is seized. Can one do such a thing?"

"Do calm yourself, dearest Father," said Elly. "He'll never come."

"But if he should come here, Elly? If in some way he has got this address?"

Elly wanted to say what that question had suddenly made quite clear to her: that she would have to help him, come what might. However, to spare her father she simply repeated: "He won't come."

177

The paperhanger sat in brooding thought. "May misfortune pass my door! May his flight be successful! May he be captured before. . ." No, he wouldn't wish that even to his worst enemy. But why must he of all people be tormented with questions like these, questions to which he knew no answer? It had all come about through a silly girl's being in love. He got up and said in a changed voice: "This fellow who was in your room last night, who the devil was he?"

In the hallway he turned back. "Oh, yes. Here's a letter for you."

This letter had been slipped under his kitchen door a short while before. Elly looked at the address: *For Elly.* She opened the envelope after her father had gone. There was only a movie ticket, a blank piece of paper folded around it. From Else, probably. She got cut-rate tickets now and then. This little green ticket had come fluttering down from Heaven itself. If it hadn't come, she might have sat all night on the edge of her bed, her hands in her lap. "But is it right?" she thought to herself. "If one is plunged as deep in sorrow as I am, does one still go to a movie? Nonsense, that's what the movies are for. Now all the more!"

"There are still two cold cutlets from last night," said the landlady. "Now all the more," repeated Elly to herself. "These cutlets are tough as leather, but they aren't poisoned." Puzzled, Frau Merkler watched the delicate, sad young woman sitting quietly at the kitchen table consuming two cold cutlets, one after the other. "Now all the more," thought Elly again. She went to her room, took off the clothes she was wearing, made herself fresh and clean from head to foot, put on her best lingerie and dress, and brushed her hair until it was sparkling and flying. For this pretty curlyheaded Elly who looked at her with sad brown eyes from her mirror, life was somewhat easier to bear. "If they are actually shadowing me as my father says," she thought to herself, "very well; but I won't give myself away."

"Nothing but idle gossip," said Mettenheimer at home to his frightened wife. "Elly is in her room; there's nothing the matter with her."

"Why didn't you bring her along?"

The few members of the Mettenheimer family still living under the old man's roof sat down to supper. Father and mother; Elly's youngest sister, the pug-nosed Liesbeth whom Mettenheimer had not considered a suitable champion in matters of faith; and Elly's child, his grandson, an oilcloth apron tied around his body, slightly uneasy because of the general silence which made him wave his big spoon at the steam rising from the dish.

Mettenheimer ate slowly, his eyes on his plate, to avoid questions from his wife. He thanked God that she did not have brains enough to comprehend the doom hanging over them.

As a matter of fact, George was only about half an hour's walk away from Mettenheimer's home. He got off the streetcar and took another car to Niederrad. The nearer he came to his goal, the stronger grew the impression that he was being awaited, that his bed was now being made, his dinner prepared. At this very moment his girl would be listening for a sound on the stairs. When he got off the car, he was filled with a tension akin to despair; as if his heart struggled against actually taking the way he had walked countless times in his dreams.

He passed through a few quiet streets with front gardens as one strolls through memories. Consciousness of the present was erased within him, and with it consciousness of danger. Had not the dry leaves at the roadside rustled that day? he asked himself, not aware that his own shoe was disturbing the leaves. How his heart struggled against entering the house! This was no longer a pounding, it was a furious rattling! He leaned out of a window on the stairs. The gardens and courtyards of many houses came together here. The tops of walls and balconies were thickly covered with the endlessly falling leaves of a mighty chestnut tree. A few of the windows were already lighted. This sight so calmed him that he was able to continue his climb. Hanging at the door was still the old sign bearing the name of Leni's sister, and below it a new one, a little intarsia work, with a strange name. Should he ring or knock? Didn't that use to be a children's game? He knocked softly. "Yes?" said a young woman in a striped sleeved apron. She only opened the door a crack.

"Is Miss Leni at home?" asked George, less softly than he had intended, because his voice was hoarse. The woman stared at him, and into her healthy face and her round blue eyes, sparkling like glass marbles, came an expression of alarm. She tried to shut the door, but he put his foot in it. "Miss Leni at home?"

"No one here by that name," said the woman hoarsely. "See that you get out of here immediately."

"Leni," he said calmly and firmly, as if he wanted to implore his own Leni of the past to leave for his sake the body of the buxom, prosaic, aproned woman into which she had been bewitched. It was in vain. The woman kept staring at him with the unabashed fear of a person bewitched who stares at those who have remained unchanged. Quickly he pushed open the door, elbowed the woman back into the hall, and closed the door behind him. The woman went back toward the open kitchen door. She held a shoebrush in her hand. "Why, Leni, listen to me. It is I. Don't you know me?"

"No, I don't," said the woman.

"Why were you startled then?"

"If you don't get out of this flat at once – " all of a sudden she was bold and saucy – "you'll get all you're looking for. My husband will be here any moment."

"Is that him?" asked George. On a little bench stood a pair of highly polished black top boots, beside them a pair of women's low shoes. There was also an open tin of shoe polish and a few rags.

"Yes, it is." Now she had barricaded herself behind the kitchen table. "I'll count three," she said. "By three you'll be gone or else. . ."

George laughed. "Or else what?" He pulled the sock from his hand, a filthy black sock he had found somewhere on the way and pulled on glovelike to hide his bandage. She watched him with open mouth. He circled the table. She shielded her face with her arm. With one hand he grabbed her by the hair, with the other he jerked down her arm. In a voice one might use to speak to a toad which one knew had once been a human being, he said: "Stop it, Leni, and recognize me. I am George."

Her eyes became saucers. He held her fast, endeavoring at the same time to wrest the shoebrush from her hand, disregarding the pain in his own injured hand. Imploringly she said: "But I don't know you."

He let go of her and took a step backward. "Very well," he said. "Just give me the money and the clothes."

For a moment she was silent; then, again quite bold and with renewed sauciness, she answered: "We give nothing to strangers. Only directly to the winter aid."

He stared at her, but in another way than before. The pain in his hand subsided, and with it the consciousness that all this was happening to him. He felt only faintly that his hand had begun to bleed again.

The blue-checked tablecloth on the kitchen table was set

for two. Clumsy little swastikas were carved in the wooden napkin rings, an amateurish job. Slices of sausage, radishes and cheese were neatly decorated with parsley. A couple of open boxes contained pumpernickel and Swedish toast. He thrust his uninjured hand here and there on the table, stuffing in his pocket whatever came into his grasp. The glassmarble eyes followed his movements.

His hand on the latch, he turned round once more.

"You wouldn't make me a fresh bandage, would you?" She shook her head twice, quite seriously.

Going down the stairs, he leaned against the same window. He crooked his elbow and drew the sock back over his hand. "She won't say anything to her husband because she is afraid. She must never have known me. Almost all the windows are lighted now. Just look at all these leaves from the chestnut tree." As if autumn itself were dwelling in this tree, powerful enough to cover the whole city with foliage.

Slowly he shuffled on along the edge of the pavement. He wanted to make himself believe that another Leni with long swinging steps was coming to meet him from the other end of the street. Suddenly he became aware that never again would he be able to go to Leni and, what was infinitely worse, that he could never again even dream he was going to Leni. That dream was now utterly destroyed. He sat down on a bench and, without a thought, began to munch a slice of toast. As it had become cool and dusky and was much too conspicuous to keep on sitting there, he got up presently and trudged on, following the rails, for he no longer had the price of carfare. Where to go now, before nightfall?

iv

Overkamp closed the door to have a few minutes' solitude before Wallau's questioning. He arranged his slips of paper, looked over his notes, sorted them, underscored words, and connected various items by a certain system of lines. His questionings were famous. Fischer had once said that Overkamp could get information from a corpse. His notes for an examination were comparable only to intricate musical scores.

Beyond the door, Overkamp could hear the scraping jerky sound that accompanies a military salute. Fischer came in and closed the door behind him. In his face, anger and amusement struggled for supremacy. He immediately sat down close to Overkamp. With only a lift of his eyebrows the latter warned him of the guard's presence beyond the door and of the partly open window. "Anything else the matter?"

In a low voice Fischer said: "This affair has affected Fahrenberg's brain. He'll certainly go insane over it. Perhaps he is already. He'll be fired anyway. We'll put some steam behind that. Just listen to what he's been up to again.

"We can't have three separate steel chambers built expressly for these three captured fugitives, can we? We made an agreement with the fellow, didn't we, that the three men were not to be touched until we had all of them safely back again? After that he can make sausage meat of them, as far as we are concerned. He had the three men brought before him once more. There are some trees standing in front of his quarters – I mean the things that used to be trees – he had them all trimmed this morning. Well, as I was going to say, he had the three men stood against the trees, so – " here Fischer spread out his arms – "after he'd had the trunks

183

studded with nails so that the men couldn't lean against them. He had all the prisoners lined up and made them a speech. You should have heard it, Overkamp. He took an oath that every one of the seven trees would have its occupant before the new week began. And do you know what he said to me? 'You see, I'm keeping my word – not a blow.'"

"How long is he going to keep them standing that way?"

"That's what caused all the rumpus. Will the men be fit for questioning after an hour or an hour and a half? Well, all right. He'd only exhibit the men to the camp once a day. That'll be his last fun in Westhofen. He thinks if he gets all seven back, he'll be allowed to stay."

"Even if this fellow Fahrenberg falls down the ladder now, he'll land at the bottom with such a bounce that it'll land him several rungs up another ladder," said Overkamp.

"As for this Wallau," continued Fischer, "I plucked him from Fahrenberg's third tree." He got up suddenly and opened the window. "Here they come. You'll excuse me, won't you, Overkamp, for giving you some advice now?"

"Which is?"

"Have them bring you a raw beefsteak from the canteen."

"What for?"

"Because you'll sooner knock a deposition out of that beefsteak than out of the man they're bringing in here now."

Fischer was right. Overkamp knew it as soon as he saw the man. He might just as well have torn up the slips of paper on his table. This fortress was impregnable. What Overkamp saw was an exhausted little man with an ugly little face, dark hair coming to a point on his forehead, heavy brows, and between them a furrow cleaving the forehead. Inflammation had made the eyes look smaller; the nose was broad and somewhat bulbous; the lower lip was bitten through and through.

Overkamp fastened his eyes on that face, the scene of the

approaching action. This was the fortress which he was now to penetrate. If, as was alleged, it was impervious to fear and threats, there were other means of taking a fortress unawares, provided it was famished and weakened by exhaustion. Overkamp was familiar with all these means and he knew how to use them. He'd start with asking questions. In an effort to ascertain the weak points of the fortress he'd begin with the simplest of questions. He would ask for the date of birth and at once be informed of the star under which the man was born. Overkamp watched the prisoner's face as an officer watches a terrain. He had already forgotten his first sensation at Wallau's entrance. He had returned to his fundamental principle: there are no impregnable fortresses. Taking his eyes off the man's face, he looked at one of his slips. With his pencil he stabbed a little point behind a word and gazed back at Wallau. Politely he asked: "Your name is Ernst Wallau?"

Wallau replied: "I shall from now on refuse to answer any question."

To which Overkamp said: "So your name is Wallau. Let me point out to you that your silence will be interpreted as affirmation. You were born in Mannheim, on October 8, 1894."

Wallau remained silent. He had spoken his last words. If a mirror were held to his lips, not a breath would cloud it.

Overkamp did not take his eyes off Wallau. He was almost as motionless as the prisoner himself. Wallau's face had become a shade paler, the line cleaving the forehead a little blacker. The man's gaze was directed straight ahead, right through the affairs of a world that had suddenly become glassy and transparent, right through Overkamp and the board partition and the guard posted outside, right through to the core that is impenetrable and able to withstand the gaze of the dying. Fischer, a similarly motionless witness of the questioning, turned his head in the direction of Wallau's gaze. All he could see was the luscious everyday world that is not transparent and without core.

"Your father's name was Franz Wallau; your mother's Elisabeth Wallau, maiden name Enders."

Instead of an answer, silence came from the bitten-through lips. Once there had been a man named Ernst Wallau. That man was dead. Hadn't we just witnessed his last words? He had had parents whose names were as cited. One might as well place beside his father's tombstone that of his son. *If it is true that you can get depositions out of a corpse, I'm deader than all your dead.*

"Your mother lives in Mannheim, Mariengaesschen 8, with her daughter Margarete Wolf, maiden name Wallau. No, stop: used to live... This morning she was transferred to the Home for the Aged at An der Bleiche 6. Following the arrest of her daughter and her son-in-law because they are suspected of having aided your escape, the flat at Mariengaesschen 8 was sealed."

When I was still alive I had a mother and a sister. Later I had a friend who married my sister. As long as a man lives he has all kinds of connections and family ties. But this man is dead. And no matter what strange things happen to these people in this strange world after my death, they need no longer concern me.

"You have a wife, Hilde Wallau, maiden name Berger. The fruit of this marriage was two children, Karl and Hans. Let me point out to you again that I am taking your silence to mean Yes." Fischer stretched out his hand, shifting the shade of the 100-watt lamp so that the light fell full in Wallau's face. Still the face remained as it had been, steeped in a dull evening light. Not even a 1000-watt lamp can reveal traces of torment and fear or hope in the hopeless finality of dead men's faces. Fischer pushed the shade back again.

When I was still alive I also had a wife. We even had chil-

186

dren. We raised them in our common belief. What a joy it was for husband and wife to see the teachings take root. How sturdily the little legs swung at their first political demonstration! The pride in the little faces, and the anxiety lest the heavy flags in their fists tip over! When I was still alive during the first years of the Hitler régime, when I was still doing all the things that meant life to me, I could without fear reveal my hiding places to these boys, at a time when other sons were betraying their fathers and teachers. Now I am dead. Let the mother worry about providing for the fatherless waifs.

"Your wife was arrested yesterday with your sister for having aided in your escape. Your sons were handed over to the Educational Institute at Oberndorf, to be brought up in the spirit of the National Socialist State."

When the man whose sons were now mentioned was still alive, he tried in his way to take care of his family. Now it would soon become apparent what that care was worth. Others who were far stronger than two foolish children have given way. And the lies are so luscious, and the truth so dry! Strong men have sworn their lives away. *Bachmann has betrayed me. But two young boys – that, too, is said to happen occasionally – will not deviate a hair's-breadth from the way of truth. My fatherhood, at any rate, has come to an end, no matter what the final outcome may be.*

"You fought in the World War as a soldier at the front."

When I was still alive I went to war. I was wounded three times – at the Somme, in Roumania, and in the Carpathian Mountains. My wounds healed, and I was sound when I came home. Even though I am dead now, at least I did not fall in the World War.

"You joined the Spartakus League in the month it was founded."

The man, while he was still alive in October 1918, joined the Spartakus League. But what of that now? They might as well summon Karl Liebknecht to be questioned; he would answer as much and as loudly. Let the dead bury their dead.

"Look here, Wallau, do you still cling to your old ideas?"

They should have asked me that yesterday. Today I am no longer able to answer. Yesterday I should have been compelled to shout Yes! Today I keep silent. Today others are answering in my stead; the songs of my people, the judgment of posterity. . .

It was growing cool around him. Fischer was feeling chilly. He would have liked to tell Overkamp to have done with this useless questioning.

"And so you were hatching plans for an escape, weren't you, Wallau? Ever since you were assigned to the special work squad?"

Several times in my life I was compelled to flee from my enemies. At times the flight was successful; at others it miscarried. Once, for instance, it ended badly. That was when I wanted to escape from Westhofen. Now I have been successful. I have escaped. In vain do the dogs sniff at my trail, it has been lost in infinity.

"And then, first of all, you told your friend George Heisler about your plan, didn't you?"

When I was still a living man, in the life I used to live, I met a young fellow named George at the very last. He was much younger than I. I became attached to him. We shared our sorrows and joys. Everything in this young man was dear to me. Everything in life that was dear to me I found again in him. Now he has no more to do with me than any living man has with a corpse. May he remember me occasionally, if he finds time for it. I know that life is busy and crowded.

"You made Heisler's acquaintance only at the camp?"

No flood of words, but an icy flood of silence came from the lips of the man. Even the guards listening at the door shrugged their shoulders uneasily. Was this a questioning? Were there still three of them in there? – The man's face was

188

no longer pale, but alight. Overkamp suddenly turned away. He made a dot with his pencil and broke the point.

"You'll have yourself to blame for the consequences, Wallau."

What consequences could there be for a dead man who was being thrown from one grave into another? Not even the towering monument of the final grave is of any consequence to the dead.

Wallau was taken away. Within the four walls the silence held; it would not depart. Fischer, sitting motionless on his chair as if the prisoner were still there, looked steadfastly at the place where Wallau had been standing. Overkamp sharpened his pencil.

George had reached the *Rossmarkt*. He walked on and on, although the soles of his feet were burning. He must not detach himself from the crowd, he must not sit down anywhere. He cursed the city.

Before he had thoroughly weighed the pros and cons, he found himself standing in a side street off Schillerstrasse. He had never been there before. Suddenly he decided to take advantage of Belloni's offer. Wallau's voice counseled him to do so. The little artist with the serious face no longer seemed to him impenetrable. Impenetrable – the people passing him were impenetrable! How familiar Hell had been compared with this city!

Even while he stood in the flat Belloni had indicated, his old distrust returned – what a strange odor! Nothing in all his life had ever smelled like this! The old jaundiced woman whose hair was the color of shoe blacking looked him over sharply and silently. "Perhaps she is his grandmother," thought George. The likeness stemmed from no family relationship, however, but from their common profession.

"Belloni sent me," said George.

Madame Marelli nodded. She seemed to find nothing extraordinary in that. "Wait here a moment," she said. The room was cluttered with wearing apparel of all kinds and colors. The odor, stronger even than in the hallway, almost suffocated him. Madame Marelli cleared a chair for him and went into the next room. George looked around. His gaze went from a coat sparkling with black paillettes to a wreath of artificial flowers, from a white hooded cloak with rabbit ears to a little dress of lilac-colored silk. He felt too exhausted to make sense of these surroundings. He looked down at his stockinged hand. He started up at the sound of whispering in the next room. He expected to be seized and to hear the click of handcuffs. He jumped up.

Madame Marelli returned, her arms loaded with clothing. "Go ahead and change," she said.

Hesitating, George admitted: "I have no shirt."

"Here's one," said the woman. . . "What's the matter with your hand?" she asked suddenly. "Oh, I see, that's why you had to quit."

"Never mind," said George. "I don't want to undo this. Just let me have a rag."

Madame Marelli brought him a handkerchief. She looked him over from head to foot. "Yes, Belloni gave me your measurements. He has a tailor's eye. You have a true friend in him. A good man."

"Yes. That's right. He is."

"You were on the same bill with him?"

"Yes."

"If Belloni can only carry on! He didn't look good to me this time. And you? How are things with you?" Shaking her head, she looked at his emaciated body, but with no other curiosity than that of a mother who has borne a number of sons so that, no matter what the occurrence, whether it concerned body or soul, she was ready to compare. She was the type of woman who could make the Devil himself feel at ease. She helped George change his things. Unfathomable though her little black paillette eyes remained, George lost his distrust.

"Because Heaven has denied me children," said Madame Marelli, "I think about all of you all the more when I am sewing and mending things. As for you, you must take care of yourself so that you'll be able to carry on. A nice pair of friends you are! Why don't you look at yourself in the looking glass?" She led him into the next room in which stood her bed and her sewing machine. Here, too, everything was cluttered up with the strangest wearing apparel. She moved the side parts of the large, almost luxurious three-winged mirror into place. George could see himself now from the side, from the front, from the back, in a brown-felt hat and a brownish overcoat. His heart had for some hours behaved quite reasonably, but now it began to beat furiously at the sight.

"Now you can hold up your head again. If you make a bad appearance, you're all the more certain not to make a hit. We have a saying that where one little dog has done his job, others will soon come and do theirs. Now I'm going to make a little package of your old rags." He followed her into the first room. "I've fixed up a little statement here," said Madame Marelli, "although Belloni thought it unnecessary. It goes against his grain to settle accounts. Look at this cape, for instance – almost three hours' work. But decide for yourself: would I be justified in taking a quarter of his pay from a man for sewing a rabbit costume he needs for one evening? Look here; I got twenty marks from Belloni. I was all for refusing the job at first, for as a rule I don't repair street clothes. I don't think twelve marks is excessive. So here are eight marks. Give my love to Belloni if you meet him."

"Thank you," said George. Walking down the stairs he again became suspicious – the street door might be watched.

He had almost reached the bottom when the woman called after him that he had forgotten his package. "Mister! Mister!" she called. He paid no attention, but rushed out into the street. It was empty and quiet.

"Apparently Franz won't be at home at all tonight," they were saying at Marnet's. "You'd better divide his pancake among the children."

"Franz isn't what he used to be," said Augusta. "Since he's been working in Hoechst, he doesn't turn a hand for us."

"He's tired, that's all," said Frau Marnet who liked Franz well enough.

"Tired?" croaked her shriveled little husband. "I'm tired, too. If I only worked regular hours – but I work eighteen hours a day."

"Tut, tut," said Frau Marnet. "Just remember that when you were working in the brickyard before the war you used to come home all twisted up every night."

"As for Franz," said Augusta, "he isn't staying away because he's overworked. Oh, no, quite the contrary. I bet he has some attraction in Frankfurt or Hoechst." All eyes were turned upon Augusta who, filled to the bursting point with gossip, was sugaring the last pancake.

"Has he said anything?" asked her mother.

"Not to me, he hasn't."

"I always thought," said her brother, "that Sophie was kind of sweet on Franz. If that were the case, he'd certainly fallen into something soft."

"Huh, Sophie and Franz?" sneered Augusta. "Why she's much too fiery for him!"

"Fiery?" There was astonishment in everybody's face. Twenty-two years ago it was that Sophie Mangold's diapers were hanging on the line in the next-door garden. And now she was supposed to be "fiery," according to her friend Augusta.

"If she's fiery," said old wrinkles with glittering little eyes, "she'll need a little kindling."

"You're the right one to talk about kindling," thought Frau Marnet to herself. She had never been able to stand her husband, though not for one minute in their married life had she permitted this to make her unhappy. Only people who are fond of somebody can ever be unhappy, she had told her daughter before her wedding.

While his Cousin Augusta was dividing his pancake into as equal halves as she could, Franz was entering the Olympia. The lights had been lowered, and people grumbled when he squeezed awkwardly past them to his seat, because he made them miss some of the weekly news.

Franz had noticed at once that the seat next to his was occupied. Then he had caught sight of Elly, her face white and rigid, her eyes wide open. Watching the weekly news, he pressed his elbow close to his body, for it was Elly's arm that was propped on the elbow rest between their seats.

Why couldn't the years be erased? Why couldn't his hand close round her wrist? He let his gaze travel along her arm, her shoulder, her throat. Why couldn't he brush a caressing hand over her thick brown hair? It looked as though it needed a caress. In the lobe of her ear gleamed a small red point. Had no one given her any other earrings in all these years? He frowned. He must be careful of every word and thought! If later, during the intermission, he were to speak to the pretty little trick that happened to be sitting next to him, nobody could suspect anything even if she were being trailed at the movies.

"I'm going to buy some burnt almonds," he thought, as

the lights went up. He had to pass in front of Elly to get to the aisle. She looked at him, but even at this short distance failed to recognize him. "So Else couldn't come after all," thought Elly. Had the ticket come from her? "Perhaps the old lady beside me is her mother. At any rate, it's good to be sitting here." She wished the intermission were over, and the lights would go down again.

She looked at Franz when he came back. A faint ray of recognition flashed through her mind. . . . Vague recollections. She couldn't even tell whether they were joyous or mournful. "Elly," said Franz. She looked at him with astonished eyes. Even before she definitely recognized Franz she felt comforted. "How are you?" he asked. A frown passed over her face. She forgot to answer his question. "I know. I know all about it," he said. "Don't look at me now, Elly, but listen carefully to what I say. Keep on reaching for the almonds and chewing. I was at your house last night – look at me now and laugh a little. . ."

Elly acted quite cleverly. "Eat," Franz said. "Eat." He spoke quickly and softly. She had only to answer Yes or No. "Try to think of his friends. Do you know any I don't know? Think! Whom did he use to know here? Perhaps he'll come into town after all. . . . Look at me and laugh. We can't be seen together after the show. Go to the big market early tomorrow morning. I'll be helping my aunt. Order some apples. I'll deliver them, and we'll be able to talk. Do you understand?"

"Yes."

"Look at me." In her young eyes there was almost too much confidence and peace of mind. "I wouldn't have minded if there'd been something else in them, too," thought Franz. She gave a forced laugh. When the house was dark she looked at him quickly again, her expression real, her face serious. Perhaps she herself would have liked to grasp his hand now, if only because of a feeling of anxiety.

Franz crushed the empty paper bag in his hand. It occurred to him that there could be nothing between him and Elly as long as George was still in the country. He ought to be satisfied if he could see her again briefly without endangering her or himself.

But now she was sitting beside him. She was alive and so was he. The stir of happiness, no matter how feeble and brittle, was stronger than anything that burdened him. He was asking himself whether she actually saw the film her wide-open eyes were staring at. He would have been disappointed had he known that Elly, forgetting herself and everything else, was following with all her heart the wild ride through the snowbound landscape. Franz stopped looking at the screen. He looked down at Elly's arm and, now and then, fleetingly at her face. He was startled when the picture was over and the lights went up. Before separating in the crowd their hands met lightly, as do those of children who have been forbidden to play with each other.

v

George felt both more at ease and strange in his overcoat. "I have much to apologize to you for, Belloni." What now? The streets would soon grow empty as the people went home from coffee houses and movies. The night stretched before him. An abyss, where he had expected to find a shelter. He moved on, almost unconscious from exhaustion, a dressed-up dummy set in motion by a spring. He had intended to send Leni to one of his old friends tomorrow, to Boland. Now he would have to go himself. There was nothing else to do. It was fortunate that he at least had these clothes. He tried to figure out the shortest route to take. To map out a way, to make his mind follow short cuts and turns while he yearned only for sleep, was as tormenting as actually to trudge through those streets. He arrived shortly before half-past ten. The street door was open because two women were volubly taking leave of each other. George had no doubt about Boland being the right man for him. He was the first choice among all those who could be considered. The first choice by so wide a margin that one need not rack one's brain about it again. "He is the right one," George repeated to himself while he was mounting the stairs. His heart was beating regularly, because he would no longer harbor useless warning; perhaps, too, because there was nothing to warn him about.

He recognized Boland's wife. She was neither old nor young, neither handsome nor ugly. Once, George recalled, when there was a strike she'd taken care of another child in addition to her own. Someone had brought the child – its father was probably in prison – to their meeting place that evening. Boland had put its hand in his own, taken it to his flat to consult his wife, and come back without it. The evening's business had proceeded – some talk, if George remembered correctly, about a planned demonstration. And in the meantime the child had acquired parents, brothers and sisters, and supper. "My husband isn't in," said the woman, "he's at the inn across the way." She was a bit surprised, but not distrustful.

"May I wait for him?"

"I'm sorry, but I'm afraid not," she replied, not angrily, but with decision. "It's late, and I've a sick child in the house."

"I'll have to watch for him," thought George to himself. He came down to a lower floor and sat on the stairs. Would the street door be locked now? Someone might come in ahead of Boland and find him and question him. "What if Boland is with someone? I'd better wait for him in the street, or perhaps go over to the inn. Boland's wife didn't

196

recognize me, and this morning the teacher took me to be as old as his father." He slipped out between the two women who were still at their farewells.

Could it be the same inn to which they'd brought the child that evening? Everyone seemed about to leave. They were all slightly tipsy and they laughed so heartily that sounds of Sh! came from some of the open windows. Almost all the men were SA; only two were in civilian clothes, one of them Boland. He too was laughing, though in his familiar noiseless, good-natured way. He had not changed. Leaving the others, he walked away between two SA men. The laughter of the three men had already diminished to an amused smile. Apparently they lived in the same house, for one of them unlocked the door – the two women were actually gone by this time – and the other two followed.

George knew that the company Boland kept need have no actual significance. He also knew that the shirts Boland's companions wore were equally insignificant. He had heard enough about such things at the camp to know what to think about them. He knew that a change had come into people's lives – their outward appearance, their companions, and the forms their struggles took. He knew all that, just as Boland must know it if at heart he had remained the same. He knew it all, but he did not feel it.

George felt as he always had recently, and as one gets to feel in Westhofen. He had no time now to let his reason tell him why their brown shirts were indispensable to Boland's companions, and why these companions were indispensable to Boland. At their sight he felt only what he had felt at Westhofen. There was no sign on Boland's forehead to identify him as trustworthy. George had no feeling about it. He might be, and then again, he might not.

"What am I to do?" George asked himself. He had already done something: he was no longer in Boland's street. The town came alive once more. It was the last outbreak of noise before the quiet of the night would descend.

"They had to arrest the Bachmann woman in Worms."

"Why?" asked Overkamp crossly. He had been against the arrest; it would only arouse people's curiosity and excitement, whereas any obvious leniency on the part of the police would have isolated the Bachmann family most effectively.

"When Bachmann's body was cut down in his attic, she shouted he should have done that yesterday before the questioning – that it was a pity to ruin a perfectly good clothesline. She didn't calm down even after the body had been removed. She made everybody in the neighborhood crazy with her shouts that she was innocent, and so on, and so forth."

"What was the neighbors' attitude?"

"Well, fifty-fifty, I guess. Shall I ask for detailed reports?"

"Oh, Lord, no," said Overkamp. "That's none of our business. Let our colleagues in Worms worry about that. We've got enough to do here as it is."

George could not very well vanish into thin air. He decided: "The first slut that comes along." But when he saw her come out from behind the shed that stood midway in Forbach-strasse, in back of the freight station, she looked so much worse even than his imagination had pictured her that he felt he could not bear to touch her with his finger tips. Her flesh on her longish head was shrinking. In the feeble light of the street lamp he couldn't tell whether the tan-colored tuft on top was growing from her head or was merely sewed on to her hat as an ornament. He started to laugh. "That isn't your hair, is it?"

"My hair? Why, yes." She looked at him uncertainly, the trace of a human emotion crossing her cadaverous face.

"Well, no matter," he decided.

She looked at him again, with a sideways glance. Then she stopped at the corner of Tormannstrasse, hesitating professionally, but ostensibly to give a final touch to her face and hair. With a show of heartiness, he took her arm. They walked along quickly. It was she who first spotted the policeman at the corner of Dahlmannstrasse and pulled George into a doorway. "Everything's so strict now," she said. Carefully avoiding police patrols, they walked through several streets arm in arm. At last they arrived. It was a small square, neither angular nor round; it was like a circle drawn by a child. The square and the overlapping slate roofs seemed suspiciously familiar to George. "Wonder if I lived here once with Franz."

On the stairs they had to squeeze past a small group – two fellows and two girls. One of the girls was knotting the bow tie of a young chap two heads shorter than she. She twirled the ends up, Shorty immediately turned them down, the girl yanked them up again. The other fellow had a smooth shaven face, was somewhat cross-eyed, and very well dressed. The other girl wore a long black dress. She was surprisingly good-looking – a little white face in a cloud of shimmery pale gold. One of the fellows called out: "Good night, sweetie!"

"Good night, cockeye!" George's woman called back.

As she was unlocking the door, Shorty shouted: "Have a good time!"

"Shut up, shrimp," she retorted.

"Is that supposed to be a bed?" asked George.

The woman let out a flood of abuse. "You'd better go to the Englischer Hof, or to Kaiserstrasse. . . ."

"Do be quiet and listen to me," said George. "I've had some trouble, and it's none of your damn business either what it was. I've been beside myself with worry and I haven't had a wink of sleep ever since. If you can manage to make me fall asleep, I'll treat you right. I don't mind spending a little money, and I have some to spend."

She looked at him with surprise. Into her eyes came a glow, as if a light were lit in a death's-head. Then she said with the utmost determination: "Done!"

There came a thump at the door, and Shorty stuck his head in the room. He looked about as if he had left something. The woman ran toward him, scolding, but stopped her abuse when, with a mere lift of his eyebrows, he motioned her outside.

George could hear the five of them beyond the door whispering back and forth with a labored softness that made the whispers all the more audible. In spite of it, George couldn't catch a single word. A hissing – it stopped abruptly. George put his hand to his throat. Had the room shrunk? Had the four walls, the floor, the ceiling contracted? He said to himself: "Get out of here!"

She came back presently and said: "Don't look at me so crossly, please don't." She chucked him under the chin but he pushed her hand away.

Later – what a miracle! – he actually slept. Hours? Minutes? Had Loewenstein in his desperate indecision turned on the faucet a third time? Slowly George returned to consciousness. Consciousness would certainly bring in its wake excruciating pains in at least six places in his body. Still, he continued to feel surprisingly fresh and clear. So he had actually slept! "I'll give her everything I have," he thought. What had awakened him? The light had been switched off, and only the feeble glow from the lamppost in the yard came through the little window at the head of the bed. As he sat up, his giant shadow sat up on the opposite wall. He was alone. He listened – waited. It seemed to him he heard a noise on the stairs, a faint creaking made by bare feet or by a cat. He felt unspeakably oppressed by the presence of his shadow which, mammothlike, reared into the ceiling. At one time the shadow gave a violent start as though it wanted to hurl itself upon him. A flash through his brain: the four pairs of piercing eyes behind him as he had come up the stairs! The short fellow's head in the crack of the door! The lifting of the eyebrows! The whispers on the landing! He jumped out of bed, through the window, and into the yard, landing on a pile of cabbages. He stumbled on and smashed a pane – a foolish thing to do because the bolt could have opened much more quickly. He knocked down something that came in his way, becoming aware seconds later that it was a woman. Two faces came crashing together. Two eyes were staring into his, a mouth roaring into his mouth. They rolled on the pavement as if horror compelled them to clutch at each other. Taking a zigzag course, George ran across the square and into one of the side streets, which suddenly turned out to be the street on which he had lived happily years ago. As in a dream, he recognized its paving stones, the bird cage above the cobbler's shop, the door in the yard that opened on other yards and from them to Baldwinsgaesschen. "But if the door is locked now," he thought, "everything is lost." The door was locked. But what did a locked door matter when what was pursuing him lent him the strength to hurl himself against it? No use measuring anything by old forces that had lost their power. He ran through the yards, turned gasping into a doorway, and listened. Everything here was still quiet. He drew back a bolt. He found himself in Baldwinsgaesschen. He could hear the whistles, but they were no nearer than Antonsplatz. Again he was running through a maze of little streets. Again it seemed like a dream – a few places were the same, others were changed. The image of the Holy Virgin was still hanging there over the gate, but next door the street suddenly came to an end – there was a strange square, wholly unknown to him. He crossed the strange square and came into a section honeycombed by innumerable little streets. He was in another quarter of the city. The smell of earth and gardens was in the air. George climbed over a low fence into a corner formed by yew hedges. He sat down and drew a few deep breaths. Then he crawled a little farther and lay down, for his strength had suddenly given out.

How bell-like was the clarity of his wakefulness, and how sad it was to be so fully awake! He was so miserable, forsaken as he was by all his good spirits.

The route of his flight had presumably been learned by now, and his exact description flashed everywhere. His distinguishing features were possibly even now being impressed continuously upon everybody's brain by radio and newspapers. In no town was he in greater danger than here. The silliest and most common of all reasons had brought him to the verge of utter ruin: he had put reliance on a girl. Now he could see Leni as she had actually been at the time: neither romantic nor prosaic, but quite ready to go through fire for her lover of the moment, to cook his meals, or to distribute propaganda literature. If in those days he'd been a Turk, for his sake she would have aided in having the Holy War proclaimed in Niederrad.

Steps were approaching on the path beside the fence. A man with a cane passed. The Main was probably quite near, for George had come to realize that he was not in a garden but on an embankment. Now he recognized beyond the trees the smooth white houses of the Obermain Quai. He could hear the rumbling of the trains and, though it was still quite dark, the clanging of the first streetcars.

He would have to get away from here. His mother was undoubtedly being shadowed. The woman, Elly, who bore his name was also sure to be shadowed. In this town anybody who had ever so much as set a tiny tile in the mosaic of his life might be shadowed – most likely his few friends, his teachers, his brothers, his former sweethearts. The whole town was a tortuous net in which he was already caught. He would have to slip through the meshes. True, he was now at the end of his rope. His strength was barely enough to get him over the fence. How was he to get out of the town? The same way he'd entered it yesterday? How was he to get twenty times farther to the frontier? He might as well cower here until he was found. His mind rebelled madly, as if someone had actually made this proposition to him. If there remained in him only the strength for one tiny movement in the direction of freedom, no matter how senseless and useless the movement, he would still want to make it.

A short distance away, at the nearest bridge, a dredger was already at work. "My mother can probably hear that," he thought to himself. "My little brother, too, is hearing it now."

Chapter IV

i

Even before his sleepless night had come to an end, Peter Wurz, former Burgomaster of Oberbuchenbach, now burgomaster of the united villages of Ober- and Unterbuchenbach, got up from his bed of pain, stole through the yard into the stable, and in its darkest corner sat down on the milking stool. He wiped the perspiration from his forehead. Ever since the radio had listed the names of the fugitives yesterday, everyone in the village – men, women, and children alike – had tried to get at him. Was he actually green in the face? Had he actually got the gout? Had he actually suddenly shriveled up?

Buchenbach lies up the Main a few hours' walk from Wertheim, but removed from the highway as well as from the river, as if it wished to withdraw from all traffic. Formerly it had consisted of two villages, Oberbuchenbach and Unterbuchenbach, that bordered upon a common road. As the result of administrative reforms and ground adjustments, Ober- and Unterbuchenbach were united.

Whenever an earthquake destroys a prospering town, there always are in the debris a number of decayed walls that would have crashed anyway, sooner or later. Seeing that the brazen fist in its ruthless suppression had also suppressed a number of ancient purposeless customs, the sons of Old Man Wurz and their SA companions showed a bold and rebellious front to the peasants who opposed the union of the two villages.

Wurz on his milking stool wrung his hands till the joints cracked. Since it was not milking time yet and their udders did not hurt, the cows failed to be impressed. Every few seconds Wurz gave a violent start and pulled himself together, only to start again. He thought: "He could sneak in here, too, he could waylay me here..."

The man whose coming he so dreaded was Aldinger, the old peasant whom George and his friends in Westhofen had considered somewhat queer and deranged.

Wurz's eldest son had at one time been as good as engaged to Aldinger's youngest daughter. It had been mutually agreed that they would wait a few years before getting married. The two families' acres had joined each other, and so had the two little vineyards across the Main which, since grapes were no longer profitable, could someday be put to other uses. At that time, Aldinger was burgomaster of Unterbuchenbach. In 1930, his daughter fell in love with a fellow who was working on the Wertheim road-building project. Aldinger did not oppose the match; on the contrary he rather favored it since the young man was earning regular wages. The couple went to live in the city. In February 1933, the son-in-law made a brief appearance in the village, but little attention was paid to his visit. Like many other workingmen in small towns whose political convictions were only too well known he preferred to spend that first period of arrests and persecutions with relatives in the country.

He had disappeared again when Wurz, following his sons' advice, reported his visit to the State Police.

In the meantime, Aldinger, knowing of the proposed union of the two villages, had rallied around him a group of men who held that if he could no longer be Burgomaster, Wurz, too, should relinquish his office, and a third man be appointed to govern the combined villages. This group was supported by the village priest, who lived and preached in Unterbuchenbach, where his church and parish were located.

There had actually been a search for the son-in-law who for years had been collecting dues for his trade union and also for a small workingmen's paper. The Buchenbachers, although as a rule greatly prejudiced against outsiders, never found anything to criticize in the quiet man who lent Aldinger a hand at harvest time in return for bread and sausage for his family, which now numbered five. The only quarrel he ever had was at the inn with Wurz's sons who even then were leaning toward the SA. This tendency led them later to advise their father.

Wurz had almost been frightened at the speed with which his action in accordance with his sons' advice bore fruit. Aldinger had been taken away. Wurz had only wanted to have him out of the way until he himself was safe in office. It would have been fun to gloat over Aldinger's discomfiture. But somehow this part of the plan miscarried, and Aldinger, for inexplicable reasons, failed to return.

Wurz, sitting on his stool, thought: "That fellow Aldinger was at the end of his rope, anyway. Where did he keep himself at the last? Nobody was giving him any thought any more."

What had puzzled people in Buchenbach most was the matter of the demesne. It had always been the demesne. Now a model village was being established there, and thirty families from a great many villages in the vicinity were being settled there. They were mainly peasants who were proficient in some trade and had large families. There was the blacksmith from Berblingen, the shoemaker from Weilerbach. From many of the villages only one family had been chosen; next year more would be settled. Every village entertained hopes. It was like the big prize in a lottery – everybody seemed to know a family who had won it. Slowly it dawned upon several who had opposed Wurz because of Aldinger that Wurz, in permitting his sons to join the SA, had backed the right horse. If one wished to have a claim on the demesne village, if one wished to be justified in entertaining even the slightest hope of being settled there, it would be well not to show too openly one's opposition to Wurz, through whose hands all the applications had to pass. One should not even visit the Aldingers too frequently. They soon became isolated. People stopped asking after Aldinger's whereabouts; perhaps he was already dead. His wife was always dressed in black, her lips always compressed. She went to church a good deal, but she had always done so. His sons never came to the inn.

When the escape had been broadcast yesterday, everything had been changed again. Now there was no one who could have wished to change places with Wurz. Aldinger was a robust man and he'd know how to get hold of a rifle if he actually got to the village. What this fellow Wurz had done – bearing false witness against one's neighbor – was certainly wrong. It was on his account that the whole village was now guarded. The SA squad to which Wurz's own sons belonged was guarding the farm. That wouldn't do him much good. Aldinger knew the lay of the land. Suddenly he'd be there, and as suddenly Wurz would have a bullet in him – and nobody would be surprised. All the guards in the world couldn't help him. Someday he would have to cross the Main, someday he would have to go to the wood.

Wurz started. Somebody was coming. By the clatter of her milk pails he recognized his eldest daughter-in-law, Alois's wife. "What are you doing here?" she asked. "Mother is looking for you." Through the stable door she watched him slinking through the yard as if he himself were an intruder. She twisted her mouth. Ever since her marriage into the family Wurz had ordered her about. Now she rather gloated over the man's discomfiture.

ii

Although, as far as it concerned Westhofen, the Belloni case was closed by the man's death, there was still a lot of "unfinished business" concerning other departments. The documents covering this business were far from dust and decay, sharing the usual fate of such papers. While Belloni himself was decaying, his case remained alive. Who had given the man sustenance? Who spoken to him? Who were these people who obviously could be found only in the city? By listening carefully to the gossip in places frequented by performers, the police learned Madame Marelli's name as early as Wednesday evening. Everybody seemed to know the woman. The night had not yet ended – Wurz, the Burgomaster of Buchenbach, was still sitting on his milking stool – when Madame Marelli had some visitors. She was not in bed, but was sewing metal sequins onto a skirt. It belonged to a woman who had that evening performed at the Schumann Theater and who had to leave by an early morning train to fill a Thursday engagement. When the police arrived and informed her that she would have to come along at once for questioning in a matter of the utmost urgency, Madame Marelli was greatly perturbed, but only because she had faithfully promised the dancer she would have her skirt ready by seven the next morning. The questioning itself was a matter of indifference to her; she had already been through a few of them. Besides, the SS and SA uniforms made as little impression on her as the shiny shields the Gestapo agents displayed. Possibly she was one of the few people who are entirely lacking in consciousness of guilt, or else her profession had taught her that outward adornments and interchangeable costumes were apt to produce astonishing results. She put a little bag of sequins and her sewing things with the partly finished skirt, wrote a note, and tied the package to the outside knob of her door. Then she quietly followed the two policemen. She asked no questions, her thoughts still occupied with the skirt and her doorknob. She began to be surprised, however, when she found herself at a hospital.

"Do you know this man?" asked one of the two commissars. She drew back the sheet. Belloni's regular, almost handsome features were marred only slightly. One could almost say they were befogged. The commissars expected one of the outbursts of wild grief, simulated or genuine, which the living seem to think they owe the dead on such occasions. But the only sound from the woman was a low-voiced "Oh!" as if she were saying, "What a pity!"

"So you do know him?" asked the commissar.

"Naturally," said the woman. "It's little Belloni."

"When did you see this man last?"

"Yesterday – no, day before yesterday, in the morning. I remember I was surprised to see him so early. I had to sew a few stitches in his coat. He was going through. . ."

Instinctively she looked around for the coat. The commissars were watching her closely. They communicated their impressions to each other by nods – the woman was obviously sincere, although one couldn't be too sure. They waited calmly for her words to trickle out. "Did it happen at a rehearsal? I didn't expect him to rehearse here. Or did he make another appearance before leaving? He expected to take the noon train for Cologne."

The commissars were silent. "He told me," she continued, "he had an engagement in Cologne. I remember saying to him: 'Are you back in form again, my dear little fellow?' How did this thing happen?"

"Frau Marelli," shouted the commissar. The woman looked up with surprise, but without fear. "Frau Marelli," repeated the commissar, with the coarse and unnatural seriousness affected by police officials when giving out information whose importance lies not in its essence but in the effect it produces, "Belloni was not the victim of a theater accident. He was a fugitive."

"A fugitive? Fugitive from what?"

"A fugitive from Westhofen, Frau Marelli."

"What did you say? When? Why, he was at the camp two years ago. Wasn't he discharged long ago?"

"He was still at the camp. He escaped. You mean to tell us you didn't know that?"

"I did not know," said the woman simply. She spoke in a tone of voice that definitely convinced the commissars she had known nothing of the whole affair.

"Yes, a fugitive. He lied to you yesterday."

"The poor fellow!" murmured the woman.

"Poor?"

"Well, he wasn't rich, was he?" asked Madame Marelli.

"None of your impudence now!" said the commissar. The woman frowned. "Well, sit down, sit down. I'll have some coffee brought in. You haven't eaten anything yet this morning."

"Oh, I don't mind," replied the woman with quiet dignity. "I can wait till I get home."

"Now tell us exactly, please, the circumstances of Belloni's visit – when he came, what he wanted of you. Every word he said to you. Wait a moment! Belloni is dead, to be sure, but that does not prevent you from being seriously, very seriously, suspected. Everything depends upon you now."

"Young man," said the woman, "you are probably deceived about my age. My hair is dyed. I am sixty-five years old. I have worked hard all my life, although many people unfamiliar with our profession have a wrong idea of our work. Even now I have to work hard. What are you threatening me with, I'd like to know?"

"With jail," said the man drily. Madame Marelli opened her eyes wide, like an owl. "You see, your little friend here, whose escape you may have abetted, had a good deal to answer for. If he hadn't broken his own neck. . . perhaps. . ." He moved his hand horizontally through the air. Madame Marelli gave a start. Presently, however, it became apparent that she had started because something had occurred to her. With an expression on her face as if in all this talking the most important thing had been neglected, she walked back to Belloni's bed and drew the sheet over his face. One might have inferred that she was not rendering this service for the first time.

Then her knees sagged. She sat down and said calmly: "You'd better get me some coffee after all."

The commissars were growing impatient, for every second counted. Standing at the right and left of Madame Marelli's chair and well trained to each other, they fired alternate questions at her.

"Exactly when did he come? How was he dressed? Why did he come? What did he want? What did he say? How did he pay you? You still got that note that you gave him change for?"

Yes, she had it with her in her handbag. The number was noted, and the change compared with the money found in the dead man's pocket. There was quite a difference. Could Belloni have made some purchases before embarking upon his pleasure trip across the roofs? "No," said the woman, "he left some money with me because he owed it to somebody."

"Have you already spent it?"

"You don't think I'd steal a dead man's money, do you?" asked Madame Marelli.

"Has it been called for?"

"Called for?" she repeated in a slightly less assured tone, suddenly realizing she had said more than she had meant to.

The commissars stopped her. "Thank you, Frau Marelli. We'll take you home again in our car. We might as well have a look-see in your rooms."

Overkamp did not know how to express his feelings when he got the report that the sweater, which the fugitive George Heisler had obtained from the riverman in exchange for the velvet coat, had been found in Madame Marelli's flat. By now Heisler would be safe in Westhofen again, if one hadn't given credence to the deposition of that fool gardener's apprentice. Not to recognize one's own jacket! Was that possible? Was there anything suspicious in that quarter? And if so, what? So Heisler had after all gone back to his own town. The search was resumed with renewed vigor. All means of egress from the town – crossroads, railroad stations, bridges, ferries – were watched closely, as if war had broken out. A reward of five thousand marks was placed on the head of each fugitive.

As George had foreseen that night, his home town and all the people who had ever been connected with his life – that brotherhood which sustains every being and surrounds him with blood relatives, loves, teachers, masters, and friends – had changed into a network of living traps.

The net grew tighter and more artfully woven with every hour of police effort.

"This little tree," said Fahrenberg, "was expressly grown for Heisler. The crossboard is a little lower so the fellow will have to stoop a bit. Here, an inner voice tells me, he can rest over the weekend from his hardships."

"That inner voice of yours!" said Overkamp a bit contemptuously. He glanced at Fahrenberg with the eyes of a professional inquisitionist. The man was utterly done for.

Fahrenberg was still a comparatively young man when, during the war, he took unto himself a "war bride." His elderly wife and her two almost grown-up daughters made their home with his own parents in that house on Market Square, the ground floor of which was occupied by the plumber's shop. Fahrenberg was expected to enter the business, since his older brother, the plumber, had fallen in the war. Fahrenberg had at first intended to study law, but war conditions and the troubled times had prevented him from making up through diligence what his natural talents did not make any too easy for him. He decided that rather than help his aged father lay pipes in Seeligenstadt he would help in building up a new Germany; he and his SA squad would try to win little towns for the cause, especially his home town which had formerly considered him a good-for-nothing. It was his ambition to shoot off his gun in the workmen's quarters, to beat up Jews, and finally to put to shame his father's and the neighbors' gloomy prophecies by coming home on furlough with bars on his shoulders, money in his pocket, a following, and power.

Of all the specters that had haunted Fahrenberg during the past three nights, the most horrible was that of a ghost-like Fahrenberg in blue plumber's overalls blowing out a clogged pipe. His eyes burned from lack of sleep. The latest report – the finding of the sweater – seemed the answer to all his nightly prayers to sustain him in his hour of need, to bring back the prisoners, and not to punish him with what to him was the most fearful of punishments – the loss of power.

"First of all," said George to himself, "I'll have to get something to eat or I'll be done for in another hundred steps. A few minutes' walk from here, where the tram stop is, there ought to be an automat." He felt a piercing pain in the pit of his stomach, almost as he were being stabbed and were keeling over. His head began to swim. It was the same sensation he had had at the camp after especially trying ordeals. He had always been disappointed later when it passed off, as if the point had not remained in the wound but had been drawn through it smoothly. Now he was angry. He had had a different idea of perishing: to go down fighting, roaring defiance at people.

"What's the use?" he asked himself. He was on his feet again. He shook out his overcoat which had got damp and crushed, and crossed the city's Obermain section. It would have been funny, wouldn't it, if he had been lying dead behind a fence while they were searching the whole town for him!

How young the town looked all at once, how still and clean! "Perhaps Wallau is already out of the country," he thought. "Belloni is sure to be. Apparently he had plenty of resources here... What mistake have I made, that I got stuck here?" The outlying streets were still empty. Beyond the Playhouse life began to pulse, as if the day were spreading from the inner part of the town. As George stepped into the automat, got the smell of coffee and soup in his nostrils, and saw bread and food displayed behind the glass panels, hunger and thirst made him forget fear and hope. At the cashier's desk he changed one mark of Belloni's money. With tormenting slowness the sandwich turned toward the opening. Ah, to have to wait until the thin stream spurting out of the faucet filled his cup of coffee!

The automat was rather crowded. Two young lads wearing gas-company caps had taken their cups and plates to one of the tables against which their tool kits were leaning. They ate and exchanged small talk, when one of them suddenly stopped. He did not even notice that his companion looked at him with surprise, turning to see what had attracted his attention.

George in the meantime had eaten his fill. He left the automat without looking to either right or left. He brushed against the young chap who had given such a start at seeing him. "Do you know the fellow?" asked the other.

"Why, you know him too. You used to." His companion looked at him uncertainly. "I am sure that was George," the first one continued quite frankly, unable to contain himself "Yes, Heisler the fugitive."

With a faint smile and an oblique look the other one said: "Lord! You could have earned a nice bit of money."

"Could I? Could you?"

Suddenly they looked into each other's eyes with the terrible look one sees in the faces of deaf-mutes or very clever animals, in the faces of all creatures whose reason is locked in for the duration of their lives. The flash that came into the second lad's eyes untied his tongue. "No," he said, "I couldn't have done it either." They picked up their kits. They had been good friends formerly, until the years when they refrained from talking about the things that mattered, for fear of putting themselves at the other's mercy in the event that the other had changed. Now it had become clear that both of them had remained as they had been. Friends again, they left the buffet.

iii

Ever since her discharge, Elly had been watched night and day in the hope that she would lead her former husband to his doom if he was still in town and tried to get in touch with his family. The night before, at the movies, she had not been out of the sight of watchful eyes for a second. Her street door was under observation the entire night. The net hanging over her pretty head could not have been tighter. But even the tightest net, so the saying goes, consists mainly of holes. While they had seen that Elly permitted herself during the intermission to be drawn into conversation with the man in the next seat, on the way to the movie and in the theater itself she had chanced upon half a dozen acquaintances, one of whom had waited for her and escorted her home. He had turned out to be the harmless son of an innkeeper.

The Marnets were surprised at Franz's offer to accompany his cousin and his aunt and their apple baskets to market before he went to work. This was quite a change from his recent attitude.

Franz was already busy loading the truck when the others came down. "Plenty of time to drink your coffee," said Augusta, mollified. When the truck rattled down the hill, the moon and the stars were still in the sky.

In his attic, still apple-scented although the fruit had been packed the day before, Franz had racked his brains all night long. "If I were in George's place, supposing he is still here, to whom could I turn?"

Just as the police used their documents and card indexes and records to acquire knowledge of the fugitive's former life and enable them to draw a net over the whole city, so Franz too laid a net that from hour to hour became tighter as his memory conjured up everyone who to his knowledge had at one time been connected with George. Among them were some who had never left a trace on any registration blank or any other official document. It needed knowledge of a different kind to get on their track. Others there were whose names undoubtedly were known to the police. "If only he doesn't go to Brand," thought Franz. "The fellow is said to have worked here four years ago. And not to Schumacher either. He might even report him." Who else was there? The fat cashier girl whom he had seen him sitting on a bench with after he had broken with Elly? Stegreif, the teacher, whom he used to visit occasionally? Little Roeder, his school and soccer chum, to whom he had been greatly attached? One of his own brothers? Doubtful fellows, these, and besides unquestionably under observation.

Robust Augusta helped Franz to unload. Frau Marnet set out her goods. A little knife in one of her hands and a piece of apple for a sample in the other, she was at once on the lookout for the expected wholesale buyers.

"If Elly actually intends to come," thought Franz, "she ought to be here now." For quite some time, here and there, he had seen a shoulder, a hat, or something else that could have turned into Elly, if only it could have made up its mind to come in his direction. At last he saw her face, pinched and pale with fatigue – at least he thought he saw it. Quickly it disappeared again behind a pile of baskets. He was afraid he had been mistaken; but then he saw her approaching him jerkily, as if his heart's desire were to be fulfilled only reluctantly.

Elly greeted Franz only with her eyebrows. He was astonished to see how well she had grasped his hurried instructions and how cleverly she pretended actually to be buying apples. As if she did not know that Franz belonged to the Marnet outfit, she persistently turned her back on him. Deliberately she tasted a piece of apple. She bargained for the apples that would be left over after the expected whole-sale order was filled. Like all good deceptions this pretended transaction was successful because, as a matter of fact, Elly was to a slight extent really interested in it. The sample she had tasted pleased her palate, and she did not care to get the worst of a bargain. Even had she known how closely she was being watched, she could not have made a better pretense.

The mustachioed young man, whom Elly might have noticed, had been replaced by a stout woman who looked like a nurse or a sewing teacher. This did not mean that the young man had withdrawn; on the contrary he was still one of the group entrusted with trailing her. He had been sta-tioned at the confectioner's. Several times on her way Elly had looked back to see if she were really being followed as her father and Franz had assumed. She thought that as a matter of course her pursuer would follow at her heels and be a man. She had noticed nobody except the worthy stout woman, but even she had disappeared, for the very good reason that at a prearranged place she had turned Elly over to another agent for further observation. Everything went smoothly, however; Franz had not yet attracted anybody's attention. Without betraying the least uneasiness, Elly was transacting a business deal that was unlikely to cloak any-thing else. She did not exchange a word with Franz. The only time Franz spoke was to Frau Marnet: "We might leave the apples with the Behrends and I'll deliver them after work, seeing that I have to go to town anyway." This overreadiness gave Augusta food for thought, but she could not possibly have guessed that this very purchaser was the girl who was drawing Franz to the city twice in one day. As for her opin-ion of Elly, it had solidified long since – thin as a bean pole, a hat like a little toadstool, a curly-headed asparagus stalk. If she runs around in a blouse like that on a weekday at six, what'll she put on of a Sunday? When Elly left, Augusta said to Franz: "Doesn't need much material for a skirt, that's one advantage she has, anyway." Franz swallowed his feelings. "Not everybody can have Sophie Mangold's behind," he answered.

George waited at the Playhouse for a streetcar. Out of the city by all means! He felt his throat contract. Belloni's overcoat, which yesterday had given him a certain feeling of security, was burning his shoulders. Take it off? Shove it under that bench?

He boarded his car. "I'll have to get out anyway. I must not ride to the end of the line, for there are sure to be guards there." George picked up a stray newspaper and unfolded it to hide his face behind it. The headlines jumped at him, and now and then a phrase or a picture.

Neither electrically charged barbed wire nor long lines of guards nor machine guns had been able to prevent events that happened in the outside world from finding their way into Westhofen. It was because of the kind of men that were interned there that even far-distant events were known there more intimately, if not more thoroughly, than in many of the scattered villages throughout the country, and in many flats. A certain natural law, or a mysterious circuit, seemed to connect this group of chained-up miserables with world centers. Thus, when George looked at the paper – the fourth morning of his flight was part of that week in October when the Teruel battle was raging in Spain and Japanese troops invaded China – he thought casually, but without being unduly surprised: "So that's how it happened!" These were the headlines of old stories that had pulled at his heartstrings. Now he lived only for the moment. When he turned the page his gaze was arrested by three pictures. They were painfully familiar. Quickly he looked away again. Still the pictures stayed before his eyes: Fuellgrabe, Aldinger, himself. He hurriedly folded his newspaper into a small square and put it in his pocket. He glanced quickly to the right and left. An old man standing beside him looked at him – very sharply, so it seemed to him. George got off the car suddenly.

"I'd better not get on a car again," he thought to himself "A fellow is imprisoned there. I'll walk it." As he passed police headquarters his heart gave a mighty jump. He put his hand to it, but presently it was beating normally again. He plodded on steadily, without fear, without hope. He trudged past the museum and a small street market. He trudged through Eschenheimergasse and past the building of the *Frankfurter Zeitung*. He trudged as far as the Eschenheimer Tower, crossed the street, and quickened his pace because for the past few minutes the sense of being in danger set his skin tingling. His brain evolved a single thought: "I am being watched!" He felt no fear; on the contrary he was rather calmer and more reassured because the enemy came in sight. As though his other sensations were the more acute the duller his head felt, he seemed to feel boring into his neck a pair of eyes which, from the safety island at the Tower, followed him incessantly. Instead of continuing to follow the tracks, he ran into a little park.

He stopped suddenly. He simply could not resist turning round. A man stepped out of the group of people at the Tower tram stop and walked toward George. They grinned at each other and shook hands. The man was Fuellgrabe, the fifth of the seven fugitives. He looked as neat as a shop-window dummy. It was George who finally said: "Let's go in here."

They sat down on a sunny bench. Fuellgrabe dug at the gravel with the toe of his shoe. His shoes were as fine as his clothes. "Wonder how the fellow got all these things so quickly," thought George.

Fuellgrabe said: "Do you know where I was heading for?"

"No. Where?"

"Mainzer Landstrasse."

"Why?" asked George. He drew his overcoat round him so as not to have it touch Fuellgrabe's. The thought flashed through his mind: "Is this really Fuellgrabe?"

Fuellgrabe drew his overcoat around him. "Have you forgotten what is on Mainzer Landstrasse?" he asked.

"I suppose I have," said George tiredly.

"The Gestapo," said Fuellgrabe. George remained silent, waiting for the strange apparition to vanish.

Fuellgrabe began: "Listen, George, do you know what's going on at Westhofen? Do you know that everybody has been recaptured except you, myself, and Aldinger?"

On the bright sunlit ground in front of them their shadows melted into each other. "How do you know?" asked George. He moved a little to one side so as to create two neatly separated shadows.

Fuellgrabe answered: "I suppose you haven't read the papers. Here – look! For whom are they looking? You, me, and Grandpa. I daresay he got one on the head long ago and is lying in some ditch. He couldn't have held out long. That leaves the two of us." Quickly he rubbed his head against George's shoulder. George closed his eyes. "If they were still looking for anyone else, he'd be in the papers, too. No, no, they've got the others all right. They've got Wallau, and Pelzer, and – what was that fellow's name? – Belloni. As for Beutler, I was there to hear his screams."

George meant to say, "Me, too," but his open lips couldn't utter a sound. What Fuellgrabe had said was right – mad but right. "No!" George exclaimed.

"Sh-sh!"

"That isn't true," said George. "That's impossible. They couldn't have caught Wallau. He isn't one to let himself be caught."

Fuellgrabe laughed: "Then how did he get to Westhofen in the first place? My dear George! We were all crazy, and Wallau was the craziest of all." He added: "But that's enough of that."

"Enough of what?" asked George.

"Of this madness. I, for my part, am cured. I'm going to give myself up."

"Give yourself up where?"

"I'm going to give myself up," Fuellgrabe repeated stubbornly. "In Mainzer Landstrasse. I'm throwing in the towel. That's the most sensible thing to do. I want to keep a head on my shoulders. I can't stand this fools' dance another five minutes – and in the end they catch you anyway. You can't buck it." He spoke quite calmly – getting calmer all the time. He strung one little word to another, simply and monotonously. "It's the only way out. To get across the border is impossible. The whole world is against us. It's a miracle that we two are still at large. Let's put a stop to the miracle of our own free will before they catch us, or else it's curtains for us. You can imagine what Fahrenberg is doing to those who are brought back, can't you? Do you remember Zillich? And Bunsen? Do you remember the Dancing Ground?"

George was conscious of a horror against which there was no struggling. He felt paralyzed already. Fuellgrabe must have shaved quite recently. His thin hair was brushed and smelled of the barber's. Was it really Fuellgrabe?

"You do remember, don't you?" Fuellgrabe went on. "You remember what they did to Koerber who they said intended to escape! He hadn't even intended. We actually did."

George began to tremble. Fuellgrabe watched his trembling for a moment and then continued: "Believe me, George, I'm going there at once. It's the best thing to do. And you'd better come along, too. I was on the point of going there. God Himself has led us to each other. I am sure of it!"

His voice had become a drawl. His head nodded twice. "I am sure of it!" he said again. Again his head nodded.

George gave a sudden start. "You're mad," he said.

"We'll see which of us is mad, we'll see, we'll see," answered Fuellgrabe in his deliberate manner. At the camp it had earned him the reputation of being a good-natured sensible fellow who never raised his voice. "Just use the little brain you've got, my lad. Look things in the face. Yours will be a sudden and quite disagreeable end unless you come along with me, my friend. Sure. Come on!"

"You are mad," said George. "You seem to think they'll hold their bellies with laughter when you approach. Is that what you think they'll do?"

"Laugh? Let them laugh. As long as they let me live. Get wise to yourself, brother, there's no other way out for you. If they don't grab you today, they will tomorrow, and nobody will give a damn what happens to you. My lad, this world of ours has changed, let me tell you that. Nobody gives a damn for us any more. Come on – do as I do. It's the very, very, very cleverest thing to do, the only thing to save us. Come on, George!"

"You are utterly mad."

Until now they had had the bench to themselves, but now a woman in a nurse's uniform sat down at the other end. With one hand she rocked a perambulator gently and expertly. It was a mammoth pram full of pillows and lace and pale-blue ribbons. The tiny baby in it was apparently not yet sound asleep. She turned the carriage obliquely to the sun and took out her sewing after a quick glance at the two men. She was what is generally called businesslike, neither old nor young, neither pretty nor homely. Fuellgrabe returned her glance, not only with his eyes, but with a somewhat forced smile, a horribly spasmodic contraction of his whole face. Seeing it, George felt quite faint.

"Come on!" said Fuellgrabe. He got up. George grabbed him by the arm. Fuellgrabe tore himself loose with a motion that was more violent than George's grip was firm; his arm touched George's face. "He that will not be advised cannot be helped. Good-by, George!"

"Don't! Wait a minute," said George. Fuellgrabe actually sat down again. George said to him: "Don't do such a crazy thing, don't walk right into their trap. You'd get yours quickly, believe me. Have they ever shown anyone any mercy? Nothing is likely to impress them... Why, Fuellgrabe! Fuellgrabe!"

Moving close to George, Fuellgrabe said in a sad, changed voice: "My dear friend! Come along. You've always been a decent lad. Why won't you come with me? It's so horrible to go there alone."

George looked at the mouth from which these words had issued. He noticed that the teeth which seemed unnaturally large because of the gaps between them looked like the teeth in a death's-head. Fuellgrabe's days were certainly numbered. Probably even his hours. "He's already out of his senses," thought George, wishing fervently that he would go away quickly and leave him, alone and sound. Probably at the very moment Fuellgrabe was thinking the same thing about George. He looked at George with consternation, as though he had only now become aware of with whom he was talking. He got up and hurried away, disappearing so quickly behind the bushes that George had the feeling the meeting had just been a dream.

Presently he was seized with an attack of fear, as sudden and wild as in that first hour when he had cowered at the edge of the camp among the willow bushes. A cold shudder that shook body and soul with quick jerks went over him.

Suddenly the attack passed. He wiped the perspiration from his forehead as if he had been through a struggle. As a matter of fact, he had, although he thought he had only been shuddering. *What was it that just happened to me? What tale was I told? Can it be true, Wallau, that they got you? What are they doing to you?*

Calm yourself, George! Do you think they would have mercy on YOU – *anywhere? Would you have gone to Spain if you had had the chance? Do you think they would have shown us mercy* THERE? *And do you think it would be better to be hanging from a barbed-wire entanglement or to get a bullet in your belly? This city that is afraid to take you in today – when there is a rain of bombs from Heaven, it will know what it means to be afraid. . .*

But Wallau, look here; I'm alone, I could not be so alone in Spain, not even in Westhofen. Nowhere could I be so utterly alone. . .

Be calm, George! You have plenty of good company. It is somewhat scattered now, I know, but that doesn't matter. Heaps of company – dead and alive.

Behind the large bed of asters, behind the lawn, behind the brown-and-green bushes, on a playground perhaps or in a garden, a swing could be seen indistinctly moving up and down. George thought: "I'll have to start all over again and reason out everything. To begin with, shall I really try to get out of this town? What good would it do me? How would I get anywhere? To try to get over the border without help would mean to court capture a thousand times. My money will soon be gone. To make my way from chance to chance without money would be too much for me in my weakened condition. Here in town there are at least people I know. All right, a girl refuses to take me in. So what? There must be others. My family, brothers, my mother? Impossible – all being watched. Elly, who came to see me in Westhofen? Impossible – being watched most surely. Werner, who was at camp with me? Also being watched. Father Seitz, who is said to have helped Werner after his discharge? Impossible – being watched most likely. What other friends are there?"

Before he went to prison, in the life before death, there had been people upon whom he could rely absolutely. Franz was one of them – but Franz was far away, George thought. Still, he let his thoughts dwell on him for a moment. A waste of the minutes left to him for reflection. It was some consolation anyway to be able to say that a man, such as he needed now, actually existed. If he did exist, his being alone was merely accidental. Yes, Franz would have been the right man. And the others? He weighed them, one after another. The weighing was surprisingly simple. A number of people were passing in review in his head. They were probably attending to their work or fussing with a meal; they could not have the faintest inkling of how fearfully they were being weighed at that moment. A last judgment without trumpet blasts, on a clear autumn morning. In the end, George found four who passed the test.

He was firmly convinced that he could find shelter with any of the four. But how to reach them? Suddenly he imagined that at that very moment guards had been posted at the four doors. "I must not go there myself," he said to himself. "Someone else must go in my place. Someone whom nobody could suspect, who has nothing at all to do with me, and who would yet do everything for me." Again he began to let them all pass in review. Again he felt entirely alone, as if he had never had parents, had never grown up with brothers, had never played with other boys or fought beside comrades. A multitude of faces – old ones and young ones – floated through his mind. Exhausted he peered into the congeries he had evoked – followers half of them, pursuers the other half. Suddenly a face came back to him; covered with a profusion of freckles, it was neither old nor young; for truly, in school Paul Roeder had looked like a little man, and at his wedding like a boy about to be confirmed. When they had been lads of twelve, they had got their first football partly by fraud, partly by work. They had been inseparable until – until other thoughts, friendships of another type, had come to rule George's life. During the year he had spent with Franz he had never been quite able to rid himself of a certain feeling of guilt in connection with little Roeder. He had never been able to explain to Franz why he was ashamed because he himself could understand thoughts which Roeder would never understand. There had been times when he would have liked to shrink down and unlearn everything so that he could get back to his school chum's level. It was all a tangled skein of recollections from which a single smooth thread presently emerged. "I'll go to Bockenheim at four. I'll go and see the Roeders."

iv

Franz was so tired that he felt as if the belts were whirling through his head. Nevertheless he made no mistake, probably because for the first time he was not afraid of making one. To the exclusion of everything else, he was thinking of his chances of seeing Elly alone when he delivered the apples.

While he was thinking of how in a few hours he would again be facing Elly, the selfsame Elly he had always loved, it flashed through his mind that all his dreams might become realities.

For a moment, a single moment only, Franz asked himself if this simple happiness did not outweigh everything else. A slice of ordinary happiness now, instead of the terrible and relentless struggle for a final happiness of some humanity of which he would most likely no longer be a part. "All right, now we can bake some apples in our own oven," he'd say. The wedding would be celebrated in November to the tune of fiddles and pipes, and their two cozy little rooms in the Griesheim settlement would be waiting for them. Going to work in the morning, he'd be conscious all the way of Elly's waiting for him in the evening. Annoyances? Wage deductions? Drudgery? In the evening, in their neat little flat, all such things would roll off of him. Standing as he was even now, punching piece after piece, he would be able to think incessantly: "In the evening... Elly." Flags out? Swastika in the buttonhole? Render unto Hitler the things that were Hitler's. Don't mind them! Elly and he would get their fun out of everything they did together: love and Christmas trees, the Sunday roast and the sandwiches in his dinner pail, the little privileges granted to newlyweds, their tiny garden and the workingmen's excursions. They'd have a son. To be sure, it would be a matter of putting something by and postponing their adventure into "Strength through Joy" until the following year. The new wage scale was still generally satisfactory. They must have figured that out pretty cleverly, seeing that in spite of everything the output continued to increase. By and by, of course, the continuous hustling would get on one's nerves. "Don't grumble so much," Elly would say. "Don't let's have any trouble, Franz – least of all now." For they were now expecting their second child. It was lucky that Franz was made foreman; now they could pay off the small loan they'd had to take from Elly's father. If only Elly weren't so afraid of having another child! "I hope we're not going to have any war babies," said Franz. This time Elly cried continuously. They figured back and forth, calculating every expense on the basis of the various benefits granted heads of large families. But even while he was figuring, Franz felt his heart grow heavy – why, he did not exactly know. It was as if he were darkly conscious of a certain illegality in that kind of figuring. In the end, everything passed smoothly. Yes, now they could put in their application for the ship excursion – Mother would take care of the boy, and they would leave the baby with Elly's sister. It was this sister who was teaching the boy the Hitler salute. Elly was still pretty; she'd lost none of her bloom. "I hope she'll have something good for me to eat," thought Franz during the day, "not some of that warmed-up hash again."

Franz's thoughts strayed back to the morning when he came to the factory and found instead of Noggin a strange lad sweeping off the waste dust. "Where's Noggin?" Franz asked. "He's been arrested," one of the men answered. "Arrested? Why, for Heaven's sake?" "Because he spread rumors." "What kind of rumors?" "About Westhofen. There was a jail break on Monday." "What, in Westhofen?" asked Franz with surprise. "Didn't know there were any still alive there." To this, one of the punchers, a quiet, dry man with sleepy features, said: "Why, did you think they croak them all up there?" Franz had never paid much attention to this man, but now he started and stuttered: "No, no – I just thought they'd all been discharged." The puncher smiled vaguely and turned away. "If only I didn't have to go home tonight," thought Franz. "If I could only talk once more to one like him." He realized suddenly that he'd known the puncher before. Somewhere in his past life he'd had some connection with this puncher – he'd known him for a long time, even before Elly, before. . . Franz started violently, ruining one of the plates. But why take it out on Snapper, the lad everybody praised because after only three days on the job he could sweep the dust from under one's arms as skilfully as Noggin who'd done this work for a whole year?

George, standing on the platform of a streetcar, thought: "Wouldn't it have been better to walk? Skirt the town?"

Hadn't he attracted more attention this way? *You shouldn't worry over what you failed to do, counseled Wallau. It's a useless waste of energy. You shouldn't jump off suddenly, and try this, and then that. Pretend to be calm and secure.*

"What good is all the advice, if you yourself haven't been able to profit by it?" He had lost the sound of Wallau's voice.

Immediately George began to speculate on who his pursuer might be. The man with the goatee and glasses, who looked like a teacher? The lad in the plumber's overalls? The old fellow who was carrying a little tree that was carefully wrapped up and was probably intended for his garden plot?

During the past few seconds the sound of marching music had detached itself from the conglomerate noise of the city. It approached quickly, growing stronger, and imparting its precise beat to every noise and movement. Windows were thrown open, children came running; the street was quickly lined with people. The motorman jammed on the brakes.

The very pavement began to vibrate. Shouts of acclamation could be heard from the end of the street. The Sixty-sixth Infantry Regiment had been quartered in the new barracks for several weeks. Whenever it marched through any section of the town it was given a new reception. Here they came at last: trumpeters and drummers, the drum major whirling his stick, the showy horse ambling. Here they were at last! People were jerking their arms up, holding them out in stiff salute. The old fellow saluted, supporting the little tree with his knees. His brows jerked to the beat of the march, his eyes sparkled. Had he a son in the regiment? That was the march that stirred the people's very heart, making their skin tingle and their eyes shine.

What magic was this, brewed from equal parts of age-old memories and total oblivion? One could have believed that the last war these people had fought had left only happy memories, had carried in its wake nothing but joy and prosperity. Women and girls were smiling as if their sons and lovers were invulnerable.

How well the boys had learned the step in just a few weeks! At the sound of that march, mothers who were justified in scrupulously counting their every penny and in asking, "What for?" would readily give up their sons, or pieces of their sons. What for? What for? That was the question they would ask themselves softly as soon as the music died away. Then the motorman would start his car again, and the old man would grumble about a twig on his tree that had been broken. The police spy – if there actually was one – would come back to earth with a start.

For George in the meantime had jumped off the car. He'd walk to Bockenheim. Paul lived at Brunnengasse 12. Neither blows nor kicks had been able to dislodge that knowledge or the name of Paul's wife: Liesel, maiden name Enders.

Nearing his goal, George walked quickly and surely, without once turning around. He stopped in front of a show window on a street leading into Brunnengasse to catch his breath. The sight of his reflection in the mirror made him hold fast to a railing. How white the face of that man who was clinging to the railing with one hand – a man with a brownish coat and a felt-hatted head!

"Dare I, after all, go up and see the Roeders?" George asked himself. "What justification is there for my belief that I have shaken off my shadow – if I really was being shadowed? And Paul Roeder – why should he of all men assume such a tremendous risk? How did I come to be sitting on that bench a while ago?"

V

On the third-floor-left door, Roeder's name was painted on a small piece of cardboard, dainty and exact, inside an escutcheonlike circle. George leaned against the wall and stared at the name as if it had pale-blue eyes and freckles, short arms and legs, intelligence and a heart. While he was devouring the sign with his eyes he realized that the formidable but rather indefinite noise he had heard at the foot of the stairs was coming from this selfsame flat. He heard a child's toy being wheeled about, a child's voice call out the stations, and another child shouting "All aboard!" – all to the accompaniment of the whirring of a sewing machine. Suspended over all these noises was the sound of a woman's voice singing the chorus of the *Habañera* from "Carmen." So strong, almost powerful, was the voice that George at first thought it was coming from the radio until it broke unexpectedly on a high note. All these sounds were heightened rather than drowned out by the sounds of the identical march he'd heard in the street a little while ago; he thought this music was coming from outside until he realized that a band was playing it on the radio in the flat opposite the Roeders'.

George recalled that, as a girl, Liesel had occasionally sung in the chorus at the Opera. Paul had taken him to the gallery from time to time to admire her in the ragged skirt of a smuggling lass or the knee breeches of a page. Liesel had always been what is usually called a good fellow. The chasm which had suddenly separated him from Paul when he took up with Franz, that unintentional but impassable chasm, had first impressed itself on his awareness in connection with Roeder's wife and Roeder's home. Living with Franz meant not only studying, absorbing certain thoughts, and taking part in certain struggles, but also carrying oneself differently, wearing different clothes, hanging different pictures, and judging different things to be beautiful. Would Paul be able to stand his waddling Liesel all his life? Why did they stuff their place with all that trash? Why had they saved two long years to buy a sofa? George had felt bored at the Roeders'; hence he stayed away. And then Franz too had bored him, and their room had seemed bare to him. Suffering from this confusion of unfermented feelings and partly conscious thoughts, George, at the time hardly more than a boy himself, had more than once brusquely quit his friends and companions. This had gained him the reputation of being an unpredictable fellow. The way he figured it, one action could be invalidated by another, one sentiment be extinguished by another, opposite one.

George, still listening to all the sounds, put his thumb on the doorbell. Not even in Westhofen had he ever been seized with so poignant a feeling of homesickness. He withdrew his hand. How could he enter here, where they would welcome him innocently without any suspicion? Could not a single pressure on this bell disperse the family inside like chaff before the wind? Bring in its wake imprisonment, torment, and death?

George's mind was filled with a piercing light. "My exhaustion was to blame," he said to himself, "for having suggested the idea to me." Had he not been convinced, no less than half an hour ago, that he was being followed? Did he really think that a man like himself could shake off his shadowers so easily?

George shrugged his shoulders and descended a few steps. At that moment somebody came in from the street. His face turned toward the wall, George let Paul Roeder pass him going upstairs. He dragged himself to the nearest stair window and leaned against it, listening.

Roeder, however, instead of entering his flat, also stopped

and listened. Suddenly he turned and walked downstairs. George went down another few steps. Roeder leaned over the banister. "George!" he called. Without answering, George went on downstairs. Roeder, at his side in two leaps, again said: "George!" He grabbed him by the arm. "Is it you, or isn't it?"

Paul laughed and shook his head. "Were you up at our place? Didn't you recognize me just now? I thought to myself: 'Good Lord, isn't that George?' But you're changed, man. . ." Suddenly he sounded hurt: "It has taken you three years to remember Paul again. Oh, well – come along anyhow."

Without saying a single word to all this, George followed his friend. Now they were standing at the large stair window. Roeder gave George an upward glance. No matter what Paul was thinking, his face was too thickly freckled to allow any suspicion of a gloomy expression.

"Well," said Paul, "you look a bit green about the gills. Tell me, are you still the George I used to know?" George moved his parched lips. "You are, aren't you?" Roeder asked quite seriously. George laughed shortly. "Come on, man, come on!" said Roeder. "It's really surprising that I recognized you on the stairs."

"I was ill a long time," said George quietly. "My hand hasn't healed yet."

"Any fingers missing?"

"No. I was lucky."

"Where did that happen? Have you been around here all this time?"

"I was a chauffeur in Kassel," said George. In a few calm sentences he described the place and the circumstances as he recalled them from a fellow prisoner's tale.

"Now we'll have some fun," said Paul. "Liesel's face'll be a study." He pressed the doorbell. Even while the fine piercing sound of the bell still echoed, there came a thunderstorm of banged doors, children's loud voices, and Liesel's "Well, I'll be darned!" Clouds of flowered dresses and wallpaper were swirling, intermingled with pictures and faces with thousands of freckles and frightened little eyes – then darkness and quiet.

The first thing George was conscious of was Roeder's voice ordering angrily: "Coffee! Coffee! Do you hear? Not dishwater!" George sat up on the sofa. With a tremendous effort he came back from his unconsciousness, in which he had felt so secure, into Roeder's kitchen. "That still happens now and then," he explained. "Nothing serious. Liesel needn't bother about coffee."

George stretched his legs under the kitchen table. He put his bandaged hand on the oilcloth between the plates. Liesel Roeder had grown into a stout woman who would no longer look so well in a page's breeches. The warm, rather heavy gaze of her brown eyes rested briefly on George's face.

"All right," she said. The best thing you can do now is eat. We'll have the coffee later." She set the table and prepared the meal.

Roeder got his three oldest children seated around the table. "Wait, I'll cut it for you, George. Can you spear it all right? I hope you don't mind our simple fare. Do you want some mustard? Some salt? He who eats well and drinks well keeps body and soul together."

"What day is today?" asked George.

The Roeders laughed. "Thursday."

"Why, Liesel, you've given me your own two sausages," said George, who was using every ounce of his will power to fit himself into an ordinary evening, he who had had to fit himself into utmost danger. As he was eating with his uninjured hand and the others were eating, he caught brief looks, now from Liesel and now from Paul, that made him feel that he was fond of them and that they, too, were still fond of him.

Suddenly he heard somebody coming up the stairs –
higher and higher. He listened. "What are you listening to?"
asked Paul. The steps grew fainter. On the oilcloth near his
injured hand was a faded circle that had probably been made
by a hot plate. George pressed his beer glass on the faded
spot like a stamp: "Let things take their course!" Paul, interpreting George's motion in his own way, poured some more
beer in the glass. Slowly they finished the meal.

"Are you staying with your parents again?" asked Paul.

"Temporarily."

"How about Elly?"

"We don't see each other any more. . ." George pulled
himself together. He looked about him, at all the curious
little eyes. "Well," he said, "you seem to have accomplished
quite a lot in the meantime."

"Why, don't you know that the German nation must
quadruple?" asked Paul, his eyes dancing. "You apparently
don't listen to the *Führer*'s speeches."

"Oh, yes, I do, but I never heard him say that little Paul
Roeder of Bockenheim must do the job all by himself."

"Well, it isn't so difficult nowadays to have children,"
said Liesel Roeder.

"It never was."

"Oh, George," Liesel laughed, "now you're getting back
into your stride again."

"No, I meant it. There were four of us at home. Fritz,
Ernst, myself, and Heinie. And you, Paul?"

"I was one of five. . ."

Liesel interrupted him: "Nobody ever cared a straw about
us; but now, at last, things are different."

Paul said laughing: "Liesel got an official message of
congratulation. . ."

"I certainly did. Yes, sir!"

"Well, but how about Paul? Shouldn't he have been congratulated on his fine performance?"

"Joking apart, George, look at all the allowances and the extra pay. Seven pfennigs an hour is not to be sneezed at. Then there's the exemption from wage deductions and the free supply of diapers. As if the Social Welfare knew that a succession of three little behinds would completely wear out the old ones."

"Don't listen to him," said Liesel. "He's quite satisfied with things as they are. Last August on our vacation he was as spry as on his honeymoon. . ."

"Where'd you go?"

"To Thuringia. We went to the Wartburg, and Martin Luther, and the Contest of Minnesingers, and the Venusberg. That, too, was a kind of official reward. I tell you, never before in all history has anything like it been tried."

"Never," said George. He thought to himself: "Such wholesale trickery? No, never!" Aloud he said: "And you, Paul? How are you getting along? Are you satisfied?"

"Oh, I can't complain," answered Paul. "Two hundred and ten marks a month. That's fifteen marks more than I got in '29; that was the best year since the war, and then I only got it for two months. But this time it'll last. . ."

"Why," said George, "it's obvious even on the street that everything's going full blast." His throat grew ever more constricted; his heart felt heavy.

"Well," said Paul, "what do you want? That's the war."

"Isn't that a funny feeling?" mused George.

"What?"

"What you said. Just think that you are manufacturing the things that'll kill thousands of others over there."

"Oh, well," Paul replied, "what's an owl to one is a nightingale to another. If we're going to worry our heads over such things... ah, there you are, Liesel! Now for our coffee. George will have to come again soon and have another fainting spell."

"This is the best coffee I've had in three years," said George. He patted Liesel's hand. He thought: "Out of here – but where?"

"You always were given to brooding, Georgie, weren't you?" Paul said. "And what's it got you? Now, I suppose, you've settled down. Before, you would have told me exactly everything I had on my conscience." He gave a short laugh. "Do you remember, George, how you came to see me once and you were all in a stew? I was out of work, but nothing would do – I had to buy something from you – something Chinese. I, of all men – a little booklet – from the Chinese, of all people!... And don't start telling me about your Spaniards either," he said harshly, although George had remained silent. "Don't do it. They don't need Paul Roeder's help to settle their hash. They offered resistance, didn't they? And now they are licked. My few little percussion caps won't make any difference." George still said nothing. "You always used to start the damnedest arguments – about the most farfetched things."

"As long as you admit making the caps, it isn't so far-fetched, is it?" asked George.

In the meantime Liesel had cleared the table and got all the children ready for bed. "Say good night to Father. Say good night to George."

"I'll put the children to bed," said Liesel. "You don't need a light yet for your arguing."

George thought: "What else is there for me to do? I have no other choice." "I say, Paul," he said casually, "can you put me up for tonight? Do you mind if I stay?"

Roeder, somewhat surprised, said: "Why, no! Why should I mind?"

"You see, I had a row at home, and I want to let it blow over."

"Stay here as long as you want," said Roeder.

Resting his elbows on the table, George covered his face with his hands. He looked at Roeder between his fingers. Paul would have looked serious if his face weren't so merrily freckled.

"Are you still getting into rows about one thing or another?" asked Paul. "What schemes and plans you used to have! Even then, if you remember, I used to say to you, 'Leave me out of it, George. I have no use for futile dreams. I'd rather be sure of my bread and sausage.' And those Spaniards, they're a bunch of Georges too. I mean as you were before, George. Now, it seems, you're taking it easier. Look at your Russia, what a mess they've made of things! At first it looked like the real thing, and a fellow was tempted to think: 'Perhaps – who knows?' Now. . ."

"Now?" George urged him on.

Although he covered his eyes quickly, Paul had been struck by one of the piercing looks that darted between George's fingers. He faltered. "Now. . . Well, you know. . ."

"What?"

"How topsy-turvy everything is over there. One 'liquidation' on top of another."

"Who, for instance?"

"Oh, I don't know. . . I can't remember those jawbreaking names."

Liesel came back into the room. "You'd better go to bed now, Paul. Don't be angry, George, but – "

"George wants to stay here tonight, Liesel. He had a row at home."

"You're a fine one," she said. "What's happened?"

"Oh, that's a long story. I'll tell you all about it tomorrow," evaded George.

"All right! Enough talking for one evening, though. Paul will be knocked out tomorrow."

"I can well imagine," said George, "that they don't handle him with kid gloves."

"Better to be driven hard and earn a few extra marks," replied Paul. "I'd rather work overtime any day than do air-raid practice."

"And how about growing old more quickly?" asked George.

"You'll have a chance for that as soon as the next war comes. And besides, George, the whole thing isn't so wonderful that you'd want to look forward to it forever and ever. I'm coming, Liesel." He looked around and said: "The only thing, George, what'll we give you for a blanket?"

"Just give me my overcoat, Paul."

"What a funny coat you've got, George. Put that rug under your feet, so's you won't dirty Liesel's roses." Suddenly he asked: "By the way, just between ourselves, what was the row about? Girl?"

"Oh, because..." floundered George, "because... because of the little one, Heinie. You know how fond of me he always used to be."

"Oh, by the way, I met that Heinie of yours the other day. I suppose he's about sixteen – seventeen, eh? All you Heislers were good-looking fellows, but Heinie beats you all. I hear they put a bug in his ear about joining the SS later."

"What, Heinie?"

"Well, I suppose you know more about it than I do," said Roeder. In spite of Liesel, he had sat down again at the kitchen table. Seeing George's face again squarely before his own, the same foolish thought that he'd had on the stairs flashed through his mind again: "Is that really George?" George's face had suddenly changed again. Roeder would have been at a loss to describe the nature of the change in a face that had remained so still. But that's exactly what it was: the change in a clock that stops suddenly. "There used to be rows with your family because Heinie stuck to you, and now..."

"Is that really true about Heinie?" asked George.

"How come you don't know anything about it? Haven't you been home?" asked Roeder.

Suddenly little Roeder's heart began to beat furiously. He scolded: "That's the limit. You've been telling me stories. Three years you don't come to see me, and now you tell me stories! You always were that way – you still are. Telling stories to your Paul! Aren't you ashamed of yourself? What have you been up to? Must have been something. Don't take me for an absolute fool. So you haven't been home! Where have you been all the time? You seem to be in a fine mess. Ran away? What's the matter with you anyway?"

"Perhaps you can spare me a few marks," said George. "I've got to get away from here right away. Don't let Liesel notice anything."

"What's the matter with you?"

"You have no radio?"

"No," said Roeder, "seeing what a fine voice Liesel's got, and all the noise in the house anyway – "

"Well, I'm big news on the radio," said George. "I escaped." He looked squarely into Roeder's eyes.

Paul had suddenly grown pale, so pale that his freckles seemed to glisten. "Where did you escape from, George?"

"From Westhofen. I... I..."

"From Westhofen? You? Have you been up there all this time? You're a fine one, I must say. They'll kill you if they catch you."

"That's right," said George.

"And in the face of that you want to leave here? You must be out of your mind, man!"

241

George was still looking into Roeder's face. Sprinkled with stars, it looked like Heaven itself to him. "My dear, dear Paul!" he said quietly. "I can't, don't you see? You and your whole family... Here you are all happy, and I... Do you realize what you're saying? If they should come up here – perhaps they are on my trail as it is."

Roeder said: "Then it's too late anyway. If they come I'll say I didn't know anything. These last few sentences have never been spoken. Do you understand? The words were never spoken. An old friend has a right to turn up unexpectedly, hasn't he? How was I to know what you've been up to in the meantime?"

"When did we see each other the last time?" George asked.

"The last time you were at the flat was in December '32, on Christmas Day. I remember you ate up all our cinnamon stars."

George warned him: "They'll question you and question you. You don't know what new tricks they've invented." In his eyes flashed the tiny pointed sparks that Franz had been so afraid of as a child.

"Don't talk of the devil or he'll appear. Why should they hit on our flat? They didn't see you come in, or they'd have been here long ago. You'd better think of the future, and of how you're going to get away from here... You'll excuse my saying so, George, but I like you better outside the place than in."

"I've got to get out of town, out of the country. I have to find my friends."

Paul laughed. "Your friends! First you'd better find the holes they've crawled into."

George said: "Later, when there is more time, I'll tell you about some of the holes they've crawled into. For instance, out there in Westhofen there are a few dozen men whom no one knows anything about.... Oh, I can tell you about it...

that is, if by that time we ourselves, you and I, haven't crawled into some of those holes ourselves."

"See here, George," said Paul. "I've been thinking of one particular fellow: Karl Hahn of Eschersheim. At that time he – "

George interrupted him: "Never mind!" He too was thinking of one particular man. Was Wallau already dead? Dead, in a world whirling on all the more madly the more inert he lay there? Once more he could hear him say "George!" – a single word that had traversed not only space but also time.

"George!" It came from little Roeder.

George gave a start. Paul watched him anxiously. For a moment, George's face had been strange to him again. His voice strange, too, he asked: "Yes, Paul?"

Paul said: "I could go and see these people tomorrow, so's to get rid of you."

"Let me think once more who's living in the city," answered George. "It's been more than two years, you know."

"You wouldn't have got yourself into this jam," said Paul, "if you hadn't been so taken up with that fellow Franz. Do you remember? It was him that got you in properly, for before that. . . Well, we all used to go to a meeting once in a while or take part in a demonstration. We'd all been worked up now and then. And hopeful, too. But that Franz of yours, he was the real article."

"It wasn't Franz," said George. "It was something that was stronger than everything else. . ."

"What do you mean, stronger? Stronger than what?" asked Paul, while he opened the footboard of the kitchen sofa to make George comfortable for the night.

vi

That same evening, Elly's nieces and nephews were hanging out of the window so as not to miss the arrival of the apples. Their father was that SS commander of whom his father-in-law, old Mettenheimer, had boasted at his questioning.

Elly's sister was a big-breasted woman, a few years older than Elly; she had rather coarse features which, unlike Elly's, showed no trace of melancholy but were always cheerful. Her husband, Otto Reiners, was a bank clerk during the day, an SS man in the evening, and at night – whenever he was at home – a mixture of both.

The hallway was dark, and Elly had not noticed when she came in the expression of dismay and perplexity on her sister's face, so like her own. As the children swarmed away from the window and up to Elly – they all loved her – Frau Reiners made a motion with her arm as if now it was too late to guard them against contamination. She murmured: "So here you are, Elly!" When Elly had phoned her about the apples, Reiners had ordered her either to refuse to accept them or to pay for them herself. At any rate, Elly must not come to see them again. When his wife had asked him if he were out of his mind, he took her by the hand and explained to her why there was nothing for her to do but choose between Elly and her own family.

Seeing Elly surrounded by the children, who relieved her of her hat, played with her earrings, and nearly pulled her arms out of their sockets, she began fully to realize what had happened during the past few days and of what far-reaching importance her husband's command was. "What nonsense to have to choose between Elly and my children! Why do I have to choose at all? Can there be such a choice?" With sudden harshness she told the children to leave Elly in peace and be off.

When they were alone, she asked Elly the price of the apples and counted the money on the table, forcing it into Elly's reluctant hands which she kept firmly pressed between her own. Then she began to talk to her earnestly. "You understand, don't you?" she asked finally. "We can see each other at our parents'. . . . Today he was on the radio again. . . . Oh, Elly, my dear, if you'd only accepted my brother-in-law at the time! He was quite gone on you. Now there's nothing you can do; you know how Reiners is – you can't be sure of what may still be in store for you."

Under other circumstances, Elly's heart would have stood still at her sister's words. Now her one thought was: "If only she doesn't make me go before Franz comes with the apples." Calmly she said: "What could still be in store for me?"

"Reiners says that it's possible they may even lock you up again. Has that ever occurred to you?"

"Yes," answered Elly, "it has."

"And that bothers you so little that you can still go on and buy winter apples."

"Do you think my chances of not being locked up would be better if I didn't buy them?"

Her sister thought: "Elly always used to go around half-awake, her eyes downcast, and her long lashes screening her thoughts like curtains." Aloud she said: "You needn't wait for the apples."

Quickly and firmly Elly replied: "No! I ordered them, and I'm going to see that we don't get cheated. Don't let Reiners make you goofy. I won't pollute your flat in these few minutes. As far as that's concerned I have already done so."

"Do you know what?" said the sister after brief thought. "Here's the key to the attic. You go on up and dust the shelves and put the jam jars on top of the closet. Put the key under the mat when you've finished." She was quite pleased at having found a solution that would enable her to get Elly out of the flat without actually putting her out of the house. She drew her sister into her arms to kiss her, something she normally did only on her birthday, but Elly turned her face, and the kiss landed on her hair.

When the door closed behind Elly, her sister went over to the window. Fifteen years since she had first come to live in this quiet little street! To her matter-of-fact eyes these familiar, ordinary houses tonight looked like houses one sees from a moving train. Her sober heart was attacked by a faint doubt, though it took on the familiar form of housewifely pondering: "What's it all worth, anyway?"

In the meantime, Elly had opened the attic window to let out the stale air. On the labels of the jam jars her sister had neatly written the kind of jam, and the year. Her poor sister! Elly felt a strange inexplicable pity for her older sister, although fortune seemingly had smiled on her. She sat down on a trunk and waited, her hands folded in her lap, her eyes lowered, and her head bent, just as one short day before she had waited on her prison bed and on the morrow would wait God knows where.

Franz came rumbling upstairs with his baskets of apples. "Here's a friend, after all," said Elly to herself. "Everything isn't lost." Hurriedly they unpacked the baskets, their hands reaching across each other. Elly looked at him with a quick sidelong glance. He had little to say and he listened constantly – somebody might come up here under some pretext. Probably Hermann wouldn't be too pleased to learn of this meeting, not even if everything went smoothly.

"Have you thought it over?" asked Franz. "Do you think he's here in the city?"

"Yes, I think he is."

"Why? After all, he'd have had to do quite some traveling. . . And everybody knows him here."

"Yes, but he too knows a lot of people. Perhaps he has some girl here he can trust. . ." A certain rigidity came into her face. "Three years ago, shortly before he was arrested, I saw him once from a distance in Niederrad. He didn't see me. He was walking with a girl. Not only arm in arm, but holding hands; perhaps one of those girls. . ."

"Perhaps; but can you be sure?"

"Yes, quite sure. Because he has somebody here, a girl or a friend. Even the Gestapo think so because they are still after me all the time, and above all. . ."

"Yes? Above all?"

"Because I feel it," said Elly. "I feel it here – and here. . ."

Franz shook his head. "My dear Elly, not even the Gestapo would pay any attention to that."

They sat down on the trunk. Only now did Franz look squarely at her. For a moment his look absorbed her from head to foot – a moment that he snatched from the few they had to themselves, from the terribly scant time that patterned their lives. Elly lowered her eyes. Even though, until now, she had forgotten Franz entirely, even though she felt as if she were walking on a tightrope with nothing but empty space underneath, even though it was a matter of life and death that had brought them together here in the attic – could she help it if her heart was fluttering with the expectation of love?

"Elly dear," said Franz, taking her hand, "I'd like nothing better than to stow you in one of my empty baskets, carry you downstairs, put you on my truck, and drive away. God knows that it's what I'd like above all to do, but it's impossible. Believe me, Elly, all these years I've wanted to see you again. . . But for the time being we mustn't meet any more."

247

Elly mused: "All kinds of people tell me how much they like me, but that they mustn't meet me again!"

Franz said: "Has it ever occurred to you that they may arrest you again, just as they do frequently with wives of fugitives?"

"Yes," she replied.

"Are you afraid?"

"No! What good would it do?"

"Why is she of all persons not afraid?" thought Franz. He had a faint suspicion that she still liked the idea of being tied to George one way or another. Without any apparent connection, he asked: "By the way, who was the man they arrested at your house that evening?"

"Oh, just an acquaintance," Elly replied. To her shame, she had almost forgotten Heinrich, but now she hoped the poor fellow was back home again with his parents. She knew him well enough to be sure that after such an experience he'd never see her again. He wasn't made of such stuff.

Hand in hand, the two still stared in front of them, their hearts wrung by a sadness that would not be denied.

In an entirely changed voice, Franz said drily: "Well, Elly, have you thought who of his former acquaintances – people he knew when he was living here – would be likely to take him in?"

She began to recite a few names, among them two or three people whom Franz had known previously. But no – if George were still in his right mind he wouldn't turn to any of them. Two or three entirely strange names made him feel uneasy; then she mentioned a schoolmate, this little Roeder, whom Franz himself had wondered about, and then an old teacher who long since had been pensioned off and had moved away.

"There are two alternatives," Franz reflected: "Either

George is done for and is utterly incapable of thinking, in which case all our planning is useless and nothing is predictable; or else he can still think, in which case his thoughts must run parallel with ours. Besides, Hermann will know whom he associated with last, just before his arrest. But I mustn't go to see Hermann right after I leave Elly. That means another loss of hours and hours." Forgetting Elly, he jumped up; he had released her hand, and it slid down from his knee. Quickly he put one empty basket – one of those into which he had wanted to put Elly – into the other. Elly paid for the apples, and he gave her the change, remembering to say: "If they should question us, say you gave me a fifty-pfennig tip." He was expecting to be stopped when he left the house.

Only when the tension was over, when Franz had left the house and driven the empty rattling truck out of the street, did he realize that he hadn't even said good-by to Elly. Only then did he realize that he had failed to discuss the possibility of seeing her again.

Back at the Marnets', he gave them the money for the apples, not omitting to mention the tip. "That's yours," said Frau Marnet, feeling extremely generous. When he had eaten a few bites and gone up to his attic, Augusta said: "It's plain as the nose on your face that somebody's sent him packing today."

"I bet someday he'll go back to Sophie," her husband answered.

Whenever Bunsen entered a room people felt like apologizing to him because the room was so small and the ceiling so low. On such occasions his bold, handsome features would have a certain condescending assurance: *Think nothing of it! I'm only staying a second.*

"I saw your light was still on," he said. "Well, we've had a nice day of it, all of us."

"Yes. Have a seat," said Overkamp. He was by no means enchanted at this visitor's arrival. Fischer vacated the chair he usually occupied during questionings and moved to a bench against the wall. Both men were dog-tired.

"Do you know what?" said Bunsen. "I've got some corn brandy in my room." He jumped up, flung open the door, and shouted into the night: "Hey... hey..." The clicking of heels could be heard. As if the world outside had burned down and were still smoking, fog came rolling over the threshold. Bunsen went on. "I was glad to see the light here. Frankly, I can't stand this any longer."

Overkamp thought: "My God, what next? Questions of conscience take at least an hour and a half." "My friend," he pontificated, "this world of ours, such as it is, offers comparatively few alternatives. Either we keep a certain category of men behind barbed wire and take good care – much better care than we've taken up to now – that they all stay there, or else we'll find ourselves inside, and the others in charge. And since the former condition is more desirable, to insure its permanency we must see to it that certain – er – not always pleasant precautionary measures are observed."

"You voice my own sentiments," replied Bunsen. "What I can't stand any longer is Old Man Fahrenberg's drivel."

"My dear Bunsen," said Overkamp, "that's entirely your affair."

"Now that Fuellgrabe is back in the fold since this afternoon, he's absolutely convinced that he's going to get them all back. What do you think, Overkamp?"

"My name is not Habakkuk, it's Overkamp. I'm not one of the minor prophets, nor one of the major ones either. I've got hard work to do here." To himself he thought: "This fellow still has quite an exalted opinion of himself because

Monday morning, on his own authority, he issued some simple routine instructions that were called for by the regulations."

The corn brandy and some small glasses had been brought in on a tray. Bunsen poured himself a drink, drained it at a gulp, then a second and a third. Overkamp watched him with a professional stare. The liquor had a peculiar effect upon this man. Perhaps he never got really drunk; but, even so, the third glass brought about a slight change in his attitude and language. Even the skin on his face loosened a bit.

"You know," he said, "I don't think our four beauties feel anything at all; as for the fifth one, our Signor Belloni, he certainly doesn't feel anything any longer because only his cap and his old full-dress coat are hanging there. But the rest of the prisoners — when they are lined up, they feel plenty. You ought to see them when they are taken to the Dancing Ground; they don't want to watch and yet they are compelled to. The four main actors have a very good idea of what they're in for later, but... I've heard that if a man has such an idea he becomes totally indifferent and no longer feels anything. Well, anyway, they just have to stand in an uncomfortable position — the nails don't really hurt them. Fuellgrabe was the only one who let out a howl of disappointment. I wonder if he'll get another turn tonight. If he does, I'd like to be there."

"Nothing doing, my dear fellow."

"Why not?"

"Rules and regulations — a ticklish matter, you know."

"Ah, you and your regulations!" said Bunsen, his eyes shining. "Just let me have your Fuellgrabe for five minutes, and I'll tell you whether he met Heisler just by accident."

"He'll probably tell you he met Heisler by appointment if you kick him in the belly. But I still say it was an accident... Why? Because one only has to shake Fuellgrabe and information falls down like plums. Furthermore, because I have formed a definite picture of Fuellgrabe, and a definite picture of Heisler. Heisler, as I picture him, would never make an appointment with Fuellgrabe in a city in broad daylight."

"If he remained seated on the bench, as Fuellgrabe told you, he must have been waiting for somebody. Has his picture been given to all the janitors and block wardens?"

"My dear Bunsen," said Overkamp, "do be thankful for the worries other people have to contend with. Here's how!" They clinked glasses.

"Couldn't you take Wallau's cute little head apart? I know that's where we'd find who Heisler was waiting for. Why don't you gang up on Fuellgrabe and Wallau?"

"My dear Bunsen, your idea is like Mary, Queen of Scots: beautiful but unhappy. In case you are particularly interested, we have examined Wallau very thoroughly. Here is the record of it."

He took a blank piece of paper from the table. Bunsen stared at it and smiled. His teeth, the little teeth of a mouse, were too small for his boldly proportioned face. "Just you leave your Wallau in my hands until tomorrow morning!"

"Why don't you take this paper with you," said Overkamp, "and make him spit blood on it?" He poured another drink for Bunsen. Like everyone who is three quarters drunk, Bunsen was clinging to one face. He never even noticed Fischer. Fischer, who never drank, was sitting on his bench, holding his full glass carefully so as not to spill anything on his trousers. Overkamp signaled at him with his eyebrows. Fischer got up, carefully circled Bunsen, walked over to the table, and took one of the receivers off its hook. "Oh, excuse me," said Overkamp. "Duty before pleasure."

"And he looks like an archangel in armor, like Saint Michael," said Fischer, as soon as Bunsen had left happily.

Overkamp picked up a switch lying near the chair, looked at it briefly just as he was in the habit of looking at hundreds of similar objects: carefully, so as not to smudge any fingerprints. Then he said: "Your Saint Michael has left his sword behind." He called for the guard at the door. "Clear up here! We're through for the day! Guards to remain!"

For the third time this evening Hermann asked his Else if Franz hadn't left any message. For the third time Else told him that Franz had asked for him day before yesterday and hadn't been back since. "How does that hook up?" thought Hermann. "At first he's so excited about the escape that he can hardly talk of anything else, and then he stays away. If only he doesn't do anything on his own hook. Could anything have happened to him?"

Else was busying herself in the kitchen, humming in a deep, somewhat rough voice that at times sounded as if a bee were buzzing round a heath rose. Every evening this buzzing went far to reconcile Hermann's conscience to the fact of having married a mere child who knew nothing about him or about anything. Tonight Hermann had to admit to himself that, in his solitude and tension, life without the child would have been hard to bear. He had already learned of Wallau's capture. He turned his thoughts to the still uncaptured fugitives, especially to George Heisler, the fellow who hailed from this district and might conceivably try to find shelter here. What Franz had told him about George had been entirely too jumbled up with unsettled sentiments to suit Hermann's taste. What others had told him about Heisler had enabled him to picture the man he had never met personally: a man who does not spare himself and is ready to lose in order to gain. What he might still have lacked could have been supplied by Wallau, Hermann thought. Wallau himself he knew slightly. Here was a man he need not bother to analyze. Money and papers should be got ready, reflected Hermann. He pondered the advisability of next day approaching the only quarter whence, in a case of the utmost urgency, such aid would be forthcoming. "That's all I can do for the present, and I'll do it," he determined, and felt calmer for it. In the kitchen, the bee was humming "The Millwheel." "Without Else," thought Hermann, "I'd probably be more upset." Everything has its uses and advantages.

Chapter V

i

The law in accordance with which people's feelings flame up or grow cold was not applicable to the fifty-four-year-old woman who was sitting at the window of a room in Schimmelgaesschen, her ailing legs extended onto a second chair. This woman was George's mother.

Since her husband's death, Frau Heisler had shared her flat with her second son and his family. She was even stouter. Her sunken brown eyes held the expression of fear and reproach one sometimes sees in the eyes of a drowning person. Her sons had become accustomed to the expression and to the brief sighs that came from her open lips like the steam given off by thoughts. They were convinced that their mother no longer fully understood what was said to her or, at least, didn't grasp its real significance.

"If he comes, he'll surely not come up the stairs," said the second eldest. "He'll come through the yards. He'll climb the balcony, as he used to do. He doesn't know that you aren't sleeping in your old room any longer. You'd better stay where you are. Go on to bed."

The woman twitched her shoulders and legs; she was too heavy to get up by herself. Her youngest son said: "You'll lie down, Mother, won't you, and take some valerian, and shoot the bolt on your door?" The other one said: "That's the best thing for you to do." His large head was cropped, and his brows and lashes had recently been singed by the flame of a soldering torch. This gave a dull expression to his face. At one time he had been a good-looking lad, like all the Heisler boys. Now, everything in him coarsened and thickened, he was a regular specimen of an SA man. Heinie, the youngest, was just as Roeder had described him. His stature, the shape of his head, his hair, his teeth – all were as if his parents had created him in strict accordance with racial precepts. With a forced laugh, the oldest son went toward the mother as if he were about to pick up her and the two chairs and carry her to bed. He stopped short at the formidable look in her eyes – a look that probably cost her a tremendous effort to muster. He let go of her chairs and bowed his head. Heinie said: "You've understood me, Mother, haven't you? What do you say?"

The old woman said nothing at all, but kept looking from her youngest son to her oldest and back again to her youngest. How strong the lad's armor must be to withstand her look! His older brother went to the window and looked down on the dark street. Heinie, however, had no trouble withstanding his mother's look; he never even noticed it.

"Won't you please go to bed?" he said. "Go on, and put the cup beside your bed. Whether he comes or not is none of your business. You shouldn't even think of him. You have the three of us, haven't you?"

His brother was listening to him, his face turned to the street. He was amazed at the language Heinie, George's little darling, had acquired. "He's taking part in the hunt as if it meant nothing at all to him. Wants to prove to the boys in the street, and to the grownups, too, that George means nothing to him, though he used to stick to him like a leech." They'd turned young Heinie inside out even more thoroughly than they had him, and Lord knows they'd done enough to him! A year and a half ago, shuddering at his previous five years of unemployment, he'd joined the SA. This shudder was one of the few exercises of his dull and unenterprising brain. He was the most immature and stupid of all the Heisler boys. "You'll lose your job tomorrow," they'd tell him, "if you don't start today." His clumsy dull head still harbored the shadow of an idea that all this to-do about a New Order was only partly valid and that the final verdict was still to come. The whole thing was but a phantasm that would have to pass. How? Through whom? When? To all this he had no answer. When he thought of the bold frigid tone in which Heinie talked to his mother, the same Heinie whom George had carried on his shoulders to all the party demonstrations and who now had grandiose notions about *Führer* schools and SS and motorized SS, he felt his heart turn over. He turned away from the window and stared at the youth.

"I'm going down to see the Breitbachs, and you are going to bed, Mother," said Heinie. "You have understood everything, haven't you?"

"Yes," answered their mother to their surprise.

The old woman had actually come to the end of her thoughts. Quite heartily she said: "Bring me my valerian." "I'll take it," she thought to herself, "so that my heart won't play me any tricks. I'll lie down so that they will leave. Then I'll sit down at the door, and as soon as I hear George coming through the yards, I'll shout: 'Gestapo!'"

For three days now they had been explaining to her, especially Heinie and her second son's wife, how large her family was; not counting George, there were three sons and six grandchildren, all of whom would be ruined by her thoughtlessness. The old woman had said nothing. In the old days George had been only one among her four sons. He had caused her a great deal of sorrow. There had always been complaints from teachers and neighbors. He was forever quarreling with his father and his two elder brothers – with the second-born, because what got George stirred up left him indifferent; with the oldest, because both of them were stirred up by the same things, but their opinions about them differed.

The oldest son lived with his own family at the other end of the city. Newspapers and radio had informed him of George's escape. Though not a day had passed since George's arrest that he had not thought of him, now he hardly thought of anything else. If he had known of some way to help him, he would have considered neither himself nor his family. A dozen times at work he'd been asked whether that fellow Heisler was any relation of his. And each time he had answered, in a voice that dropped silence all around him: "He is my brother!"

Their mother at times had shown a preference for her oldest son and at others for her youngest one. She was also greatly attached to her second-born; he had always been good to her – perhaps, in his dull and simple way, he was better than all the others.

All this had now been changed. For, contrary to life's usual experience, the longer George stayed away, the less they heard from him, and the fewer people asked about him, the more distinct became his features and the more accurate her recollections. Her heart withdrew from all the plans and tangible hopes of her three boys whose lives were normal and healthy. Gradually it became filled with plans and hopes for the absent and almost lost son. At night she would sit up in bed, recalling details that had long since faded in her memory – George's birth, the trifling accidents of his childhood, the serious illness that had almost taken him off, the war years when she'd made grenades and had had a hard time to make ends meet for herself and her three sons, the time when George had been in trouble because he'd robbed some field, his little occasional triumphs, the scanty wages, the teacher who had praised him once, the master who thought he was handy, his victory in an athletic contest.

As if somebody were trying to prove to her that she had only three sons and that the fourth was better considered unborn, she invented thousands of counterproofs. How often had Heinie explained to her that the street was closed off tight, the flat under observation, and the Gestapo on the alert? She ought to think now of her other three sons.

She gave up these three sons. They would have to get along without her. George alone she did not give up. The second-born noticed that his mother's lips were constantly moving. She was praying: "Lord God, You must help him. If You really are, help him! If You are not. . ." She turned her face from the uncertain helper. She sent out her prayers not only to all humanity as far as she knew it, but also to the darkest and most nebulous zones, zones of which she knew nothing, but where perchance there were people who might be able to help, her son. Perhaps there was someone – somewhere – whom her prayers would reach.

The second-born son came over to her chair again and said: "I didn't want to mention it while Heinie was in the room, because you never can tell what he'll do or say. I saw Zweilein, the tinsmith. . ." She looked at him brightly. Quickly and easily she put her feet down on the floor. "Zweilein's got a slick flat. He can look out on two streets. If George does come, he's sure to come from the direction of the Main. Of course I didn't talk with Zweilein much – just with my thumb and one eye." He demonstrated to his mother how, with thumb and eye, he had spoken to the tinsmith. "He answered me the same way. He's going to stay up and watch out for George so that he won't come running into our street."

These words brought a brilliant light to the old woman's eyes. Her features a moment ago had had the flabbiness of rolled dough, but now they became firm and vigorous as if her flesh had been revivified. She groped for her son's arm to pull herself up.

Then she said: "And if after all he comes from the city?" Her son shrugged his shoulders. Speaking rather to herself, the old woman continued: "Suppose he takes it into his head to go to Lore. She's on Alfred's side, and they'll be sure to report him."

"I wouldn't be so sure about that," her son answered. "But he'll come from the Main anyway. Zweilein will watch out for him."

The woman sighed. "If he comes here he is lost."

Her son said: "Even then he is not entirely lost."

ii

Day was dawning, though it was hardly noticeable through the dense fog that enveloped the villages along the river-banks. The lamp was still burning in the kitchen of a house at the edge of Liebach, when a girl carrying two pails stepped into the yard. Shuddering, she walked to the gate and put her pails down. Her face quiet and relaxed, she waited for the lad to whom she was engaged.

While the girl, tired of waiting, crossed the yard with her pails, the little shop bell tinkled in the distance – Kohler was buying some tobacco. Fritz waited in front of the door. He had received the new summons yesterday. They would not stop asking him questions about the jacket. "But it isn't yours at all, is it?" his mother had asked. Her, too, he had answered with a firm "No!"

He had lain awake all night worrying about what they would ask him now. In the morning he had fussed with the radio. When the fugitives had been described – only two of the original seven were still at large – he felt himself grow hot with anxiety. Perhaps they had already captured the one he called his man. His man might have said: "Yes, that's the jacket."

Why did he suddenly feel quite alone in the world? He dared not ask advice of his father or mother, or of his friends. He couldn't even ask Martin, his squad leader, in whom he had implicit faith. Last week everything had been all right, his mind cool and at rest, and the whole world at ease. Last week, if Martin had ordered him to shoot at the fugitive, he would have done so. If Martin had ordered him to hide in the shed until the fugitive sneaked in to steal his jacket, he would have killed him with his dagger before he'd even had a chance to commit the theft.

Kohler, the gardener, was walking along the road – a man old enough to be his father, an old grouch smoking a vile pipe – and Fritz fairly ran after him. One could talk about a lot of things to this man.

"They've sent me another summons." Kohler glanced quickly at the boy, but said nothing. Silently they walked to the shop. Fritz waited until Kohler came out, stuffing his pipe. They walked on. Fritz had forgotten his girl as if she had never existed. He said: "Why do you think they're sending for me again?"

"Well, if it isn't your jacket. . ."

"Why, I told them exactly where my coat was different. Suppose they've captured the man whom the coat belongs to... There are only two left!" Kohler remained silent. He who asks no questions receives the most explicit answers. "And suppose he says: 'Yes, that's my coat.'"

At last Kohler said: "Could be... They might have used pressure to make him say it." He peered sharply at the boy from under his lowered lids; he'd been watching him the past two days.

Fritz frowned. "Oh, do you think so? And what about me?"

"Why, Fritz, there are hundreds of such jackets."

They trudged on toward the school, sure of their way in spite of the fog. No single thought but a flood of them rushed through the man's head. He could not have said how the boy at his side differed from the other boys, he couldn't even be sure that he did. And yet, there was something here he couldn't account for. He had as little doubt as Overkamp himself that there was something queer about this coat mix-up. He thought of his own sons. They belonged partly to him, and partly to the new State. At home they were his, they sided with him when he said that tops were still tops in the State, and bottoms were still bottoms. Away from home, though, they wore the regulation shirts and shouted, "*Heil!*" at the proper moment. Had he done all in his power to strengthen their resistance? By no means! That would have meant the dissolution of the family – jail – himself the victim of his sons. He would have had to choose – and there was the break. Not only for him, Kohler, but also for many others. How could a man make such a decision, how bridge such a break? Just the same there were some in the country who could, and even more of them outside. Take all those people in Spain who were said to have been vanquished but were obviously still unconquered. All of them had made the leap. Hundreds of thousands of them! Former Kohlers all! If a coat belonging to one of his sons had been stolen, how would

262

he have advised him? Was it right for him to advise Fritz, the son of other parents? What a decision! What a world!

He said: "All the hundreds of coats made by that factory were undoubtedly alike. The Gestapo need only telephone. The zippers are all alike to the sixteenth of an inch. The pockets are all alike. But if for instance a key or a pencil had worn a hole in the lining, the Gestapo could never prove that it hadn't. That's the difference that you must obstinately hold to."

iii

In Westhofen, Fuellgrabe had been awakened five times during the night for questioning, at the exact moment when he was on the point of falling asleep from exhaustion. Since his voluntary return had proved that sheer funk had been the most powerful incentive in his decision to give himself up, the means of curing him was indicated if he showed any signs of stubbornness. At last Overkamp had got hold of a tangible piece of evidence definitely connected with Heisler, after having had to follow dubious trails and alleged pieces of clothing. Even at his fifth questioning Fuellgrabe showed signs of obstinacy when grilled about his meeting with George, although he had divulged it himself when strongfisted threats had forced him to account for every hour of his flight.

Fuellgrabe jerked and fidgeted on his chair. Something seemed suddenly to be impeding the machinery of the grilling – up to that point it had run quite smoothly. Some conflicting emotion seemed all at once to have got mixed up with the fear that had lubricated every minute part of the man's brain. But all Fischer needed to do was to take up the phone and call Zillich; his very name would act as a separating agent. The feeling of fear became separated from secondary feelings; visualization of a painful death from the fact of actually being alive; the Fuellgrabe of today, gray and trembling, from a long-forgotten Fuellgrabe who had still known bursts of courage and the contagion of hope. Evasions and irrelevancies became separated from the true record.

On Thursday, shortly before noon, I met George Heisler at the Eschenheim Tower. He led me to a bench in the park, on the first path to the left of the large bed of asters. I tried to induce him to give himself up with me. He wouldn't listen to me. He wore a brown overcoat, a brown-felt hat, low shoes that weren't brand-new or worn-out. I don't know whether he had any money. I don't know why he was in Eschenheim Park. I don't know whether he was waiting for somebody. He stayed there on the bench. I do think that he was waiting for somebody because he led me to that bench and because he stayed there. Yes, I turned around once, and he was still sitting there.

Instructions had already been issued to the city authorities on the basis of this deposition when, early in the morning, Paul Roeder left his flat. Several block wardens had already received their orders, but they had not yet passed them on to the janitors. After leaving radio sets and telegraph wires, events fall back again into the hands of human beings.

Roeder's janitress was surprised to see him leaving for work so much earlier than usual. She mentioned it to her husband when he came into the hallway with a pail of soft soap to give her a gob of it for her washtub. Neither the janitress nor her husband had any feeling for or against the Roeders. There were complaints now and then about Frau Roeder's singing at untimely hours, but all in all they were pleasant people, easy to get along with.

Roeder hurried to the tram stop through the hazy streets, whistling to himself. Fifteen minutes into town, fifteen minutes back, left him half an hour for two calls, supposing the first one was not successful. He had told Liesel that he had to get away early to catch his friend Melzer, the Bockenheim goalie. "Take care of George till I get back," he said as he left. All night he had lain quietly and wakefully beside Liesel; finally, toward dawn, he had slept a bit.

Roeder stopped whistling. His lips were dry because he'd had no coffee. The dawn, his thirst, the pavement itself seemed to be replete with threats: "Take care! Think what you're planning to do!" Roeder thought to himself: "Schenk, Moselgasse 12; Sauer, Taunusstrasse 24." He would have to see these two men now, before they left for work. George considered both of them as being unshaken and beyond question. Both must and would help him with advice and shelter, with papers and money. Schenk used to work at the cement works, at least in George's time. He was a quiet, clear-eyed man; neither his outward appearance nor his inner self had any salient characteristics. He gave the impression of being neither particularly foolhardy nor particularly witty; his courage was spread over his whole life, his wit over all of his reflections. But to George, Schenk had been a symbol of all that signified the movement, the very essence of his life.

About a month before George's arrest, Sauer had found a job at the municipal building office after five years of unemployment. He was still a young man. The fact that he was gifted in his profession made him all the more desperate at his idleness. Through several hundred books, through several hundred meetings, slogans, sermons, speeches, and talks his reasoning processes had finally led him to the point at which he met George. George considered him as safe, in his own way, as Schenk. Sauer followed his mind in everything, and his mind never let go what it had found. He was incorruptible and steadfast, even if every so often his heart urged him to yield a little and to dwell for a time where life was easier, so that he could rise again rested and ready with any number of justifications for his letdown. "Sauer, Taunus-strasse 24," Paul repeated to himself. "Schenk, Moselgasse 12." Turning a corner, he ran into Melzer, the man he'd used as a pretext to Liesel. "Hello, Melzer! The very man I want to see! Got a couple of tickets for us for Sunday?"

"I guess I can fix it," said Melzer.

"Do you really think, Paul," a small still voice within him was asking him softly and slyly, "do you really think you'll need the tickets Sunday? That you'll have any use for them?" "Yes," said Paul aloud, "I want them." Melzer prophesied the probable outcome of the contest "Niederrad-Westend." Suddenly he interrupted himself – he'd have to hustle to get home before his mother woke up, he explained. He was on his way home from his fiancée, who worked at Cassella's, and his mother, who owned a tiny confectionery store, could not stomach her. Paul knew the little store and its owner, and he also knew the girl; the knowledge made him feel at home and secure. Laughing, he watched Melzer hurry away. Then he heard the soft sly little voice again: "You may never see Melzer again." Furious, Roeder thought to himself: "Nuts! A thousand times nuts! I'll even go to his wedding."

Fifteen minutes later he was walking down Moselgasse, whistling. He stopped at Number 12. Fortunately, the street door was already open. He went quickly upstairs to the fourth floor. When he saw a strange name on the door plate he made a wry face. An old woman in a faded morning jacket opened the opposite door and asked whom he was looking for.

"Don't the Schenks live here any more?"

"The Schenks? Somebody here asking for the Schenks," she said in a peculiar voice to someone inside the flat. A

266

younger woman leaned over the railing of the top floor. "He's asking for the Schenks," the old woman shouted up to her. An expression of dismay came over the younger woman's tired, puffy face. She wore a flowered dressing gown and had big, loose breasts. "Just like Liesel," thought Paul. All in all, the stairway was not unlike his own. His next-door neighbor, Stuembert, was also one of these partly bald elderly SA men, like this one here who wore his uniform unbuttoned and was in his stocking feet, probably because, just home from a night drill, he had thrown himself down as he was. "Whom do you want to see?" he asked Roeder, as if he could hardly believe his ears.

Paul explained. "The Schenks still owe my sister money for some dress material. I am doing the collecting for my sister. I came at an hour when I'd be likely to find people in."

"Frau Schenk hasn't lived here for three months," said the old woman. The man added: "You'll have to go to Westhofen if you want to collect." He looked quite wide-awake now. It had cost him a lot of effort before he finally caught the Schenks listening to a foreign broadcast, but by using a number of tricks he had finally succeeded. How tame and innocent these Schenks had acted! It was *Heil Hitler!* here, and *Heil Hitler!* there. *But you can't deceive me about people who live next door to me.*

"You don't say!" exclaimed Roeder. "Well, *Heil Hitler!*"

"*Heil Hitler!*" responded the shoeless man with a slight lifting of the arm, his eyes shining with the enjoyment of a delectable memory.

Behind him, Roeder could hear the man's laugh. He wiped his forehead, astonished to find it damp. For the first time since he had seen George again, perhaps even since his childhood, he felt a chill in the pit of his stomach, a sensation to which he refused even now to give the name of fear. He had a feeling as if he, who all his life had enjoyed perfect health, were suddenly threatened with a contagious disease. It was most annoying, and he fought against it. He stamped his feet on the stairs to rid himself of the weak feeling in the bend of his knees. On the lowest landing he met the janitress. "Who did you want to see?"

"The Schenks," said Roeder. "I'm doing the collecting for my sister. The Schenks owe her money for some dress material."

The woman from the top floor was coming down the stairs with her garbage pail. She said to the janitress: "He was asking for the Schenks." The janitress looked Paul over from head to foot. In the entrance he could still hear her saying to someone in her flat: "There was a fellow asking for the Schenks."

Roeder stepped into the street. He wiped his face with his sleeve. Never in his life had people looked at him so strangely. What evil spirit had advised George to send him to the Schenks? How was it that George didn't know Schenk was in Westhofen? "Curse this fellow George," counseled the smooth inner voice. "That'll make you feel easier." "He couldn't help that," thought Roeder, "it wasn't his fault." Whistling again, he hurried on. As he passed through Metzgergasse, his face cleared. Through an open doorway he stepped into a large yard surrounded by tall houses. In the rear of the yard was the garage which was part of his Aunt Katharina's trucking business. He could see her standing in the middle of the yard, shouting at the truckmen. There had been a time, the Roeder family used to say, when his aunt had been delicate and soft-spoken, but while she was still quite young, she had fallen in with Grabber, the truckster, a drunken sot; she herself had taken to drink and grown coarse and sullen.

Roeder had always felt drawn to this aunt, partly against his will, partly out of curiosity. Fond of the merry side of life himself, he loved to look at her big scowling face, into which life had graven such deep lines, though they were mostly evil ones. For minutes he even forgot George and himself while, with a smile, he listened to the woman spouting curses that were quite new to him. "She's the last person in the world I'd want to work for," he thought to himself. All the same, he had talked to her about one of Liesel's brothers and got from her a half-promise of a job for the unlucky fellow – he'd been deprived of his driver's license after an accident. "I must talk to her again, but that'll keep until the evening," thought Paul. Unable to resist his thirst, he entered the tavern through the rear door from the yard, merely waving to his aunt and uncertain if, what with her cursing, she had even seen him. A little old man in the back room, a perennial tippler, raised his glass to him. "*Prosit*, Pauley!" "Tonight I'll have a few myself," thought Paul, "as soon as I attend to this other matter."

At this time yesterday he had been hurrying to the grocer's for two pounds of flour for his wife. "By the way, she hasn't baked the cake yet," thought Paul. "I hope she makes it today." He found himself in front of Taunusstrasse 24. He looked about him with surprise, for the staircase was rather pretentious; the stairs were covered with carpet held in place by brass rods. He felt a faint doubt as to whether help for his kind could be found in such a house.

Roeder breathed more easily when from the stairs he recognized the names, embossed in Gothic letters on a metal plate; he touched the plate gingerly before he rang the bell. SAUER, ARCHITECT. Roeder was annoyed by the beating of his heart. The good-looking white-aproned girl wasn't the Frau, of course, but only the servant. Presently Frau Sauer herself came out; she also was young and good-looking, but sans apron and as brunette as the first one was blond. "What? My husband? At this hour?"

269

"Professionally; only two minutes." His heart had ceased to bother him. He thought: "This fellow Sauer seems to be quite a swell."

"Come in," said Frau Sauer.

"In here!" called the man. Roeder glanced to right and left. He was by nature of a curious disposition. Even now he was intrigued by the glass tube against the wall – it was a lighting fixture – and the nickeled bedsteads. Following the voice, he went through a second door. In spite of the heaviness of his heart, he had time to marvel at the sunken tub, into which one did not step but fell plump, and the three-sectioned mirror above the washstand. "*Heil Hitler!*" said the man without turning around.

Roeder saw him in the mirror, a towel tucked under his chin. A thick lather covered the unfamiliar face like a mask. The eyes in the mirror swept him with a sharp glance that showed nothing but intelligence. Roeder tried to collect his wits. "Yes?" said the man. He stopped the razor with the utmost care. Roeder's heart beat violently, and so did Sauer's. He had never seen this man before in all his life. He had never been connected with the municipal building department; of that, Sauer felt sure. Unknown visitors at unusual hours might mean anything... Best to know nothing and nobody. Never be caught unawares. "Well?" he said again. His voice was rough, but Roeder was unfamiliar with his usual voice.

"I am bringing you the regards of a mutual friend," said Paul. "I wonder if you still remember him. He was with you once on a nice canoeing excursion on the Nidda."

"The test will be," thought the other man, "whether or not I cut myself." He began to shave with a loose wrist. He did not cut himself, neither did he tremble. "Well, that's done with," thought Paul. "Why doesn't he wipe his face or and talk to me sensibly? I am sure he doesn't usually scrape his face as long as this. I bet it's usually a fast swish-swish..."

"I fail to understand," said Sauer. "What do you want of me? Whose regards are you bringing me?"

"Your canoeing companion's," repeated Roeder, "on the little boat *Annemarie*." He caught an oblique look that Sauer threw him over the edge of the mirror.

A speck of lather got into his eye and he removed it with the corner of the towel. Then he went on shaving. Without really opening his mouth, he said: "I still don't understand at all. Excuse me. Besides, I am rather in a hurry. I am sure you must have the wrong address."

Roeder had advanced a step. He was much shorter than Sauer. He could see the left half of Sauer's face in the side of the mirror. He peered under the lather, but could see only the thin neck and the extended chin. Sauer thought: "How he is watching me! But I won't let him see my face. Let him watch. How the dickens did he hit upon me? So they do suspect, and I am actually being watched. How the little rat is sniffing all around!"

Aloud he said: "Well, your friend must have put you in touch with the wrong man, that's all. I'm in a great hurry. Don't bother me any longer, please. Hedy!"

Paul gave a start – he had not noticed that there were three of them. Beyond the door, pulling a little neck chain through her teeth, stood a child who had probably been watching him mutely all the time. "Show him the door!" Roeder followed the child and thought: "The bastard! He understood everything all right. Doesn't want to take any risk, perhaps because of this brat here. Haven't I any children, I'd like to know?"

When he heard the door slam, Sauer went over his face with a swish! just as Roeder had surmised he would. Breathing hard, he rushed to the bedroom window and raised the shade quickly. He caught sight of Roeder as he was crossing the street. *Did I act correctly? What will he report about me?*

Quiet! I certainly am not the only one. They may be trying to pump any number of suspects today. What a funny pretext! This escape, of all things! Well, it isn't such a stupid pretext. Something must have led them to think that I used to have some connection with Heisler. Or do they ask everybody the same thing?

Suddenly a shudder went down his spine. What if it was on the level and not one of the Gestapo's ruses? If George actually had sent this man? If he had not been one of the Gestapo's stool pigeons? Oh, pshaw! If it really was not just a rumor that George Heisler was on the loose in town, they'd have other means of getting in touch with him. This funny little fellow just wanted to do a little spying. Clumsy and bungling! He drew a long breath and went back to the mirror to comb his hair. His face had grown pale the way dark faces do – as if the skin were withering. Light-gray eyes were staring back at him from the mirror, looking deeper into him than any strange eyes ever could. Stale air! That damn window is always stuck fast! Quickly he lathered his face again. *At any rate, they must have some reason for sending this red herring up to me. Ought I to leave town at once? Can I still even ask whether I should flee, without jeopardizing others?* He began to shave, but now his hands trembled, and almost at once he cut himself. He swore.

Ah, well, I'll still have time to go to the barber's – Court of Popular Justice, and it's all over – two days after the arrest. Don't carry on so, dearest. Imagine, darling, if I'd been in a plane crash!

He tied his necktie. A healthy, thin, confidence-inspiring man of about forty. He looked at his teeth. No longer ago than last week he had said to Hermann: "These brass-band guys will lose their jobs before we ever lose ours. I bet I'll yet build you a few decent roads right across the new republic."

He went back to the bedroom window and glanced

down into the empty street through which the little fellow had walked a while ago. He felt cold. The man didn't look like a spy. He didn't have the manners of a spy. His voice, too, sounded quite sincere. *In what other way could George have reached me? It was George who sent this man to me.*

Then again he thought: "It may have been a spy after all. The name of the boat? They could have found that out long ago. They didn't need to know my name. And certainly George hasn't given anything away." There came a knock. "Herr Sauer, the coffee is served." "What?" "The coffee is served." He shrugged his shoulders, slipped into his jacket which was adorned with a party button and the ribbon of the Iron Cross. He peered about him as if he were looking for something. There are moments when even the most familiar room and the most ornamental household goods are changed into a sort of dumping ground for a multitude of trash that could not possibly be utilized by anyone. With an expression of repugnance, he picked up his brief case.

When the hall door slammed a second time, Frau Sauer asked: "Who was that?"

"Herr Sauer, I suppose," said the maid, pouring the coffee.

"That's impossible," said Frau Sauer.

"Why, that's impossible," thought Sauer's wife. She was sitting at the breakfast table with her child. "Without his coffee, without saying good-by?" She tried to control herself. Hedy was looking at her, saying nothing; even she had at once sensed the icy current of air that had flowed from the short, freckled man.

Roeder jumped onto a tram and got to work just in time. Not for a second did he stop cursing Sauer. Both his softly spoken and silent curses were radically changed when, toward the end of the first hour of work, he scorched his arm. That had not happened to him in a long time. "Hurry to the first aid," Fiedler advised him. "If you don't you won't get any compensation if it gets worse. I'll do your work in the meantime." "Aw, shut up," said Roeder. Fiedler looked at him with surprise from behind his protective goggles. Moeller turned around. "Hey, you over there!"

Gritting his teeth, Paul went on with his work. "What did the bastard mean: 'Hey?' How did he get to be foreman, anyway? Ten years younger than I am. He just grew older a little faster, George would have said. George! He's waiting now in my flat, waiting, waiting. If only Liesel will think to bake the cake. At least a piece of cake," thought Paul, watching the indicator closely and, his lips compressed, letting metal pour into the pipe. When Fiedler signaled him that the plug cap was pressed home, he would open the pipe and at the same time quickly raise his left leg, a motion that was not at all necessary but one that he had adopted from the first. Among the half-naked, strongly developed men Paul looked like an alert and ageless gnome. Everybody liked him because he was forever cracking jokes, and he didn't mind a practical joke himself. "For twenty years you've liked me," Roeder thought wrathfully. "Now you can lump me. You can look for another joker. I'll go crazy if I don't get something to drink soon. Can it be possible, only ten?" Haller suddenly appeared beside him, smeared some salve on his arm with incredible speed, and topped it with a piece of gauze. "Thanks, Haller, thanks." "Don't mention it." "Fiedler put him up to it," thought Paul. "They're all good fellows, and I don't want to lose this job. I want to be standing here again tomorrow. If this goddamn Moeller ever gets anything on me! And Haller? If he knew who's sitting in my flat! Haller's all right. Well, up to a certain point. He bandaged my arm, but if it had been a question of burning his own fingers. . . Fiedler?" He cast a lightning glance in his direction. "Yes, he's different," he thought, as if suddenly and with one look he had discovered something new in the man who worked beside him the year round.

"Still more than an hour to go! If George doesn't get a better idea, he'll have to stay another night at my flat. George was ready to swear by Sauer. Good thing he's got a Paul."

"You could at least stir with one hand, even if you can't do anything else," Liesel said to George. "Hold the bowl between your knees."

"What's this going to be? I always have to know first what I'm doing."

"It's going to be a cake. A cake with icing."

"In that case you can keep me stirring until tomorrow morning."

He had no sooner started to stir, however, than he began to perspire. He was still extremely weak. All last night, in spite of the quiet, he had just drowsed restlessly. "He must have gotten hold of one of them," thought George, "either Schenk or Sauer." Schenk or Sauer, he stirred, Schenk or Sauer!

From the street came the sound of rolling barrels and the age-old counting-out song intoned by the rollicking voices of little children: –

> *Maikaefer flieg,*
> *Der Vater ist im Krieg,*
> *Die Mutter ist in Pommerland,*
> *Pommerland ist abgebrannt. . .*

When was it that he had yearned – ah, so bitterly – to be a welcome guest in some everyday home? He had been standing in a dark gateway in Oppenheim, waiting for the driver who had eventually kicked him off his truck.

"Come on, Liesel, why don't you darn some stockings and sit down here beside me for a change?"

"Stockings? Now? This pigpen has got to be cleaned, unless you like to be choked by all the dirt."

"Have I done enough stirring?"

"Keep on until the batter gets bubbles in it."

If she knew the truth about me, would she throw me out? Perhaps she would, and perhaps she wouldn't. Harassed Liesels like her, used to all kinds of trouble, usually have courage.

Liesel took the washtub from the stove and put it on the washing stool. She started to scrub clothes so vigorously on the washboard that strands of muscle stood out on her round arms. "Why are you in such a rush, Liesel?"

"You don't call this rushing, do you? Do you expect me to spin on my heel every time I finish a diaper?"

Well, at least, I've seen all this once more from the inside. Does it go on this way all the time? Will it always go on? Liesel was already hanging a few pieces of laundry on a line stretched across the kitchen. "So! Now let's have your mixing bowl. See? That's what I meant by getting bubbles." Her guileless, coarse features wore an expression of childlike pleasure. She set the bowl on the stove and spread a cloth over it.

"Why do you do that?"

"It must not be exposed to the slightest draft of air; don't you know that?"

"I had forgotten it, Liesel. It's a long time since I watched a cake being made."

In the canteen of the Griesheim Railway Shops, Hermann, his beer in front of him, opened Else's sandwiches: mortadella and liverwurst, always the same. His deceased first wife had shown more imagination about sandwiches. Except for her clear eyes, she had not been a good-looking woman, but she was clever and determined, well able to get up in a meeting and express her opinion. How would she have borne these times? Hermann ate his sandwiches with the four exactly cut slices of sausage that always aroused thoughts of this kind in him. At the same time he listened to right and left.

"Now there are only two of them left; yesterday they were still talking about three."

"One of them knocked down a woman."

"Why?"

"He was stealing washing from a line, and she caught him at it."

"Who was stealing washing from a line?" asked Hermann, although he'd heard everything.

"One of the fugitives."

"What fugitives?" asked Hermann.

"The ones from Westhofen. Who else?"

"He kicked her in the belly."

"Where is that supposed to have happened?" Hermann wanted to know.

"They didn't say."

"How can they tell that it was one of the fugitives? Perhaps it was only some linen thief."

Hermann looked at the last speaker. He was an elderly welder, one of those who during the past year had grown so silent that one was apt to forget them although one saw them every day.

"Well, suppose it was one of them," said a young man. "He can't go and buy his shirts at Pfueller's. If he gets caught stealing by such a woman he can't say to her: 'Won't you be kind enough to iron this for me?'" Hermann's eyes turned toward this man. He was comparatively new at the plant, and it was he who had said to him yesterday: "The main thing for me is to hold a soldering iron once more in my hands. We'll see about everything else later."

"The fellow must feel like a wild animal," said still

another, "knowing that if he's caught – good night!" Hermann looked at this man too; he cut the air with the flat of his hand as he finished speaking. Everybody gave him a quick glance, then silence, for the most important thing was still to come – or nothing at all.

The new young man shook everything aside and said: "That'll be a big affair on Sunday."

"The fellows from Mainz have a reputation for doing things handsomely."

"We'll go at least as far as Binger Loch."

"They're even going to have a kindergarten nurse on the ship; what do you think of that?"

Hermann put in a question, just as one hammers a nail into something slippery that tends to get away: "Which two are left?"

"Left of what?"

"Of the fugitives."

"An old fellow and a young one. And the young one is supposed to be from this district."

"That's just people's imagination," said the welder, who popped up again as if he had just come back to his folks after a long journey. "Why should he flee into his home town where hundreds of people know him?"

"That has its advantages. People will report a stranger much more readily. Imagine, for instance, reporting me!"

Occasionally, in the last three years, Hermann had tried to sound out discreetly the man who had just spoken, but the fellow never seemed to understand. Hermann suddenly got the impression that the man understood more than was apparent.

"I'd report you without the slightest hesitation. Why not? If for any reason you cease to be my comrade, it will happen long before my reporting you makes me cease being yours." The speaker, Lersch, the Nazi liaison man in the plant, had spoken in the peculiarly distinct tone of voice used by people who want to state a matter of principle. Little Otto, his boyish face tense, was staring at him fixedly. Lersch was the boy's instructor; he was teaching him how to handle a soldering iron as well as how to play at spying. Hermann looked Otto over briefly. Though he was first squad leader of the Hitler Youth, he was not arrogant, but rather quiet; he smiled rarely, and was exceptionally tense in all his movements. Hermann often thought of this boy who was so blindly devoted to Lersch.

"That's right," said the elderly man calmly. "Before anybody reports me he'll have to find out whether I've done anything to make me cease being his comrade."

After leaving the canteen, most of the men quietly retired to some corner of their workrooms. Hermann had nothing more to say.

He smoothed out his crumpled sandwich paper and put it in his pocket so that Else could use it again tomorrow. He was almost certain that Lersch was watching him, scenting an intangible something that, by one word or at some particular time, would someday define itself. Everybody was relieved when the bell shrilled the end of the lunch hour, for the signal put an outside end to something which, from the inside, could never be ended.

That noon, a group of small boys, skipping through one of the streets of Wertheim, started a quarrel which was really more of a game, formed two sides, and fought. Most of them had thrown their school things to one side.

Suddenly one of the young fighting cocks paused, bringing the whole fracas to a standstill. An old ragged man was standing at the edge of the pavement, digging in the pile of school things. He had come across an unused bread card. "Hey, you. . ." shouted one of the boys. The old man shuffled off, tittering. The boys left him in peace. Whereas on other occasions they were like little devils, whenever any mischief was done, now they contented themselves with gathering up their belongings. The tittering old man with the wild hairy face had been exceedingly repugnant to them, so much so that, as if by agreement, they never even mentioned him again.

The old man left the village in the opposite direction. Passing an inn, he paused, laughed, and entered. The proprietress stopped serving several truckmen for a moment to hand the old man the glass of schnapps he had asked for. Presently he got up again, tittered, and walked out without paying, his head and shoulders jerking. The woman shouted: "Where's that fellow going?" The truckmen started out after him, but the innkeeper stopped them all. He did not care to have any disturbance just then for it was Friday and he had to hurry to the fishdealer. "Aw, charge it to profit and loss."

Undisturbed, the old man went on his way. He walked through the little place, not on the main street, but by way of the little market. With rather a show of reassurance, holding himself more erect than before, his expression calm, he went between the gardens at the edge of the village and walked up the hill.

Where the houses stood, the street was still paved, with occasional steps at the steepest places; but in the hills it became a common field path that led away from the Main and the highway into the interior. At the edge of the town, a similar path branched off and joined the highway some distance away.

The old man was Aldinger, one of the two fugitives still at large after Fuellgrabe had given himself up. Nobody in Westhofen would seriously have thought that Aldinger could get even as far as Liebach. If he weren't caught in the next hour, he would be in the next one after that. In the meantime, Friday had come, and Aldinger had reached Wertheim. Nights he had slept in the fields, and once a moving van had given him a four-hour lift. He had eluded all the patrols, but it had not been due to a cunning of which his poor old head was no longer capable. Even at the camp there were doubts as to his sanity. For days, he wouldn't speak a word; then he'd start tittering suddenly at some command. Hundreds of little accidents might have led to his arrest any hour – the smock he had stolen barely covered his convict's clothing – but none of them had happened.

Aldinger knew nothing about reflection, nothing about calculation. He only knew directions. The sun above his village would lie so in the morning, so at noon. If, instead of putting in motion the intricate and powerful machinery for capturing fugitives, the Gestapo had drawn a straight line from Westhofen to Buchenbach, they would soon have caught up with their man at some point on this straight line.

Above the town, Aldinger stood still and looked about him. The twitching of his face ceased, his gaze hardened, and his sense of direction, an almost superhuman sense, dulled because there was no longer any need of it. Here Aldinger was at home. On this spot, once a month, he had halted his cart, and his sons had taken the baskets down to the little market. While he was waiting for them he had contemplated the landscape. How familiar to him were the partly wooded, partly cultivated little hills whose reflections were mirrored in the water, the river itself which caught up everything only to leave it behind again, the very clouds drifting on high, and the little boats carrying their load of humanity! . . . What was the use of it all? Though his own village was not far away, all these things he had contemplated represented to him an alien and digressive world. He had escaped from Westhofen because he wanted to return to the life of his past. "Past" was the name of the land out-side the town. "Past" was the name of his village.

During his first days at Westhofen, when the first curses and blows had rained down upon his aged head, he had known the feeling of hatred and rage, and also the desire for revenge. But the blows had come faster and harder, and his head was old. Shattered before long was his desire to be avenged for all the atrocities showered upon him, shattered even the memory of those atrocities. What the blows had left, however, still held all its power and strength.

Aldinger turned his back on the river and trudged on between the cart ruts in the path. From time to time he looked around, not furtively, but in order to ascertain his direction by means of some fixed point. His face had lost some of its wild look. He jogged down one little hill and up another. He went through a small fir wood and a patch of young trees. The country seemed deserted. Aldinger crossed a stubble field, then a turnip acre. It was still quite warm. Not only the day, the very year seemed to stand still. Even now, Aldinger felt the Past in all his bones.

Today Wurz, the Burgomaster of Buchenbach, had not gone out to his field as he had intended, or at least boasted he would. Instead he had betaken himself to his office, the name he had given to his living room, a stuffy, cluttered lit-tle room that served him as Burgomaster's and Registrar's office. His sons, desirous of having a heroic father, had tried to persuade him to go to the field without fear. Wurz, how-ever, had submitted to his wife and her endless wailing.

Buchenbach was still surrounded by guards, and a spe-cial guard had been assigned to Wurz's farm. People were inclined to laugh about this. Aldinger would surely never think of walking right into the village. He'd look for another opportunity – and find it – of drawing a bead on Wurz.

How long would His Honor insist upon having a bodyguard? A costly whim, indeed! After all, the SA lads entrusted with the guard duty were all peasant boys who were needed on their farms.

Schulz, the grocery woman, having seen Wurz in his Registrar's office, informed her niece's fiancé of the fact. The young man helped her in the store that sold everything a village was likely to need. A few hours earlier than he was expected he had arrived from his home in Ziegelhausen with a few boxes of nondescript merchandise, in the veterinary's motorcar. He had intended to ask Wurz this evening to publish the banns. When his aunt said that Wurz was in the Registrar's office, he put on his collar, and Martha started to change her clothes. The young man was ready before she was and went on across the street. At the door stood the SA guard who knew him. "*Heil Hitler!*" The bridegroom was a member of his storm troop, not because the brown shirt was essential to his happiness, but because he wished to work in peace and be able to marry and inherit, all of which would otherwise undoubtedly have been impossible. The SA guard, guessing that the young man was calling about his banns, laughed while he knocked at the living-room window. But Wurz did not reply.

Wurz had been sitting at his desk under Hitler's picture. When a shadow flitted against the window, he cowered in his chair, and at the knock he slid down, crawled around the desk and behind the door. "Why don't you walk in, the two of you?" asked the guard outside, Martha having arrived in the meantime. The young man knocked at the door and, failing to hear a "Come in!" turned the knob; but the door was bolted from the inside. The guard came up, banged with his fist, and shouted: "A publication of banns!"

Only then did Wurz shoot the bolt. Puffing, he stared at the young man as he spread out his papers. He pulled himself together sufficiently to rattle off his little say about the roots of national existence, the importance of the family in the National Socialist State, and the sanctity of the race. Martha listened to everything earnestly; the young man nodded. When he and Martha were again outside, he said to the guard: "Nice kind of a worm you have to guard here, Kamerad!" He broke off one of the yellow roses and put it in his lapel. Then, his bride's arm in his, they walked down the street, round the village square, past the Hitler Oak – it was not yet big enough to shade children and children's children; the most it could cover was some snails and sparrows – and on to the parsonage, where they presented themselves as a prospective bridal couple.

Aldinger had the next-to-the-last hill behind him. It was called Buxberg. He walked now very slowly, like one dead-tired but knowing that there is no rest for him. No longer did he turn around, for he knew every inch of the way. Already some Buchenbach fields were intermingled with the last fields of Ziegelhausen. Even though the ground-regulation ordinance had caused a good deal of talk, from up here the land still looked as checkered as the darned aprons of peasant children. Aldinger climbed the little hill with infinite slowness. His gaze was vague, but it was not a dull and fidgety vagueness, but the reflection of an unexpected and indeterminable goal.

As was customary at this hour, the guard down in Buchenbach was changing. The man at Wurz's house had been relieved. He went to the inn, where he was presently joined by two other comrades just off duty. The three were hoping that on the way back from the parsonage the prospective bridegroom would come in and stand them a round of drinks.

Noon and the fright he had experienced had made Wurz

feel tired. He laid his head on his desk, on the papers of the bridal couple, on their pedigrees, and on their certificates of good health.

Aldinger had at last come up to the top of the hill. This point was not particularly high for a young person, even though the village could be seen lying down below. For the space of a few yards the way was lined with hazel bushes, and Aldinger sat down between two of them. Partly in the shade, he was very quiet for a while. Sections of roofs and fields glistened between the twigs. He was just dozing off, when he gave a slight start. He got up, or rather tried to get up. He glanced down into the valley. But the valley did not reveal itself to him in its usual noonday splendor, in the sweet everyday light. A cool, sharp brightness lay over the village, a brilliance tempered by wind, so that its outlines showed up distinct as never before, but also, and for that very reason, estranged. Then a deep shadow fell over the land.

Later that afternoon two peasant children came along to gather hazelnuts. They screamed and ran headlong to their parents out in the field. Their father, after looking at the man, sent one of the children to the next field to get Neighbor Wolbert. Wolbert said: "Well, if it isn't Aldinger!" Then the first peasant also recognized him. Young and old stood among the hazel bushes, looking down upon the dead man. Finally the two peasants improvised a stretcher on which they carried him into the village, past the guards.

"Who are you bringing here?"

"It's Aldinger. We found him." Where else were they to take him but to his own house? To the guards in front of Aldinger's door they likewise said: "We found him." And the guard was entirely too bewildered to stop them.

When the body was brought into the room, Frau Aldinger's knees gave way, but she recovered herself, as she would have had to do had he been brought in dead from his work in the field. Before her door the neighbors had already assembled; there was also the guard who had been stationed at her house, and the two newly posted guards from the edge of the village and the three S A men from the inn and the couple from the parsonage. Only at the other end of the village were guards still on duty and also around the outskirts, for they of course had not yet heard the news. There was still a guard in front of Wurz's door to protect the Burgomaster against any act of revenge.

Frau Aldinger turned back the bed clothes on the bed that had been kept ready with a clean set of linen all the time; but when she saw how dirty and untidy he was, she made them put him on her own bed. After she had put some water on the stove, she sent her eldest grandchild to call the rest of the family from the field.

The people at the door made room for the child to pass. Already the boy had the close drawn lips and the downcast eyes of people whose house harbors a corpse. Presently the child returned with his parents and uncles and aunts.

Altogether, everything assumed a normal aspect. Those who entered the house no longer shouted "*Heil Hitler!*" and jerked up their arms, but uncovered their heads and shook hands with the others. The S A guards who had come within a hair's breadth of chasing and killing an old man returned for the time being to their fields with unsullied hands and a clear conscience. Those who passed Wurz's window did so with curling lips. They made no secret of their contempt, or feared they might forfeit an advantage for themselves or one of their own. Likely, they asked themselves why it was Wurz, of all people, who held the power. They no longer saw him surrounded by the luster of his might, but as they had seen him during the past four days, trembling in his wetted trousers. No more cringing before Wurz!

Her two daughters-in-law helped Frau Aldinger bathe

her husband, cut his hair, and put good clothes on him. They stuffed his convict's rags into the fire. They had to heat a second tub of water before they could get his body clean. Then they bathed themselves and put on their Sunday clothes.

The Past to which Aldinger had so wished to return opened its gates wide. He was now laid upon his own bed. Mourners began to arrive, and each one was offered a piece of cake. Martha's aunt hurriedly opened the nondescript boxes the young man had delivered to her, for now the Aldingers were sure to need soap, black ribbons, and candles. Everything was now in order: the dead man had succeeded in outwitting the guards that had surrounded the village.

Fahrenberg received the report: Sixth fugitive found. Found dead. How? That no longer concerned Westhofen. That was the Good Lord's affair and the affair of the Wertheim officials, the peasant officials of Aldinger's district, and the local Burgomaster. Fahrenberg then went to the square that was known as the Dancing Ground. The SA and SS who were detailed to this particular service were already lined up. Commands grated. Deathly tired, heavy with dirt and despair, the column of prisoners still moved quickly and softly like a wind made by departed souls. The two plane trees left intact at the right of the door to the commander's barrack were resplendent in their autumn red and the sun's last rays; for the day was declining, and from the boggy country the fog was rolling up to the accursed place. Cherub-faced Bunsen was standing in front of his SS squad as if he were awaiting his Creator's orders. Of the dozen or so plane trees that had stood to the left of the door, all but the seven that were needed had been cut down yesterday. Zillich, commanding the SA, ordered the four recaptured fugitives to be tied to the trees. Every evening when this command was given a tremor passed through the ranks of the prisoners, feebly and inwardly, like the last shiver before rigidity sets in, for the vigilant SS would permit no one to move as much as a finger.

The four who were tied to the trees did not tremble. Not even Fuellgrabe trembled. His mouth open, he stared straight ahead as if Death himself had commanded him to behave decently at the last. On his face too there was a gleam of that light compared with which Overkamp's torture lamp was but a miserable contraption. Pelzer had closed his eyes; his face had lost all its delicacy, all its timidity and weakness; it had grown bold and sharp. His thoughts were collected; they did not dwell on doubts and evasions, but on the comprehension of the inevitable. He felt Wallau's presence at his side.

On Wallau's other side was that man Beutler who had been recaptured immediately after the escape. At Overkamp's instructions he had been patched up again, though only superficially. He, too, did not tremble; he, too, had long since ceased to do so. Eight months ago, when his coat had been lined with foreign currency, he had betrayed himself at the border by his trembling. Now he was hanging suspended rather than standing in his strange place of honor at Wallau's right, which even his wildest imagination could never have pictured to him. His damp face was spotted with light. Of all the men's eyes, only Wallau's were purposeful. Whenever Wallau was led up to the crosses, his almost petrified heart gave a new leap. Would George be one of them? What he was staring at now was not death but the column of prisoners. He could even discover a new face among the familiar ones – Schenk's who had been in the hospital, Schenk to whose house Roeder had gone that very morning to obtain shelter for George.

Fahrenberg advanced. He ordered Zillich to draw the nails out from one of two trees. Bare and empty stood the two trees, two veritable crosses for graves. Now there was but one unoccupied studded tree, the one at the extreme left, at Fuellgrabe's side.

"The sixth fugitive found!" announced Fahrenberg. "August Aldinger. Dead, as you see. He has only himself to blame for his death. As for the seventh, we won't have to wait long for him, for he is on his way. The National Socialist State relentlessly prosecutes anyone who transgresses against the national community. It protects those who deserve protection, it punishes where punishment is due, and it destroys what ought to be destroyed. No longer does our country offer a haven for fugitive criminals. Our people is healthy; it shakes off the diseased and kills the insane. No more than five days have elapsed since the escape. Here – open your eyes wide, and impress this on your minds!"

This said, Fahrenberg returned to his barrack, and Bunsen ordered the column of prisoners to advance two yards. Now only a narrow space separated the trees and the first line. During Fahrenberg's speech and the commands that followed it, daylight had completely vanished. On its right and left the column was firmly hemmed in by the SA and SS. Above and beyond lay the fog. It was the hour when all gave themselves up for lost. Those among the prisoners who believed in God knew He had forsaken them. Those who believed in nothing at all let their souls decay; for decay can set in while the body is still alive. Those who believed in nothing but the strength inherent in man thought that this strength lived only in their bodies, that their sacrifice had been in vain, and that their people had forgotten them.

Fahrenberg sat down behind his table. What day was today? True, the day was practically over, but there were still three days left of the time he had set himself. If six could be found in four days, one must be found in three. Besides, this one was already surrounded and wouldn't have another minute's sleep; neither, unfortunately, would Fahrenberg.

It was almost dark in the barrack, and Fahrenberg switched on the light. This light shining from his window made the shadows of the trees reach the front line of the column. How long had the men been standing there? Was it night already? And still no command came, and the tied-up men's sinews were burning. Suddenly a man in the next to the last row of the column screamed. At the scream the four crucified ones gave a violent start that thrust them against the nails. The man pitched forward, brought the man in front down with him, and rolled screaming on the ground, blows and kicks already raining on him. The SA swarmed everywhere.

At that moment, from the center of the camp, came the two commissars, Overkamp and Fischer, hatted and rain-coated, brief cases under their arms, and accompanied by an orderly with their bags. Overkamp's activity at West-hofen had come to its end. The hunt for Heisler had nothing to do with his further presence there.

The two men went into the commander's barracks and came out again presently and again walked down the line. This time, Overkamp's gaze rested briefly on the trees. Wallau's eyes met his. Overkamp hung back almost imperceptibly. Into his face came an expression, a mixture of recognition, of "Sorry!," of "It's your own fault!" Perhaps in this mixture there was even a little kernel of respect.

Overkamp knew that as soon as he had left the camp these four men were lost. At best they might be kept alive until the seventh man was brought in – unless, of course, someone bungled or lost his patience.

When the motor started, it could be heard on the Dancing Ground, a sound that made hearts turn over. Of the four tied-up men, only Wallau was able to realize clearly that now they were doomed. But what of George? Had he been found? Was he on his way here?

"This fellow Wallau will be the first to bite the dust," said Fischer. Overkamp nodded. He had known Fischer a long time. They were nationally-minded men with a profusion of war decorations. Even under the System they had occasionally worked together. In his profession, Overkamp was in the habit of following the usual police methods. Grueling questionings, when harsh means were called for, were for him all in the day's work; they did not amuse him one whit, nor did he have any predilection for them. To him, the men he had to prosecute were always enemies of order, according to his own conception of order. Thus far everything was quite clear. Things grew muddled only when he started reflecting on for whom he was working.

Overkamp forced his thoughts away from Westhofen. There was still that Heisler case. He looked at his watch. He and Fischer were expected in Frankfurt in an hour and twenty minutes. The fog kept the speed of their car down to twenty-five miles. Overkamp wiped the window.

George did not have to ask Paul any questions when he came home from work. Paul's face showed plainly the result of his search for a hiding place.

Liesel expected to be complimented on her cake. But instead of hearing *Ah's* and *Mmm's*, she had to watch the men chew it as if it were plain cabbage. "Don't you feel well?" she asked Paul.

"What? Oh yes, I had a little accident." He showed her his burned arm. Liesel was almost relieved to know that there was a definite reason for the ungrateful silent munching. After inspecting the scorched skin – from childhood she had been used to all kinds of workingmen's accidents –

she went to fetch a little box of ointment. George said suddenly: "I don't need a bandage any longer. While you're playing the doctor, you may as well give me a bit of plaster."

Paul watched in silence while his wife undid the gauze bandage without any fuss. The older children were watching the procedure from the back of George's chair. George caught Paul's look – Roeder's eyes were severe and cold. "You were lucky, George," said Liesel, "that the splinters didn't get into your eyes."

"Lucky! Lucky!" repeated George. He looked at the palm of his hand. Liesel had applied the plaster rather skilfully; only the thumb was bandaged now. If he held his hand naturally, it looked uninjured. Liesel shouted: "Stop! Don't!" She added: "We might have washed that." George had got up quickly and stuffed the soiled bandage into the stove where some embers still glowed from the cake baking. Roeder watched him motionless. "Phew!" said Liesel and flung open a window. A little wisp of evil-smelling smoke wafted out into the air of the city, air to air, smoke to smoke. Now the doctor could rest easily. What a risky undertaking it had been to go to his office! How skilful his hands had been! How revealing of heart and skill!

"I say, Paul," said George quite gaily, "do you remember Old-Clothes Morris?"

"Do I!" replied Paul.

"Do you remember how we used to pester the old fellow to death, and he complained to your father, and your father gave you a beating, and he watched it and finally shouted: 'Not on the head, Herr Roeder, or he'll grow up stupid! On the arse! On the arse!' That was quite decent of him, wasn't it?"

"Yes, very decent. Your father must have given you the wrong kind of beating," said Paul, "or else you'd be cleverer."

For three minutes they had felt easier; but now things

as they actually were weighed down upon them again with all their irrevocable and unbearable heaviness. "Paul!" said Liesel anxiously. Why did he keep staring in front of him? She paid no attention at all to George. While she cleared the table she darted quick glances at Paul and gave him another one from the door when she went to put the children to bed.

"George," said Paul when the door had closed behind her, "that's that. We'll have to think of something better. Tonight you'll have to sleep here again."

"Do you realize," said George, "that by now all the precincts have my picture? That it will be shown to all the block wardens? And by the block wardens to the janitors?"

"Did anybody see you go up yesterday?"

"I can't swear to it; the hallway was empty."

"Liesel," said Paul, when his wife came back into the room, "you know, I have such a thirst. It's unbearable. I can't imagine why I should be so thirsty. Won't you run down and get us some beer?"

Liesel got the empty bottles together. She was glad to go. Good Lord, what was eating the man?

"Shouldn't we tell Liesel something?" asked Paul.

"Liesel? No. Do you think she'll let me stay here?"

Paul was silent. Suddenly in his Liesel, whom he had known from childhood, and so very thoroughly, there was one spot that was unknown to him, unfathomable. Both men pondered deeply. "Your Elly," said Paul at last, "your wife. . ."

"What about her?"

"Her family's in comfortable circumstances. . . people like them know others. . . wonder if I shouldn't drop in there."

"No! She's undoubtedly being watched. Besides, you don't know how she feels."

Liesel came back with the bottles, quite excited. "Funny," she said, "somebody's been asking for us at the inn."

"What? For us?"

"Asked Frau Mennich where we lived. The man can't know us though, if he doesn't know where we live."

George got up. "I have to be going now, Liesel. Thanks for everything."

"Won't you have some beer with us before you go, George?"

"Sorry, Liesel, but it's late already. Well. . ."

She switched on the light. "Now, don't let such a long time go by again, George."

"I won't, Liesel."

"Where are you going?" Liesel asked Paul. "First you send me for beer. . ."

"I'm just going to the corner with George – I'll be back right away."

"No, you stay here," said George.

"I'll go with you as far as the corner. Don't try to stop me."

In the door Paul turned around once more. "Liesel," he said, "listen to me. You are not to mention to anybody that George was here."

Liesel grew red with anger. "So he's in trouble after all. Why didn't you say so right away?"

"When I come back I'll tell you all about it. But keep your mouth shut, or else it'll be bad for me, and for the children too."

Liesel stood transfixed after the door slammed. Bad for the children? Bad for her Paul? Hot and cold by turns, she went over to the window. She could see the two of them – one tall, and one short – walking between the lampposts. She was afraid. It was quite dark now. Seated at the table, she waited for her husband's return.

"If you don't leave me here at once. . ." said George in a low voice, his face contorted with rage. "You're ruining yourself without doing me any good."

"Shut up! I know what I'm doing. You'll go now where I take you. When Liesel came up just now, and terror struck us to the bone, I had an inspiration. I have a great idea. If Liesel keeps mum – and I'm sure she will because she's afraid for us – you'll be out of danger at least for tonight."

George said nothing. His head felt empty, swept clear of thoughts. He followed Paul into town. Why think, if it doesn't lead to anything? Only his heart went on pounding as if it were asking to be let out of its inhospitable abode. How like two nights ago, when he had been about to call on Leni! He tried to calm his heart. *You can't compare this; now it's Paul who is at stake. Don't forget that. That has nothing to do with love affairs. This is friendship. Can't you trust anybody? It takes courage to put confidence even in a friend. Pipe down, will you? You can't keep on beating that way. You disturb me.*

"We won't ride," said Paul. "Ten minutes more or less won't matter. Let me tell you where I'm taking you. I passed here once this morning when I was going to see that damn Sauer. My Aunt Katharina lives here. She has a trucking business – nothing big – just three or four trucks. One of Liesel's brothers – he comes from Offenbach – is supposed to start working for her. He was in jail. . ."

"And how about papers? And tomorrow?"

"Why don't you get into the habit of counting two-one-three instead of one-two-three? You've got to do something. You've got to find shelter for the night. Would you rather start by being dead tonight and have an authentic set of papers tomorrow? I'll slip in there tomorrow. Little Paul always gets an idea."

George touched Paul's arm. The little chap looked up at him, made a face as one does to children one wants to keep from crying. His forehead was lighter than the rest of his face because it wasn't so freckled. The bare fact of his company reassured George. "If only he doesn't suddenly turn back."

"We may be picked up any moment, you know," said George.

"Why bring that up?"

The town was bright and crowded. Paul occasionally met an acquaintance, greeted him, and was greeted in return. On such occasions George turned his head away. "You mustn't always turn away," said Paul. "Nobody'll recognize you anyway."

"You recognized me right away, didn't you, Paul?" They came to Metzgergasse, a street with two repair shops, a tanking station, and a few taverns. Paul was in that neighborhood frequently and he was hailed repeatedly. It was *Heil Hitler!* here, and *Heil Hitler!* there; *Hello Paul!* here, and *Hello Paul!* there. There was a little delay at the gate – some SA men, two women, and the little man from the back room, whose nose glowed tonight like a carbuncle.

"We'll be at the Sun. Come in for a while, Pauley."

"Let me first say good night to Aunt Katharina."

"Wheee!" whistled the old man; the mention of her name sent chills down his spine.

When they finally entered the truck yard, there was Frau Grabber, Aunt Katharina herself, standing square in front of them, for she had just dispatched a truck. Long-distance trucking started at night.

"This is him!" said Paul.

"This fellow?" asked the woman. She glanced briefly in George's direction. She was robust and broad-shouldered, but more bony than fleshy. The white shaggy hair topping a wickedly bumpy forehead and the shaggy white brows atop a pair of sharp sinister eyes gave her not the appearance of an old woman, but rather of some creature nature had endowed with a white mane. She gave George a second brief glance. "Well?" She waited a moment, and then rather casually knocked his hat off "Off with it! Hasn't he got a cap?"

"His things are still at our place," said Paul. "He was to have spent the night with us, but Paul Junior is fretting, and Liesel thinks it may be measles."

"What fun!" said the woman. "Well, what are you standing in the gate for? Either come in or stay out."

"So long, Otto, take care of yourself," said Paul, who was still holding the hat she had so summarily removed from George's head. "Good-by, Aunt Katharina. *Heil Hitler!*"

George in the meantime had taken a good look at the woman's face, the terrain through which he would have to find his way during the next few hours. She was now looking him over for the third time, this time quite thoroughly. He didn't flinch from her gaze – there was no occasion on either side for kindness.

"How old are you?"

"Forty-three."

"Then Paul lied to me. My business is not a home for the infirm."

"Why don't you find out first what I can do?"

The woman's nostrils distended. "Oh, I know all right what you fellows can do. Well, make it snappy and change your clothes."

"Lend me a pair of overalls, Frau Grabber, will you? My things are still at Paul's place."

"Hm?"

"How was I to know that you work at night?"

The woman now began to curse, keeping up a full head of steam for several minutes. George would not have been surprised had she actually hit him. He listened to her in silence, on his lips a faint smile which she either noticed and disregarded or failed to notice in the scanty light. When she finally came up for air, he said: "If you haven't any overalls for me, I'll work for you in my underdrawers. How am

I supposed to know what's what around here, seeing that this is my first time here?"

"You'd better take him right back home again!" shouted the woman at Paul, who had suddenly reappeared, George's hat still in his hand. He had been hurrying down the street, answering any number of *Heils!* and waving his arm, when he had suddenly been reminded of the hat. Paul, startled, made a wry face. "Give him a chance until tomorrow. I'll come back then and you can tell me what's what." He hurried away as fast as his legs would carry him.

"Without a fellow like Paul," the woman said now more calmly, "chaps like you would go to the dogs. My business is not for weak people. Come along now, you!"

He followed her through the yard, which was much too brightly lighted and too crowded to suit him. People were constantly coming and going through the back door of the tavern and the other houses. There were already glances in his direction. A policeman was standing in the open garage near an empty car. "Just my luck that the man could not have attended to his business here a little earlier," thought George, perspiration breaking out all over him. The policeman was asking for some sort of document and paid no attention to George. "Pick out some work clothes," the woman said to her new employee. Inside the garage there was a windowed recess that was used for an office. The policeman watched George disinterestedly while he picked out one of the greasy overalls that lay strewn about. Then he looked up at the bright open window and the woman's large white head. "Some female!" he muttered. When he had gone, the woman stuck her head out of the window, leaning her arms on the sill in a manner that plainly showed this window to be her conning tower. She cursed and shouted: "Get out of here and into the yard, you faking loafer! That car has to be ready for Aschaffenburg in an hour and a half. Get busy!"

George stood beneath the window. Looking up at her, he said: "Will you be kind enough to explain to me quietly just exactly what I am to do?" Her eyes narrowed. Her pupils bored into the face of the man who she'd heard was a rather dissolute fellow who neglected his family. But no matter how hard she bored, she could make no impression on that face which, so she thought, some smash-up had disfigured. Though her stare usually froze whatever it hit, for the first time she herself now felt an icy breath. She began quietly to explain matters to George, telling him what had to be done to the car. She watched him closely. After a while, she came out, stood at George's side, urging him on. The wound in his hand, only partly healed, soon opened again. When he knotted a filthy rag around it with his teeth and his left hand, she said: "If you are cured step lively; if not – get out!" He made no answer, nor did he look at her again. "That's the way she's gaited," he thought to himself. "You've got to take her as she is. After all, everything comes to an end."

He worked on quickly and doggedly, and was soon so exhausted that he could no longer fear or even think.

In the meantime, Liesel sat waiting in her dark kitchen. When ten minutes passed and Paul had not returned, she knew he had gone farther than the corner with George. What had happened? What were the two men planning? Why had Paul not told her anything?

The evening was deathly quiet. The hammering on the fourth floor, the cursing on the second, march music from the radio, and the laughter across the street from window to window could not drown out the quiet nor, above all, the light steps coming up the stairs.

Only once in her life had Liesel had anything to do with the police. When she was a child of ten or a little more, one of her brothers – perhaps the one who later had fallen in the

299

war for the family never spoke of it again, it had been buried with him in Flanders – had gotten into some mischief. But the fear that had gnawed at her heart at that time was still in her blood: the fear that is entirely dissociated from the conscience, the fear of the poor, the fear of the chicken before the hawk, the fear of being pursued by the State. It is the age-old fear, indicating more exactly who the State served than all the constitutions and historical works in the world. Liesel decided she would defend herself, protect herself and her brood with tooth and claw, with cunning and perfidy.

When the steps had passed the last landing and were undoubtedly coming in her direction, she jumped up, switched on the light, and began to sing, her voice dry and choked. She said to herself that singing and light were the best indications of a clear conscience. The person at the door actually hesitated before he rang the bell.

The man wore no uniform. Liesel's light shone upon an insipid, dull face that was unfamiliar and impressed her as dishonest. "Surely a copper," thought Liesel to herself. In her thoughts she used expressions like this; she must have picked them up somewhere, because Paul hardly ever spoke to her about such things. "I bet he's got his dog license pinned to the inside of his coat."

"Are you Frau Roeder?" asked the man.

"And suppose I am?"

"Is your husband at home?"

"No," said Liesel, "he's out."

"About when will he be back?"

"I really couldn't say."

"Well, he'll be coming home sometime."

"Couldn't say."

"He isn't out of town, is he?"

"Yes, he's out of town. His uncle died." Partly hidden behind the door, partly in the shadow, she noticed the strange face twitch, apparently with disappointment. "Well, what are you waiting for?" she thought.

The man was about to leave but turned around once more: "Has he been gone long?"

"Rather."

"Well, *Heil Hitler!*" Even his back looked disappointed as he shrugged his shoulders.

Liesel had a second fright. Suppose he asked the janitor.

She tiptoed out on her stocking feet and watched, but the man did not stop. When she went back to the kitchen window, she saw him walking away along the quiet street.

What had impelled Franz to call at the Roeders' that evening was a half hope, a sort of sense of direction for what was possible. As he was walking through the quiet streets toward his streetcar stop he felt disappointed and downcast. He rode to the opposite edge of the town where he had left his bicycle at an inn. Then, at last, he went in the direction of Hermann's house.

Hermann had been so sure of Franz's coming that he grew uneasier every minute. Franz rarely stayed away so many evenings in succession. Hermann suddenly realized that he himself, to whom Franz came for advice, was more in need of Franz than he had been aware of. This advice, which Franz used to ask for quietly and with a quiet look before he followed it exactly, needed Franz himself to make it detach itself and come forth. When, at last, they heard the noise of the bicycle under the window, Else wiped the oilcloth-covered kitchen table with her apron, and Hermann brought the chessboard from the drawer, hiding his gratification.

But tonight Hermann's gratification lasted only until Franz was seated at the table. Franz was different from his usual self; furthermore, he remained silent much longer.

Hermann let him take his time. Finally Franz would break out, or things would break out of him. Hermann listened merely attentively at first, then surprised, finally worried. Franz told him what had happened to him, how he had met Elly three times – at the movies, in the market, and in the attic. How together they had searched through George's life and had dug up people out of their memories; how he had followed these leads, obsessed by the idea of finding George himself. How everything had miscarried altogether!

"What do you mean – altogether?" But Franz had relapsed into silence, and Hermann had to wait.

Again Franz began to talk, but differently than Hermann expected.

"You see, Hermann, I am quite an ordinary man. All I desire of life is the most ordinary things. For instance: to be able to stay here where I am, for I like to be here. The urge so many others have – to go away as far as possible – is lacking in me. As far as I am concerned, I could stay here forever. This sky – not too glaring and not too gray. One becomes neither countrified nor citified. There is something of everything – smoke and fruit. If I could have had Elly, I would have been overjoyed! Others may have a hankering for any number of women, for all manner of adventure, but not I. I would have been true to Elly, though I realize fully that she's not exceptional in any respect. She's nice, that's all. Still, I would have been satisfied if I could live with her until we are old and gray. As it is, I can't even see her again. . ."

"Certainly not," said Hermann. "It was too risky to see her at all. . ."

"It surely is nothing out of the way to want to go out with Elly on Sunday, but I mustn't do it. No. Don't look at me so surprised, Hermann. I can't have Elly! Whether I'll be able to stay here long is questionable. Who knows but what even tomorrow I'll have to be off.

"All my life I've wished for only the simplest things – a meadow or a boat, a book, friends, a girl, to be surrounded by quiet. Then this other thing – this yearning for justice – came into my life. It happened when I was still quite young. Slowly my life has changed; now it is only outwardly quiet."

"Well, it's good to know about all this," said Hermann. "But tell me, what does this Roeder, George's friend, look like?"

"Short," said Franz. "Looks like a boy from a distance. Why?"

"If the Roeders were hiding someone they would not behave any differently from what you tell me. But probably they are not hiding anybody."

"When I came, Frau Roeder was alone with the children," said Franz.

Hermann thought: "Franz has got to be kept out of it altogether." The three words "like a boy" had almost frightened him. It was the second time he had heard them today. *If only I had some time. Bacter will be in Mainz early this week. Time is the only thing I lack. We could get the lad out all right, but the time... the time...* "Where has this Roeder been working?"

"At Pokorny's. Why do you ask?"

"Nothing particular." But Franz felt, or thought he felt, that Hermann was keeping his thoughts from him.

That night, Paul and Liesel were sitting side by side on their kitchen sofa. He stroked her head and her well-rounded arm as if he were back to his attempts when he was first making love to her. He kissed her face. When he felt the tears on it, Paul told her some of the truth. George was being sought by the Gestapo because of some old affairs. They carried terrible penalties, according to the new law. How could he possibly have sent George away?

"Why didn't he tell me the truth? To eat and drink at my table!"

Liesel had scolded at first and stamped about in the kitchen, her face crimson with rage. Then she began to cry, but that too had ceased. Now it was past midnight. Every ten minutes she asked: "Why didn't he tell me the truth?" as if it were the crux of the whole matter.

At last Paul said in a changed, dry voice: "Because I didn't know how well you could stand the truth." Liesel pulled her arm away from his hands. When she said nothing, Paul continued: "If we had told you everything, if we had asked you beforehand whether he could stay, would you have said Yes or No?"

Liesel replied vehemently: "I should certainly have said No! What of it? He's just one, but there are four of us – five, even six counting the one we're expecting; we didn't even mention this one to George because he teased us about how many we've had. And you really should have said to him: 'My dear George, there's just one of you, but there are six of us' – "

"Liesel, it was a matter of his very life – "

"Yes, yes, I know; but it was a matter of ours, too."

Paul was silent, utterly miserable. For the first time in his life he felt entirely alone. Things could never again be the same as they had been. These four walls, what for? These children tumbling about – what for? Aloud he said: "And then you expect us to tell you everything. Tell you the truth. If you had shut the door in his face and two days later I showed you the paper and you found him – George Heisler – under NATIONAL COURT NEWS and under JUDGMENT PUT INTO EFFECT AT ONCE, wouldn't you have felt any remorse? Would you close the door in his face again, if you could know that beforehand?"

Paul had moved away slightly from his wife. She began

to cry again into her folded hands. Then, sobbing violently, she said: "Now you think I am bad. Bad! Bad! Never before have you thought I was so bad. And now you would like to be rid of bad little Liesel – your Liesel. Yes, I know that's what you are thinking, and that you are quite alone, and that you don't give a damn about us. George is the only one you care for. Yes, if I could have known beforehand that everything would turn out that way, that I'd find his name under that heading, oh yes, then I certainly would have taken him in. And perhaps I would have taken him in anyway. I can't tell now. That's always a hair-trigger decision. Yes, I think now that I should have taken him in."

Paul said, more quietly: "You see, Liesel, that's why I didn't tell you anything, because at first you might not have let him stay, and then afterwards, when I had explained everything to you, you would have felt sorry."

"But something terrible might still happen, and then you'd be held responsible."

"Yes," said Paul, "I'd be responsible. It was up to me to decide, not up to you. I am the man of this house, and the father of this family. And I can say Yes to something right away, whereas you would have said No at first, and then Perhaps, and finally Yes. But then it would have been too late. I can make my decisions at once."

"But what will you tell Aunt Katharina tomorrow?"

"We'll talk about all that later. Make me some coffee now, like you made yesterday when George keeled over."

"That fellow's turned everything here topsy-turvy. Coffee at midnight!"

"If the janitor asks you tomorrow who was here today, tell him it was Alfred of Sachsenhausen."

"Why should he ask me?"

"Because they themselves are questioned by the police, and they might question us."

305

At this, Liesel was up in arms again. "Questioned? By the police? My dear Paul, you know very well that I'm a poor liar. Anyone can find me out. Even as a child I couldn't lie. Even when others were lying, my face gave them away."

"What do you mean, you can't do it? Didn't you lie a little while ago? If you can't lie to the police, everything here will be ruined. You'll never see me again. But if you lie exactly as I tell you to, then I promise you that we'll be able to use our free tickets next Sunday for the Westend-Niederrad match."

"Oh, will there be free tickets?"

"Yes."

Shortly before midnight, George stretched out at the garage but was called again almost immediately because the chauffeur of the car he had overhauled had some complaint. Frau Grabber berated him, this time her voice low and her remarks caustic. When he had finished and was ready to lie down again, the second Aschaffenburg car had to be fixed. This time Frau Grabber did not budge from his elbow; she watched his work closely, commenting on every awkward move, as well as on all his misdeeds during his life. This fellow Otto, whose place he was taking, must have had a rather shabby, vicious life. No wonder he was playing sick, trying to postpone the drastic treatment in store for him. George was ready to lie down a third time, but now the tools had to be overhauled and the garage swept. Morning was near. For the first time, George had time to look up. The woman stared at him. Was this fellow entirely indifferent to what wheels ran over him? Perhaps the wheels under which he had now come seemed even gentle in comparison. Astonishment brought quiet to her, and through her to the man. Frau Grabber left him, returning once more to her office window. George curled up on a bench. She thought: "Perhaps

I'll be able to get along with him after all." Dead-tired, George lay under Belloni's coat. Though sleep was out of the question, his thoughts were racing through his brain smoothly, without gap or ending, in a dreamlike procession. "What if they do not bother about me any more? If Paul simply leaves me here? In place of that fellow Otto?"

He tried to imagine his life if he had to stay here permanently, if he were powerless to leave the place. Never to get out of this yard again, forgotten by everyone. Best to try to get away through his own efforts – and as quickly as possible. But what if help did come? And he was gone – to be captured a few hours later? What if he were taken back to Westhofen?

"If they catch me and take me back," he said to himself, "let it be while Wallau is still alive. If it has to be, let it happen quickly so that I can die with Wallau. That is, if he is still alive." At that moment the end seemed inevitable to him. What normally is spread over the span of a lifetime, over a number of years, an exertion of all of one's powers to the breaking point, the relaxing and yielding and painful straining again – all this took place in his mind in the space of an hour – while minutes changed. At last, burned out, he dully watched the day break.

Chapter VI

i

Fahrenberg was lying on his back fully dressed, his booted legs dangling over the edge of his bed. His eyes open, he listened to the night. He put his head under the covers. Now, at least, there was a noise – the surf seething in a person's soul. No longer to be forced to listen! He was consumed with yearning to hear a sound, some alarm of which one could not tell beforehand where it would come from, thus making the self-consuming listening perfect. A motor humming far away on the highway, the shrill ringing of a telephone in the Administration Building, even steps coming from that building toward the commander's quarters, could have put an end to this waiting. But the camp had been still, deathly still, since the SA had finished celebrating the commissars' departure after their own fashion.

Several times during the night Fahrenberg had given a violent start. Once a car had gone in the direction of Mainz, two more toward Worms; there had been steps in the Dancing Ground but they had gone past his door toward Bunsen's; shortly after two the telephone in the Administration had shrilled and he had expected the report – but it was not the report that would be handed to him at any hour of the day or night: the return of the seventh.

Almost choked, Fahrenberg drew the covers from his head. How still the night was! Instead of being filled with the sound of sirens, pistol shots, and motors, with the turmoil of a tremendous search in which everybody was taking part, it was the stillest of all nights, an ordinary night between two workdays. No searchlights darted through the skies. For the villages of the district the autumn stars were lost in the mist; only the soft but penetrating light of the waning moon could find those who longed to be found. After a hard day's work everybody was in a quiet sleep.

"I am going to sleep now," said Fahrenberg to himself. "Overkamp has long since reached his destination. Why was I foolish enough to fix a time limit, and why did I let it be known? If they don't capture Heisler now, no one can put the blame on my shoulders. At any rate, I've got to get some sleep now."

He sat bolt upright. It was five o'clock. There was a confused noise outside. Yes, the thing had happened. From the highway, from the entrance to the camp, came the noise of motors, the sharply uttered commands that accompanied the reception of prisoners. Then followed the dark and unevenly mounting noise that had not as yet found its proper pitch or assumed its bittersweet flavor. No blood had as yet been shed.

Fahrenberg switched on a few lamps; but when the light seemed to interfere with his hearing, he switched them all off again. Ready to go out, he hesitated, listening for something over at the entrance of the camp, beset by his tormenting, now almost fulfilled hope.

Fahrenberg's next reactions were rather human – he placed his hand over his heart, his lower jaw sagged, and his

309

face was flabby with disappointment. To his ears, all this was a reasonable, otherwise definable sequence of sounds.

New commands were heard from outside. Fahrenberg, pulling himself together, switched on lights again. He pressed buttons and shifted plugs.

When, a few minutes later, Bunsen crossed the Dancing Ground, he could hear Fahrenberg raging like one possessed even through the closed doors. Zillich had just finished his report: Eight new prisoners, all of them from Opel Ruesselsheim; all of them had opposed something or other. Here for only a brief cure that would make them find their new piece wages more palatable later.

Zillich expected and suffered a new flood of invective with an impenetrably gloomy face. The roaring that was his master's usual way of letting off steam could not bowl him over. Ah, but this time there was not a single word about old times and solidarity, not even the slightest allusion to it. His large head dropped on his chest, Zillich waited despondently. With his uncanny faculty for following his master's every emotion, he knew only too well that Fahrenberg's manner toward him had changed sadly during the past week. On Monday after the escape they had both still shared the feeling of a jointly suffered misfortune, but during the next few days Fahrenberg must have shut him out. Would his master forget him entirely?

Fahrenberg's close-set eyes – by no means fear-inspiring, by no means intended by nature to fathom great depths, but only to peer into clogged-up pipes and funnels – gazed at Zillich coldly, even with hatred. Now Fahrenberg actually believed that this clumsy lout was chiefly responsible for his misfortune. Several times in the course of the week such a thought had flashed through his mind; now it was growing into a certainty.

Zillich used the breathing spell for a slight advance, a sort of test of confidence. *"Herr Kommandant* – I beg to request your consent to the following changes in appointments, relating to the changes to be made in the squads detailed to guard duty over the special column. . ."

Bunsen could hear Fahrenberg's second fit of bellowing. "Well, there won't be many more occasions for so much fun." The commission investigating events before and after the escape had so far not made any official announcement, but it was noised about among the SS that the old man would not last another week.

A second breathing spell. Bunsen entered, smiling only with his eyes. Zillich, looking like a bull with his horns cut off, was dismissed. In the voice of a man whose power of command, reckoned by scope and duration, was incontestable, Fahrenberg said: "The new arrivals are subject to all punitive measures imposed upon every prisoner since the day of the escape." In the same tone he enumerated these measures. With every enumeration they grew more stringent. "Many of the fellows who are on the brink now will certainly keel over," thought Bunsen. "This man is giving himself a nice last fling."

Zillich went to the canteen. Coffee was being served. Distracted, he sat down in his own place at the narrow end of the table. Ever since Fahrenberg had bellowed out the news that the responsibility for the special column was no longer his but Uhlenhaut's, there had been a fog in front of his eyes. The mood in the canteen was that of hungry robust young fellows who like to put their strong teeth into good healthy food: country bread and plum jam. Everything was plentiful in the neighborhood. The larder was especially well stocked this week because of the punitive reductions in the prisoners' fare. Back and forth across the table went the large cans of coffee and milk. The guards who had accompanied the transport were the guests of the Westhofen SA. The men

311

were laughing and chewing. Zillich stared in front of him, stuffing bread into his mouth.

ii

Some of the fog had drifted away; a few tatters still hung suspended between Marnet's and Mangold's apple trees. Franz on his bicycle bumped over a couple of ridges in the road. Today, instead of giving him pleasure, the jolting jarred his empty weary head. The mist felt soft and cool on his tired face as he rode through it.

As he was skirting Mangold's farm, the sun tried to peep through the shrouding haze. But now the denuded trees gave back no sparkling reflections. Beyond this farm the land sloped down into infinite loneliness. One was apt to forget that the Hoechst factories were down there in the fog, that the nation's largest cities were not far away, and that cyclists would soon come down the road in droves. Here was the dreariness that had been rankling under the soil. Here was the old solitude, not more than three hundred yards from the environs of the cities. The land was doubly bare where Ernst and his sheep had passed. This desolation was still unconquered; who was there who wanted to conquer it? Everybody had to go through it, everybody wanted to leave it behind. A fire would be welcome at home tonight. Franz had never had any particular liking for Ernst; but today he missed him, as if life itself had gone with him into another realm.

"If only I could go on riding here forever," thought Franz, "if only this road would never get to Hoechst!" But already the air about him was full of tinkling sounds. There was Anton Greiner at the soft-drink stand. "I hope I live to see the day when this fellow goes by here without spending anything," thought Franz. Into his face, which only a little while before had mirrored nothing but autumn's solitude and desolation, came a narrow, niggardly expression. Presently it passed, and his face saddened. The thought of Anton's fiancée led him to thoughts of Elly.

From the window of the soft-drink stand came a gust of warm air. The young woman in there had lighted her stove. She even had put in an innovation: a hot-plate for coffee for the workmen from distant villages.

"How can you drink coffee again," Franz asked, "after just coming from your home?"

"I suppose you want to save my money as well as your own," was Anton's retort. Ill-humored they cycled downhill. They were already in the midst of the pack. At the sudden warning sound of a horn, everybody crowded to one side, and a motorized S S man flashed by, Anton Greiner's cousin. "Funny lot of nonsense that fellow talked last night," said Anton. "He even asked about you." Franz gave a start. "Wanted to know if you were feeling good and laughing in your sleeve."

"Why should I feel good?"

"That's what I asked him. He was already three sheets to the wind, and a fellow in that condition is worse than if he were blind drunk. But the motorcycle is his own now, he's made his last payment on it. Every man with a motorcycle has been put on duty, he said, to search the city. Cordons have been drawn around whole blocks."

"What for?"

"Because of the fugitives."

"With such widespread control," said Franz, "it really ought not to be hard to find one solitary man."

"That's what I said to my cousin; but he said such control was not as easy as one might think."

"How's that?"

"That's what I asked him. Says he, control like this is hard to control. By the way, he'll soon be getting married. Guess who..."

"Now you're asking too much of me, Anton. How am I to know who your cousin wants to marry?" He tried to hide his agitation. Had this SS cousin really been asking about him?

"He wants to marry Little Mariechen of Botzenbach."

"Why, isn't she Ernst's girl?"

"Which Ernst?"

"The shepherd."

Anton Greiner began to laugh. "Why, Franz, that fellow doesn't count. There's not one man who's even jealous of Ernst."

Again there was something that Franz could not understand, nor did he find an opportunity to have it explained, for at the Hoechst town limits they had to separate. Franz got on a street that was blocked by two gasoline trucks. Everybody had to get off their bikes and push them ahead in single file. The faces were as gray as the air; only from metal surfaces – the handle bars of the bicycles, a bottle protruding from somebody's pocket, the curved tops of the trucks – was any light reflected. Right ahead of Franz a row of girls in gray and blue aprons were walking. When Franz pushed his bicycle past them they grumbled. Had one of them said his name? He turned around. From a dark eye darted a sharp look. Didn't he know this girl, with her evilly drooping mouth and the lock of hair above her badly disfigured face? Hadn't he met her once before, early that week? She nodded to him derisively.

In the locker room, the men were buzzing and whispering: "Noggin... Noggin..."

"What's the matter with Noggin?"

"He's back again."

"What? Where? Here?"

"No, no! Perhaps Monday he'll be here."

"How do you know all that?"

"Last night I was at the Anchor when his daughter comes in, the lame one. 'He's back again,' she says, so I goes right up to the house with her. Noggin is sitting up in bed, and his wife is making him compresses. There's one around his head. 'Jesus, Noggin,' I says, '*Heil Hitler!*' 'Yes, *Heil Hitler!*' he says. 'It's nice of you to come and see me right away.' 'What's nice about it?' I ask. 'Come on now and tell us a thing or two. What have they been doing to you? Come on, tell me.' So he says, 'Karl,' he says, 'can you keep your mouth shut?' 'Surest thing you know.' 'Well, so can I,' he says. And that's all he would say."

iii

Elly kept her brown eyes fixed unflinchingly upon the man who, after almost an entire night of questioning, was no longer a stranger to her – Overkamp. "Do be kind enough to collect your thoughts, Frau Heisler. Do you understand me? Perhaps when you are all by yourself your memory functions better than when you are allowed to mingle with others. That could easily be ascertained, you know."

Her thoughts were withered by the glaring light; she could think only of what she saw. She thought: "Three of his upper teeth are certainly false."

Overkamp planted himself directly in front of her, the harsh glare from the light striking his own shaved neck so that her face was for once in the shade. "Did you under-stand me, Frau Heisler?"

In a low voice, Elly replied: "No."

"If you can't make anything occur to you while you are enjoying liberty – for which, by the way, you are indebted only to the fact that you and Heisler parted on bad terms – prison, and if necessary the dark cell, may have a salutary influence on you. Do you understand me now, Frau Heisler?"

Elly said: "Yes." When her forehead was in the shade, she could think. "What would I be missing if he did lock me up? The office? Typing two dozen letters a day to stocking manufacturers. . . The dark cell? Anything's better than this light that cuts one's head in pieces."

Overkamp stepped to one side. Elly quickly closed her eyes against the white light that took her breath away. He contemplated her again with painstaking minuteness – no lover could have done better. She had been sitting there for several hours. Last night he had had about a dozen people, Elly Heisler among them, summoned out of their first sleep. To all his questions Elly had said nothing but her soft Yes or No. Her little face seemed to melt away in the murderous light.

Overkamp drew up a chair and began once more: "Well, my dear Frau Heisler, let's start again at the beginning. During the early days of your married life – do try to recall it – while the fellow was still in love with you – no wonder, by the way – and then, when love began to disappear the least little bit – of course, there were quick reconciliations that made things doubly sweet – that's how it was, wasn't it, Frau Heisler? – Well, as I was saying, when the fires of love slowly – oh, very slowly – refused to burn properly – when your husband became estranged from you – at that time, when you yourself had by no means got over it – when your heart still used to ache at the thought that your great, great love was about to go to the dogs – do you remember?"

"Yes," said Elly softly.

"Yes, you do remember. When first one and then another of your dear women friends gave you a dirty dig – when he

316

stayed away for an evening the first time and then, without so much as a by-your-leave, made it three or four days – and with that woman, of all persons. . . You do remember, don't you?"

Elly replied: "No."

"What do you mean, No?"

Elly tried to turn her head to one side, but the harsh light had the power to root people to one spot. She said softly: "He stayed away, that was all."

"And you mean to tell me that you don't remember even who with?"

"No."

Quite as Overkamp had foreseen, when the questioning came to this point unwelcome thoughts hurtled in droves through Elly's mind. There fluttered, like spectral moths beneath the glaring police lamp, the fat cashier, two or three nice young women, a slatternly thin neighbor in Niederrad, and still another one – she had first been jealous of this one and it had lasted, probably because she had had no cause for it – Liesel Roeder.

Thus it appeared that, as usual, Overkamp's edifice of questions had been constructed quite correctly. His questions had dug out of Elly's memory what they had been intended to dig out. The trouble was that the woman who was sitting before him, so gentle and quiet, kept everything locked within herself. Overkamp had the feeling that the questioning had, as they said among themselves, bogged down. That was the devilish thing about the most beautifully planned grilling, and a thing that had often proved a stumbling block to even the most astute policeman: instead of loosening up just before it disintegrated under the persistent hammering of hundreds of questions, the human ego contracted suddenly at the last minute and grew firm again. The hammering, instead of shattering one into pieces,

317

had a solidifying effect. Besides, if this young woman's strength was to be broken, she must first be allowed to gather some strength. Overkamp switched off the lamp. A mild indirect light filled the almost bare room.

"You may go now. Hold yourself in readiness at any minute. We shall need you again today or tomorrow. *Heil Hitler!*"

Elly went into town, swaying with fatigue. At the nearest baker's she bought a warm bun. Entirely at a loss where to go, she automatically went toward her office. Her hope of finding nobody there except the cleaning woman and of sitting unmolested in a corner until nine o'clock was not realized. The office manager, an inveterate early bird, was already there. "Ah, 'Early to rise – early to rise' – that's my motto – and really, Frau Elly, if it were anybody else, I'd swear you'd been out on a spree... Aw, you needn't blush, Frau Elly. If you knew how becoming this is to you – a certain something, delicate and drooping, at the tip of your little nose, and the blue circles under your eyes!"

"If only, once in my life, I could have a real lover," thought Elly. "George – even if he still existed – wouldn't love me anymore. As for Heinrich, I don't even want to think of him. Franz is out of the question. This afternoon, when I leave the office, I'll go and see Father. He, at least, is glad to see me. He has always been good to me, and he always will be."

iv

"They have forgotten me here in this yard," thought George. "How long have I been here – hours – days? This witch will never let me out again. Paul won't ever come back."

People were coming out of their doors on their way to

the city. "Well, Mariechen, be good to yourself." "Up so early? *Heil Hitler!*" "Don't be in such a rush, Herr Meier, your work won't run away." "Morning, sweetheart!" "Well, Alma, see you tonight."

Why are they all so gay? What gives them so much pleasure? Because another day has come, and the sun is shining once more. Have they been gay, I wonder, all the time and through everything?

"Well?" said Frau Grabber, when he paused the space of one hammer beat. She had been standing behind him for several minutes.

George thought: "If Paul actually forgot me and I had to stay here forever in his brother-in-law's place – at night on the bench in the garage – here in the yard during the day. . . That was to have been the brother-in-law's lot."

"Listen, Otto," said Frau Grabber, "I spoke to your brother-in-law Paul about your wages – that is, if I decide to keep a fellow like you, which is by no means sure – 120 marks. . ."

"Well?" she said again, when he seemed to hesitate. "Go on with your work. I'll deal with Roeder, seeing that he's your sponsor." George said nothing. The hammering inside him was so loud and hard that he thought the whole street must hear it. He thought: "Will Paul come before Sunday? What if he doesn't come even then? How long shall I wait for him? Perhaps I should get out of here on my own hook. I don't want to think in circles all the time, I don't want my thoughts to be my ruin. Have I confidence in Paul? Yes. Then I must wait until he comes."

Frau Grabber was still standing behind him. George had entirely forgotten her. She said suddenly: "By the way, how did you manage to keep your driver's license?"

"That's a long story, Frau Grabber. I'll tell you all about

it tonight – that is, if we come to an understanding and I'm still here tonight."

V

Paul at his work, standing straddle-legged when the caps were pressed home and storklike on one leg when he pulled down the lever, was cudgeling his brain in search of the right man to help him today.

There were sixteen men in his shop, not counting the foreman; he was out of the question entirely. Their bare, steaming torsos – lean or fat, young or old – bore the marks of every kind of wound a human being can sustain, some from birth, some from a fight, some from Flanders or the Carpathian Mountains, some from Westhofen or Dachau, and some from work. A thousand times Paul had seen Heidrich's scar below his shoulder blade. It was a miracle indeed that, pierced by a bullet from back to front, the man had been saved – to be a welder at Pokorny's. But no wounds could have bled Heidrich as did the ensuing years of peace; unemployment, hunger, family worries, the crumbling of all rights, the cleaving of the classes, the waste of precious time, squabbling about who was right instead of doing the right thing at once, and then, in January '33, the most terrible blow of all. The sacred flame of faith – of faith in oneself – burned out! Paul wondered why he had not noticed a change in Heidrich. As Paul saw him this morning, he was certainly unwilling to lose another hair of his head, and he wished for nothing better than to be allowed to work steadily for the rest of his life. What was the use of it all?

"Perhaps Emmrich is the man," thought Paul. Emmrich, the oldest man in the shop, had white bushy brows above severe eyes, and a little tuft of white hair on the top of his head. Once upon a time he had been a staunch member of the organization and had made it a point to hang out the red May Day flag on the evening of April 30th so that it could wave in the very first breeze of the morning. Paul suddenly remembered this. Such matters as people's whims and peculiarities had not carried much weight with him before. Presumably Emmrich had escaped a concentration camp because he was one of the indispensable expert workmen; moreover, he was rather old. His teeth had probably become dull, and he wouldn't nibble at any bait. But then Paul recalled that he had seen Emmrich twice at the Erbenbeck Inn with young Knauer and his friends though they never talked to one another at the shop, and that Knauer had several times been seen coming from Emmrich's house of an evening. Suddenly Paul could understand the whispering of people, just as the man in the fairy tale could understand the birds' songs after he had eaten a certain food. Yes, these three belonged together; Berger, too, was one of them, and possibly also Abst. Emmrich might have furled his flag, but his severe eyes still had an expression of watchfulness. "He and his comrades will undoubtedly know of a shelter for my George," thought Paul, "but I don't dare ask them. They stick together, they won't let anyone come near them, they don't know me, and they are distrustful. Well, aren't they right? Why should they trust me? What, after all, am I to them? Just little Paul."

Whenever anybody approached Paul, he had said: "Just leave me out of it. All I want to be sure of is that my Liesel has my soup ready at night, even if at times it isn't as strong a soup as it might be."

And now? Tomorrow? He could hear George's abrupt, hoarse voice again, more real and enduring even than the guest himself whose gray face and bandaged hand had rested on his kitchen sofa.

He is lost if I can't find someone today. I mustn't think of anything else. But how in the world can I find somebody? The bad ones will betray me, and the good ones are hiding. They hide themselves entirely too well.

There, on his powerful legs, stood Fritz Woltermann, as if he were cast in a mold. A blue serpent with a girl's head tenderly encircled his big round torso; his arms too were tattooed with little serpents. The man had formerly been a welder on a man-of-war.

He was a daring fellow, got a great deal of satisfaction out of being daring, and knew other daring men. He would not balk at the risk of getting himself smashed up; on the contrary, it would tempt him. Paul thought: "Woltermann! Yes, he's the one." He felt easier.

But for minutes only. Then his heart was heavy again. All at once it seemed impossible for him to put the most precious thing he had in the world at the mercy of these bold, serpent-twined arms. Woltermann might be indifferent to the risk of getting himself smashed up; but to Paul it was not a matter of indifference. Woltermann was out of the question.

It would soon be noon. Ordinarily he heaved a sigh of relief when the sun came up over the rooftops. He knew that when the brass cap of his indicator sent out a sparkle, the noon hour was not far off. He thought: "I mustn't wait beyond the noon hour to speak to him – to him who doesn't even exist."

How about Haller? He was the best-natured of them all. If two of the men were quarreling, he'd make peace between them. If somebody was in trouble, he'd help him out. Yesterday he had bandaged Paul's arm like a mother.

Perhaps he was the right one. Almost a saint. And always

322

quiet. "Yes – he," thought Paul. "I'll speak to him in just a little while." Struck by the rays of the noonday sun, the little pointed metal cap gleamed bright. Fiedler called out softly: "Hey, Paul!" For once Paul had failed to pull down his lever at the right second.

"No," thought Paul. Something warned him, although as a rule he was neither sharp-witted nor given to presentiments. "Haller – he'll consider himself much too important. He'd use some big words if I said anything. . . Give some kind of a saintly excuse. He'd want to go on putting on hundreds of little plasters, settling hundreds of petty disputes, and comforting hundreds of little sorrows."

For the second time Fiedler warned him quietly: "Paul!"

Ah, Fiedler – he wouldn't do either. No later than last week, when Brand had had him up on the carpet and had reminded him that formerly he had been in every strike and in every demonstration, he had declared openly that times change and we change with them.

Without turning his head, Paul glanced at Fiedler out of the corner of his eye. "This is the second time that Paul has looked at me strangely," thought Fiedler. "Is anything troubling him?" Fiedler, who was about forty, looked firm and strong, for rowing and swimming were his favorite sports. He had a broad calm face, and his eyes also had a calm expression.

"Fiedler's answer to Brand really doesn't mean a thing," Paul mused. "It's nothing against him. Nothing but air! Take a handful of it, and what have you?" Yes, Fiedler had been decent. There was the story of the elevator over at the plant – a horrible thing. Two men from Paul's own shop had been sent for just after the elevator had been installed, and they and two others had been the first to use it. A rope had jumped its track – presumably this had been Schwertfeger's fault – and the four men had sustained severe injuries. Fiedler himself had a broken collarbone. They could have asked for heavy damages, and they could have ruined Schwertfeger; after all, he'd been to blame for everything. It had been Fiedler who induced the three others to represent the whole thing as a trifle, his own fracture included, and not to make trouble for Schwertfeger.

"Does this alone justify me in having confidence in Fiedler?" Paul wondered. Perhaps Brand would have acted similarly – out of community spirit, or whatever the Nazis called it now. Perhaps, on the other hand, Brand would have held that responsibility must not be shirked, that negligence is one of the shortcomings of community spirit, and that Schwertfeger ought to be punished.

In plant meetings, Fiedler had always asked quiet questions. He had always made sure that the men got everything they were entitled to. In that respect, too, he had been of one mind with Brand.

The brass cap on the indicator still gleamed. The whistle would sound presently.

Something crossed Paul's mind, something that had involved no action and no speech, something so casual that he had never given it any thought. In the spring, when word went around that all the men were to go to the Main Hall after work to listen to the *Führer*'s speech, someone had said: "Hell, I have to go to the station." Another answered: "Go ahead, nobody'll notice it." A third one had added: "It isn't compulsory, you know." Paul himself had said: "If it isn't compulsory – me for Liesel! We all know anyway what he'll say." All at once quite a few had left – that is, they'd wanted to leave, for they soon discovered that every one of the three gates was locked. Somebody recalled that there was a little door near the gatekeeper's lodge. The door was not bigger than one on a doll's house, and there were twelve hundred men in the plant. As things happen occasionally, all of the men had tried to get through it at once, including Paul himself. "You are crazy, fellows," the gateman had warned them. When someone in the crowd said: "I suppose this is the needle's eye through which a camel would sooner pass than..." Paul had turned around. He saw a triumphant gleam in Fiedler's calm eyes and a light spreading over his serious, reserved features.

The ray of sun had faded from the point of the cap. The sun now shone on the piece of wall between the yard windows. The noon whistle sounded.

"I must speak to you for a moment." Paul had waited for him in the yard. Fiedler thought: "So something is troubling him. I wonder what could affect a nature like Paul's."

Paul hesitated. Fiedler was surprised to notice that, at very close range, Roeder looked quite different from what he had imagined. His eyes in particular were different. Far from being waggish and childlike, they were cold and severe. "I need your advice," Paul began.

"Well, shoot!" said Fiedler.

Again Paul hesitated. Then he went on, speaking connectedly and very quietly and plainly: "It concerns the men from Westhofen... You know what I mean, Fiedler... It's about the fugitives... About one..."

He grew as pale at what he was saying as he had two days before when George had told him. Fiedler, too, had blanched to his very lips almost at Paul's first words; he even closed his eyes. How the yard roared! Into what turmoil had they both been hurled?

Fiedler asked: "Why do you come to me, of all people?"

"I can't say why. Confidence, I guess."

Fiedler took a firm grip on himself. He asked some questions between his teeth harshly and gruffly, and Roeder's answers were equally harsh and gruff so that one might have thought they were quarreling. Their wrinkled foreheads

325

and their pale faces expressed hatred and strife. At last Fiedler tapped Paul lightly on the shoulder and said: "Be at the Finkenhof Inn forty-five minutes after work. Wait for me. I'll have to think all this over. I can't promise you anything now."

It was the strangest work period they had ever experienced – that second part of their shift. Paul managed, once or twice, to turn in Fiedler's direction. Was he the right man? He'd have to be.

"What made the man hit on me?" thought Fiedler. "Is anything still evident from my behavior? O Fiedler! Fiedler! Here you were taking such good care to prevent anyone from drawing any conclusions that in the end what was not concluded had ceased even to exist, had been extinguished. So there should have been no danger of anyone drawing any conclusions.

"But all the same," he continued to say to himself, "in spite of every precaution and without any intention on your part, something must have remained. It is there, and Roeder has sensed it. Ought I to have said: 'Roeder, I can't help you either. You are mistaken in me. I no longer have connections with any party leaders or with comrades. I got out of touch with my own people long ago, though perhaps I could have traced them and renewed the contact. But I didn't care to bother – I am out of touch. I am on my own now, and I can't help you.' Should I have said these things to Roeder after he showed so much confidence in me? How is it that I suddenly find myself alone and isolated? I couldn't keep in touch with things after the countless arrests and after all the contacts were severed one by one. Or was I really no longer so keen on reestablishing these contacts? Had I ceased to regard them as one regards something without which he can neither live nor die? But I could not possibly have sunk so low – not quite so low. I am not entirely callous and indifferent, and I still belong to the movement, for how else could Paul have found me out? I can also find my comrades again and renew my contacts. Even without them I've got to help him in this. It is not always possible to wait and to ask questions. The trouble was that I was so desperately tired when everything went wrong all at once. We tell ourselves: 'If things go wrong, the best that can happen is six or eight years in the C C; the worst – off comes the head!' No wonder, then, that one gets for an answer: 'What you want of me, Fiedler, isn't worth risking my neck for.' And before you know it, you yourself have given such an answer. It was almost a knockout blow to me when our party headquarters went up in smoke and George was nabbed. Then I quit. But now – I feel it – everything will turn out all right."

vi

As Hermann was walking through the yard after the noon hour, he noticed that Lersch was issuing brief orders with an expression on his face that Hermann instinctively disliked. Hermann looked up. Little Otto, suspended from ropes, was dangling between the wheels of a railroad car, awkwardly turning the heavy axle. The yard was below the street level. A car could be upended with cranes or moved so that it protruded over the yard. The boy, swinging lightly, held fast stiffly. Occasionally he gazed down into the yard which from his height seemed far below him; at other times he looked up at the car which seemed on the point of toppling over on top of him. The young workman who was manipulating the cranes called out something to him that did not sound short or derisive, but gay and lively. Otto was obviously the victim of an attack of fear and awkwardness, not unusual to an apprentice.

Continuing on his way, Hermann heard the young workman give a short laugh. Lersch gave Otto one of his short commands in a tone more suitable to a barrack square than a factory yard. Hermann turned around quickly. The boy's face was pale with the fear of being found wanting on an occasion much too trifling for either commands or ambition. "What would become of a lad," Hermann wondered, "who considers kindness nothing but talkativeness, and solidarity medieval nonsense? A second Lersch perhaps, or a worse one, to judge by his apprenticeship."

Hermann crossed the two yards at the street level and entered the deafening noise of the shop, the incessant white and yellow welding flashes. Here and there a smile met him, not unlike a grimace in the blackened faces – glances from oblique eyes whose white eyeballs seemed to roll – threateningly – like the eyes of Negroes – a few shouts that were drowned in the thunderous din.

"I am not alone," said Hermann to himself. "What I was thinking about the boy just now was nonsense, utter nonsense. He is a boy like all the other boys. I'll be his Godfather – a kind of secret Godfather. I'll snatch this boy from under Lersch's nose, and I will succeed. We'll see who is the stronger. Yes, but that will take time. Will I be granted the time?" From the time-consuming task he had suddenly set himself – so suddenly that it seemed to have been set him – his thoughts returned to the most burning task that might wreck everything – himself, Otto, and unknown future tasks.

Yesterday, Sauer, the architect, had waited for Hermann at a place which they had agreed was to be used only in cases of the utmost urgency. Sauer was tormented by doubts whether he had been justified in summarily dismissing his caller; his description of him – short, blue-eyed, freckled – tallied exactly with Franz Marnet's description of Paul Roeder.

If this man Roeder was still working at Pokorny's, there was a good man there who might sound him out – an elderly man, firm and reserved, who had escaped persecution because, during the two years prior to Hitler, he had been somewhat aloof and was considered to be on bad terms with his former associates. This man might be able to approach Roeder on Monday. Hermann, who knew him well, was convinced that he could be entrusted with money and papers for Heisler, if George was still alive. While he himself became one with the roaring and flaming of an ordinary workday, Hermann considered whether it was right to risk so much on behalf of one person. The man who was to sound out Roeder was almost the only wholly reliable person at Pokorny's. Was it permissible to jeopardize one man because of another? If so, under what conditions? Once more Hermann weighed everything carefully. Yes, it was permissible. Not only permissible, but imperative.

vii

Zillich went off duty at four o'clock in the afternoon. Even in normal times he was at a loss as to what to do with his spare time. He cared nothing for his comrades' excursions to near-by towns, and was not interested in the way they amused themselves. In this respect he was still a peasant.

At the entrance of the camp stood a rattletrap car filled with SA men who had gotten together for a trip up the Rhine. Although they urged Zillich to get in, they would undoubtedly have been astonished, probably even disappointed, had he accepted. From the glances that followed him and from the sudden stopping of their gay laughter it was evident that there was a certain distance even between them and him. Zillich tramped over the brittle dry ground on the field path to Liebach. He crossed the road that connected the highway with the Rhine. In front of the vinegar factory a guard was stationed even today – Westhofen's most advanced outpost. The man saluted, and Zillich acknowledged the salute. He walked on for a short distance in back of the factory. He looked at the drain through which Heisler had probably crawled and also looked at the place where, according to Pigwidgeon's deposition, the fugitive had vomited. The Gestapo had reconstructed rather accurately the man's route to the Darré School. Zillich had covered it several times before.

He walked along the field path under the cool afternoon sun. As the river was not visible from here, the land looked to him exactly like his own homeland. Zillich was a near neighbor of Aldinger's. He had grown up in one of the remote villages beyond Wertheim.

Here and there he could see the blue-and-white kerchiefs of women bending over the earth. What month was it? What would they be harvesting now? Potatoes? Turnips? In her last letter his wife had asked him if he would not come home, for she was anxious to give their tenant farmer notice to quit. The money they had saved could be profitably invested. They could live more economically now, in view of the fact that he was an old-front soldier with many children and therefore entitled to a number of privileges. Now that the farm was in fairly good shape, as soon as he came back, part of the section they had been forced to farm out could be plowed up, partly left in clover for the cows they could buy now. The two oldest boys were already almost as strong as their father, but they could not replace him; he was the head of the family.

Zillich set one of his top boots on the spot where George had found the hair ribbon. A few minutes later he came to the fork where the grandmother, Bagatelle, had turned off. He did not walk up to the Darré School, but descended into Buchenau, for he was thirsty. Zillich was not a regular drinker; he drank at intervals, periodically.

He could see a spade glinting here and there in the fields. At the approach of a man, a peasant woman would raise her head from her work at the roadside, wiping the perspiration out of her eyes with her fists, the better to look after the retreating figure. As Zillich walked across the quiet land that basked under a pale-blue sky, his very soul revolted at the thought of going home to stay. But if Fahrenberg dropped him, or were himself dropped with such a crash that he would be unable to hold anybody else, what other place was there for him to go?

His memories were tormenting him. In November '18, when he had come back from the war to his neglected farm, he had been appalled by the decay and the flies, by the brats – one for each furlough – that had been added to the original two, and by his wife who had grown as dry and hard as stale bread. Timidly and with gentle eyes she had asked him to make the windows tight, especially in the stable, because the wind blew in. She had brought him the rusty tools. It was then that he'd realized that this was no furlough after which, when he'd taken care of a few nails and such things, he could go back where there was no tightening to do and no nails to be driven in, that now it meant staying at home, hopelessly and inescapably.

During the next few years, too, they had put up with him around the village out of compassion for his wife. When they saw that the woman was working herself to death before their eyes, they had at first come with offers of this and that – the free use of the threshing machine or the loan of some tool. But Zillich had spurned them. "I'd rather die in the gutter than accept anything from these bastards!" His wife had asked: "Why bastards?" Zillich had replied: "They couldn't run back fast enough to their potatoes. . ." In spite of her burdens and sorrows, Frau Zillich's fear was not un-mixed with a certain admiration. But the farm went to ruin; the crisis hit guilty and innocent alike. Zillich cursed in uni-son with those whose tools he had refused to accept. He had to abandon his farm and move to a tiny one owned by his parents-in-law. That year, when they were penned up like so many pigs, had been the most terrible year of all. How the children had trembled when he came home in the evening! Once, when he had gone to the Wertheim market, someone had suddenly hailed him. A fellow-soldier had said to him: "Come on, Zillich, come with us. That's the right thing for you to do! You're a comrade, you're a fighter, you're a nationally minded man, you're against the scoundrelly rab-ble, against the system, and against the Jews."

"Yes, yes, yes," Zillich had replied, "I am *against*. . ." From that day on, Zillich had been able to snap his fingers at every-thing. No more oily peace for him; Zillich would show them!

Before the dismayed eyes of the village, a motorcycle had fetched Zillich evening after evening; sometimes it was even a motorcar. If only that evening the bunch from the brick-yard had not happened into the inn where the SA hung out! A look had led to a word, a word to a knife thrust.

True, it had not been much worse in prison than it was in that suffocating mouse hole he called home; it was a bit cleaner and more entertaining. His wife was terribly ashamed and wailed at the dishonor, but even she had to rub her eyes and stare when the SA squad came marching into the village to celebrate his return. Speeches – *Heil!* – Drunken orgies. How the innkeeper and the neighbors gaped!

Two months later, at the big SA parade, Zillich saw Fahrenberg, his old lieutenant, on the reviewing stand. In the evening he inquired where he was staying. "Does the *Herr Leutnant* still remember me?"

"Good Lord, it's Zillich! And we're both wearing the same shirt!"

And now he – he, Zillich! – would have to trifle his time away with the damn cows again! The mere sight of the village street, which so reminded him of the one at home, filled his soul with a dull fear. The very doorknob at the inn reminded him of home by its shakiness.

"*Heil Hitler!*" shouted the innkeeper, with an excess of zeal. In his usual innkeeper's voice he added: "There's a nice sunny place in the garden. Perhaps the *Herr Genosse* would like to sit in the garden."

Zillich glanced quickly through the open door into the garden. Speckled autumn light was falling through the chestnut trees on empty tables, freshly covered with red-checked tablecloths in anticipation of the coming Sunday. He turned away. Even this reminded him of the many commonplace Sundays, his past life, and the vilest of all peaces. He stayed at the bar and asked for a glass of new wine. The few people at the bar who, like Zillich, had ordered the year's new wine, all inched away and eyed him with a frown. Zillich failed to notice the sudden silence in the room. He was soon at his third glass, the blood already singing in his ears. But again his hope for relief was shattered. On the contrary, the dull fear that had filled him to the bursting point still seemed to be growing in him. He wanted to roar.

In the war Zillich had found the one thing that could bring him ease. He did not become frenzied at the sight of blood, as it is claimed murderers do. That would still have been a sort of intoxication. The sight of blood quieted him. He grew as quiet as if his own blood were gushing from the deadly wound. It was like a self-inflicted blood-letting. He would look, become quiet, and go away. His sleep would be undisturbed.

At the table in the inn parlor several Hitler Youths were sitting, among them Fritz and his leader, Martin, the same Martin to whom only last week Fritz would have accorded blind obedience in everything. Martin, a deeply tanned alert boy with shrewd eyes, already knew how to maintain a certain almost imperceptible distance between himself and the others. The innkeeper was his uncle. The lads were drinking sweet cider. On the table there was a plate of nuts that they were cracking one against the other. They threw the kernels into the cider so they would soak up the liquid. When the glasses were empty, the nuts would taste sweet. The boys were making plans for a Sunday excursion.

Ever since Zillich's appearance in the inn, Fritz had taken part neither in the deliberations nor in the nut cracking. He too knew Zillich by sight. His eyes were glued to his back. He had heard many rumors about the man, but had not bothered his head about them.

Fritz had been summoned to Westhofen that morning; after a sleepless night he had answered the summons, his heart beating wildly. A great surprise had awaited him. He had been told to go home again, that the commissars had left, that the summonses still outstanding were null and void. Immensely relieved, Fritz had gone on to school. Everything was perfect now except for his jacket, and he was more than willing to forfeit it as the price of his peace of mind. How he had buried himself in his work, in the Youth Service, in comradeship! He avoided Kohler, the gardener. What a fool he had been to open up to the old fellow, the silly pipe sucker! All that day Fritz had been the old Fritz of the week before. Why had he been so uneasy anyway? What had he done? A few stammered words. A feeble No. There had been no consequences at all. And may not that which has no consequences be considered as having never happened at all? Fritz had been the gayest one of the boys around the table – until about five minutes ago. "Are you boring holes into the air with your eyes, Fritz?" He started.

Who is that Zillich? What has he to do with me? What can I have in common with a Zillich? What has he to do with us? Is it true what people say of him?

Perhaps it really was not the right jacket. There are people who are as like as two peas, why not coats also? Perhaps by now all the fugitives have been recaptured, mine too. Perhaps he has disclaimed the jacket as his own. Is this Zillich really one of us, the same as Martin, and is everything true that people are saying about him? What do we need him for? Why did my man have to be caught? Why did he flee? Why was he arrested in the first place?

He kept staring at the powerful brown back. Zillich was now at his fifth glass.

Suddenly a motorcycle stopped at the inn. An SS man, without taking his left leg off the seat, called into the tap-room: "Hey, Zillich!" Zillich turned around slowly. "Get up here," said the SS man. "They're looking for you everywhere. I would have been willing to bet I'd find you here."

Zillich walked from the inn somewhat heavily, but erect and firm. His fear had evaporated, for it gave him considerable satisfaction to be needed and looked for. He swung himself onto the pillion, and the two men were off.

Altogether, the whole scene had not lasted more than three minutes. Fritz had shifted his position so that he could watch the departure. Zillich's face had frightened him, and so had the look the two men had exchanged. He was chilly. Something stirred in his young heart, a warning or a doubt – something that some people claim is born in a man, others claim is not born in them but comes into existence gradually; still others claim there is no such thing at all. But it kept stirring and trembling in the lad as long as he could hear the rat-tat-tat of the motorcycle.

"What do you want me for?"

"It's because of Wallau. Bunsen is giving him the once-over again."

They went to the barrack which early that week Overkamp and Fischer had made their headquarters. In front of the door stood a loosely formed group of excited SS and SA men. Bunsen, who had obviously assumed Overkamp's position, called a few men by name after each stage of his questioning. Whenever he opened the door, the men were anxious to learn whom he would need next.

When Wallau was taken to the barrack he had entertained a feeble hope that Overkamp had not left and that he was facing merely a resumption of the useless grilling. But he had found only Bunsen there, and that fellow Uhlenhaut who was slated to be Zillich's successor as head of the punishment squad. And in Bunsen's face it was written that the end had come.

All of Wallau's sensations were now merged into one – thirst. What a terrible thirst! Never would he be able to quench it. Every bit of perspiration had been drained out of him. He was drying up. What a fire! Smoke seemed to be pouring from all his joints. Everything had turned to steam as if the whole world were coming to an end, not just he – Wallau.

"You didn't care to say anything to Overkamp. All right. But we two will get along better. Heisler was your intimate friend. He told you everything. Quick – what is the name of his girl?"

"Ah, so they still haven't got him," thought Wallau, once more drawn out of himself, out of the exclusiveness of his own extinction. At the flash in Wallau's eyes, Bunsen's fist shot out, and Wallau reeled against the wall.

In a voice alternately soft and loud Bunsen said: "Uhlenhaut! Attention! – Well, what is her name? Her name! – Forgotten so soon? That can be remedied quickly!"

While Zillich was being driven across country to Westhofen, Wallau was lying on the floor of the barrack. He did not feel as if his own head were bursting, but as though the whole brittle world were being shattered to pieces.

"Name! What was it? – There! Elsa? – There! Erna? – There! Frieda? – There! Amalia? – There! Leni. . ."

Leni – Leni – in Niederrad! Why did George have to tell me that? Why does that have to come into my mind now? Why don't they go on with their THERE *–* THERE! *Have I said anything? Has it slipped out?*

"There! Katharina? – There! Alma? – There! – Stop a moment and make him sit up!"

Bunsen looked out of the door, and the sparks in his eyes lighted similar sparks in all the eyes turned toward him. When he saw Zillich, he waved him inside.

Covered with blood, Wallau was sitting propped against the wall. From the door, Zillich looked over at him calmly. A faint light over his shoulder, a tiny blue corner of autumn, told Wallau for the last time that the structure of the world held firm and would continue to hold firm regardless of what struggles might come. For a moment Zillich stood rigid. Never before had anybody awaited him with so much calm, with so much dignity. "This is death," thought Wallau. Slowly Zillich pulled the door shut behind him.

It was six in the afternoon. Nobody else was present at Wallau's last ordeal. But the following Monday morning, a slip of paper went from hand to hand in the Opel works near Mannheim, where Wallau in the old days had been shop committeeman. *Our former committeeman, Delegate Ernst*

337

Wallau, was murdered in Westhofen on Saturday, at six o'clock. This murder will have to be heavily paid for on the Day of Judgment.

A noticeable trembling went through the column of prisoners on Saturday evening, when they noticed that Wallau's tree was empty. The leaden pressure over the whole camp, Zillich's sudden return, subdued noises, the concentration of the SA – all these symptoms had prepared them for the truth. The prisoners were no longer able to obey, even though their very lives depended on it. Some collapsed in the column, others couldn't stay in step. These were minute irregularities which, in the aggregate, broke through the rigid order. Incessant threats, increasingly heavy penalties, the excesses of the SA who were now raging through the prisoners' barracks every night, had lost their power to intimidate anybody because everyone considered himself already lost.

Wallau's death had made something snap in the SS and the SA that for a few days past had prevented their going to the utmost lengths. The utmost had been Wallau's death. Only now came the unimaginable, the undreamed-of, that succeeds the utmost. Pelzer, Beutler, and Fuellgrabe were not murdered as quickly as Wallau had been – a slower process was used for them. Uhlenhaut, who was now in charge of the special column, wanted to prove that he was a second Zillich. Zillich wanted to prove that he was still Zillich. Fahrenberg wanted to prove that he still retained the power of command over the camp.

There were other voices among the mighty of Westhofen. They declared that the conditions in Westhofen were untenable. Fahrenberg would have to be dropped as quickly as possible, and with him the clique that he had partly brought with him and partly assembled. Those who voiced these opinions had no desire to see the Hell end and justice begin; they merely wanted order even in Hell.

Fahrenberg, no matter how wild his actions, had tolerated rather than instigated Wallau's murder and all that followed in its wake. His thoughts had long since been centered on a single individual, and they could not tear themselves away from him as long as he continued to exist. As though he himself were the pursued, he neither ate nor slept. What was to be done with Heisler once he had been brought in alive was the only thing to which, with all its details, he would give his personal attention.

"Time to knock off, Herr Mettenheimer!" called out the chief paperhanger, Fritz Schulz, in his usual brisk and animated tone. For fully half an hour he had prepared himself for this remark. Nor did Mettenheimer fail to make the expected answer: "You can leave this to me, Schulz."

"My dear Mettenheimer," said Schulz, smothering a laugh – for he was rather fond of the old man who was squatting there on his ladder with so severe a face and so sad a mustache – "Herr Brand, the Troop Leader, will end up by presenting you with a decoration. But do come down now, everything is really finished."

"Everything finished?" repeated Mettenheimer. "There is no such thing. But it is finished to the extent that Brand won't know what hasn't been done."

"What more do you want?"

"My work must be perfect, whether it's for Brand or for Sondheimer."

Amusement in his eyes, Schulz looked at Mettenheimer; up there like a squirrel on a branch, filled entirely with the consciousness of doing his duty before the eyes of a strict but invisible customer.

Schulz walked through the empty, already brilliantly colored rooms. When he reached the staircase he heard the workmen grumbling, and Stimbert, the Nazi, mumbling something about overstepping limits, and work hours, and calling to account. Calmly and with laughing eyes Schulz asked: "Aren't you willing to add half an hour for your Troop Leader?" The others snickered. Stimbert's face changed immediately. Some of the others were pleased or embarrassed.

On the threshold of the first room that opened on the staircase stood Elly; she had come up the stairs quietly. The little apprentice had been sweeping up; he was behind her, grinning. "Is my father still here?"

Schulz called out: "Herr Mettenheimer, your daughter!"

From his ladder, Mettenheimer asked: "Which one?"

"Elly!"

"I wonder how the man knows my name," thought Elly.

Like a youngster, Mettenheimer climbed down from his ladder. It had been years since Elly had called for him at his place of work. Pride and pleasure rejuvenated him as he saw his favorite daughter standing there in the large, empty, ready-to-be-moved-into house, one of the many he had papered for her in his dreams. He immediately saw the sorrow in her eyes and the fatigue that made her face look even more delicate. He took her around, showing her everything. "Look out you don't get yourself dirty!" he said.

The little apprentice, the first to regain his wits, clicked his tongue, and Schulz smacked him. The others said: "She's a peach! How'd the old guy manage to bring anything like her into the world?"

Schulz changed his clothes quickly. At some distance he followed father and daughter as they walked down Miquelstrasse arm in arm.

"That's how it happened last night," said Elly, "and they'll come for me again, perhaps even tonight. Every time I hear a step I jump. I'm so tired."

"Be calm, my child. You know nothing, that's all there is to it. Keep thinking of me. I will never forsake you. But for the next half hour you mustn't think of anything. Come on, let's go in here. What kind of ice cream would you like? Mixed?"

Elly would much rather have had a cup of hot coffee, but she didn't want to spoil her father's pleasure – he'd always treated her to ice cream when she was a little girl. He asked: "Have another cookie?"

At that moment, Schulz, his chief paperhanger, came into the shop and over to their table. "You'll be at the building again tomorrow, Mettenheimer, won't you?" he asked.

Surprised, Mettenheimer answered: "Why, yes!"

"Well, then, I'll be seeing you," said Schulz. He waited a second to see whether Mettenheimer would ask him to sit down. He shook hands with Elly, looking her straight in the eye. Elly would not have objected to the company of a man who looked so brisk and handsome and had such a decent and frank face. To be alone with her father was gradually becoming oppressive. But Mettenheimer only looked sourly at Schulz until the latter took his leave.

viii

"Have you two had a fight at home, Herr Roeder, that you seem to enjoy being here with us so much?" asked mine host of the Finkenhof.

"My Liesel and I do not fight. All the same, she wouldn't let me in tonight if I did not bring home the free tickets. Tomorrow, you know, is the final Westend-Niederrad match.

That's why I'm letting you make some money out of me so early in the day, Herr Fink." Paul had been waiting for Fiedler at the Finkenhof for over an hour. He looked out into the street. The lights were already lit. Fiedler had intended to be there at six, but he had told Paul to wait indefinitely.

"The best thing for me to do now," thought Paul, "is to eat spareribs and sauerkraut." But to keep Liesel waiting and eat up her Sunday money – no, he couldn't do it. He ordered another glass of light. Someone on his way through the taproom asked: "Are you here still or already?" "There comes Fiedler," flashed through Paul's mind, "and he hasn't found anybody." Fiedler's face was severe and tense. He didn't seem to notice Paul right away. But while he was standing indifferently at the bar, he could feel Paul's persistent look. Only when he was about to leave did he give Paul's shoulder a pat and casually sit down on the edge of the nearest chair: "At eight-fifteen at the Olympia, where everybody parks, a small blue Opel car. Here's the number. He's to get in at once. He'll be expected... Now listen carefully, I want to see that everything is taken care of. If my wife came to your flat, what reason could she give Liesel for her call?"

Only now did Paul turn his eyes away from Fiedler. He looked in front of him, then said: "The recipe for the cake with icing."

"Tell your wife you let me taste a piece of your cake. If my wife comes to get the recipe and everything is O.K. with Heisler, tell her you hope we'll enjoy the cake; but if something has gone wrong, tell her we mustn't upset our stomachs."

"I'll go and see George at once," said Paul. "Don't send your wife before an hour or so."

Fiedler rose immediately and left. Again his hand pressed Paul's shoulder lightly. For a little while, Paul continued to sit motionless. The slight pressure of Fiedler's hand still lingered, that faint hint of wordless respect and brotherly confidence, a touch that penetrated deeper than any display of affection. Only now did he fully comprehend the scope of the news Fiedler had brought him.

He got up. He didn't have the patience to wait for the streetcar; he preferred to walk to the city. As the streets and people flitted past him he felt that, after all, he was having his share in the course of events. He waited in the dark gate until he had become quiet, flattening himself against the wall to let a group of people from the inn pass him. From the street came the noise of a Saturday evening. He, too, had tried to get away from Liesel on such an evening for a few hours at the inn, for there was a long Sunday of companionship ahead of them. He could see George squatting on the ground, hammering in the light from a street lamp. It was about the same time that it had been last night when he brought him here. The lighted window of the garage office meant that the woman was in.

George bent lower as he always did when he heard steps approaching from behind him. He hammered the piece of tin – what had long been straight had become bent – and straightened it out again. He felt somebody stop in back of him. "Hey, George!" He looked up quickly, and as quickly down again; with a loose wrist he gave two light blows with his hammer. "It's O.K., George," he said. "Be at the side exit of the Olympia at eight-fifteen. A small blue Opel car. Here's the number. Get in at once."

George hammered the straightened edge crooked again. "Who is it?"

"I don't know."

"I don't know whether to do it."

"You must. Be calm. I know the man who has fixed it up."

"What's his name?"

Hesitating, Paul answered: "Fiedler." George rummaged

343

in his memory – a host of names and faces that went back years. But no recollection came to him. Paul urged: "The man is absolutely trustworthy."

"I'll do it," said George.

"I'll go in now," said Paul, "and settle things with my aunt, so you can go and get your things right away."

Paul was relieved when Frau Grabber made no objections. She retired behind the table which filled the room almost completely. The lamp, drawn far down below the ceiling, shone upon her thick, white flaming mane. On the table lay the ledger and charts and a few letters under a malachite paper weight. A malachite mountain housed not only a clock but also an inkwell and a groove for pens and pencils. It was the most ordinary table in the world, in a most ordinary yard office. There was nothing strange there except the woman herself. She had made of this place, to which an ill wind had driven her, all that could be made of it. The whole yard had watched her husband beat her unmercifully. The whole yard had watched when she got the idea of doing some of the beating herself. The war had taken from her both her husband and her lover. Her child, too, had been dead these twenty years, choked during a spasm of whooping cough, and buried in the part of the Koenigsberg cemetery that is cared for by the Ursuline nuns. When she had come back that time she had known from the gaping and leering of the yard people that all of her secrets were public property. Her trucksters had thought that she'd got all she'd bargained for. She had stamped her foot and roared: "Are you paid to gape? Get to work! Get on with it!" From that moment, nobody around her had known the meaning of rest, herself least of all.

Perhaps she felt a shade mellower tonight. Should she forbid this man to get his things from Roeder's? Why hadn't Paul brought them, and be done with it? Well, let him go and bring his trash. *And about the wages, that will be taken care of when he's settled here definitely. I like him. I'll curb his tongue all right. There's something about him that reminds me of home. He must come from a district where it blows so cold that afterwards every little breeze seems gentle. I'm tempted to say he is a fellow countryman. Let him sleep in the shed of the garage. He can set up Grabber's bedstead – a practical use for it.*

Paul had gone back to George. "Well, George. . ."

George replied: "Yes, Paul?" Paul hesitated about leaving him; but when George urged him he went without taking leave, without a look, stepping quietly into the street. In their hearts both felt immediately and simultaneously that subtle and unappeasable burning that people experience when they have a presentiment that they will never meet again.

George placed himself so that he could keep an eye on the clock in the back room of the inn. After a while Frau Grabber came out of the office. "Quit now," she said, "and get your trash."

"I'd rather finish up here," said George. "Then I can spend the night at Roeder's."

"There's measles there."

"Oh, I've had the measles; you needn't worry about me."

The woman still stood behind George, but she found no reason to urge him on. "Come on," she said suddenly, "let's drink to the new job." He started. Only in that part of the yard that fronted the garage did he feel comparatively safe. He was afraid of some unforeseen incident at the last minute. "Since my hard-luck accident I've made up my mind to give up drinking," he replied.

Frau Grabber laughed. "How long are you going to stick to that?"

He seemed to reflect upon that for a moment; then he said: "Another three minutes."

They had a noisy reception in the crowded taproom; the

woman was a regular customer. After a brief flood of welcoming shouts she and George attracted no further attention. They stood at the bar.

"*Prosit!*" said Frau Grabber. They clinked glasses. "Now he can't get out of it," she thought. "Now it's settled."

"So! And now I'm off to Roeder's. Thanks, Frau Grabber! *Heil Hitler!* See you again!"

He crossed the yard and changed his clothes, folding the borrowed overalls neatly. He hesitated a moment in the gate before going out on the street. He had the feeling that he'd left something behind him in the yard, something important, something indispensable. He thought: "I've left nothing. Here I am, already in the street. I've already passed three streets. So I must have left the yard, after all. Too late for anything else."

He walked along Schaefergasse past the parked cars. He spotted the blue Opel and compared the numbers. They checked. "If only the whole thing checks! If only Paul has not let himself be duped. I should certainly bear you no grudge, Paul, for better men than you have been duped. But what a pity if things go wrong now at the last minute!"

The door of the car was opened from the inside as George approached. The car started up at once. What a strange smell in this car, so sweet and heavy. They drove through several streets to the Zeil. George glanced at the man at the wheel. The driver paid as little attention to him as if he were not in the car at all; he sat there stiff and silent. The glasses on a longish thin nose, the jawbones grinding with suppressed excitement – what the devil did all that remind George of? They drove toward the East Station. "Why don't you say something?" thought George. "Where are we bound for?"

As if he yielded to the man's wish – as if he had never got in the car at all – George had not asked these questions aloud. Not a single look did the driver give him. He sat in an awkward position, as if George's presence would become real only if he touched him.

They left the East Park behind them. George thought: "The trap might be sprung any minute now... No! A man who was setting a trap would behave differently; he'd be talkative and oily, and would try to lull you into a feeling of safety. Pelzer, in a similar situation, might have acted as this man does... But if it's a trap after all, then..." They drove to the Riederwald settlement and stopped in a quiet street before a yellow house. The man got out. Even then he did not look at George; he only motioned to him with his shoulder to get out, go into the hallway, and from there into the room.

"This is a school chum of mine on the way through, so I brought him along. I suppose he can stay the night with us?"

Entirely indifferent, the woman said: "Why not?" George shook hands. They looked at each other briefly. The man stood stiffly, watching them, as if his passenger only now were beginning to change from a dream into something tangible. "Would you care to go to your room first?" she asked.

George glanced at the man, who nodded imperceptibly. Perhaps it was the first time that he actually looked at George. The woman made as if to show the way, but the man stopped her with a motion of his hand. He preceded George from the room. On the stairs he said: "I am Dr. Kress. Some of your friends know me from attending a chemistry course of mine."

No sooner had a certain sense of safety enveloped George – not certainty, but a hope of safety – than he found pleasure in the colored rugs on the stairs, in the gleaming white paint, in his host's matter-of-fact manner, in the woman's attractive looks.

What a miracle that he was allowed to be alone in this room and to think. When Kress had gone, George locked the

347

door. He turned on the faucets, sniffed the soap, and drank a little water. When he looked at himself in the mirror, he found himself so strange that he refrained from looking a second time.

At about this time, Fiedler entered the flat of his parents-in-law, in which he and his wife had a room. He would probably have taken in Heisler himself, if he'd lived by himself. As it was, he had thought of Dr. Kress. The man had formerly been with Pokorny, and later with Cassela. Fiedler had also run into him in an evening school for workmen where Kress was teaching chemistry. They met off and on, and it was Kress who learned from his pupil. Although quite timid by nature, Kress in '33 had bravely stood by what he considered right. It was then that he had given Fiedler the fateful answer: "My dear Fiedler, don't come to me with your collection lists, and don't bother me either with your banned newspapers. I don't feel like risking my life for a pamphlet. When you have something that is worthwhile, come to me." Three hours ago, Fiedler had taken him at his word.

"At last!" thought Frau Fiedler, when she heard her husband's steps on the stairs. Although she disliked nothing so much as waiting, she was too proud to join the others in the kitchen.

While Fiedler was still in the hall, she saw that his face was animated and his eyes shining. "Listen well, Grete," he said. "You are to call on the Roeders now. You know the woman by sight, don't you? The stout one with the large breasts? You are to ask her for a cake recipe. She'll write it down for you and, in addition, say something, something to which you must pay particular attention. She'll either say: 'I hope you'll enjoy it,' or 'Don't eat too much of it.' All you have to do is to tell me what she said. In any event, take a roundabout way both going and coming. You must leave at once."

Grete nodded and went out. How bright his eyes had been! So, one was no longer in a state of suspension! The old ties had been fastened again, or perhaps they had never been sundered. No sooner had she started on her roundabout way to Roeder's flat than she had the impression that others, too, now unafraid, must have started after a long pause.

Frau Roeder did not recognize Fiedler's wife immediately, for her eyes were swollen with weeping. In despair, she stared disappointedly at the strange visitor whom she had hoped forlornly would change into her Paul.

Frau Fiedler grasped at once that something had gone wrong here. She would not go home, though, without her information. "*Heil Hitler!* Forgive me, Frau Roeder, for breaking in on you in the evening. And it seems I have come at a rather inopportune moment. But I wanted your recipe for the cake with icing. Your husband gave mine a taste of it. They are friends, you know. I'm Frau Fiedler. Don't you recognize me? Didn't your husband tell you that I was coming over for the recipe?

"And now, do calm down, Frau Roeder, and sit down. As long as I am here, and seeing that our husbands are friends, perhaps I can be of some help. Don't stand on ceremony, Frau Roeder; there is no necessity for that between us. Least of all in such times as these. Do stop crying, won't you? Come on, sit down over here. Tell me, what's the trouble?" By this time they had reached the kitchen and the sofa. Instead of stopping, Liesel's tears streamed afresh.

"Frau Roeder! Come, come, Frau Roeder!" said Frau Fiedler. "Rest assured, things are never half as bad as they look. So, your husband didn't tell you anything? Didn't he come home at all?"

Weeping, Liesel replied: "Only for a moment."

"Anybody call for him?" asked Frau Fiedler.

"He had to go by himself."

"By himself?"

"He had to," replied Liesel in a tired voice. She brushed her bare arms sideways over her face. "The summons was here when he came, and he was so late!"

"Then he can't be back yet," Frau Fiedler said. "Get a grip on yourself, my dear."

Liesel shrugged her shoulders. Tired out, she said dully: "Yes, he can. He'll either come back or the Gestapo will keep him there; they'll surely keep him there."

"But how can you be sure of that, Frau Roeder? He is certain to have to wait; there are always so many people there, day and night, like an endless chain."

Liesel was staring in front of her with brooding eyes; for a few minutes at least, she had stopped crying. Suddenly she turned to her visitor. "What kind of recipe? The cake with the icing? No, Paul didn't say anything about it. He was so alarmed at the summons that he rushed off right away." She got up and started to rummage in the drawer of the kitchen table. Frau Fiedler would gladly have questioned her further, for she felt that she could get anything she wanted out of Liesel. But she shrank from asking about things that her husband was keeping secret from her.

Liesel in the meantime had found a stub of a pencil and torn a page from her expense book. "I am trembling all over," she said. "Couldn't you write it down yourself?"

"Write what down?" asked Frau Fiedler.

"Five pfennigs' worth of yeast," Liesel answered, weeping; "two pounds of flour, add milk till it stiffens, a little salt. Knead well. . . ."

On her way home through the night-covered streets, Frau Fiedler could have told herself that now all the innumerable vague coincidences, all the semi-real and semi-imaginary threats, were becoming tangible and assuming definite shape; but she no longer had any time for such thoughts. To the exclusion of everything else, she gave her attention to taking the proper detours and seeing that nobody was following her. She drew a deep breath. This was the old air again, cool with danger, that touches one's brow as if it were laden with frost. The old darkness, too, under whose protection bills were posted, slogans painted on board fences, handbills slipped under doors. If someone had asked her this noon about labor conditions or the prospect of the struggle, she would have shrugged her shoulders exactly as her husband would have. Although now she had experienced nothing but a useless visit to a weeping woman, she had taken her place again in the old life. All at once everything was possible, quickly possible, for suddenly it was in her power to hasten the march of events. Everything was possible in the time that had just now begun; a sudden change in all relations, her own included, quicker than one had dared to hope, while one was still young enough jointly to partake of some happiness after so much bitter suffering. True, it was also possible that Fiedler would be destroyed, more quickly and more terribly than they had anticipated, in the fight they had undertaken. Only when nothing at all is possible any longer does life pass by like a shadow. But the periods when everything is possible contain all of life – and of destruction.

"Are you sure that nobody was trailing you?"

"I can swear to it."

"Listen now, Grete, I'll pack the most necessary things. If anybody asks where I am, I've gone to the Taunus. As for yourself, you do the following: Go to the Riederwald Settlement, Goetheblick 18. That's where Dr. Kress lives; he has a fine yellow house."

"Is that the Kress from evening school? The one with the glasses? The one who always quarreled with Balzer about Christendom and class struggles?"

"Yes. But if anybody asks you, you've never seen Kress in

all your life. Give him this message from me: 'Paul is in the hands of the Gestapo.' Give him a little time to digest this. Then ask him to tell you where he can be reached from now on. Grete dear, be careful. Never in all your life have you been implicated in such a risky affair. Don't ask me anything, please. I'm on my way now. But I'm not going to the Taunus as yet. Tomorrow morning you are to go out to the bungalow. If the police have come to the house during the night, put on your sports coat. If not, wear your new outfit. If you don't show up I'll know they've taken you. If you are wearing your new outfit – don't worry about how I'm going to find out what you are wearing – I won't need to fear going to the bungalow, and will know that things are not as bad as they might be. Is there any housekeeping money left?"

Grete gave him the few marks she still had. Silently she packed his few things. They did not kiss when they parted, but held fast to each other with both hands. As soon as Fiedler had gone, Grete put on her outing jacket. Her practical turn of mind told her that she would hardly have time to change if things took a nasty turn. If the night passed peacefully she would have plenty of time in the morning to put on her new outfit.

Kress was still standing in the same spot in the dark part of the room. Without looking at him, the woman sat down again in her chair and opened the book to where she'd been reading when the arrival of the two men had interrupted her. Her smooth blond hair, somewhat dull in daylight, shone more brightly than the electric light that illuminated it. She looked like a slender boy who has put some helmet on for fun. Speaking down to her book, she said: "I cannot read if you keep staring at me."

"You had time for reading all day. Talk to me now."

Without looking up from her book, the woman asked: "Why should I?"

"Because your voice soothes me."

"Why should you need to be soothed? There's no lack of quiet here."

The man continued to look at her steadily. She turned two or three pages. Suddenly, in a changed voice, he called her name: "Gerda!"

The woman frowned. She pulled herself together, both from habit and because she told herself that Kress was her husband, was tired from his work, and the evening together had begun. She put the open book face down on her knee and lit a cigarette. Then she said: "Whom did you pick up? A strange fellow."

Kress did not answer. Instinctively she contracted her brows and looked at her husband sharply. She was unable to distinguish his features in the dusk. What made his face shine so? Was he really as pale as that? Finally Kress said: "I suppose Frieda will be gone until the morning."

"Until the morning of the day after tomorrow."

"Listen, Gerda, you are not to tell a soul that we have a visitor. If somebody asks you, say it's a schoolmate of mine."

Without showing any surprise, she answered: "All right!" The man came close to her. Now she could see his features plainly. "Have you listened to the radio? About the West-hofen escape?"

"I? Radio? No."

"They've recaptured all of them. . ."

"Too bad."

"Except one."

A gleam came into the woman's eyes and she raised her face. Only once had it been so bright – at the beginning of their life together. Now, as then, the brightness passed quickly. She looked her husband over from head to foot. "Just think of that," she said. He waited. "I would never have given you credit for that. Just think of it!"

Kress stepped back. "What? Not given me credit for what?"

"For that! For all that! Well, really – I apologize."

"What are you talking about?" Kress asked.

"About us."

In his room George thought: "I must go downstairs. What was I hoping for up here? Why must I be alone?" Why torment himself in this blue-and-yellow locked hole, covered with hand-woven mats, with its running water from nickeled taps, and a mirror that mercilessly impressed upon him the same thing the darkness did: himself?

From the low white bed came the cool odor of freshly bleached linen. Though he was ready to drop with tiredness, he walked up and down, from the door to the window, as if he'd been deprived of his bed as a punishment. "Is this to be my last shelter? My last – before what? I must go downstairs, be with human beings." He unlocked the door.

From the stairs George could hear the voices of Kress and his wife, not loud but impressive. He was surprised. They had struck him as being almost mute, or at least extremely taciturn. Hesitating at the door, he heard Kress say: "Tell me, why do you torment me?"

The woman's rather deep voice replied: "Is that really torment to you?"

More quietly, Kress said: "I'll tell you something, Gerda. It's all the same to you why the man is in danger, all the same who he actually is – that's all the same to you. The danger is what impresses you most. Whether it is an escape or an automobile race – it makes your spirits soar. That's how you used to be, and that's how you still are."

"You are partly right, partly wrong. Perhaps I used to be

354

that way, perhaps I am again that way. Would you care to know why?" She waited a moment. Regardless of whether Kress wanted to know everything, or preferably nothing at all, his wife went on determinedly: "All the time you kept saying: 'There's nothing one can do; one is powerless against it; one has to wait.' Wait, I thought to myself! He wants to wait until everything that once was dear to him is trampled under foot. Do try to understand me. When I left my people to marry you, I wasn't yet twenty. I left home because everything there was repulsive to me – my father, my brothers, and that awful quiet every evening in our living room! But here, eventually, it was just as quiet as at home."

Kress was listening; possibly he was even more surprised than George at the door. For countless evenings he had had to pull words out of her very teeth.

"And another thing. At home nothing was ever permitted to change. It was pride that wanted everything to stay as it was. And then you! You, who suddenly told me that even in stones nothing remains stony for even a second, and least of all in human beings. Except me, of course! Isn't that so? For you say of me: 'That's how you were, and that is how you are.'"

Kress waited a second or two to see if she had finished. She had again assumed her air of indifference, even obstinacy. He put his hand on her head and grasped her hair instead of stroking it. She was both tender and tough; ready to be loved, to be taught, perhaps – who knew – to be changed. He began by shaking her gently.

George entered the room. Kress and his wife stepped apart quickly. Why the devil did Kress have to tell everything to his wife? The indifference disappeared from her face, giving way to a cool curiosity. George explained: "I can't sleep. May I stay down here with you?"

Kress, leaning against the wall, stared at him. No doubt

355

about the guest being here or the invitation having been accepted beyond recall. Assuming the manner of the master of the house, he asked: "What would you like to drink? Some tea? Schnapps? Perhaps some fruit juice? Or a beer?"

"He must be hungry," said Frau Kress.

"Tea and schnapps," said George, "and as for food, whatever you have in the house."

This sufficed to keep husband and wife in motion for several minutes. The table was laid. Large and small dishes were put down, bottles opened. Ah, to eat from seven plates and drink from seven glasses. Nobody was feeling quite at ease; the Kresses only pretended to eat. George put the white napkin in his pocket – make a good bandage for his torn hand. He pulled it out again and smoothed it. He was full now, and ready to drop with fatigue. If only they would leave him alone. He pushed knives and forks and plates aside and laid his head on the table.

It was much later when he raised his head again. The table had long since been cleared, and the room was full of smoke. George couldn't get his bearings. He felt chilly. Kress was leaning against the wall once more. For God knows what reason, George tried to smile at him; the answering smile on his host's face seemed equally oblique and labored. In the meantime Frau Kress had left the room, a fact which George rather welcomed. Kress said: "Now we'll have another drink or two." He brought back the bottles and poured out the liquor. His hand trembled slightly and he spilled a few drops. It was this very trembling that reassured George entirely. "A decent man, this – it required a great deal of effort on his part to give me shelter. But he has done so."

The woman came back into the room, sat down at the table, and smoked silently. The men, too, had grown silent.

The gravel in the path crunched under light footsteps. The steps halted at the front door. One could hear shoes shuffling on the flagstones while someone was looking for the doorbell. The two men gave a violent start, although they expected the ringing. "You met me accidentally in front of the movies," George said softly but firmly. "You had known me in the chemistry course." Kress nodded. Like many timid people he was calm in the face of actual danger. His wife got up and went to the window. Her face wore an expression of haughtiness and the slight scorn it always displayed at any risky undertaking. She raised the shade, peered out, and announced: "A woman."

"Open the door for her," said George, "but have her wait outside."

"She wants to speak to my husband personally. She looks quite decent."

"How does she know I'm at home?"

"Because you spoke to her husband at six o'clock."

Kress went outside. His wife sat down again at the table with George. She went on smoking, now and then glancing at him shortly as if they were both caught on a sharp turn of the road or against an ice-covered, extremely difficult steep mountainside.

Kress returned, and his face told George that the worst had happened. "I am to tell you, George, that your Paul is at the Gestapo. To be on the safe side, the woman's husband has already left his home. We must tell her where we are going now – or you, George, if you go alone – so that one can get in touch with you." He poured himself a drink.

"He hasn't spilled anything," George thought. His head felt entirely empty as if, instead of having been stuffed with new food for thought, it had been swept bare as a board.

"We could take you somewhere in the car. . . or should we all go? The three of us in the car? Where? Straight to the East Station? Or just far out into the country? To Kassel? Or, better yet, shall we separate at once?"

"Do keep quiet for a moment, please. . ."

The thoughts came pouring back into his empty head. So Paul had been nabbed. Stop! Why nabbed? Had somebody reported him? Had he been summoned? Nothing had been said about that. At any rate, they've got him by the collar. And Paul himself? If they could prove that Paul had sheltered him, if they could actually prove that. . . Paul would never divulge George's new hiding place. Did Paul even know it? Well, not the hiding place itself. If the go-between was reliable, really one of our own men, he gave no names. But Paul knew the car number, that was enough. George recalled others who had been stronger than Paul, men with the strength of giants, their craftiness and experience gained in all the battles they had witnessed since their youth. Even they had been worn down, and deathly fear had made every bit of information ooze out through the cracks. But Paul would not betray him. The daring thought that took shape in George's mind required all his courage and a quick decision. He had confidence in Paul. His teeth gritted, he would be lying where others before him had lain, and his obstinate silence would in time become effortless and final.

Perhaps, too, it was just an ordinary questioning. He'd stand there, short and stupid, giving harmless answers in a carefully shrewd manner. "We'll stay!" George announced.

"Wouldn't it be better to go away?"

"No. Anything else would only get us into difficulties. Here I was to have received instructions, money, and papers. If I have to go away, I am lost again."

Kress was silent. George guessed his thoughts. "If you want to get rid of me because you are afraid. . ."

"If I were afraid," said Kress, "it would not be the cause of my sending you away. You alone know this man Paul. It's all up to you now."

"All right," said George, "tell the woman out there that we'll stay where we are."

Kress went out at once. George liked him better every minute.

He appreciated the readiness with which the weaker part of Kress's nature subordinated itself after a brief struggle to the stronger, even the honesty of his fear which did not for a second try to hide behind bragging and talk. George liked him better than he did the woman. She had finished the last of her cigarettes and was blowing smoke into the air. He imagined that she had never had anything that she feared losing.

Kress returned. They listened to the steps receding in the direction of the settlement. When all was quiet again, the woman said: "Let's go upstairs for a change."

"All right," said Kress. "We couldn't sleep anyway."

Under the eaves, Kress had made himself a den with the aid of a few hundred books. From the window one could see that the house stood at the end of a new street, a little way from the Riederwald Settlement. The sky was clear. It was a long time since George had seen a cloudless starry sky – it had been foggy near the Rhine. He looked up as do all who are in deadly peril, as though the sky were a protecting arch over him and his kind. Frau Kress drew the shades and turned on the heat, things that Kress himself was in the habit of doing when he came home early of an afternoon. She swept the books off some chairs and the corner of a table. "Now Paul is being tortured," thought George, "and Liesel is sitting at home waiting." His heart contracted with fear and doubt. Had he been justified in giving his life into Paul's hands? Was Paul strong enough? Well, it was too late now, he couldn't get out of it now. The Kresses were silent; they were probably thinking that he was about to fall asleep. But

George, his hands shielding his face, was seeking counsel from Wallau. *Be calm! Remember what is at stake here, and that its being labeled George for a week is but incidental.*

With a sudden excess of cheerfulness, George turned to his host and asked him his age and profession. He was thirty-four, said Kress, and his profession was physical chemistry. George wanted to know what that was. Kress, relieved, tried to explain. At first George listened attentively, but then his thoughts returned to Paul, to Paul covered with blood, and to Liesel waiting. Kress put his own interpretation on George's silence. "There'd still be time," he said softly.

"Time? For what?"

"To get away from here."

"Haven't we decided to stay here? Don't give it another thought, please."

George turned to the woman and asked her casually about her home and her childhood. She gave a slight start, something Kress had never known her to do. At once she began: "My father joined the Army when he was still quite young. He didn't show any particular aptitude, so that when he left the service at the age of forty-four, he was only a major. There were five of us, four brothers and myself, and he had a chance to torment us until we were grown up."

"And your mother?" George was never to know anything about Frau Kress's mother because a motorcar stopped so near that all three held their breath. The car drove away, but it had killed all further desire for talk. George was thinking of Paul again; he asked his pardon for having been frightened a moment ago, as if, like Kress, he were prepared for every eventuality. Just the same, at the sound of the next automobile he gave an equally violent start. They had ceased talking. The night dragged on interminably in the smoke-filled room.

Chapter VII

i

At last the night was over. Both men had been startled whenever a car came up from the Riederwald Settlement, or they heard the steps of the policemen on patrol. As the night wore on, these attacks of fright had become more violent and lasting, as if their bodies had lost their weight.

When the woman raised the blinds, opened the window, and turned back into the bright room, it seemed to her that the two men had aged and grown thin during the night, her own husband as well as the stranger. She shuddered slightly. A glance at the flat nickeled bottom of the table lamp showed the reflection of her own face, unmarred except for the slight paleness of her lips. "The night is over!" she announced. "I, for my part, am going to bathe and put on a Sunday dress."

"And I am going to make some coffee," said Kress. "How about you, George?"

There was no answer. When the bracing morning air had rushed into the room through the open window, George had been overcome by the cumulative effect of sleepiness and exhaustion. Kress went over to the chair in which he had slumped down, his forehead against the edge of the table. Noticing that the edge was cutting into George's flesh, Kress raised the head of the sleeping man and turned it a bit. A corner of his mind began to question him as to how long he would have to shelter this guest. Ashamed that such a question should even have been thought of, he gruffly ordered this part of his ego to keep quiet. "You are mistaken," he said to himself. "I'd shelter even his corpse."

It was not long before George roused himself, perhaps at the slamming of a door. Still befuddled by sleep, he yielded to his old compulsion to account for the various noises in the house: this was the coffee grinder, that the running bath water. He wanted to get up and join Kress in the kitchen. He wanted to fight the sleep that was trying to engulf him again, an unsatisfactory sleep. But there, it had already come over him. His last conscious thought was that it was only a dream that threatened him; he would resist being drawn into it. But now it was stronger than he. . . .

So he was caught after all. They threw him into Barrack VIII. He was already bleeding from many wounds, but fear of what was bound to come made him forget his pain. He said to himself: "Courage, George!" But he knew that here in this barrack the most gruesome of fates loomed ahead of him. And there it was!

Behind a table covered with electric cords and telephone apparatus, but otherwise not unlike a table at an inn – between the cords he could see a few cardboard disks that they put under beer glasses – sat Fahrenberg himself, staring at him with his narrow piercing eyes and his frozen smile. At his right and left sat Bunsen and Zillich, their heads turned toward him. Bunsen laughed loudly, but Zillich was as gloomy as always. He was counting out cards from a deck. The room was dark, except for the slight glow above the table, although George could see no lamp. One of the wires was wound three times round Zillich's powerful body; this sent icy showers of horror down George's spine. All the same, his thoughts were quite clear: "They are actually playing cards with Zillich." So after all there were tables where class distinctions were disregarded!

"Come closer," said Fahrenberg. But George stayed where he was, from obstinacy as well as because his knees were shaking. He waited for Fahrenberg to roar at him, but Fahrenberg only winked at him with incomprehensible understanding. George, startled, looked from one to the other. Suddenly he noticed that the flesh on Zillich's cheek that was turned toward him was apparently rotting away, one ear on Bunsen's handsomely shaped head was crumbling off, and so was his forehead in one place. George realized that the three men were dead and that he himself, whom they received in eternal concord, had likewise already died.

He screamed at the top of his voice: "Mother!" With one hand he grasped the base of a table lamp; it catapulted over one of his legs and crashed down onto the floor. The two Kresses came rushing into the room. George was wiping his face and looking about the bright disordered room. He offered his embarrassed apologies.

Frau Kress with her thin bare arms, and wet, shaggy hair, looked exceedingly comforting, young, and clean. They led him to the table, sat him between them, poured him some coffee, and filled his plate. "What are you thinking of now, George?"

"Of the thing that has such power over us. How long do you think I could stay here if worse comes to worst?"

"Until your relief comes," Kress said firmly, as if he had not been asking himself at the time how long he could stand this waiting.

ii

At that hour, Fiedler was sitting in the bungalow in the Taunus which he and his brother-in-law had leased. Before going there he had made sure that his wife was wearing the clothes that had been agreed upon if the night had passed uneventfully.

So Roeder as yet had betrayed nothing. He had not given away his middleman. If he had, the pack would already be on his trail. Not as yet! That merely signified a certain degree of steadfastness, nothing lasting.

Frau Fiedler had lighted the little stove that served for both heating and cooking. The frame hut was painted neatly on the outside; inside it was so orderly that it seemed the Fiedlers no longer expected to do a lot of moving. Especially during this last and more peaceful year, Fiedler had put in a good deal of work on the bungalow. Frau Fiedler served his coffee on the table that he himself had planned and built. It was many-hinged and could be folded in various ways to suit requirements. The wood was ordinary pine, but Fiedler's planning and polishing had given it a nice grain.

Through a small bright windowpane, which he himself had put in the sash, he looked out upon the distant spires of the city through a loose hedge sprinkled with innumerable dog roses. If Roeder had not talked during the night, it was possible that he would begin tomorrow; perhaps he was talking at this very moment. Suppose when Roeder came to the shop tomorrow he was followed by two shadows, and he pointed out Fiedler to them? "No," said Fiedler aloud. Even the Roeder of his imagination refused to be drawn into this imaginary betrayal. "What do you mean, no?" asked Fiedler's wife.

Fiedler only shook his head with a strange smile. Under

no circumstances could Heisler stay where he was for very long. Counsel and help were needed. Had not Fiedler protested to himself all through the year that he was entirely alone and knew no one to whom he could turn? There was possibly one, but only one – Reinhardt. Although this one possibility worked at Fiedler's own plant, he had steadfastly avoided him. Why? For a variety of reasons, among which – as is always the case when there is a variety of reasons – the main one was lacking. For instance, Fiedler thought he ought to avoid this man so as not to burden someone who perhaps had great responsibilities at Pokorny's. Another time Fiedler decided to avoid him because they had known each other before and Reinhardt might talk about him carelessly. Thus his reasons for avoiding him were contradictory – distrust, the utmost confidence. Now, however, that Heisler was at stake, he could lose no more time; not a single minute must be spent fussing about his reasons. Suddenly Fiedler realized what the real reason was: he knew that, once face to face with this man, there was no escaping from him; he would have to decide definitely whether he meant to stay away forever – withdraw from everybody and everything – or continue to belong. In his own way, this man likewise had the power to possess himself of a man's inmost soul.

The man in whom Fiedler put so much confidence was lying in bed in a darkened room, enjoying his Sunday rest and listening sleepily to the noises in his flat.

In a corner of the kitchen his wife was feeding their grandchild, for their daughter had gone off on a Strength through Joy excursion to some vintage festival. He had been quite young when he married. His hair was of a mottled gray, as if it were only now beginning to turn or had long since been white and was now discolored by metal dust. His lean, ageless face was not remarkable in any respect unless one came within the range of his eyes, and then only if something in that person excited their attention. Then they would shine with a mixture of kindness and distrust and love of sarcasm, and perhaps the hope of having found a new friend.

Although he had been awake a long time, he kept his eyes closed. Another minute, and he would have to get up. This Sunday, his rest would have to be abandoned. He must try to find the man of whom he'd been thinking for an hour. Perhaps this man had gone off on a workingmen's excursion. Reinhardt had heard about little Roeder from Hermann and he knew him when he saw him; but it would be impossible in this semidarkness of rumors and conjectures to approach him directly when so much was at stake. The man he'd been thinking about was the very man to sound Roeder out.

Perhaps it was all his imagination. True, names and places had been mentioned in the police reports. A few streets had been combed, a few flats searched. Perhaps they were using this rumor of an escape only as a pretext for some arrests, for some random grillings. Since yesterday the radio had been strangely silent. Perhaps Heisler had already been captured and was chasing through the city only in people's gossip, keeping under cover in imaginary hiding places, escaping again and again by means of countless ruses – a dream known to many. To him, Reinhardt, this solution seemed highly probable. In this case, the yellow envelope Hermann had handed to him was intended for a spectral George – a borrowed passport for a shadow. In these times, when people's lives were confined within suffocatingly narrow limits, everything that came within the scope of wishes and dreams was possible.

The last minute of his Sunday morning rest was over. With a sigh he put his feet on the floor. He must see this man in Roeder's shop immediately; he would be able to determine what part of this story was actually flesh and blood. He must be prepared for the story of the escape to vanish into thin air, but at the same time he must take it seriously enough for immediate action. Even Hermann, his dearest friend, had, in spite of all his doubts, acted without delay, as if no doubts were admissible. From the first minute he had busied himself with securing money and papers. Reinhardt's eyes shone at the thought of Hermann: a man who gave one not only the strength to do many extremely difficult things, but also the strength to do many extremely difficult things in vain. His gray eyes dulled and he knitted his brows as he thought of the man whom he had to see, the man in Roeder's shop.

It was true that this man would be able to give him some general information about Roeder, for he had worked with him at Pokorny's for several years. He would also keep silent about being questioned. But the man was likely to hesitate, as he had hesitated for a long time. Reinhardt had studied him closely. Would he be able to lift the intimidated frightened man out of himself this morning?

He sat down on his bed and put on his socks. The doorbell rang. There must be no interference now because Monday might be too late; he would have to go today, at once. His wife came to his door to announce a visitor. "It's me," said Fiedler as he entered the room. Reinhardt pulled up the shade, the better to see his caller. Fiedler was now conscious of Reinhardt's eyes being turned upon him – those eyes of which he had stood in awe a whole year. Yet it was Reinhardt who was the first to lower his and to say with dismay and embarrassment: "You, Fiedler? I was on the point of going to see you; I've got myself in a position where I have to confide in somebody. I don't know, though, whether you understand why I've kept away so long."

"I, too, have kept away," replied Fiedler, "and I feel I ought to explain. . . "

Reinhardt quickly assured him that he understood everything. As if it were his turn to apologize, he told about an
episode that had occurred in '23. He had been stationed in
the vicinity of Bielefeld when General Watter had marched
in. He'd been so beside himself with terror that he had kept
himself hidden for weeks. Finally, when the terror had
passed, his shame and anger at having been so terror-
stricken made him keep on hiding.

After Reinhardt had thus spared him an explanation of
his own behavior, Fiedler proceeded at once with the story
of what had brought him here. Reinhardt listened quietly.

After Reinhardt had been told everything, he left Fiedler
alone for a couple of minutes so that the latter in turn might
have an opportunity fully to realize the gravity of the step
he had taken, a step which had proved so easy and so hard
at the same time. When Reinhardt returned he laid a tough
yellow envelope in front of Fiedler. It contained papers made
out in the name of the nephew of a captain on a Dutch tugboat; the young man usually accompanied his uncle on the
trip to and from Mainz. Luckily he had been reached in
Bingen; he'd gladly yielded his papers and passport, especially since he still had in his pocket a regular permit to
cross the border. The passport photo had been touched up
with the utmost skill so that it would resemble the picture
in the warrants for Heisler's arrest.

Inside the passport were several banknotes. Fiedler flattened the envelope as much as possible with the edge of his
hand, a motion which was as practical as it was tender.
Within this envelope was the result of a vast amount of
dangerous and painstaking work; it represented innumerable errands, information, lists, the work of past years, old
friendships and connections, the Association of Seamen
and Dock Workers, a whole network that spanned oceans
and rivers. But the life of the man whose fingers were now

368

touching this network was narrow and heavy; the few banknotes represented an enormous sum for these times – the
District Leader's emergency fund for special cases. Fiedler
put the envelope in his pocket.

"Are you going to take it to him yourself?"

"No, my wife will."

"Are you sure she's all right?"

"Even more so perhaps than I myself."

Her eyes blinded with tears, Liesel Roeder fed and dressed
the children after a sleepless night. "Why, it's Sunday," said
the oldest boy when she gave him bread instead of a roll.
On Sundays, Paul usually brought in warm rolls from the
baker's across the street. This memory made Liesel's tears
flow anew. The children dunked and munched, intimidated,
uncomprehending, and offended.

Well, Paul had not come home, and their life together
had come to an end. Judging by the sobs that shook Liesel,
life with the vanished Paul must have been incomparably
happy. Liesel had put all her strength not into their future,
not even into the children's future, but in their present life
together. As she looked down into the street with her unsee-
ing swollen eyes, she hated everybody who had dared to lay
hands upon that life, be it with persecutions and threats, or
even with promises of better things to come.

The children at the table were finished eating, but they
stayed there, strangely silent.

"Will they beat him?" Liesel asked herself. She saw her
own ruined life in all its details, and all that was to follow.
The other person's ruined life was more difficult to visualize, even though that other person was Paul. "What if they
beat him until he confesses where George is? If he confessed,
would they let him come home? Could he come home at
once? Could everything be again as it had been before?"

Liesel's thoughts stopped. Her tears ceased. Her heart was struck by a foreboding that for her even to continue her train of thought was not permissible. Nothing could ever be as it had been. Ordinarily, Liesel had no comprehension of anything outside her orbit of life. She knew nothing of the shadow behind the border posts of reality, and less than nothing of the strange proceedings that take place between the border posts: when reality fades into nothingness and can never return, or when the shadows show a desire to come crowding back in order to be taken for real once more.

At that moment, though, even Liesel understood the meaning of an imaginary world, an illusory Paul who, even though he returned, was not Paul any more, a family that could no longer be called a family, and a life together which, because of a few words of confession spoken in a Gestapo cellar on an October night, had ceased to be a life.

Liesel shook her head and turned away from the window. She sat with her children on the kitchen sofa. The eldest boy she made change his dirty stockings for the clean ones that had been drying on a stick over the kitchen stove. She held the girl on her knee and sewed on a button.

iii

Mettenheimer told himself that he was still being shadowed continuously, but the thought no longer filled him with the old fear. "Let them trail me," he said to himself with a kind of pride, "for only in that way will they get to know what a really honest man is like."

Even so, he continued to pray that George would vanish from his life without bringing any harm to Elly, but also without his needing to heap sin upon his own soul.

Perhaps the shabby little fellow who sat down beside him on the bench was replacing that bowler-hatted man who had almost driven him to despair last week. All the same, Mettenheimer waited calmly for the caretaker's family to return from church and unlock the house. "A splendid house," thought Mettenheimer. "The people who built that had no venom in their spleen."

The two-storied white house with its low, slightly curved roof and its beautiful portal, curved with the same arc, looked larger from the top of the sloping garden than it actually was. Originally it had been outside the city, but the spreading city had overtaken it. For its sake, the street had been given a slight curve, for the house was too fine to be torn down. It was a house for a loving couple who relied on the constancy both of their feelings and of their outward circumstances, and who anticipated grandchildren even on their honeymoon.

"A nice house," said the shabby little man. Mettenheimer looked at him. "It's a good thing that it's being fixed up a bit," continued the man, "and that others are going to move in for a change."

"Why, are you the new tenant?" asked Mettenheimer.

"Good Lord! Me?" The little man had a laughing fit.

"I'm the paperhanger here, you know," said Mettenheimer drily. The little man looked at him respectfully. Since Mettenheimer was less than talkative, he soon got up, gave his *Heil Hitler!* and left. "That surely wasn't even a police spy," thought Mettenheimer.

He was on the point of getting up to assure himself that he had not accidentally missed the caretaker's family when he saw Schulz, his chief workman, come from the streetcar stop. Mettenheimer was surprised to see Schulz display so much zeal on the Sabbath.

371

Schulz seemed to be in no hurry, though, to go to the house. He sat down in the bright sunshine beside Mettenheimer. "A fine autumn day, Herr Mettenheimer."

"Mmm!"

"Weather won't last very long though. The sky was very red last night."

"That so?"

"Herr Mettenheimer," said Schulz, "your daughter, Elly, who called for you yesterday. . ."

Mettenheimer turned around abruptly. Schulz grew embarrassed. "What about her?" asked Mettenheimer, annoyed for some reason or other.

"Why, nothing, nothing at all," said Schulz, quite confused. "She's really quite good-looking. It's surprising she didn't marry again, long ago."

Mettenheimer's eyes grew angry. "That's Elly's affair, I suppose."

"Partly," said Schulz. "Has she divorced Heisler?"

Mettenheimer's wrath was now fully aroused. "Why don't you go ask Elly herself?"

"The man really has difficulty in understanding," Schulz thought. "I could do that," he said quietly, "but I thought you'd like it better if the two of us talked things over first."

"What things, for Heaven's sake?" Mettenheimer asked with dismay.

Schulz sighed. "Herr Mettenheimer," he began in a different tone of voice, "I have known your family for nearly ten years, almost as long as you and I have worked together for the same firm. In past years your Elly used to come to where we were working once in a while. When I saw her again yesterday, it went through and through me."

Mettenheimer sucked in his mustache and began chewing it. "At last!" thought Schulz. He continued: "I am a man without prejudices. There's that story about George Heisler that is going the rounds. Well, I never knew the man. Confidentially, Herr Mettenheimer, I – I hope with all my heart that he will succeed in getting away. I say now what others are merely thinking. Then your Elly could immediately enter a plea of desertion. And there's Heisler's child, too. Yes, I know. If he's a nice child, well, there'll already be a child."

Softly, Mettenheimer said: "He is a nice child."

"All right. If I were Heisler I'd say to myself, 'It's better to let Schulz take care of the child – after all, he's a man like myself – than to let him fall into the hands of those scoundrels and be made into a scoundrel himself.' By the time Heisler's boy is ready to join us on the job, the reign of the scoundrels will have come to an end."

Mettenheimer, startled, looked around, but as far as he could see they were alone in the autumn sun. "If, on the other hand, Heisler should be captured," Schulz said softly, "or has already been captured – there was nothing on the radio about him either yesterday or today – then there is no escape for the poor devil; his life is gone, and Elly won't even have to enter a plea of desertion."

They were looking in front of them. Scattered over the quiet sunny street lay the leaves from the garden. Mettenheimer thought: "Schulz is a steady worker; he's got a heart and a brain, and he's good-looking. I've always wanted a man like him for Elly. Why didn't he become a member of my family long ago? We might have been spared much."

Schulz went on. "A long time ago, Herr Mettenheimer, you were kind enough to ask me to call on you. I didn't take advantage of your invitation then. Will you permit me, Herr Mettenheimer, to make up now for my neglect? But you must promise me, Herr Mettenheimer, to say nothing to Elly about our conversation. If I call, Herr Mettenheimer, and your daughter Elly happens to be in the room, why, it will be just an accidental meeting. Girls of her type don't like to

373

have things prearranged. They want to be wooed by a man who knows his own mind and is ready to storm the fortress."

When a man is condemned to wait, when the waiting is a matter of life and death, and he is not able to foresee how long it will last or how it will end, he will take the strangest measures against time. He will try to catch the minutes and annihilate them. He will try to build a kind of dike against time, and continue to plug up the holes in it though the water has started to seep through long ago.

George, who was still sitting at the Kresses' table, had made such attempts in the beginning. Soon, however, he had withdrawn imperceptibly. He was determined to stop waiting. Kress told how and where he had made Fiedler's acquaintance. George listened unwillingly at first, but then with real interest. Kress described Fiedler as an unchangeable man who was open to no doubts or fears. A Babel of voices outside the window made Kress stop, but it was just an ordinary Sunday excursion. Kress got up and twirled the knobs of the radio. The fag end of a morning concert killed a few minutes. George asked him to bring a map and tell him about several things he was determined to find out. Barely two weeks ago, a newly arrived prisoner at Westhofen had fashioned a Spain from some splinters of wood on the damp ground and marked the scenes of the war with his forefinger. George remembered how the man had rubbed the thing out with his wooden shoe at the guard's approach. He was a little printer from Hanau. George stopped, and time came rushing in. Suddenly, as if someone had commanded her to say something, Kress's wife volunteered the information that one of her brothers had gone to Spain on Franco's side, and that Benno, her childhood friend and her brother's friend as well, had wanted to go with him. She kept on talking so as not to give time another chance, like a person that grasps the first thing that comes to hand to stop a gap.

"I hesitated a long time whether to take you or Benno."

"Me or Benno?"

"Yes. On the whole, I felt more at home with him. But I wanted to go somewhere else." Her efforts were useless; the few words she spoke took hardly any time at all.

"Go on and work, Kress, or do whatever you were planning to," said George. "Or why don't you take your wife out for a nice Sunday walk? Forget for a few hours that I am here. I'm going upstairs." Much to the couple's surprise, he got up.

"He's right," said Kress. "Or rather, he would be right if one could really do that."

"Of course one can," answered his wife. "As for me, I'm going out in the garden to transplant the tulip bulbs."

"Roeder will never betray me," said George to himself when he was alone, "but he may make a false move. He doesn't know how to answer, he doesn't know how to act. He mustn't be blamed for anything. When one is weakened by blows and ill from lack of sleep, his quick-wittedness is apt to forsake him. Then even the shrewdest man becomes dull and stupid. Paul was certainly seen with Fiedler every day. The Gestapo didn't have far to look. But Paul ought not to be blamed."

Every enclosed space being odious to him, he went to the window. He saw the white road that bisected the settlement. Beyond it – the settlement resembled an all-too-clean village – he could see parks and forests.

He was overcome by a feeling of abject homelessness that was almost immediately followed by a feeling of pride. Was there any man who could look with the same eyes at the wide steel-blue sky and the road which, for him only, led into a perfect wilderness? He contemplated the people who were passing – people in their Sunday clothes accompanied by children and old women and strange packages; a motorcyclist with a girl on the seat behind him; two youths; a man with a folding-boat sack on his back; an SA man leading a child; a young woman carrying a bunch of asters.

Presently the doorbell rang. "Never mind," said George to himself. "I suppose there are any number of rings here in the course of the day." House and street remained quiet. Kress came up the stairs. "Come out on the landing a minute." With knitted brows George looked at the young woman with the asters who was suddenly standing there in Kress's house, three steps below him.

"I am to hand you something," she said, "and in addition I am to tell you that tomorrow morning at half-past five you are to be at the Kastella Bridge landing in Mainz. The ship's name is *Wilhelmine*. You are expected."

"Good!" said George, but he didn't budge.

Without letting go of her flowers, the woman unbuttoned the pocket of her jacket. She handed George a thick envelope. "Now I have delivered this envelope to you." From her attitude it could be assumed that she took George for a comrade who had to hide, but that she did not know his identity.

"All right!" said George.

Liesel, grinding some malt coffee for the children, had failed completely to hear the key turn in the lock. In his hand Paul carried a paper bag of rolls he had brought on the way home. "Come on, Liesel," he said, "wash your face with vinegar water, change your dress, and we'll be in time for the match. Why, Liesel, what is there to bawl about now?"

He laid his hand on her hair, for she had put her head on the table. "Come on. Stop. That's enough. Didn't I promise you I'd be back?"

"Oh, Lord!" sobbed Liesel.

"He hasn't anything to do with it, or at least not more than He has to do with everything. He surely has no extra

376

dealings with the Gestapo. Everything was as I expected it to be. A great hocus-pocus. They sweated me for hours. What I never dreamed of was that they'd let me sit down through it all and that they'd take down all I spouted. In the end I even had to sign my name to it to prove that it was all my own. When had I known George, where, how long; who were his friends, who mine. And they also asked me about my visitor day before yesterday.

"They threatened me with every imaginable thing that can be used as a threat. Hell-fire was the only thing they left out. But in every other respect they apparently wanted me to think they were the Day of Judgment... But they are a long way from knowing everything. They only know what they are told."

Later, when Liesel felt a little cleaner, had put on her own Sunday clothes, changed the children's clothes, and washed her face, Paul began again: "What surprises me is that those people talk so much. Why? Because they think they know everything anyway. I said to myself: 'Nobody can prove that George was actually at my flat. Even if somebody saw him, I could still deny it. Nobody has any proof that it was he, except George himself. Well, if they've got him, everything's over anyway. But if they had him they wouldn't be asking me so many questions.'"

Twenty minutes later, they left for town. They made a detour to leave the children with Paul's family for the afternoon. The smallest one had been left with the janitress, in accordance with an arrangement made several days ago. Although Paul strongly suspected the woman of having reported him, he knew that, generally speaking, she was obliging and fond of children.

Suddenly Paul asked Liesel to wait with the children – there was something he had to attend to. He went through a gate. The little window in the garage was lighted as usual,

377

although there was full daylight in the yard. In order not to keep his family waiting, he went quickly to the window to settle this disagreeable matter. "Aunt Katharina!" he called.

When Frau Grabber's head appeared he said quickly and without stopping: "My brother-in-law sends his apologies. The police in Offenbach sent him another summons. He had to go home again, and it's doubtful whether he'll come back. I'm very sorry, Aunt Katharina, but it wasn't my fault."

After a minute's silence, Frau Grabber roared: "For my part, he can stay away altogether! I was going to kick him out anyway! Don't ever dare bring me such trash again!"

"Well, well, well," said Paul, "after all you haven't lost anything by it. You've had your cars overhauled gratis. *Heil Hitler!*"

Frau Grabber sat down behind her desk. The red date on her calendar told her it was Sunday. On Sundays the moving vans usually remained at their destination. She no longer had any family; if she'd had any she wouldn't have gone to see them. Her disappointment was out of all proportion to the unimportant fact that Paul's brother-in-law was not going on working for her. This summons was probably just an excuse; he hadn't liked it here. But then he shouldn't have had a drink with her last night. "He shouldn't have done that," she thought, furious. "That was a mean thing to do."

She looked about her in the immeasurable desolation of the Sunday, a veritable deluge of desolation on which a few objects were floating – a little mountain of malachite, a lamp, a ledger, a calendar.

Frau Grabber rushed to the window and shouted into the yard: "Paul!" But Paul was already far away with Liesel, headed for the Niederrad Stadium.

Partly happy and partly with a guilty conscience, Hermann watched his wife making herself pretty, singing the while. They had been invited to the Marnets this Sunday.

With her damply brushed hair, her candid eyes, her neck chain, and her stiffly ironed dress she was not unlike a robust child about to be confirmed. Although it was only a ten-minute walk up the hill, she put on her hat – "Just to show the Marnets." That Else, silly little Else, had got this well-paid elderly railway worker for a husband still stuck in Cousin Augusta Marnet's throat.

Amused, Hermann watched Else's face as they approached Marnet's house. He knew every one of her emotions, just as one soon becomes familiar with the emotions of a little bird. How proud she was of a marriage that she considered indestructible. "Why are you looking at me in that funny way?" Was it good or bad that she had begun to ask questions?

The whole Marnet family and their guests were seated around the table in Marnet's damp hot kitchen. Once a year, after the apple picking, they had applecakes up here in tins that were as big as the table. Every mouth was shiny with juice and sugar, the children's no less than the soldiers', and even Augusta's thin, stingy lips. The huge coffee pot, the somewhat smaller milk pitcher, and the onion-patterned cups on the table looked like a family themselves. A whole clan was gathered round the table: Frau Marnet and her diminutive husband; her grandsons – little Ernst and Gustav; her daughter Augusta; her son-in-law and her eldest son – both of them in SA uniform; her soldier boy – new and shiny; Messer's second son – a recruit; his youngest son, in SS uniform (Applecake is applecake!); Eugenie – handsome and proud; Sophie Mangold – a bit exhausted. Ernst was there, without his neckcloth, but wearing a tie – his mother was tending his flock; Franz, who jumped up when he saw Hermann and Else come in. At the head of the table, in the place of honor, sat Sister Anastasia of the Koenigsberg Ursulines, the white wings of her headdress fluttering.

Else sat down proudly among the women of her family.

Her firm childish hand, adorned by her wedding ring, reached delightedly for the applecake. Hermann sat down next to Franz. "Last week Dora Katzenstein came to say good-by to me," said Sister Anastasia. "I used to buy material for my orphans in her store. 'Don't tell anybody, Sister,' she said, 'but we'll be going away soon.' She cried too. Yesterday Katzenstein's shutters were closed and the key was under the door mat. When the door was opened everything inside was bare. Only the yardstick was lying on the counter."

"Well, they were careful not to go until the last yard of calico was sold," said Augusta.

"If we had to go away we'd wait ourselves until the last potato was gathered," said her mother.

"Why, you don't mean to compare our potatoes with Katzenstein's calico?"

"There are comparisons between everything."

Messer's SS son said: "Well, one Sarah less!" and spat on the floor. Frau Marnet would have preferred him to spit almost anywhere else than on her clean kitchen floor. At any rate, it was not easy to spread horror in Marnet's kitchen. If the Four Horsemen of the Apocalypse had come rushing by on that Sunday, they would have tied their horses to the garden fence and behaved like rational guests.

"It didn't take you long to get a furlough, Fritzchen," said Hermann to Marnet, his cousin by marriage.

"Didn't you read about it in the paper? Every mother is to have her joy on Sunday by seeing a brand-new recruit in the house."

Eugenie said: "One's son is a joy no matter what he wears." Everybody looked at her with a little embarrassment, but she went on calmly: "A new coat is naturally nicer than an old one with holes, especially if the holes go deep."

The others were glad when Sister Anastasia bridged the awkward pause by reverting to her earlier subject: "Dora was quite a decent person."

. "She couldn't carry a tune," said Augusta, "when we were at school together."

"Quite decent," said Frau Marnet. "I'd like to know how many bolts of calico she's carried on her back." Dora Katzenstein was already on the emigrant ship when the tender obituary flag was hoisted in Marnet's kitchen in her honor.

"I suppose you two will be getting married soon?" Sister Anastasia asked.

"Us?" exclaimed Sophie and Ernst. They moved away from each other with decision. How strange that from her place of honor the Sister seemed to be able to look not only across the table but under it as well.

"When are you going to be called up for service?" asked Frau Marnet. "That would be a good thing for you, Ernst, you wouldn't get out of things so easily."

"Why, he hasn't been at a military drill for months," said the SA Marnet.

"I'm excused from all the drills," countered Ernst, "because I'm with the Air Raid Protection."

Everybody laughed except the SS Messer; he looked at Ernst with disgust. "I suppose you have to fit your sheep with gas masks."

Ernst turned suddenly to Messer, whose gaze he had felt. "Well, what about you, Messer? I suppose you'll find it hard to exchange your fine black coat for an ordinary soldier's tunic."

"Won't have to," growled Messer, but before an awkward pause could occur or worse be said, Sister Anastasia interrupted: "You have learned that from us, Augusta, putting grated nuts on the applecake."

"I'm going to get a breath of air," said Hermann. Franz went with him into the garden. The sky arching over the plain was changing color, and the birds were flying low.

"The good weather will be gone tomorrow," said Franz. "Ah, Hermann. . ."

"What are you ah-ing about?"

"Neither yesterday nor today was there anything on the radio – nothing about the escape, nothing about the warrant of seizure, nothing about George."

"I wish you'd stop worrying about that, Franz. It'd be better for you and better for everyone. It takes up entirely too much of your thoughts. Everything that could be done for your George has already been done."

For a second an expression of animation crept into Franz's face that showed clearly that he was not at all slow and sleepy but was capable of feeling and doing everything. "Is he safe?" he asked.

"Not yet. . ."

iv

Fahrenberg stood in front of the column which, Sundays and weekdays, was lined up at six P.M. Zillich no longer headed the SA; this place was held by his successor, Uhlenhaut. The SS were led not by Bunsen – he was on leave – but by Hattendorf, a man with a long, horselike face. After the tortures of the past week, though formerly they had been quick to perceive the slightest change, the prisoners were in a strangely apathetic frame of mind, dull and obstinate.

None of them could have said whether the three remaining fugitives now being dragged toward their trees were dead or still alive. All in all, the whole Dancing Ground in front of the barrack somehow resembled an intermediate landing station; the place was hardly of this earth, nor was it part of the beyond. Fahrenberg himself, as he stood facing the column, seemed as shrunk and emaciated and tormented as all the others.

Into the dulled heads of the prisoners bored a voice – detached words, something of Justice and the long arm of the Law, the people and the canker on the body of the State, the escape and the day it had occurred – just a week ago tomorrow. But the prisoners were listening to the faint sounds of drunken peasants in distant villages.

Suddenly a shock went through every man in the column of prisoners. What had Fahrenberg said just now? If Heisler had been caught, everything was finished.

"Finished," said one of the men on the way back. This was the only word that was spoken.

An hour later though, in the barrack, one man said to another through motionless lips – talking was prohibited – "Do you think they've really got him?" and the other replied: "No, I don't believe it." The one was Schenk, whom Roeder had vainly tried to visit; and the other was a newcomer, a workman from Ruesselsheim. Schenk went on: "Did you see the embarrassment on their faces? Did you see them wink at each other? The old man couldn't get his voice pitched right. No, that wasn't on the level today. They haven't got him."

Only those very near the two men could understand what they were saying, but the sense of their words spread from one man to another during the evening.

Bunsen had taken two young friends with him when he went on leave – handsome, witty chaps, though not as brilliant as himself; this made them all the more suitable for companions.

While Fahrenberg was making his speech, Bunsen and his two satellites were alighting at the Rheinischer Hof in

Wiesbaden. Followed by the two men, and taking every-thing in quickly, Bunsen entered the ballroom. It was still rather empty. The orchestra which relieved the jazz band was playing one of the old dreamy waltzes, and no more than a dozen couples were dancing on the brightly polished floor. There being ample space, the women's long skirts made every swaying motion even softer and more undulat-ing. Most of the men were in uniform, and the effect of the whole was almost that of a celebration or a victory feast, such as is customary at the conclusion of peace.

Bunsen discovered his prospective father-in-law and nod-ded to him. His fiancée's father was traveling for Henkel – "Champagne Consul," he called himself, not failing to add that he was a colleague of Ribbentrop who had once been in the same line of business. Bunsen saw Hanni, his fiancée, among the dancers. A flash of jealousy made him think she was dancing with a stranger, but he saw that her partner was her cousin, a thin, newly commissioned lieutenant. When the dance was over, she joined Bunsen. She was a girl of nine-teen, with light-auburn hair and bold eyes. Both of them sensed and were glad that they were being generally admired. Bunsen introduced his two friends, tables were joined, and the little waiter was kept busy breaking up ice with his tiny hammer. Hanni said that this was her farewell party, for tomorrow she was going to begin her six weeks' course at the school for SS brides. Nothing could be more important, said Bunsen, and went on to ask whether she intended to give her fellow students some private coaching. Hanni's father, a witty, shrewd widower, looked at him sharply, and then, almost as sharply, at his two friends. He had not been over-enthusiastic about the handsome fellow his daughter had fallen in love with; furthermore, Bunsen's command at West-hofen had seemed a rather queer job for a son-in-law. But he had gotten some information about Bunsen's parents;

they were just average, rather decent people. The man had been a petty official in the Palatinate. Hanni's father could not help thinking, while he sat in the stuffy drawing room when he was making his formal call, that for such people to have given birth to this rather extraordinary offspring could be attributed only to the genius of the race.

In the meantime the place had filled up. Waltzes alternated with one-steps and polkas. Hanni's father and all the other old people there smiled when the orchestra played a tune with which they were familiar and which recalled fond antewar memories. Such a genuine spirit of festivity and such untroubled cheerfulness were seldom seen there. Relaxation like this is to be found in all similar places, in cities all over the world, when those who have escaped from great danger – or think they have – are celebrating. Tonight's gaiety would not be spoiled by plotters or kill-joys – good care had been taken to prevent it, not only here but elsewhere too. A whole flotilla of little Strength through Joy boats floated on the Rhine. Hanni's father's firm had donated a good supply of Henkel Dry to each one of them. No wry-mouthed spectators stood at the hall's entrances. The little waiter with the inscrutable face, who broke up the ice with his tiny hammer, did not count.

The Kresses had left their Opel car at the parking place before the *Kurhaus*, after they'd dropped George at Kostheim. He would have to spend the night at a home for rivermen; for with the papers he had, he'd fit rather oddly in the blue car. During the last half hour of the ride to Kostheim, Kress had been as silent as he'd been on their earlier trip to the Riederwald Settlement. It was as if the guest who had slowly materialized were on the point of vanishing again, and it would be useless to address him. There had been no leave-taking. Even afterward, Kress and his wife had said nothing. Tacitly they had come to the Rheinischer Hof, for they were hungry for lights and for people. They sat down at a table in a corner of the room, because they were somewhat out of place in their dusty sports clothes. They watched everything there was to be seen. At last Frau Kress broke the silence that had lasted almost an hour.

"Did he say anything at the end?"

"No. Only 'Thanks!'"

"It's strange," she said, "but I feel as if I should thank him, no matter what happens to us as a result, for having stayed with us, for having paid us this visit."

"I feel the same way," her husband answered quickly. They looked at each other in surprise, with a new, and to them hitherto unknown, mutual understanding.

$\mathcal{V}$

After the Kresses had dropped him in front of an inn, George reflected briefly and walked down to the Main, instead of going into the inn. He sauntered along the embankment among a crowd of people who were enjoying the Sunday and the autumn sun. The sunny weather, they said, was like the apple wine – on the point of turning – and wouldn't last much longer. George walked past the bridge, at which a guard was posted. The embankment widened – he had come to the mouth of the Main much sooner than he had anticipated. The Rhine lay before him, and beyond it the city through which he had scurried a few days ago. Its streets and squares, witnesses of his agony, were fused into one great fortress that was reflected in the river. A flock of birds, flying in a sharply pointed black triangle, was etched into the reddish afternoon sky between the city's tallest spires, making a picture that resembled a city's seal. Presently, on the roof of the cathedral, between two of these spires, George made out the figure of Saint Martin bending down from his horse to share his cloak with the beggar who was to appear to him in a dream: "I am he whom thou pursuest."

George could easily have crossed the next bridge and hired a room at a rivermen's hotel. Even if there were a raid his passport would protect him. But, afraid of getting involved in questioning, he preferred to spend the night on the right bank of the river and board his ship early in the morning. He decided to think everything over thoroughly again, while it was still daylight. He turned about and sauntered across the meadows that bordered the Main.

Kostheim, a small village with a profusion of walnut and chestnut trees, looks down upon the river. The nearest inn was called "The Angel"; a wreath of brown leaves above the sign indicated that new wine was being served here.

George went in and sat down in the diminutive garden. It seemed the best place for resting, for looking down on the water, and for letting things take their course. He would have to make a decision.

He sat close to the wall, with his back toward the garden. When a waitress put some new wine before him, he said: "Why, I haven't ordered yet." She picked up the glass and asked: "Well, for Heaven's sake, what do you intend to order?" After a little pause, George said: "New wine," and both of them laughed. She put the glass directly into his hand. The first sip created so inordinate a desire that he drained the glass at one gulp. "Another glass, please!" "Now you just wait your turn." She served some other guests at the next table.

Half an hour passed. The waitress looked over at him briefly several times. The lack of restraint in his drinking contrasted with the calmness and steadfastness with which he contemplated the meadows. The last guests went from the garden into the taproom. The sky was red, and a fine but penetrating wind stirred the vine leaves even on the inside of the wall.

"I hope he's left the money on the table," thought the waitress. She went out to see. He was still sitting there. "Don't you want to drink your wine inside?" she asked.

George looked at her a second time. She was a young woman in a dark dress. Her face, momentarily animated, showed a Sunday tiredness. Her breasts were strong, her neck delicate. She looked familiar to him, even intimately so. Of what woman of bygone days did she remind him? Or was it just the memory of a desire? It could hardly have been a particularly unquenchable desire. "No, you may bring me my wine out here, if you will," he answered.

The garden being empty now, George sat facing the inn and waited until the waitress came back with his drink. He hadn't been mistaken, he liked her – as much as he could like anything now. "Why do you keep rushing about all the time?"

"Aw, I have a room full of customers." Even so, she stood with a knee braced against a chair and her elbows on its back. Her collar was pinned together with a garnet cross. "Do you work here?" she asked.

"I work on a boat."

She looked at him quickly but sharply. "Are you from this district?"

"No, but I have some relatives here."

"You talk almost like one of us."

"The men in my family always come here for their wives." Though she smiled, her face did not lose its trace of sadness. George looked at her; she did not seem to mind his looking.

A motorcar stopped in the street, and a whole flock of SS men walked through the garden and into the taproom. The waitress barely glanced up. Her lowered gaze was fixed upon George's hand that was grasping the back of the chair. "What's the matter with your hand?"

"An accident – didn't heal well."

She took his hand so quickly that he had no chance to withdraw it, and looked at it closely. "I suppose you got your hand in some broken glass – that place could easily open again." She let go his hand. "I've got to attend to business now."

"Such fine customers mustn't be kept waiting."

She shrugged her shoulders. "It isn't as bad as all that. We're pretty hard-boiled here."

"Meaning what?"

"Uniforms."

She walked away, and George called after her: "Another glass, please!"

The evening had already grown cool and gray. "I want her to come back," thought George.

The waitress took the customers' orders, all the while thinking: "What kind of a fellow is that one outside? What kind of trouble is he in? For he is in some kind of trouble." She served her customers with proud and adroit cheerfulness. "He certainly hasn't been on a boat long. He's not a liar, but he is lying. He's afraid, but he is no coward. Where did this happen to his hand? He was so startled when I took his hand, and yet he looked at me. I saw him clench his fingers when the SS men crossed the garden. Is there any connection there?"

At last she brought George another glass of wine. Nothing was right about him, but his eyes were. She walked away so that these eyes might have their fill of her. George sat there in the cold evening; he hadn't even touched his second glass yet. "What do you want a third glass for?"

"It doesn't matter," said George and pushed the glasses together. He took her hand. The only ring she wore was a thin one with a good-luck beetle, such as one gets as a prize at fairs. He asked: "No husband? No intended? No sweetheart?" Three times she shook her head. "No luck? Been disappointed?"

She looked at him with surprise. "Why do you ask?"

"Well, because you are alone."

She struck her hand gently against her heart. "That's where the disappointment is." Suddenly she hurried off. When she was at the door, George called her back to his table and gave her a banknote to change. She thought: "Well, so this isn't it either." When she came into the dark garden a fourth time with the money on a plate, he mustered up his courage. "Is there a guest room in the house? It would save me the trouble of crossing over to Mainz."

"Here in the house? What do you think? Only the proprietors live here."

"And how are things where you are living?"

She quickly drew back and looked at him almost frowning. He was prepared for a rough answer, but after a brief silence she said simply: "All right." Then she added: "Wait here for me. I still have some work to do inside. When I come out, follow me."

He waited. His hope that his flight might after all be successful was mingled with joyful anxiety. At last she came out, in a dark coat. She didn't turn around once. He followed her through a long street. It had begun to rain; almost stunned, he thought to himself: "Her hair will get wet."

A few hours later, George came to with a start – he didn't know where he was. "I woke you up," she said. "I had to. I couldn't listen to it any longer. Besides, you'll wake my aunt."

"Did I shout?"

"You moaned and shouted. Go back to sleep and be quiet."

"What time is it?"

She hadn't slept a wink. Because she had heard every hour strike since midnight she could say: "Almost four. Sleep quietly. You don't need to worry. I'll wake you all right." She didn't know whether he fell asleep again or just lay quietly. She waited for a recurrence of the trembling that had seized him when he first went to sleep. No, he was breathing quietly.

Fahrenberg, the camp commander, had given strict orders this night, as he had every other night, to wake him as soon as a report about the fugitive came in. The order was meaningless, for as on all other nights, Fahrenberg never closed an eye. Again he listened for every sound that could have any connection with the news he was expecting. If the past nights had tortured him with their quietness, this Sunday night tortured him with the frequent honking of horns, the barking of dogs, and the shouts of drunken peasants.

But finally everything quieted down. The countryside sank into the soundless sleep that comes between midnight and dawn. Without ceasing to listen, he tried to picture this country to himself – all the villages, the highways and roads that connected with each other and with the large cities, a triangular network within which the man would have to be trapped unless he were the devil himself. After all, this man could not dissolve into thin air! He must have left some footprints on the damp autumn soil; somebody must have gotten shoes for him, some hand must have cut his bread and filled his glass, some house must have sheltered him. For the first time the possibility that Heisler might have made good his escape occurred to Fahrenberg. But this possibility was impossible. Didn't everyone say that his friends were disowning him, that his own wife had had a sweetheart for a long time, and that his own brother took part in the search? Fahrenberg drew a breath of relief. The most probable solution was that the man was no longer alive. He'd probably drowned himself in the Rhine or the Main, and his body would be fished out tomorrow. Suddenly he saw Heisler before him after the last grilling, his mouth torn and his eyes insolent. Fahrenberg realized that his hope was futile – no Rhine and no Main would ever yield up this man's body, for he was alive and would continue to live. For the first time since the escape, Fahrenberg sensed that he was pursuing not an individual but a featureless and inexhaustible power. But only for a few minutes was this thought bearable.

"You must go now." The woman helped George dress, handing him every piece of clothing as soldiers' wives do at the end of the last night of furlough.

"I could have shared everything with her," thought George. "My whole life. But I have no longer a life to share."

"Have something hot to drink before you go." In the early light he saw what he would presently have to leave. The woman was freezing. The rain beat against the window; the weather had changed overnight. From her wardrobe came the faint smell of camphor as she pulled out something, some ugly, dark-wool thing. *All the nice things I would have bought you – red and blue and white!*

Standing, she watched him swallow some coffee. She was quite calm. She preceded him downstairs, opened the street door, and went upstairs again. In the kitchen and on the stairs she had asked herself whether she shouldn't have told him that she had an idea what his trouble was. But what for? It would only make him uneasy.

While she was rinsing his cup, the kitchen door opened, and an old woman with a gray pigtail appeared on the threshold. With incredible swiftness she scolded from within the quilt that was wrapped around her, "You silly goose! You'll never see the fellow again, I know it. You picked up something nice, didn't you? Tell me, Marie, have you gone quite mad? You didn't even know him when you left this afternoon, or did you? What? Have you swallowed your tongue?"

Slowly the younger woman turned from the sink. Her eyes fastened upon the old woman, who cowered under their brilliance.

With a quiet proud smile Marie looked away, wrapped in her thoughts. She had had her moment. But she had no witnesses except an old woman who, shaking with cold and anger, retreated quickly to her warm bed.

"What would I do without Belloni's overcoat?" thought George as, his head bent, he followed the tracks. A hard rain struck his face. At last the houses retreated. The city across the river was hidden behind a curtain of rain. Against the immeasurable dull sky the city seemed bereft of all reality – one of those cities one fashions in one's sleep for the length of a dream, and that doesn't last even that long. And yet it has withstood the rush of two thousand years.

George reached the Kastella bridgehead. The guard challenged him, and he showed his passport. When he was on the bridge, he realized that his heart had not beaten any faster. He could have passed ten other bridgeheads without trouble – one gets accustomed even to that. He felt that his heart was now proof not only against fear and danger, but also perhaps against happiness. He walked a bit slower so as not to be a minute early. Looking down, he saw his tugboat, the *Wilhelmine*, with her green load line mirrored in the water. She lay quite near the bridgehead, unfortunately not touching the bank but alongside another vessel. George was less concerned about the guard at the Mainz bridgehead than about how he would get across the strange boat. He need not have worried. He was still twenty paces from the landing place when the globular, almost reckless head of a man popped over the *Wilhelmine's* gunwale. George had obviously been expected by the man with the round, fattish face, whose wide nostrils and deepset eyes gave it a rather sinister look. It was precisely the right kind of face for an upright man who was willing to run considerable risk.

On Monday evening, the seven trees in Westhofen were cut down. Everything had happened very quickly. The new commander had assumed his duties before the change had become generally known. Presumably he was the right man to straighten out a camp in which such things had happened. Instead of roaring, he spoke in an ordinary tone of voice, but he left not the slightest doubt in our minds that at the least provocation we would be shot down like so many wild beasts. He ordered the crosses to be dismantled at once, for they were not what he went in for. Rumor had it that Fahrenberg had gone to Mainz that same Monday. He was said to have taken lodgings at the Fuerstenberger Hof and to have put a bullet through his brain – but that was only rumor. It didn't quite fit him. Perhaps it was someone else who, because of debts or a love affair, shot himself through the head that night at the Fuerstenberger Hof. Or perhaps Fahrenberg has bounced up another ladder and is now wielding even greater power.

We didn't know any of this as yet then. So many things happened later that nothing that could be learned could be believed implicitly. True, we had thought that it was impossible to experience more than we had already experienced; but once outside, we found out how much there still was to be experienced.

But on that evening when the prisoners' barrack was heated for the first time, and we watched the flames of the kindling wood that we thought had come from the seven trees, we felt nearer to life than at any time later – much nearer, too, than all the others who are under the impression that they are alive.

The SA guard had stopped to wonder how long the rain would keep up. He turned around suddenly to surprise us at something that was forbidden; he roared at us and, for good measure, distributed a few penalties. Ten minutes later we were lying in our bunks. The last little spark in the stove had gone out. We had a foreboding of the nights that were in store for us. The damp autumn cold struck through our covers, our shirts, and our skin. All of us felt how ruthlessly and fearfully outward powers could strike to the very core of man, but at the same time we felt that at the very core there was something that was unassailable and inviolable.

Afterword

Dorothy Rosenberg

ANNA SEGHERS was born Netty Reiling on November 19, 1900, in Mainz, Germany. She was the only child of a liberal, educated, cosmopolitan Jewish couple. Her father, Isidor Reiling, an internationally known art and antiques dealer, was also the curator of the art collection of the Mainz cathedral. Netty Reiling thus grew up in a middle-class family atmosphere and was sent to a private girls school. As a teenager, she was horrified by the bombing of Mainz at the end of World War I, and the civilian deaths it caused. "The First World War was cruel and cannibalistic," she later wrote, "but they only began bombing attacks on cities and people toward its end."[1]

Netty Reiling's growing awareness of, and concern for, the less fortunate was manifested in her work as a volunteer caring for small children in a "Christian Social Work Circle" while she was attending the lyceum. In a report about this period a co-worker later commented, "We understood the word Christian in its true sense, we didn't shut the others out."[2] This oblique reference to the Reiling family's religion reflects the anti-Semitism prevalent even in upper-middle-class circles in Germany in the 1920s.

After receiving her diploma in 1920, Netty Reiling left Mainz and moved to Heidelberg, where she was one of the first women to attend the Ruprecht-Karls University. Access to higher education, along with the vote, had been extended to women the year before. The violent political and economic struggles in Germany at the end the war and during the first years of the Weimar Republic affected all classes of society, but especially shocked the sheltered members the middle classes. "It was after the First World War," Netty Reiling wrote later. "Occupation, inflation. The food in the cafeteria was meager and bad for every student. The money that the families sent was paper millions, worthless by the time it arrived."[3]

The political and philosophical debates of the period dominated the attention of the students. Netty Reiling was particularly affected by her exposure to the young leftist and Communist intellectuals who had fled from southeastern Europe. "At the university," she later wrote, "I quickly got to know the emigrants who finished their studies in Germany after the bloody reaction and persecution in their countries. They opened my eyes to many political events, to the class struggle.... The White Terror had washed the first wave of emigrants through our part of the world. And its witnesses, exhausted from what they had experienced, but unbroken and daring, superior to us in experience as well as in willingness to sacrifice in large things and readiness to help in small, were real... heroes to us."[4]

At Heidelberg Netty Reiling studied history, philosophy, art history, and sinology, the latter "in order to be able to read the inscriptions on the East Asian works of art, which had been shown to [me] as a child as products of an independent culture, very different from the Greeks."[5] She spent two semesters at the University of Cologne, as an intern at the Museum for East Asian Art, and then returned to Heidelberg, where she received her Ph.D. in art history in 1924. Her dissertation was on "The Jew and Judaism in the Works of Rembrandt."[6] In the same year she made her literary debut with a story entitled "The Dead of the Island Djal: A Saga from the Dutch, translated by Antje Seghers," which appeared in the Christmas 1924 issue of the *Frankfurter Zeitung und Handelsblatt*. This was the first appearance of the pseudonym Seghers.[7] Asked much later when she had begun writing, Seghers replied:

> *I can hardly remember. Due to an illness, I was somewhat isolated as a child, left to my own devices and self-absorbed. I couldn't take part in the games and activities of the other, healthy children. Loneliness and sickness isolated me; I therefore built myself a world of my own: a fantasy world. My first written works came from the substance of my dreams when I was still quite small. Since then I have never stopped writing.*[8]

In 1925, Netty Reiling married a young Communist immigrant from Hungary, an economist named Laszlo Radvanyi (later known as Johann-Lorenz Schmidt), who had received his Ph.D. from Heidelberg in 1923. As a foreigner, revolutionary, and Marxist economist, Radvanyi's chances of an academic career in the Weimar Republic were poor. What followed were twenty years of materially difficult life, political struggle, persecution, and exile, as well as constant literary work.

Netty Reiling-Radvanyi gave up her study of art history "because otherwise I wouldn't have been able to write."[9] Her next published work, "Grubetsch," the story of a murder set in the slums of a port city, appeared as a serial in the *Frankfurter Zeitung* in March 1927, also under the pseudonym Seghers. But it was her first novel, *Aufstand der Fischer von Santa Barbara* (published in English as *The Revolt of the Fishermen*), that catapulted her to fame. Oskar Loerke, editor at Fischer Verlag, which published the book, noted that this was "a very talented, very satisfactory story by Anna Seghers. Pay attention to her!"[10] The book, "a dynamic social novel about an uprising among a group of fishermen [whose] masculine theme and vigorous treatment"[11] won Reiling-Radvanyi (henceforth known as Anna Seghers) both critical acclaim and, together with "Grubetsch," the Kleist prize (which can be compared with the Pulitzer prize). "In 1928 I received the Kleist prize for my first book," she commented. "My daughter was born the same year, two deliveries at once!"[12] According to a possibly apocryphal story published in *Current Biography 1942* (retold after Seghers had become famous with the publication of *The Seventh Cross*), the signature on the title page was simply "Seghers":

> It was assumed that the author of so robust a story must be a man. It was, therefore, with considerable surprise that the editors of the literary magazine Buecherschau, having asked this man Seghers kindly to call at their offices so that their staff artist might sketch the Kleist winner, found instead a shy young woman with a round peasant-like face, veiled, deep-set eyes, and thick pigtails wound around her broad forehead. "I am Seghers," the "man" said. "I am sorry I could not get here sooner. I was in the hospital having my baby when the book was published."[13]

In any case, it is true that the *Neue Bücherschau* printed a sketch of a heavy-browed, lantern-jawed distinctly male figure as their projection of the author.

This first novel established Anna Seghers' reputation. By 1933 it had appeared in England, France, Norway, Spain, and the United States; it was later chosen by Erwin Piscator, the famous stage director, as the basis for his first film.[14] Shortly after the book appeared in English in 1929, Seghers was invited to London by her British publisher, "but Blooms-bury found it difficult to lionize her. She discouraged inter-views and refused to be 'involved in fashionable literary circles.'"[15] According to *Current Biography*, "She refused to act the 'celebrity' . . . and did most of her 'sight-seeing' in the British Museum. At the one reception in her honor which she did attend, Frau Seghers (according to the London *Evening Standard*) 'looked just as distinguished as Charlotte Brontë must have done at Thackeray's party.'"[16]

In 1928, the same year that she received the Kleist prize, Seghers joined the Communist Party. In 1929 she joined the Bund Proletarisch-Revolutionärer Schriftsteller (BPRS – Organization of Proletarian-Revolutionary Writers), which had been founded a few months earlier. The BPRS was a section of the International Association of Revolutionary Writers, based in Moscow. The "Report of the Activities of the BPRS in 1929," written for the leadership of the Com-munist Party, noted that "Two writers who have a good name in the bourgeoisie came to us: comrade Ludwig Renn and comrade Anna Seghers. They did not come simply as 'sympathizers,' they completely accepted our literary reso-lutions."[17] What those were was illustrated in the BPRS's 1928 Action Program: "The proletarian-revolutionary writers declare with full awareness that our works shall be weapons of agitation and propaganda in the class struggle."[18]

During the next several years Seghers was very active, both politically and creatively. At the end of the 1920s, she and her husband moved to Berlin, where he first taught at the Marxistische Arbeiterschule (MASCH – Marxist Workers' School) and then served as its director from 1930 to 1933. Recalling this period later, Seghers said: "In the years of the [Weimar] Republic I worked on all the newspapers and magazines; today, to the extent they have survived, they are under Nazi censorship."[19] In addition, between 1929 and 1933 she wrote a collection of short stories, *Auf dem Wege zur amerikanischen Botschaft und andere Erzählungen* (On the Way to the American Embassy and Other Stories), and two novels, *Die Gefährten* (The Companions) and *Der Kopflohn* (A Price on His Head).[20]

During this period Seghers also published numerous articles and essays in the party newspapers and journals (*Die Rote Fahne, Der Weg der Frau,* and *Die Linkskurve*), sponsored and advised young writers in the BPRS, and took an active part in the debate over Marxist aesthetic theory that was going on within the organization.[21] In the fall of 1930 she went to Kharkhov in the Soviet Union to attend the Second International Congress for Proletarian and Revolutionary Literature, after which she visited the hydroelectric complex then being built on the Dnieper River. She returned from this visit deeply impressed by what she had seen.

Seghers was also active in, and attended conferences of, the PEN Club and the Schutzverband Deutscher Schriftsteller (SDS – German Writers' Association) and joined and supported the Society of Friends of the New Russia. She represented the "other" Germany in the emerging international peace movement and attended the Amsterdam Anti-War Congress in 1932.

Exile

Hitler was named Chancellor on January 31, 1933, and the first wave of arrests began that same evening. Many of those arrested during the first months after Hitler's rise to power were questioned and then released under surveillance; others were imprisoned. But the sudden massive influx of prisoners was more than existing jails and prisons could accommodate and concentration camps were soon opened to handle the overflow.

Anna Seghers' works were immediately placed on the Nazi "Black List" and her name was included on the preliminary list of undesirable authors printed in the *Börsenblatt fuer den deutschen Buchhandel* on May 16, 1933, six days after the spectacular book-burning in the courtyard of Humboldt University in Berlin.[22] When later asked how she had fared in this period, Seghers responded:

We were prepared for repression. But they came with unexpected brutality. The police forced their way into my apartment one night. Fortunately, my neighbors had observed everything and hidden me in time. From then on I had to live underground with the constant fear, every day, yes every hour, of being arrested and taken to a concentration camp. I succeeded in leaving Germany and reaching France only with the greatest difficulty.[23]

Seghers went first to France, which was a preferred country of exile both because it was close to Germany and because the conditions for political refugees were relatively liberal.[24] She reached Paris by way of Prague and Switzerland. She was joined by her husband and, in June 1933, by her children, Ruth and Peter.[25] She had spoken French since childhood and quickly adjusted to her new circumstances:

While most of the emigrants were still buzzing around and camping in hotels, she had already dropped anchor, only temporarily and ... ready to lift anchor at any moment, but firmly enough so she could write in rela-

tive peace. She took a furnished apartment in a little house in the suburbs. Few people knew her address. It was better that way, because of the French police, who could be disturbed by the comings and goings of lots of strangers, because of the Hitler spies who swarmed around and among the emigrants. . . . Her children went to school. Her husband continued his research in libraries and institutes.[26]

The family lived in Paris until the German invasion of the city in June 1940. Seghers' daughter, Ruth Radvanyi, later described their family life:

We lived for a long time in the Parisian suburb of Belle-vue. From France our mother traveled to Belgium, to the Civil War in Spain, or she went into the city to write in a café. . . . At the beginning of the war, she sent us to learn to swim with the last of our money. After all, we might have to travel by ship sometime.[27]

Seghers continued with her political and literary work. In 1933, she helped to reestablish the German Writer's Union (SDS) with Leonhard Frank as chairman and Heinrich Mann as honorary president (it had been dissolved in Germany by Goebbels). The group attempted to protect the material interests of its members while organizing readings, lectures, and anti-fascist demonstrations and publishing the magazine *Der Schriftsteller*. On the first anniversary of the book-burning, it founded the Deutsche Freiheitsbiblio-thek (German Freedom Library) to collect the works of authors banned in Nazi Germany and to serve as an information and research center.[28] It was a central part of the German emigré milieu. As author Bodo Uhse recalled, "The emigration was . . . [also] a cultural and political movement. We met in the smoke-filled back rooms of Parisian cafés and discussed the steps with which we could help the friends who remained in Hitler's clutches."[29]

A key problem for emigré writers was the lack of opportunities to publish. Seghers, together with Oskar Maria Graf, Wieland Herzfelde, and Jan Petersen (three asterisks were substituted for his name on the masthead since he was still in Germany working in the underground) formed the editorial board of a new magazine called *Neue Deutsche Blätter*, which was published in Prague from 1933 to 1935. In their introduction to the first issue the editors wrote:

> *There is no neutrality. For no one. Least of all for the writer. He who is silent also takes part in the struggle; he who, frightened and numbed by events, flees to a purely private existence, who uses the weapon of language as a plaything or an ornament, who serenely resigns himself, damns himself to social and artistic sterility and abandons the field to the enemy.*[30]

In addition to her political activities, Seghers continued to write prolifically. Between 1933 and 1939 she produced, in addition to countless essays and articles, a number of short stories and four novels. Descriptions of Seghers' writing in Paris all agree with that made by her friend Jeanne Stern:

> *When the household with its petty concerns bothered her, when her own four walls threatened to suffocate her, Anna Seghers packed her manuscript in a briefcase and took the next suburban train into Paris, sat down at an empty table in a café, always the same one, and, unconcerned by the surging babble, wrote.*[31]

Her next major project was a study of the February 1934 uprising against the Dollfus regime in Austria. She spent several weeks there in the spring of 1934, and on her return to Paris in June she wrote: "Café Dumesnil, 9:00 A.M. Yesterday I returned from Austria. A half dozen sessions in the trial of the men of February, which I attended."[32] Later she described another aspect of her visit: "For part of the trip I had a very specific intention. I followed the escape route of Koloman Wallisch [a Social Demacratic leader of the uprising]."[33]

After her return she quickly wrote the reportage novella *Der letzte Weg des Koloman Wallisch* (The Last Journey of Koloman Wallisch), which was published in the July issue of *Neue Deutsche Blätter*.[34] It served as the basis for the novel *Der Weg durch den Februar* (The Journey Through February), a fictional reworking of the same subject in a broader framework, which was published in Paris in 1935.[35]

At a meeting of the SDS in Paris in December 1934 Seghers suggested that the group "organize a conference of all the progressive forces in literature in Western Europe in the near future." This idea was "accepted enthusiastically and unanimously."[36] "The writers' congress is being organized," she wrote the following June. "Endless meetings. For the Germans, these preparations have a further and deeply serious meaning."[37] The International Writers' Congress in the Defense of Culture met in Paris from June 21–25, 1935. The presidium included Henri Barbusse, E. M. Forster, André Gide, Aldous Huxley, Egon Erwin Kisch, André Malraux, Heinrich Mann, Robert Musil, and Alexei Tolstoy.[38] Seghers gave a talk on "love of country," a subject of increasing concern to her and one that she was to discuss in a number of essays and develop as a major theme in *The Seventh Cross*.

This first major demonstration of international cultural support for anti-fascism was extremely important to the members of the large German delegation. Dismayed by the failure of the opposition to prevent Hitler's accession to power, many emigrants felt resigned and isolated (the suicide rate among them was very high, a subject touched upon in Seghers' 1944 novel *Transit*). The conference at least temporarily overcame some of this feeling of isolation. Members of the German delegation were also eager to demonstrate that fascism was not synonymous with German culture. For Seghers, the conference was an important example of the unity of political and artistic work, as well as an exposure to a much wider circle of colleagues; her friendships with authors such as Jorge Amado and Pablo Neruda began there.[39]

In 1935 Seghers also started work on her next novel, *Die Rettung* (The Rescue).[40] Its point of departure was a 1932 mining disaster in upper Silesia, and she visited the Borinage – the hard coal district in Belgium – to study conditions in and around the mines; but its actual theme was the effect of unemployment and its relationship to fascism. "After these men had given their utmost in heroism underground, the mine was closed and they had no more work," she wrote. "I asked myself, how did they live then, with their great inner resources?"[41] In 1936 and 1937 she also wrote two fantasy stories, "Die Schönsten Sagen vom Räuber Woynok" (The Best Stories of the Robber Woynok) and "Sagen von Artemis" (Stories of Artemis), in which she freely reworked fairy-tale and mythological motifs,[42] and her only dramatic work that was produced, a radio play called *Der Prozess der Jeanne d'Arc zu Rouen 1431*, (The Trial of Joan of Arc at Rouen), for Radio Antwerp.

The Spanish Civil War, which began in 1936, provided the first opportunity for German exiles to fight fascism actively. Many of Seghers' friends – Bodo Uhse, Ludwig Renn, Willi Bredel, Hans Marchwitza, Egon Erwin Kisch, Kurt and Jeanne Stern – went to Spain to join the International Brigades. In July 1937, Seghers attended the Second International Writers' Congress in the Defense of Culture in

Madrid.[43] When asked later what she had done as an emigré in France, Seghers responded:

> Work, write, study, fight against the Nazis. I published many articles in the newspapers. I took part in every action against fascism. In 1937 I was in Spain to attend the Writers' Congress that began in Madrid and ended in Valencia. As a representative of authentic culture, the congress won the honor of being bombed.[44]

Although Seghers wrote only journalistic pieces about Spain, the importance she attached to the defense of the Spanish Republic was reflected in *The Seventh Cross* and appeared frequently in her postwar work.[45]

The Seventh Cross

It is not clear exactly when Seghers began work on *The Seventh Cross*. When asked in an interview, she replied, "Two years before the war; I finished it as the war broke out."[46] The first written record of the book is in a letter she wrote to Ivan Anissimov, head of the Soviet publishing house for foreign literature, on September 23, 1938:

> I will finish a little novel, about 200 to 300 pages, based on an event that recently took place in Germany, a story that provides the opportunity to learn about very many levels in fascist Germany through the fate of a single man. This book should not and will not take too long; I have already begun it and want to finish it in a few months if my situation in any way permits.[47]

The structure mentioned in the above quote had been suggested to Seghers by Alessandro Manzoni's historical novel, *The Betrothed*, which had been recommended to her on her trip to Madrid. Manzoni describes the wanderings of an engaged couple through seventeenth-century Italy. In 1942, Seghers gave her impression of Manzoni's book:

> *The work of a Manzoni, classic in the traditional style, measured in its construction, in every complex sentence, shows the Italian people from inside and out as a whole. No political passion; a simple, almost banal, civilian event: the love of some nobleman for the daughter of a peasant on his lands. This event allows the author to show all of the conflicts of his people in all strata, in all individuals.*[48]

Although very different from Seghers' own work in both material and content, *The Betrothed* sparked the idea for the structure of *The Seventh Cross*: the flight of George Heisler brings him into contact with all classes in the population, making it possible to show their condition and moral conduct. His successful escape destroys the myth of Nazi omnipotence.

In a letter to Fritz Erpenbeck in the fall of 1938, Seghers reported:

> *I am now writing a small novel ... called* The Seventh Cross *... [which] should be finished around the end of March. ... The book will result from the closest collaboration with our local friends, who are already familiar with the contents and would like to see it written quickly.*[49]

Seghers' mention of "local friends" appears to be either a reference to party literary functionaries or to sources of information on conditions inside Germany that were made available through party contacts. Seghers answered the question of how she had gotten her material many times: "I was told about a number of different circumstances and events over and over again by emigrants, among them escapees from camps, described very exactly, very carefully at my request."[50] In another interview, two years later, she was more specific: "I was often in the Swiss part of the Rhine and I spoke to many refugees, and someone told me about this strange occurrence . . . which sounds extremely unlikely, namely this thing about a cross to which a prisoner who had been recaptured would be bound."[51]

Alexander Abusch, who was in Paris at the time, wrote:

Do you remember how we would come out to visit you in Bellevue near Paris when you were writing The Seventh Cross *and we brought you original reports from illegals in Germany, yes, and arranged conversations with them so that you could feel their atmosphere unmediated, draw directly from it? It is odd that from the different scenes you read us from the emerging masterpiece, the one that sticks in my memory is the conversation between the two women about whether one should iron damp or dry.*[52]

Lore Wolf, a friend who had worked illegally in Germany and sometimes acted as Seghers' secretary in Paris, describes being "cross-questioned about the fates of residents and local events."[53] Her memories of Seghers during the writing of *The Seventh Cross* echo the picture drawn by Jeanne Stern:

I often saw her in the Café de la Paix or in a small café in Montparnasse, sitting among a murmuring mass of people. Her hair hung in her face. But none of it disturbed her. She wrote and wrote. The pencil flew over the paper and the manuscript grew. Every week she brought me a bundle of pages that I typed into clean copy. It was sometimes very difficult to decipher her scribbling. . . . But I did this work gladly. Deeply moved and severely shaken, I experienced the events in the homeland.[54]

On March 27, 1939, Anna Seghers wrote to Johannes R. Becher in Moscow: "My plans: I am finishing a novel which will be printed in the IL" (*Internationale Literatur*, the journal published in Moscow which succeeded *Neue Deutsche Blätter*).[55] After listing the rest of her literary plans, she went on: "By the time I have written all this, some time will have passed and if I am then still alive, I will write a novel."[56]

Despite her regular publications, Seghers' life in Paris was not easy. In addition to the political and psychological dangers, money was a constant problem. A few months later she wrote to Wieland Herzfelde, "Dear Friend, it is absolutely necessary that I be sent money . . . my situation is now such that I really must be helped for a time."[57] Nevertheless, although well behind her original schedule, she completed the book at the end of 1939. On December 19 she wrote to Franz Carl Weiskopf in New York, "I have finished my novel and sent it to my publisher, who is in New York at the moment." In this and in a March 1940 letter, she asks that everything be done so that *The Seventh Cross* can appear quickly in English: "I hope that you will soon succeed. I would be boundlessly happy and I would hug you passionately; as I have said, this book has a special meaning for me."[58]

Seghers had offered her finished manuscript to Querido in Amsterdam. In a May 1940 letter to Wieland Herzfelde, she began confidently, "I have had no luck with *The Seventh Cross* yet. I am concerned about it, but not distressed. That means I am myself confident that sooner or later the stroke of luck will come, even if not as soon as I would like." But the tone soon shifted:

> *Querido had almost agreed and they still haven't turned it down. But I have pretty much lost hope. Do you think it completely impossible to print the book? You will per-*

haps think that I have gone off the deep end, or that I
should have asked this question a year ago. All right,
I've gone off the deep end and the timing is irrelevant.
I don't know if you're still alive. I don't know, in case you
are alive, if you feel like playing Don Quixote. Would it
help if I do without money, which doesn't exist anyway?
Perhaps I am making you . . . nervous with my tenacity,
but I really am tenacious and sometimes it's gotten me
through.[59]

Seghers' next letter to Herzfelde concerning the book was
written from the south of France in September 1940: "I
have the nicest plans. I have never, I would never have been
able to work as well as now." But in the next breath she had
to admit that she was almost at the end of her strength:
"What concerns me is that at this point I can say nothing
about what will happen to my novel. Its fate, too, will be
decided in the coming weeks."[60]

Seghers and her family had been overtaken by the war.
Ruth Radvanyi later recalled:

The war caught up with us; our father was interned.
The three of us burned our most dangerous papers and
together with thousands of French people went on the
highways fleeing before Hitler's Wehrmacht, bombed
and strafed by airplanes. We weren't too afraid; our
mother was with us. Returning to occupied Paris, we
lived in a little room on rue St. Sulpice. We lived off the
last piece of jewelry that our grandfather the antique
dealer had given us. When our friend Lore Wolf was
arrested by the Gestapo, our mother divided us up
between acquaintances and the less-well-acquainted.
With the help of Jeanne Stern we illegally crossed the
demarcation line into the not-yet-occupied part of
France. We were never completely hungry.[61]

412

Jeanne Stern later described the entire escape in a story that began as follows:

Like the ten little Indians, the troop of anti-fascist emigrants disappeared.... Anna's husband was arrested, my husband migrated into the concentration camp too. ... The Gestapo were hunting the anti-fascists. Anna was caught in a trap. She never talked about it. Why bother? It was obvious to everyone. She had left her apartment weeks earlier. She slept wherever she happened to be. She often changed quarters. Her son had found a place to stay with friends. Her daughter slept at our house....

One day Anna let me know through her daughter that I should come to meet her. She wanted to see me that evening. There was no doubt that she had a serious reason: for the first time she had given me the address of the strangers who gave her shelter.

She asked me without beating around the bush if I could help her and her children escape over the demarcation line between occupied and unoccupied France. I said yes. What could I say? If she turned to me, she had certainly carefully weighed all her possible solutions and found nothing better. It didn't say much for her situation: I possessed only the modest advantage of being a Frenchwoman among 40 million French.[62]

Seghers herself later described the same events:

My husband, a Hungarian, was immediately taken to the Vernet concentration camp, one of the most terrible in France. I stayed with my children in northern France and was taken by surprise by the Nazi invasion. When I wanted to escape it was already too late, for the Germans marched faster than we were able to flee. I had to leave the place where we had been living and move to Paris illegally. Imagine the difficulties – after all, the children were with me. In Paris I lived virtually constantly on the verge of death; I slept in a different place every night.

When asked how she was able to escape, Seghers replied:

Friends, supporters of De Gaulle, brought me to the "unoccupied" zone. Later, I was able to find quarters in a place near the concentration camp where my husband was interned. I spent about six months there, suffering a harrowing winter. No one knew where I was. Rumors that I was dead circulated because most of my friends didn't know my address.[63]

Asked about the fate of her book, Seghers said:

I had four copies: one at the house of a friend, which was bombed; other material was lost at the same time. A French friend took the second with him when he was called up; he wanted to translate the book into his own language. This friend was sent to the Maginot line. I have not seen him or the famous Maginot line or the copy again. The third fell into the hands of the Gestapo in my Paris apartment. The fourth was fortunately brought to the United States, and thus the book was saved.[64]

Seghers told a number of different stories about the fate of the manuscript of *The Seventh Cross*, all generally involving the loss of multiple copies and an uncertainty about the fate of the one copy that she had sent to New York. In fact, it appears from her correspondence that this was a dramatization. On December 19, 1929, she wrote to Weiskopf in

New York, informing him that she had finished the book and sent a copy to her editor at Querido, who was in New York at the time. In the same letter she referred to a corrected copy that she had sent "to the two of you." On January 25, 1940, she wrote to Herzfelde, who was also in the United States saying that she had sent a copy of the manuscript to her brother-in-law a week earlier and would send a copy to him the next day. And in another letter to Weiskopf, dated March 15, 1940, she mentioned that a third copy of the manuscript was en route to Berthold Viertel in Hollywood. Jeanne Stern agreed that Seghers "sent three copies of the manuscript, mailed separately, to the United States in the spring of 1940," which she "knew had arrived at reliable friends."[65]

In early 1941 Seghers and her family moved to Marseille. While she had read Balzac in Pamiers,[66] in Marseille she read Kafka.[67] Marseille in 1941 was a city filled with refugees desperate to escape the advancing Germans. Seghers had to cope with the "abstruse workings of the authorities and consulates whose card files, certificates, and stamps decided whether the anti-fascists would succeed in fleeing to another country or would end in a concentration camp"[68] and to obtain the assortment of exit, transit, and entry visas that would allow her and her family to leave Europe. She later reworked these experiences into her next and perhaps second most well-known book, *Transit*. In an interview, she described the bare details of her escape from Europe:

> *I contacted North American and Mexican friends. The North American Writers' Union took care of my exit permit and paid for the crossing for me and my family. The Mexican government granted me asylum. We boarded ship in Marseille and began a three-month journey.*[69]

Ruth Radvanyi described Marseille and beyond from her own perspective:

In Marseille she ran around to arrange the visas and tickets for America. We lived in a former flophouse, at that time an immigrant hotel. Our mother wrote on a suitcase between the bed and the gas cooker. We were, as always, sent to school. In Paris, half-illegally in Pamiers near the camp in which our father was interned, in Marseille, and later in Mexico, she always saw to it that we had an orderly daily schedule and that we went to school. Even in Martinique, the island in the Antilles which we had reached in the hold of a banana boat, she asked the commandant of our camp, which was on a peninsula, if he would take us to school on his daily trip with a motorboat. After all, we had been students at a French lyceum.[70]

On March 24, 1941, the family left for Mexico, sailing first for Martinique on the freighter the *Paul Lemerle*.[71] Arriving in Martinique, which was under Vichy rule, the family was immediately interned.[72] "It turned out that for the time being there was no direct ship. Our visas were expiring," Seghers wrote of this part of the journey. "We looked for an intermediate stop from which to go to Mexico by way of a detour."[73] New visas had to be obtained, this time for the Dominican Republic by ship from Martinique. There the family was again interned. Seghers wrote to Bodo Uhse on June 1, 1941:

I feel as if I've been dead for a year. . . . We are afraid here . . . we are completely lost here and outside of the world and must get away from here as soon as possible. I have to arrive somewhere with the children, who have been leading the wildest life for a year now.[74]

From the Dominican Republic the family took another freighter to New York, arriving at Ellis Island on June 16, 1941.[75] Here they were interned once again while Seghers tried to obtain permission for her family to enter the United States.[76] Finally, they sailed from New York for Veracruz and arrived in Mexico City in the fall of 1941.

Almost immediately after her arrival in Mexico, Seghers was once again integrated into the active political and cultural life of the German anti-fascist emigré community. In November 1941 she helped to found the Heinrich Heine Club, and was elected its president. A new German anti-fascist monthly magazine *Freies Deutschland* (Free Germany), begun a month earlier, reported the founding of the club:

> *The purpose of the club is to support free German art, literature, and science through the spoken and written word, . . . education, mutual aid, and through public events of artistic, literary, and scientific character, as well as cooperation with organizations with similar goals.*[77]

Seghers' circumstances in Mexico also encouraged her literary work. Although life was financially difficult until early 1943,[78] and although the news of her mother's deportation to a concentration camp in Poland apparently reached her at this time, the physical safety and peace of Mexico had a positive effect, as did her success as a writer. As Sigrid Bock, a literary scholar in the German Democratic Republic, has written:

> *In 1940, after finishing the novel* The Seventh Cross, *Anna Seghers was sure that she had completed something important. . . . Three years later, the worldwide response had proven her right. . . . These successes not only brought material security, which was so urgently*

needed for her work. The public recognition of her abil-
ity stimulated further creativity. . . . Anna Seghers expe-
rienced a period of intense literary creativity. She
finished the novel Transit *in June 1943; beginning in*
1944 the novellas The Excursion of the Dead Girls,
The End, Mail to the Promised Land, *and* The Sabo-
teurs *followed one another in close succession. They*
were circulated in Spanish and English in newspapers
and magazines even before Wieland Herzfelde could
publish them at his newly founded Aurora Verlag in
New York in 1946.[79]

The manuscript of *The Seventh Cross* had been making the
rounds of U. S. publishers since its arrival in New York in the
summer of 1940. After numerous rejections, Maxim Lieber,
who acted as Seghers' representative in the United States,[80]
submitted it to Little, Brown and Company in Boston. A
contract was waiting to be signed when Seghers arrived at
Ellis Island.[81] The many rejections reflect the difficulty that
many German exiles experienced in trying to publish in the
United States, where both their writing style and their subject matter were well outside the mainstream of popular
taste and the interests of the reading public.

In a recent article on the book's reception in the United
States, Alexander Stephan listed the possible reasons why
Segher's book was finally accepted:

In hindsight . . . however, the success that The Seventh
Cross *had in the United States does not seem surpris-*
ing. Books with a simple, clear plot located in the pres-
ent always easily found buyers in the United States.
The positive ending of George Heisler's story, the prud-
ery, and the focus on a single central hero were added
advantages. And finally . . . "There is not a single word

418

of theorizing in this book," noted one of the publisher's readers in praise. "Since all thought is translated into obvious action . . . there is nothing foreign to an American reader in this novel. . . . It has a chance to become a book club selection."[82]

Stephan then continued, "The reader was right: *The Seventh Cross* became . . . a typical American bestseller, which after a short, hectic success with reprintings, book club editions, illustrated versions and a film treatment is quickly forgotten again."[83]

The contract with Little, Brown was signed in June 1941; five months later John Galston delivered the translation. A number of scenes were then cut or shortened, including – to Seghers' dismay – most of the appearances of Ernst the shepherd, as well as a politically important meeting between Franz and Lotte.[84] In all, more than fifty pages were cut from the five-hundred-page manuscript.[85]

Little, Brown delivered the book to the stores in September 1942. Even before then, several Hollywood studios had expressed interest in film rights. *The New Masses* printed an excerpt, which was followed by excerpts, reprints, and condensations in, among others, *Coronet*, the publication of the Braille Institute of America, Garden City Publishing's $1.00 series, the *Daily Worker*, and the New York City Public Library's "Triangle" series. In October the Council for Books in Wartime called Little, Brown to request permission to dramatize the novel for the "Treasury Star Parade" radio program. Two years later the publisher sold the rights for an Armed Services Edition.[86] After printing, three copies were immediately sent to the Book-of-the-Month Club with a recommendation from Erich Maria Remarque. In mid-June, the selection committee accepted *The Seventh Cross* as their October choice. Copies of the translation were also sent to

England, where the book was published by Hamish Hamilton at the beginning of 1943. A Canadian edition was agreed to in September.[87]

At the end of September 1942, King Features presented a plan to distribute a comic strip version of the current Book-of-the-Month Club selection to the daily newspapers they served, which reached a total of 20 million readers, and suggested *The Seventh Cross* as the first title. Two months later the New York *Daily Mirror* printed an ad with a black uniformed SS guard, a bound prisoner, and the text: "Coming tomorrow. A Unique Pictorial Presentation . . . The book more than 300,000 Book-of-the-Month Club members have enjoyed."[88] It is not known whether Seghers gave her permission for the comic strip edition, but we do know that in the spring of 1944 Lieber, her agent, was only willing to accept a U. S. army offer to reprint the strip in a 10-cent edition if the army agreed to guarantee purchase of a quarter million copies.[89]

Figures on the total number of copies sold of the U. S. editions are not available, but 319,000 copies were sold in the first twelve days alone. Five months later the figure was 421,000.[90] In a 1943 interview Seghers referred to 450,000 copies in English, adding, "I don't know the size of the London printing. In addition the book has been printed in German, Russian, Portugese, and Yiddish. The Nuevo Mundo press is bringing out the Spanish edition."[91]

Critical Reception in the United States

The Seventh Cross was extensively publicized and reviewed in the United States. In a Book-of-the-Month Club survey of two hundred critics who were asked to list the ten best books of 1942, *The Seventh Cross* was third.[92] The *New York Times* reviewed it in both Orville Prescott's "Books of the

Times" column and in a front-page piece by Louis Kronenberger in the Sunday book review section. Prescott wrote:

As a collection of characterizations, as a demonstration of what life under Nazism does to the mind and soul of many typical Germans, "The Seventh Cross" is a searching, brilliantly skillful job. It is sharply understanding of its evil characters, in addition to being pitiless in condemnation of them. It is almost pitiful in its firm faith in the goodwill temporarily submerged beneath the Nazi surface.[93]

The *Time* magazine "Books" section devoted a full page in its September 28, 1942, issue to describing and then summarizing the story:

Author Seghers' book is a new kind of novel about the Gestapo and its victims. Geoffrey Household's Rogue Male *and Ethel Vance's* Escape *were dramatic stories of flight from the Gestapo. As a story,* The Seventh Cross *is just as good – and a lot more. . . . Author Seghers does not set out simply to tell the story of her hero. She uses him as a device to stir the fetid waters of Nazi life in order to bring to the surface of that stagnant pool those individual emotions, beliefs, and acts of courage and humanity that the Nazis like to keep concealed. This is a book of people, not of techniques of escape.*[94]

The November 1942 *Wilson Library Bulletin* printed a biography of Seghers, along with a bibliography of her works. The biography mentioned, among other things, that "she is of German-Jewish parentage. Her father died some time ago and her mother is believed to have been deported to Poland." There is, however, no reference to her political affiliations.[95]

From today's perspective, the almost total lack of comment in the popular press on the political context of the novel or on Seghers' own association with the Communist Party is striking. The *Time* review refers to "the members of George's old political party who are now underground"; Kronenberg refers to an "underground." Although reviews in the left press (the *New Republic, The New Masses,* and *The Nation*) specifically referred to "socialist revolution," or the "Communist Party," the only direct comment in the mainstream press was made by Prescott:

> *Miss Seghers has written at least four previous novels, described by her publishers as "revolutionary" without indicating whether they were orthodoxly Marxist or just dealt with revolutionary events. At any rate, combined with her "non-Aryanism," they made it necessary for her to flee.*[96]

In explanation, Stephan noted that while "some, but certainly not all, of the allusions to Heisler and his friends' membership in the Communist Party were deleted [there is no indication] that these cuts were the result of a discussion . . . of the political convictions of the author and her characters." Indeed, according to Stephan the book's editor had written that "there is not a single bit of politics in this book."

The book's politics also seems to have had no effect on Metro-Goldwyn-Mayer's decision to make a film of it. Stephan, who interviewed Helen Deutsch, the script writer, Pando S. Berman, the producer, Fred Zinnemann, the director, and Herbert Rudler, who played Franz Marnet, had commented that "none of them was able to remember that he or any of those involved in filming the book had connected the book, film, or author with Communist ideas."[97]

Judged by its massive publicity, large editions, and number of reprintings, *The Seventh Cross* was clearly one of the most important and most successful of exile novels. The film, in which Spencer Tracy played George Heisler, made it even more widely known. MGM's publicity department, worried about its $1.3 million investment in a film with "a sombre title and no love interest,"[98] organized – in an orgy of insensitivity and tastelessness – a "George Heisler man-hunt" to coincide with the film's 1944 premiere in seven American cities. A double for Spencer Tracy was to check in at seven control points, each marked with a cross. With the "unofficial blessing" of the FBI, MGM used radio announcements, billboards, and hand-out wanted posters advertising $500 war bonds as prizes:

> Be alert. Prove that no suspect can escape American vigilance. . . . This man calling himself George Heisler and other aliases will pass through this city. . . . Description . . . age 38, height 5 ft 11-½ inches, weight 190 pounds, blue-gray eyes, ruddy complexion. . . . When you see him go up to him and say "You are George Heisler. the seventh cross awaits you."

In contrast to his German model, this "George Heisler" did not escape; he was identified in Boston, San Francisco, Washington, and every other city.[99]

Reception in Germany

The Seventh Cross was one of the first books to be printed in the Soviet occupation zone of postwar Germany: the fledgling Aufbau Verlag in East Berlin printed the first German edition in 1946. By 1985 Aufbau had reprinted the book 47 times and sold nearly one million copies – in a country with a population of 17 million.[100] The book was published in the American occupation zone in 1947, by the Kurt Desch Verlag in Munich. Two other editions appeared in 1948 and 1949, but then the book disappeared from the

West German market until it was reissued in 1962.[101]

This gap in the West German publication record is not surprising – in fact, *The Seventh Cross* fared far better than Seghers' other works or books by other German writers who chose to live in the Eastern zone. By 1949, when it had become clear that Germany was not going to be reunited, Cold War anti-Communism had taken precedence over anti-fascism, postponing the discussion of the leftist literature of the Weimar Republic and the exile period for more than a decade.

In East Germany, however, this literature was not only printed but was celebrated as the exiles returned home to provide a continuity of tradition for the newly established system. In her afterword to a 1976 edition of the book, Christa Wolf, an East German writer and scholar who had been one of Seghers' postwar protegés, described her first exposure to it:

> *When* The Seventh Cross *finally came to us it was already a world bestseller in foreign languages. Toward the end of the war it had been printed in a giant edition for the armed forces of the United States. . . . At this time, no one in Germany had yet seen the book. . . .*
>
> *I can still see the odd name and the odd title written on the blackboard in the old-fashioned handwriting of my old teacher: Anna Seghers,* The Seventh Cross. *We were asked – it must have been 1948 – after having read Goethe and Rilke to go through this, since that's the way things were nowadays. Without reservation, if you please. I can still see the quickly tattered Rowohlt paperback that we then really read. – What did we read though? The breathtaking story of the escape of a person, a Communist. We hoped that his fugitive's flight would succeed – we couldn't help it. At the same time*

we were surprised. After all, we thought we knew what
it had been like in Germany in those years; at that
point we still thought our childish memories were reli-
able. Was there supposed to have been such a Heisler
beneath the smooth, to us apparently happy, surface,
had there been many like him who had run for their
lives, perhaps right past us? And had the others, the
adults, taken him in or handed him over?

The questions that the book raised in us were closely
connected with our other questions from that time.
They weighed on us, they pushed so strongly to the fore,
that we were far from really appreciating and under-
standing this book. And besides, to be able to correctly
evaluate one book, one must have read many books.
We were a long way from that too. However, the ques-
tion of what had remained alive, healthy, capable of
change in our people was posed to us directly.[102]

Greta Kuckhoff asked the same question at about the same
time, but from a very different perspective. Kuckhoff was a
member of the Red Orchestra, one of the largest and most
active underground resistance groups in Nazi Germany.
The group was organized in 1938–39 and functioned until
1942–43, when it was penetrated by the Gestapo. About
half of the 100 members arrested were executed, including
Adam Kuckhoff, Greta's husband. Her own death sentence
was commuted to life imprisonment; she was held in prisons and concentration camps until 1945. Shortly before
Seghers' return to Germany in 1947, Kuckhoff read an English edition of *The Seventh Cross* and discussed her ambiva-
lent response to it as a survivor of the German resistance:

It is lovely, how here and there ancient human kindness
shows through, how courage and faithfulness bloom in

people in unexpected places – side by side with the others who were consumed by the fear of endangering their petty lives: a warm kitchen, the possibility of a steady job, the blessing of blindness to the barbaric reality that can be felt everywhere, but rarely consciously. . . .[103]

We in Germany missed the moment at which we could have prevented National Socialism from brutally coming to power. We also failed to conquer it with our own resources. All that remained to us was to bear suffering and torture, to become fleeting and nameless. Fighters who are without victory . . . we can become objects of pity, but successors only accrue to those who win. It was our fate that this victory came from outside and our own struggle shifted to . . . correct political reconstruction and, simultaneously, a thorough reeducation to a new free thought and feeling. . . .[104]

Anna Seghers delves deep into the human soul. She "sees" people, landscapes, and things. What is missing is the reality of the freedom for which we are struggling to become visible.

In addition, there is another difficulty for German readers. Throughout the past ten years they have seen very little evidence of this secret Germany of the illegals; now it is being presented to them as if this secret Germany had reached into the lives of every strata. Here as well . . . there is a lack of perspective which would allow the reader to say: Such a thin wall separated us from all of that – maybe the searching step of a George Heisler went past our door – and we prayed: Come Lord Jesus be our guest – and didn't let him in, as he stumbled past under the weight of the cross. Only when the sense is awakened, that in these years something happened that personally concerned each one of us – each in a different way according to his own views

– only then will we succeed in melting the ice that has grown over the German people and deep into their hearts. As it is, the danger exists that this remains something which happened at a distance from them and which they now hear about the way one reads about a foreign country.

Anna Seghers has succeeded in providing insight through characterization into a good part of our life, but her wood-cut style lifts it all a bit into the legendary. One cannot be too simple in characterizing what must be said here so that those whom it concerns most are also ready to hear. . . .[105]

The fugitive George Heisler keeps finding a secret Germany. Many are afraid of course – and help anyway. Others are relieved to have help and support demanded of them. Wasn't the situation such that, at least after 1945, it had to be made clear to readers that they too ought to have taken part in the struggle – there would have been fewer victims. It seemed to be – and still does-that in a book about this time every citizen must be challenged, so that he will finally see clearly: it wasn't a question of the victims, it was a matter of clever, well-thought-out deeds. A little less fear, a little more love of life in a few hundred thousand and the war wouldn't have been possible or would have been over sooner. Sympathy for the fighters without victory only has meaning if it strikes like a bolt of insight to people who until then had been indifferent or hardened: This is your concern – it ought to have concerned you then. Don't evade the issue! You don't need to feel sorry, sympathy is evasion. It is soothing, it allows one to speak an ego te absolve over the evil deeds one did oneself or at least allowed to happen, an absolution through which nothing is basically changed.[106]

Kuckhoff's criticism of the book is based on her own experiences in Nazi Germany. It is motivated by her determination to make visible and inescapable the personal responsibility of each individual for the success of fascism and it points out the weakness of the novel as a document. Seghers had left Germany in 1933. She wrote *The Seventh Cross* in exile in 1938 and 1939, using the fragmentary reports of more recent exiles but without directly experiencing the changes which had taken place within German society. The horrors of the 1939–1945 period in Germany – the murder of the ill and the handicapped, the mass deportations of Jews, and the construction of the extermination camps – did not begin until after the book had been written. The book she wrote was intended to rally all Germans to resistance through their feelings of human decency, sympathy, and solidarity. It is by no means clear that it would have succeeded, but in any case it reached its audience too late.

Information about what was happening in Germany filtered out, but was often dismissed or simply not believed. Gradually, however, stories reached the emigrés. In May 1943 Seghers wrote:

What cripples the people is the circumstance that large segments [of the population] equate Fatherland and regime. Many Germans believe that the defeat of the Nazis would mean the final destruction of Germany. That is why the crude and demagogic propaganda is so dangerous. It is desperately urgent that we gradually separate the people from the regime, to help them to overcome their confusion and to clearly recognize their real exploiters and executioners.[107]

By 1944 Paul Merker was writing:

One may want to object: the guilty are the Nazis and not

428

the German people. But the millions who became Nazis or who let themselves be used as their henchmen, who are to blame for Lidice and Maidanek, were at the same time Germans.[108]

And Sigrid Bock has written that in 1944:

Anna Seghers looked the facts in the eye without illusion. She assumed that there would be many people who were lost, who could not be won for humanistic ideas and behavior. Therefore she regarded the German youth, "the lost sons," as her primary readers, she made a conscious choice in who her book addressed; at the same time she characterized these imagined readers as "dulled," "fascistically contaminated," "poisoned by a tremendous insanity, false ideas, a rigor mortis cramp of domination and mechanical obedience," as ruled by "senseless ideas which lead to corruption and depravity."[109]

Segher's didactic intention and her faith in ordinary people are evident throughout the novel. "Its central theme is the integrity and rectitude of the average person."[110] In 1972, the West German scholar Werner Brettschneider wrote: "However, the hero is not the one who is saved . . . but the numerous nameless people who help the escapee and thus keep something like hope alive."[111]

The same year another West German critic, Fritz Raddatz, discussed Seghers' symbolic treatment of the landscape, an outgrowth of her reflections on patriotism and love of country, and on how these genuine emotions were misused by the Nazis: "This key book of the Emigration became a novel of the homeland. In none of her other books does the landscape play such an outstanding, important role. . . . Anna Seghers fought back against an evil reality with a fictional realism and called upon . . . village and stream, and countryside as a human landscape. It is a great book of destroyed idylls."[112]

It is interesting to compare Raddatz' vision of Seghers' landscape as an idyllic context to the commentary of Christa Wolf, who focuses on the non-idyllic *people* who define and shape it:

A landscape has rarely been described so intimately. Before our eyes, occupations, actions, and thoughts weave themselves into the solid fabric of people's daily lives. Without fuss, the threads which have carried and preserved the whole fabric from time immemorial are made visible....

No one had seen it this way before. Whoever knows it will now see it this way. Whoever sees it for the first time will recognize it. "The power and glory of ordinary life," in which everything is contained: banality and poetry. The taste of daily bread and the people's everyday struggle for the bread.... This is what the book lives from, even when the memory of a Heisler, of the seven crosses and their terrible shadow over Germany no longer pain future readers as they do us.[113]

A 1982 West German dissertation on Seghers shows less political bias in analyzing Seghers' purpose and method than the earlier West German studies:

Anna Seghers leaves the reader alone with the characters. She denies herself any commentary and avoids value judgments, which could become prejudgments. The audience learns through the characters in the novel – that is, subjectively – how far the power of fascism reaches and what each individual can himself undertake against the regime. The flight of the concentration

430

camp prisoners becomes the catalyst for testing . . . the
parts of the population that are touched by it. . . .

> *The make-up of the characters in* The Seventh Cross
> *illustrates the interrelation between betrayal, fear, and*
> *resignation, of indifference and personal revenge and*
> *enrichment. Acting in combination they account for the*
> *power of the fascist Hitler dictatorship. Anna Seghers*
> *shows that the rule of terror can be broken if people*
> *make an effort to overcome their fear and resigna-*
> *tion.*[114]

Like the earlier, politically motivated, West German failure
to publish the works of leftist exiles, the Brettschneider,
Raddatz, and Buthge readings may be more reflections of
changing political climates than literary theories. However,
even Buthge, who discusses Seghers' polemical intentions,
does not mention the ultimate irony that her book only
reached her audience after its pleas for solidarity had been
rendered moot by the Allied victory.

It is clear that both the artistic level and the political significance of *The Seventh Cross* ensure that it will continue
to be discussed as one of the central works of the German
exile. It is also clear that the political nature of the novel will
continue to influence how it is discussed. Seghers became a
national hero in the GDR while she continued to be treated
as a minor author in the BRD. Her reputation has only
recently begun to rise in the West.

Return from Exile

After the war Seghers was eager to go back to Germany, but
her return was nearly as frustrating, if not as dangerous, as
her efforts to leave had been. After repeated attempts to

arrange permission and transportation, she was finally ready to travel. In a letter dated January 5, 1947, she wrote to those staying behind, "It's not even all that certain that I will get home before you do. When all of you are, hopefully soon, on your way, please look around in all the port cities to see if you still have to pick up Anna somewhere."[115]

Her route took her by way of France and Sweden and she arrived in Berlin in late April (her family followed later). While she had been deeply involved in the German opposition from abroad and was informed about the situation in Germany, her sources of information did not transmit the reality she found. Actually seeing conditions in Germany was a shock: "When I returned from emigration I traveled across Germany from the west. The cities were destroyed, and the people were just as destroyed inside. Germany then offered a 'unity' of ruins, desperation, and hunger."[116]

Segher's party membership and prominence in party-supported exile organizations made her return to the Soviet occupation zone of Berlin – rather than to Mainz in the west – a foregone conclusion. She immediately plunged into activity. In 1947 she addressed the first (and last) All-German Writers' Congress and received the George Büchner prize. In 1948 she joined the first postwar German writers' delegation to Moscow in May and attended the World Congress of Creative Artists in Wroclaw in July. She helped found the German Writers' Union and served as its chairperson until 1978 (when she became honorary chairperson); she was also a founding member of the German Academy of Arts.[117]

In addition to supporting these organizations, Seghers focused much of her attention during the postwar decade on the world peace movement. She attended the World Peace Congress in Paris in 1949 and in Warsaw in 1950, and became a member of the World Peace Council that year. After completing her epic novel *The Dead Stay Young*, which she had brought back with her from exile in manuscript, she published only short stories, articles, and essays until the appearance of *Die Entscheidung* (The Decision) in 1959.[118] Although she continued to write prolifically, *The Seventh Cross* – together with *Transit* and *The Excursion of the Dead Girls* – constituted the highpoint of her literary career.

During this period she represented the GDR at conferences and congresses in Prague, Berlin, Warsaw, and Vienna, traveled to China and the Soviet Union, and made two trips to Brazil (in the early 1960s)."[119] Artistically respected and personally well liked, she was an effective spokesperson for the new government, despite her belief that she had "no talent" for public speaking.[120] She was known as a strong supporter of the party but also as an independent thinker.

In the 1960s and 1970s she traveled less and devoted more of her time to writing and to the support and encouragement of younger writers. Christa Wolf has written:

> *"Influences," of course, but it's more than that and also something else.*
>
> *A model? – That could be awful. Our generation was obliged to follow models too frequently. This is exactly not her intent. Empty admiration, dependence, subordination, are the last things she wants. Her authority is strong, but not overwhelming. . . . A pedagogic intention is unmistakable in many of her books. This tendency in her relationship to a younger person should not be denied, but it is easily seen through and may be ignored.*[121]

Ursula Emmerich, Segher's editor at Aufbau Verlag during the last twelve years of her life, described her this way:

> *Simple and direct . . . she immediately established con-*

tact with people. She asked questions and people will-
ingly told her their life stories. Her understanding and
empathy were unique. . . . She was always in the middle
of things, always allowed people to approach her. My
children said it was actually like visiting their grand-
mother . . . first you had to have something to eat.[122]

Seghers continued to write until her death in 1983. The
staff at the Seghers Archive (located in the modest Berlin
apartment where she had lived since the 1950s) continues
to turn up previously unknown manuscripts, including a
copy of the following letter to Nico Rost, who had been her
translator at Querido. Rost was captured, and spent the war
in a concentration camp, and later wrote *Goethe in Dachau*.
Written shortly after her return to Berlin, this letter is worth
quoting at length for its illustration of both the pedagogic
and empathetic qualities described above:

Berlin, October 9, 1947

Dear Nico,

[. . .] I must admit that my life in Germany, from which,
as you know, I was far away for years, is not easy. Hitler
fascism has left terrible wounds. It didn't only destroy
the old cities, it also destroyed the people's basic beliefs,
their moral and intellectual values, to such a degree
that no matter how one tries, it can hardly be imagined
from the outside. In this darkness the points of light glow
even more brightly – the people who preserved their
belief in prisons and as fugitives, in the most terrible
situations, exposed to spies, threats, and temptations.
One needs time not only to comprehend with the mind,
but to feel through and through. What is decisive, for us
writers as well, is not the static but the dynamic, not the
circumstances, which always remain limited and acci-

dental, but the direction of events. I don't know if I have succeeded in catching something of this "direction," something of this "dynamic" in my book. After all, the events described in it took place two or three years before the beginning of the war. And it was only during the war that the fascist terror showed what it could really do. Then what we had simply taken note of when we were younger without thinking much about it became clear to us: that for humanity, as for the individual, there are only two paths, forward or back to barbarism. Things look bad enough for the main character in the book, for George Heisler. He feels himself surrounded by enemies. He only rarely comes upon a few friends, who only at the decisive moment, faced with the either-or, choose the right path. If we had observed them without George Heisler, perhaps only a week earlier, they would have appeared to be hopelessly entangled in fascism. This, Nico, is what I have understood by "direction." This is what keeps giving me new hope, even in this confused life in Germany. What we must do, particularly we writers, is put people's thinking in such a situation again and again. If we are not capable of calling such a situation to life, then we must at least bring their powers of imagination to this decisive point. That is part of the task which I believe we writers now have if we want to fight fascism. Everywhere we go here we see that while the first phase has been won, the fall of Hitler, Hitlerism has yet to be brought down. We have won the first phase, the war, but not the second, the peace, not by a long shot. The war criminals are a long way from having been disposed of by the Nuremberg trials. They are still romping quite merrily. Wherever they can, they stir up dreams of new wars unpunished. And if, as many young soldiers tell me, even in the last weeks when there were only a few kilometers of unoccupied land left in Germany they built their hopes on a fight between East and West, now that the two fronts have been brought irrevocably together into one front line, they set new hope on a falling out, on a fight between the nations that would prove the vanquished right after all.

Nico, I wish from the bottom of my heart that you will soon come here yourself and bring me your translation. Hurry, or else I will come to Holland, a country in which I have friends, in which I spent the happiest days of my youth which now seems to me to lie much further in the past than it really does. So much was packed into the past years, we have lost so much, more than a whole generation. Hopefully, it will turn out that we have also won something immense in the process: confidence in our power, the fighting power of the anti-fascists.

I embrace you and with you my friends,
Anna Seghers[123]

Notes

The translations used above are my own.

1. Frank Wagner, *Anna Seghers* (Leipzig: VEB Bibliographisches Institut, 1980), p. 9.
2. Ibid., p. 10.
3. Ibid.
4. Christa Wolf, "Nachwart," in *Anna Seghers, Glauben an Irdisches* (Leipzig, 1969), p. 372.
5. Ibid., p. 373.
6. Netty Reiling, "Jude und Judentum im Werke Rembrandts," Phil. Diss. Heidelberg, 1924.
7. She later explained that she had needed a Dutch name for the story and the works of the Dutch graphic artist of the Rembrandt period, Hercules Seghers, had suggested that name to her. See Christa Wolf, "Bei Anna Seghers," *Das Magazine* 11 (1970): 12. In numerous interviews, Seghers was asked about her pseudonym and offered a number of different versions of this story. As nearly all her answers do mention Hercules Seghers, I have chosen one of her more direct answers.
8. "Gespräch mit Anna Seghers" (Talk with Anna Seghers), in *Sinn und Form* 38, no. 2 (1986): 268; translation of an article which appeared in the Mexican newspaper *Futuro* (May 1943).
9. Letter to Kurt Batt, 23 March 1972.
10. Quoted in Fritz J. Raddatz, *Tradition und Tendenzen: Materialien zur Literatur der DDR* (Frankfurt: Suhrkamp, 1972), p. 530.
11. *Current Biography 1942*, p. 748.
12. "Gespräch mit Anna Seghers," p. 268. Although Reiling-Radvanyi was henceforth known by her pseudonym, she did not legally change her name, so the name Netty Reiling-Radvanyi continued to appear in legal documents. During exile she occasionally used other pseudonyms. To her friends she was known as Tschibi, Netty, or Anna, in some cases interchangeably. Jeanne Stern, "Das Floss der Anna Seghers," in *Anna Seghers: Ein Almanach zum 75. Geburtstag*, ed. Kurt Batt (Berlin and Weimar: Aufbau, 1975), p. 77. In literature and conversation she is invariably referred to as Anna Seghers.
13. *Current Biography 1942*, p. 749.
14. Wagner, *Anna Seghers*, p. 27. The Piscator film, *Aufstand der Fischer von Santa Barbara*, was produced in Moscow in 1934.
15. *Wilson Library Bulletin*, 17 (November 1942): 178.
16. *Current Biography 1942*, p. 749.

17. *Zur Tradition der sozialistischen Literatur in Deutschland* (Berlin: Aufbau, 1967), p. 166.

18. Ibid., p. 66.

19. "Gespräch mit Anna Seghers," p. 268.

20. *Auf dem Wege zur amerikanischen Botschaft und andere Erzählungen* (1930). The background of the title story is a demonstration protesting the execution of Sacco and Vanzetti. It and *Die Gefährten* (1932) both appeared in Berlin with Kiepenheuer. *Der Kopflohn* (1933) was completed in exile and was published by Querido in Amsterdam. In 1933 Querido set up a German section to print the works of emigre writers, with the help of Nico Rost, Seghers' Dutch translator. The director of the German section was Fritz Landshoff, the former director of Kiepenheuer; the editor-in-chief was Klaus Mann. See Kurt Batt, *Anna Seghers* (Leipzig: Reclam, 1973), p. 87.

21. She continued this theoretical discussion with Georg Lukacs by correspondence while in exile. "Brief an George Lukacs," in *Anna Seghers, Aufsätze, Ansprachen, Essays, 1927–1953* (Berlin and Weimar: Aufbau, 1984), pp. 71–88.

22. Batt, *Anna Seghers*, p. 81.

23. "Gespräch mit Anna Seghers," p. 269.

24. Batt, *Anna Seghers*, p. 84.

25. Wagner, *Anna Seghers*, pp. 27, 29.

26. Stern, "Das Floss der Anna Seghers," pp. 77-78.

27. Ruth Radvanyi, "Unsere Mutter," *Der Bienenstock* 134 (Winter 1985).

28. Batt, *Anna Seghers*, pp. 292–93.

29. Bodo Uhse, "Aus den letzten Winkeln der Erde," in Bodo Uhse, *Gestalten und Probleme* (Berlin, 1959), p. 54, cited in Batt, *Anna Seghers*, p. 293.

30. *Neue Deutsche Blätter* 1, no. 1 (1933) 3, cited in Batt, *Anna Seghers*, p. 88.

31. Stern, "Das Floss der Anna Seghers," p. 78.

32. Wagner, *Anna Seghers*, p. 30.

33. Anna Seghers, *Briefe an Leser* (Berlin: Aufbau, 1970), p. 17.

34. Anna Seghers, *Erzählungen, 1926–1944* (Berlin Aufbau, 1981), p. 365.

35. Anna Seghers, *Der Weg durch den Februar* (Paris: Editions du Carrefour, 1935). There is evidence that Seghers wrote the book on assignment for Willi Münzenberg, a well-known Communist party functionary and financial organizer who had set up the Carrefour press.

36. Johannes R. Becher, letter from Paris, 15 December 1934, in *Zur Tradition der socialistischen Literatur in Deutschland* (Berlin: Aufbau, 1967), p. 684. Becher had been chairman of the BPRS and later became the national poet of the GDR.

37. Wagner, *Anna Seghers*, p. 33.
38. Batt, *Anna Seghers*, p. 122.
39. Wagner, *Anna Seghers*, p. 35.
40. Anna Seghers, *Die Rettung* (Amsterdam: Querido, 1937)
41. "Christa Wolf spricht mit Anna Seghers," in Anna Seghers, *Über Kunstwerk und Wirklichkeit*, vol. 2 (Berlin: Akademie, 1970), p. 41.
42. "Die Schönsten Sagen vom Räuber Woynok" was published in *Das Wort* (Moscow), June 1938, and "Sagen von Artemis" in *Das Wort* (Moscow), September 1938; both were reprinted in Seghers, *Erzählungen, 1926–1944*.
43. Batt, *Anna Seghers*, p. 124.
44. "Gespräch mit Anna Seghers," p. 269.
45. Batt, *Anna Seghers*, p. 126.
46. "Gespräch mit Anna Seghers," p. 269.
47. Anna Seghers, letter to I.I. Anissimov, 23 September 1938, in Seghers, *Über Kunstwerk und Wirklichkeit* vol. 2, p. 16.
48. Christa Wolf, "Afterword" to *Das Siebte Kreuz* (Berlin and Weimar: Aufbau, 1976), pp. 425-26.
49. Anna Seghers, letter to Fritz Erpenbeck, fall 1938, cited in Alfred Klein, "Auskünfte über ein Romanschicksal," *Weltbühne* 46, no. 11 (1980): 1461; also cited by Alexander Stephan, in his article "... ce livre a pour moi une importance speciale," *Exil, Forschung, Erkenntnisse, Ergebnisse* 5, no. 2 (1985): 23, n. 45.
50. "Christa Wolf spricht mit Anna Seghers," NDL 6 (1965): 13–14.
51. Wilhelm Girnus, "Gespräch mit Anna Seghers," *Sinn und Form* 5 (1967): 1056.
52. Alexander Abusch, in *Anna Seghers: Briefe ihrer Freunde* (Berlin and Weimar: Aufbau, 1960), p. 5. Stephan, "... ce livre...," p. 5, cites a contemporary diary entry from March 1939 in which Abusch is much less specific. Stephan is generally more skeptical of Seghers' explanation of her sources.
53. Ibid., p. 15.
54. NDL 9 (1984) 45.
55. Anna Seghers, letter to Johannes R. Becher, 27 March 1939, in Frank Wagner, ... *der Kurs auf der Realitaet: Das epische Werk von Anna Seghers [1935–1943]* (Berlin: Akademie, 1975), p. 312. The opening chapters of the novel did appear in *Internationale Literatur* 6 (1939): 634, 7 (1939) 49–65, and 8 (1939): 8–25, after which publication stopped. This was obviously due to the Molotov-Ribbentrop Non-Aggression Pact, signed in August 1939, but no official reason was given. See Batt, *Anna Seghers*, p. 138, and Stephan, *Anna Seghers*, p. 16.
56. Ibid., p. 313.
57. Unpublished letter to Wieland Herzfelde, cited in *Erfahrung: Exil*

Antifaschistische Romane 1933–1945, ed. Sigrid Bock and Manfred Hahn (Berlin and Weimar: Aufbau, 1981), p. 365.

58. Cited in Wolf, Afterword, p. 417.

59. Anna Seghers, letter to Wieland Herzfelde, 9 May 1940, in Seghers, *Über Kunstwerk und Wirklichkeit*, vol.4, p. 140; cited in Bock and Hahn, eds., *Erfahrung Exil*, p. 366, and Stephan, *Anna Seghers*, p. 17. The book was finally accepted by Querido, but could not be printed until 1948, after the end of the Nazi occupation of Holland.

60. In Bock and Hahn, eds., *Erfahrung Exil*, p. 365; Stephan, *Anna Seghers*, p. 17.

61. Radvanyi, "Unsere Mutter."

62. Stern, "Das Floss der Anna Seghers," pp. 81-82.

63. "Gespräch mit Anna Seghers," pp. 269-70.

64. Ibid., p. 272.

65. See Stephan, *Anna Seghers*, pp. 16-17, and p. 24, n. 53-63.

66. Seghers, *Briefe an Leser*, p. 44.

67. Batt, *Anna Seghers*, p. 155.

68. Ibid., p. 154.

69. "Gespräch mit Anna Seghers," pp. 269-70.

70. Radvanyi, "Unsere Mutter."

71. Seghers, *Briefe an Leser*, p. 64M

72. Batt, *Anna Seghers*, p. 165.

73. Seghers, *Glauben an Irdisches*, p. 46.

74. Bodo Uhse Archiv der Deutschen Akademie der Künste, Sign. 527/7.

75. Alexander Stephan, "Ein Exilroman als Bestseller," in *Exilforschung: Ein Internationales Jahrbuch* 3 (1985): 239.

76. Seghers had previously expressed the wish to emigrate to the United States. Whether the trip by way of Ellis Island was motivated by circumstances or that wish is not clear. There is documentation of her attempt to obtain entry visas for her family and the denial of her request. See Stephan, ". . . ce livre . . . ," pp. 17-18 and p. 24, n. 64.

77. *Freies Deutschland* 1, no. 2, p. 2.

78. See Stephan, "Ein Exilroman," p. 245.

79. In Bock and Hahn, eds., *Erfahrung Exil*, p. 366.

80. Stephan, "Ein Exilroman," p. 247, n. 6.

80. Ibid., p. 234.

82. Franz Hoellering, *Evaluation*, p. 2, cited in ibid., p. 239.

83. Stephan, "Ein Exilroman," p. 239.

84. Ibid., p. 243.

85. Ibid., p. 250, n. 26. Seghers, who was in Mexico at that point, was not consulted about these cuts and expressed dissatisfaction with them. See also n. 27.

86. Ibid., p. 240.
87. Ibid., p. 241, and p. 249, n. 11.
88. Ibid., p. 241.
89. Ibid.
90. Ibid., p. 245.
91. "Gespräch mit Anna Seghers," p. 272.
92. Stephan, "Ein Exilroman," p. 244.
93. Orville Prescott, "Books of the Times," *The New York Times*, 23 September 1942.
94. *Time*, 28 September 1942, p. 92.
95. *Wilson Library Bulletin* 17 (November 1942): 178.
96. Prescott, "Books of the Times."
97. Stephan, "Ein Exilroman," p. 243. Given McCarthyism, the Hollywood Ten, blacklists, loyalty oaths, and Ronald Reagan, this could be attributed to the interviewees' reluctance to admit any association with Communism.
98. *Life*, 16 October 1944, p. 113.
99. Stephan, "Ein Exilroman," p. 246.
100. *Der Bienenstock* 134 (Winter 1985): 1.
101. Rowohlt Rotationsroman (Rororo), 1947, Büchergilde Gutenberg, 1948. Cited from Werner Buthge, *Anna Seghers: Werk-Wirkungsabsicht-Wirkungsmoglichkeit in der Bundesrepublik Deutschland* (Stuttgart: Akademischer Verlag Hans-Dieter Heinz, 1982), p. 219.
102. Wolf, "Nachwort," p. 426.
103. Greta Kuckhoff, "Begegnung mit dem 'Siebten Kreuz,'" in *Über Anna Seghers*, p. 151.
104. Ibid., p. 153.
105. Ibid., p. 155.
106. Ibid., pp. 156-57.
107. "Gespräch mit Anna Seghers," p. 271.
108. Paul Merker, "Der kommende Frieden und die Freien Deutschen," in *Freies Deutschland* 12 (1944): 8.
109. In Bock and Hahn, eds., *Erfahrung Exil*, p. 370.
110. Theodor Huebner, *The Literature of East Germany* (New York: Unger, 1970), p. 73.
111. Werner Brettschneider, *Zwischen literarischer Autonomie und Stattsdienst* (Berlin: Erich Schmidt, 1972), p. 70.
112. Fritz J. Raddatz, *Traditionen und Tendenzen: Materialien zur Literatur der DDR* (Frankfurt: Suhrkamp, 1972), pp. 228-29.
113. Wolf, "Nachwort," p. 413.
114. Buthge, *Anna Seghers*, pp. 87, 89, 93, 95, 102.
115. Cited in Wagner, *Anna Seghers*, p. 53.
116. *Über Kunstwerk und Wirklichkeit*, vol.1, p. 91.

117. Batt, *Anna Seghers*, p. 194.
118. Anna Seghers, *The Dead Stay Young* (Berlin: Aufbau, 1949); *Die Enstscheidung* (Berlin: Aufbau, 1959).
119. Batt, *Anna Seghers*, p. 194, and pp. 304-5.
120. Ibid., p. 213.
121. Christa Wolf, "Fortgesetzter Versuch," in *Über Anna Seghers*, pp. 23, 24.
122. Interview with Ursula Emmerich, Aufbau Verlag, Berlin, 31 July 1986.
123. Unpublished letter to Nico Rost, Berlin, 9 October 1947. I would like to thank Dr. Hans Baumgart, director of the Seghers Archive, for making this letter available.

A NOTE ON THE TYPE

THE SEVENTH CROSS has been set in Minion, a type designed by Robert Slimbach in 1990. An offshoot of the designer's researches during the development of Adobe Garamond, Minion hybridized the characteristics of numerous Renaissance sources into a single calligraphic hand. Unlike many faces developed exclusively for digital typesetting, drawings for Minion were transferred to the computer early in the design phase, preserving much of the freshness of the original concept. Conceived with an eye toward overall harmony, its capitals, lower case, and numerals were carefully balanced to maintain a well-groomed "family" resemblance – both between roman and italic and across the full range of weights. A decidedly contemporary face, Minion makes free use of the qualities the designer found most appealing in the types of the fifteenth and sixteenth centuries. Crisp drawing and a narrow set width make Minion an economical and easy going book type, and even its name reinforces its adaptable, affable, and almost self-effacing nature, referring as it does to a small size of type, a faithful or favored servant, and a kind of peach.

Design and composition by Carl W. Scarbrough

VERBA MUNDI BOOKS

VERBA MUNDI offers the best in modern world literature –
whether by such established masters as José Donoso and Isaac
Babel, or by some of the world's most notable young writers,
many of them making their first appearance here in English.
By offering these superbly translated, attractively designed vol-
umes – now in a uniform paperback format – we mean to invite
adventurous readers to partake in a diversity of cultures.

A Love Made Out of Nothing
& Zohara's Journey
by Barbara Honigmann

TRANSLATED FROM THE GERMAN BY JOHN S. BARRETT

WINNER OF THE KORET JEWISH BOOK AWARD FOR 2003
In these two brilliant, complementary novellas, two very different women struggle to rise from the ashes of their former selves. The narrator of *A Love Made Out of Nothing* leaves Berlin to start a new life as a student in Paris. Although she has escaped from her stifling past, she finds herself isolated, frightened, and still tied to her old existence by her complex relationship with a possessive and manipulative father. *Zohara's Journey* tells the story of a devoutly religious Sephardic Jew repatriated to southern France during the Algerian War. Married to a duplicitous rabbi, she lives alone in Strasbourg now that he has abandoned her. In her desperate efforts to locate him, Zohara comes to question both the man she thought she knew and the religion that has shaped them both. With these two intimate novellas, Godine is proud to introduce to North America a powerful new voice from Germany, one that speaks directly to the nature of isolation and, ultimately, to the necessity of self-reliance.

176 PAGES   SOFTCOVER $16.95

Human Parts
by Orly Castel-Bloom

TRANSLATED FROM THE HEBREW BY DALYA BILU

In much the way Robert Altman gave us Nashville, Orly Castel-Bloom gives us contemporary Tel Aviv, a city long plagued with terrorist ambushes and suicide bombings. And now, suddenly, the city is further plagued – by a "Saudi flu" that is overcrowding the hospitals, by a failing economy, and by hailstones as big as soccer balls. And yet, against this background of monumental affliction and institutionalized emergency, the entire population, from kibbutz to Knesset, is trying to get on with its daily life – an endeavor at once tragic and comic, heroic and banal, real and surreal. From the Israeli president to a single mother of three, from an impoverished dry cleaner to a optimistic beauty-school student, Orly Castel-Bloom gives us a cross-section of interrelated persons struggling to bring calm, continuity, and normalcy to their extraordinarily restless lives. The result is a sardonic, topical, and wholly engrossing tour de force by one of Israel's best young novelists.

256 PAGES   HARDCOVER $24.95

In the Flesh
by Christa Wolf

TRANSLATED FROM THE GERMAN BY JOHN S. BARRETT

Suffering severe abdominal pain, a woman is rushed to the emergency room. Her condition, her soaring temperature, her deepening distress – her symptoms all confound her doctors, who operate repeatedly. Drifting in and out of consciousness, she journeys through limbo, through the past, through her own memory, trying to understand the ethereal figures, signs, and portents of her twilight existence. The scene, half-real, half-hallucinated, is East Germany, a country of secrets, silences, and unexplained disappearances. The time: just before the fall of the Berlin Wall.

Christa Wolf's mesmerizing short novel, with its layers of meaning and elliptical content, is a supreme work of political and philosophical insight by one of Germany's greatest living writers. Alive with metaphor and myth, rich in symbolism and literary reference, still cooled by the chilly recollection of a monstrous regime, it draws a nuanced, witty, utterly compelling portrait of a person and a society close to death, yet still capable of recovery.

224 PAGES   HARDCOVER $24.95

Last Trolley from Beethovenstraat
by Grete Weil

TRANSLATED FROM THE GERMAN BY JOHN S. BARRETT

From the author of *The Bride Price* comes a dark and haunting story of memory, guilt, and the meaning of responsibility.

Andreas, a once-promising poet, lives with his bride, Susanne, in postwar Germany. But although surrounded by the trappings of comfort and success, Andreas is obsessed by the memory of Susanne's younger brother, Daniel, whom he had sheltered in Amsterdam, but who was eventually deported by the Gestapo. The war over, Andreas rebuilds his life in the "new" Germany, trying to recapture Daniel through marriage to his sister. But he is unable to write or to find peace, unable to forget his torture over Daniel or the harrowing days and nights of th Occupation. Finally, he returns to Amsterdam to confront his memories of the war – for it was there that Andreas first recognized the horror inflicted by his own people, as every night he witnessed the round-up of the city's Jews beneath his window. And it was there that he came to the realizations about himself, his past and his heritage that give the story its resonance.

272 PAGES   HARDCOVER $23.95

3 by Perec

by Georges Perec

TRANSLATED FROM THE FRENCH BY IAN MONK

INTRODUCTIONS BY DAVID BELLOS

George Perec, author of the acclaimed *Life A User's Manual*, is one of the great pleasure-givers of modern literature. Here, in one career-spanning volume, are three "easy pieces" from this smiling *maestro* of the typewriter keyboard. Published in 1966, "Which Moped with Chrome-Plated Handlebars at the Back of the Yard?" is a comic meditation on a serious subject: the moral imperatives of war – and of war-resistance. It tells the story of the hopelessly convoluted attempt by a group of Parisian intellectuals to save one of their fellows from being drafted into the French-Algerian conflict. "The Exeter Text" (1972) is the B-side to Perec's astounding tour-de-force *A Void* (1969), the novel in which he successfully avoided using the letter *e*. Here Perec pens the perfect reverse: he bleeds fevered, demented, clever sentences that set free the letter e's secret essence: sex. "A Gallery Portrait" (1979) was the last work Perec completed before his untimely death at the age of forty-six. It is the story of a painting – or, more precisely, of a painter and his patron – and a final exploration of many of Perec's signature themes: authenticity, forgery, valuation, mimesis, and purity of imagination.

192 PAGES   SOFTCOVER $18.95

"53 Days"

by Georges Perec

EDITED BY HARRY MATHEWS AND JACQUES ROUBAUD

TRANSLATED FROM THE FRENCH BY DAVID BELLOS

Perec was working on this literary thriller at the time of his death in 1982. He left eleven completed chapters and extensive notes, and from these his friends Mathews and Roubaud assembled the outlines of the unfinished mystery while providing the reader with a fascinating window into the author's mind as he constructed his literary conundrum. As Mathews comments, "If death had not prevented Perec from completing this book, we would today be reading a masterpiece, one in the mold of Nabokov's *Pale Fire*." But this is as close as it will get and, even unfinished, it is well worth the consideration.

272 PAGES   HARDCOVER $23.95

W, or The Memory of Childhood
by Georges Perec

TRANSLATED FROM THE RENCH BY DAVID BELLOS

From the author of *Life A User's Manual* comes an equally astonishing novel – two parallel novels, to be precise, each aesthetically complete yet casting a distant light on the other. "One of these texts," explains the author, "is entirely imaginary: a reconstruction of a childhood fantasy about an land in thrall to the Olympic ideal. The other is an autobiography: a fragmentary tale of a wartime boyhood." Each text explores the innocence of childhood, the cruelty of the childish imagination, and the child's simplistic conception of justice – the black-and-white absolutism of winning and losing, of life and death. Together, the two stories form a fictional meditation on the Holocaust, that deserves a place on the same shelf as Günter Grass's *Tin Drum*.

176 PAGES SOFTCOVER $16.95

Things: A Story of the Sixties & A Man Asleep
by Georges Perec

TRANSLATED FROM THE FRENCH BY

DAVID BELLOS & ANDREW LEAK

In these two novels, the great French novelist ponders both sides of the materialistic impulse – that is, the desire to acquire a mass of shiny new things that will give life a semblance of stability and meaning. In *Things* a young middle-class couple "wants life's enjoyment, but all around them enjoyment is equated with ownership." They are paralyzed with covetousness, caught between "the film they would have liked to live in" and the disappointment of their unglamorous daily lives. In *A Man Asleep*, a young student is paralyzed by exactly the opposite – the desire to shed all possessions "and to want nothing, just to wait, until there is nothing left to wait for." Between these extremes of acquisitiveness and asceticism lies a third way, and Perec points toward it with detachment, compassion, and a very rare sense of humor.

224 PAGES SOFTCOVER $16.95

•

The Obscene Bird of Night
by José Donoso

TRANSLATED FROM THE SPANISH BY
HARDIE ST. MARTIN & LEONARD MADES

This haunting jungle of a novel has been hailed by Luis Buñuel as "a masterpiece" and by Carlos Fuentes as "one of the great novels not only of Spanish America but of our time." The story of the last member of the aristocratic Azcoitia family, a monster protected from knowledge of his deformities by being surrounded by other freaks, *The Obscene Bird of Night* is a triumph of imaginary, visionary writing. Among the first great examples of "magic realism," its luxuriance, fecundity, horror, and energy will not soon fade from the reader's mind.

448 PAGES SOFTCOVER $18.95

Six Israeli Novellas

EDITED BY GERSHON SHAKED

This remarkable anthology, the most ambitious and representative collection of Israeli novellas ever published in English, provides readers with a matchless window onto contemporary Israeli fiction. Two of the writers, Aharon Appelfeld and David Grossman, are already contemporary classics, while the others – Ruth Almog, Yaakov Shabtai, Yehudit Hendel, and Benjamin Tammuz – here make their American debuts. From Appelfeld's modern update of the story of the Wandering Jew to Grossman's portrait of soldiers in the Yom Kippur War, from Almog's sensitive domestic realism to Shabtai's "grotesque history" of the Zionist dream, here is a literary tour of the psyche of Israel, a country where life is lived on the razor's edge, and where all the elements present in world literature are heightened and radicalized.

348 PAGES SOFTCOVER $19.95

Honeymoon
by Patrick Modiano

TRANSLATED FROM THE FRENCH BY BARBARA WRIGHT

Modiano (winner of the Prix Goncourt) constructs a deeply involving novel of suspense and longing. Jean B., a documentary filmmaker, abandons his wife and career and holes up in a Paris suburb, where his mind takes obsessive flight into the imagined life of a refugee couple he'd met years before.

128 PAGES HARDCOVER $19.95

Days of Anger
by Sylvie Germain
TRANSLATED FROM THE FRENCH BY CHRISTINE DONOUGHER
Deep in the forests of Moran, far from civilization, live families of wood-cutters and shepherds. A remote and beautiful world, it is a place where madness still reigns, murder occurs, and bloody punishments are delivered. What has happened to the body of the sensual and beautiful Catherine Corvol, wife of a rich landowner, killed not out of hatred but an excess of love? Around this central enigma, Germain has created a gothic enchantment, a dazzling rural fantasy rich in angels, obsession, and revenge where the reader is carried forward as much by the lyricism of her prose as by the macabre and fantastic turns of the plot.

192 PAGES SOFTCOVER $18.95

The Book of Nights
by Sylvie Germain
TRANSLATED FROM THE FRENCH BY CHRISTINE DONOUGHER
Winner of six literary prizes, this novel combines the timeless power of medieval legend, the resonance of Greek tragedy, and the harsh immediacy of a newsreel. Germain traces a century in the life of the Peniel family, from the Franco-Prussian War to World War II – a tale of triumph and loss, eroticism and holocaust, and the endless cycle of birth and death. *"Original and compelling. . . . Takes [magic and realism] to the outer limit and then fearlessly hurls one against the other."* – New York Times Book Review *(Notable Book of the Year, 1993)*

272 PAGES HARDCOVER $22.95

Night of Amber
by Sylvie Germain
TRANSLATED FROM THE FRENCH BY CHRISTINE DONOUGHER
In the sequel to her acclaimed *The Book of Nights*, Germain continues the grotesque, fantastic, and riveting story of the tragic Peniel family in a whirlwind novel that skillfully blends European history, myth, invention, and fantasy, tracing their fortuned from the end of World War II through the Algerian War to the frenzied Paris of 1968.

272 PAGES HARDCOVER $23.95

Five Women
by Robert Musil
PREFACE BY FRANK KERMODE
TRANSLATED FROM THE GERMAN BY
EITHNE WILIKNS & ERNST KAISER
A central figure in the modernist movement, Musil is known primarily for his magnum opus, *The Man Without Qualities*. But here, in this prequel of five short stories, as crucial to our understanding of that great work as *Dubliners* is to *Ulysses*, he displays another face, one that is by turns extravagant, sensual, mystical, and autobiographical. *Especially in the portraits of women in live, Musil is truly original. In managing scenes of physical live, he has not been approached by any writer of the last fifty years.* – V. S. Pritchett
224 PAGES   SOFTCOVER $14.95

The Christmas Oratorio
by Göran Tunström
TRANSLATED FROM THE SWEDISH BY PAUL HOOVER
A grand fresco of striving, ambition, grief, madness, and desire by Sweden's foremost contemporary novelist. Winner of the Nordic Council Prize, it unravels a three-generational saga as elaborate as a Bach cantata and engrossing as a Bergman film. *This wonderful novel is crammed with vivid and surprising incidents.... Like Bach's great musical work, Tunström's* Oratorio *offers a celebration of things that endure.* (Washington Times)
352 PAGES   HARDCOVER $23.95

Verba Mundi books are available in the finer bookstores or directly from the publisher. To order, please call 1-800-344-4771, or send prepayment for the titles desired plus $5.00 postage and handling to:
DAVID R. GODINE, *Publisher*
Post Office Box 450
Jaffrey, New Hampshire 03452
www.godine.com